Secret Confessions of the Applewoood PTA

By Ellen Meister

Secret Confessions of the Applewood PTA

Coming Soon

The Smart One

Secret Confessions of the Applewoood PTA

ELLEN MEISTER

AVON

An Imprint of HarperCollinsPublishers

FIRST EDITION

Designed by Diahann Sturge

ISBN: 978-0-06-082481-5
ISBN-10: 0-06-082481-6

The William Morrow hardcover edition contains the following Library of Congress Cataloging-in-Publication Data

Meister, Ellen.
　　Secret confessions of the Applewood PTA / Ellen Meister.—1st ed.
　　　　p.　cm.
　　1. Domestic relations—Fiction.　2. Motion picture industry—Fiction.　I. Title.

PS3613.E4355S43　2006
813'.6—dc22　　　　　　　　　　　　　　　　　　2005057688

07　08　09　10　11　WBC/RRD　10　9　8　7　6　5　4　3　2　1

This book is dedicated to Mike,
who delivers the goods

And to Fern,
in loving memory

Acknowledgments

This book would not have been possible without the creative input and gentle wisdom of Rhonda Gill and Marcus Grimm who had the patience to read through the messy first draft chapter by mucky chapter. Special thanks, too, to the folks who run my online writing workshop, and to all the brilliant friends I met there—including Terri Brown-Davidson, Don Capone, Louis Catron, Dave Clapper, Myfanwy Collins, Ray Collins, Susan DiPlacido, Kathy Fish, Glen Held, Susan Henderson, Jordan Rosenfeld, Tom Saunders, Fred Schoeneman, Robin Slick, Maryanne Stahl, Andrew Tibbetts, Leslie Van Newkirk, and David Veronese—for making me a better writer and a better person.

To all the busy professionals who took time from their hectic schedules to answer my technical and medical questions—including Dr. Charlie Goldberg, Dr. Bruce Friedman, Dr. David Kudrow, Debbie Regan, and Susan Sterling-Katz—my sincerest gratitude.

For their relentless dedication to helping me make this book all it could be, I thank my superstar editor, Carrie

Feron, and the two best agents on the planet, Andrea Cirillo and Annelise Robey of the Jane Rotrosen Agency.

To Marilyn and Gerard Meister, Andrea Meister, Stephen and Melissa Meister, and Irene Zimmerman, eternal thanks for encouraging me to the point where I actually believed I could do it. To Max, Ethan, and Emma, love and gratitude for making it all matter. And the biggest thanks of all to Mike, the love of my life, for making the world spin on its axis.

Of course, a special thanks to PTA women everywhere—but to the women of my Long Island town in particular—for their warmth, dedication, and inspiration.

Maddie, Ruth, and Lisa sit on the shiny new aluminum bleachers in their children's school yard and squint into the horizon. Ruth leans back, resting her elbows on the bench behind them. She tilts her face toward the sun.

"I bet he has great hands," she says.

"Mmm," Lisa agrees.

Ruth and Maddie look at her and laugh.

"You've thought about it?" Maddie prods Lisa, who blushes.

"I'm human, aren't I?"

"And I suppose you *never* think about getting dirty with him," Ruth says to Maddie.

"I think about making love *with* him," Maddie says.

"You think about screwing *him*," Ruth corrects.

Maddie shakes her head. "Only after he falls in love with me."

"See, that's the difference between you and me," Ruth says, "I picture him doing me first, and then *falling in love*." She turns to Lisa. "How about you?"

"Me? I, uh . . ." Lisa looks away as if she is trying to find an answer in the distance, and then actually sees something that makes her sit up straighter. "Is that him?"

Maddie and Ruth lean forward and stare at the car turning in toward the elementary school.

"It's him," Ruth says, standing. The others rise, too.

"Should we show him what this PTA is all about?" Maddie asks.

Ruth arches her back and fluffs her mane with her fingertips. "Forget the P," she says, "let's show him some T and A."

Moments later, a man emerges from the car and sees three women walking toward him, elbows linked. The one in the middle smiles proudly.

"Welcome to Applewood, Mr. Clooney."

One year earlier . . .

Chapter One

MADDIE

Maddie Schein drove into the parking lot of the North Applewood Elementary School and found a space between two massive SUVs, glinting majestically in the morning sun. She thought she saw the designer vehicles bristle at the proximity of her four-year-old, in-need-of-a-wash minivan. Ridiculous, she told herself. They're hunks of metal. And besides, even if they *could* judge her, why should she care? It's not like she even aspired to such trophies.

Still, she wished she could wear the source of her pride on the outside, like the other PTA women did. But you can't drive a law degree, or slip your IQ over your shoulders and tie it into a jaunty knot.

She slammed the van door and headed toward the building, wondering why she cared so much about impressing these women. Didn't she have enough self-esteem without their approval? Didn't she get enough reassurance from Bruce, her husband?

Well, no. And maybe that was part of the problem.

Maybe that was why she sought recognition here. It had been so long since Bruce had showered her with the kind of assurances she craved that she was starved for appreciation. And after getting that phone call this morning from his cousin, she was more than just needy. She was desperate.

She pushed open the double doors to the cafeteria where the first meeting of the year was about to start. As she scanned the room for familiar faces, Maddie wondered if she would ever feel like she had a place in this town's social strata. Little did she know that a year later she would walk into this very same room bearing the town's most important news since Mr. Abbot, the principal of the high school, was caught with Mr. McCann, the art teacher, in the janitor's closet. Only it wouldn't be about faculty. It would be about George Clooney.

Maddie scanned the room, trying to find a friendly face among the crowd of women who were still milling about, chatting in small groups. She spotted a hand waving spiritedly. It was Mary Molinari, a sweet but hypertalkative woman who managed to work into almost every conversation that she was related, however remotely, to the superintendent of schools.

Maddie also got a nod from Donna Fishbein, an icy dermatologist whose husband had recently been indicted for stock fraud.

Toward the front of the room, Maddie noticed Suzanne Podobinski, head of the PTA and one of the impeccably groomed women who gave the town's female population its reputation for high-maintenance perfection. Looking at Suzanne and her group, most of whom were actually from Applewood Estates, a more affluent hamlet to the north with multiacre zoning and long driveways, Maddie remembered a joke she had made to an old college friend.

"You've got it all wrong," she had said, "the women here run the gamut from blond to brunette, from thin to *very* thin."

It wasn't true of course, and Maddie knew it. The town had its share of diversity. If not in gene lines, then in waistlines at least. It was just that this elite group of women shone so brightly they eclipsed everyone else.

"Maddie!" Suzanne called, waving.

Widely regarded as a bitch, Suzanne sometimes seemed almost fond of Maddie, who understood it was the lawyer card working to her advantage again. And maybe it was the kind of thing everyone did, trying to find the ace that could bolster their status—like Mary Molinari and her tenuous relationship to the superintendent—but it had been so long since Maddie actually had practiced law that publicizing it was beginning to feel like a lie.

Maddie said hello to Suzanne, glancing past her to where she thought she saw her good friend Beryl Berman winding her way though the crowd.

"Who does Russell have?" Suzanne shouted over the din. Their boys were friends and eager to be in the same class.

"Mrs. Shulansky," Maddie said, referring to one of North Applewood's second-grade teachers. "How about Noah?"

"Collins," Suzanne said, pouting to illustrate her disappointment that her son was in a different class.

"We'll have to make a playdate," Maddie consoled. Suzanne was summoned by one of her fancy friends and waved good-bye.

Maddie looked back to the spot where she had seen Beryl only to discover that she stood about an inch away.

"Hey," Beryl said.

"How do you *do* that?" Maddie asked.

"Do what?"

"Appear out of nowhere."

"I tend to go invisible," said Beryl, "it's a special power I have. But it only works here in Applewood."

At five foot one, with a round shape and dark frizzy hair she had given up on, Beryl was not one of the lovelier women in the town. If you asked her about this, she would tell you it was fine with her, as she had no desire to live a life like the Applewood women who thought that the term "Miracle Mile"—a nickname for the designer shopping strip that cinched Long Island's tony North Shore—was literal.

Beryl pointed at Suzanne's group with her chin. "Look at them. Are they *all* on their way to tennis games, or are those special little PTA outfits?"

Maddie smiled. Thank God for Beryl. "If they don't show off their asses," Maddie said, "what's the point of all those hours at the gym?"

"You sound as bitter as me today. What's going on?"

Maddie sighed. "We got this wedding invitation from some distant relative of Bruce's. Since it's out of town and we barely know her, we decided not to go. So I stuck the invitation in a kitchen drawer, figuring I'd send my regrets when I had time to write a nice note. Believe me, I was thrilled we weren't going. Besides the fact that it's so hard to find someone to watch the kids for a weekend, I didn't think this wedding would be the best thing for our marriage right now."

"Why not?"

"Because I was thinking that Bruce's cousin Jenna might be there."

"You don't like her?"

"It's not that. She's kind of interesting, really. A neohippie. But Bruce, sheesh. He's starry-eyed around her. It's like I don't even exist when she's in the room. I could be standing there naked and he wouldn't notice me."

"Have you tried nipple clamps? They have light-up ones that are hard to miss."

Maddie laughed.

"Seriously," Beryl continued. "Why does this have you down if you've already decided not to go to this wedding?"

"Because," Maddie said, rubbing dirt from the corner of her eye, "Jenna called this morning. She said she'd heard we were going to the wedding and was looking forward to seeing us there. I couldn't imagine where she got that idea from, so while she talked I fished around the kitchen drawer for the wedding invitation. And guess what?"

"What?"

"The response card was missing! Bruce sent it in without telling me."

"I don't get it. Why?"

"I'm guessing he found out Jenna was going to be there and got so excited he didn't even want to pass it by me. Now it's a fait accompli and I have nothing to say in the matter."

Beryl touched her friend's arm and made her promise to call her after she confronted Bruce about it.

Maddie agreed and changed the subject back to PTA business. "Are you signing up for the public relations committee again?" she asked.

Beryl, a freelance copywriter, had signed on to that committee the year before, thinking her skills could be put to use. But all she wound up doing was writing captions for photographs of the children at various school events for the town newspaper. If you picked up the *Applewood*

Gazette and saw a picture captioned "Mrs. Hammerstein's fourth-graders enjoy a presentation on oral hygiene," Beryl probably wrote it.

"I'd rather do something *with* the kids," Beryl said. "Like the Halloween party committee or the carnival."

"Then we'd better get over to that table and see what's left." Maddie pointed to the area of the meeting room where a long table was arranged with sign-up sheets for the various committees. At the top of each page was the name of the committee, followed by numbered blank spaces for volunteers to fill in their names and phone numbers. The more personnel a committee required, the more spaces were provided for names. Once all the spaces were filled, the committee was complete.

"Oh, crap, look at this," Beryl said. "Carnival is full, Halloween is full, ice cream is full, even fifth-grade car wash is full."

"Why don't you just write in your name at the bottom, for heaven's sake?"

"I've tried that. Jacqueline Bouvier Kennedy Onassis Podobinski just *whites* it out."

"Look," Maddie said, "only one person signed up for public relations."

"Oh, God," Beryl said, rolling her eyes. "Ruth *Moss.*"

"Who's that?"

"One of Suzanne's loudmouthed friends from Applewood Estates," Beryl said, "all big hair, big teeth, big jelly-sack breasts."

"Isn't she the one whose husband had a stroke?"

"Yeah, yeah. She cried all the way to the malpractice hearing."

Maddie looked up and spotted a heavily made-up woman with an enormous mane of long, strawberry-red hair, bounding her way toward them, breasts bouncing chaotically from side to side. She wore a stylized sweat suit like Suzanne Podobinski, but instead of the intentionally sedate accessories the PTA president wore to suggest superior breeding, this woman was loudly accented with diamond jewelry, an oversized handbag, and some kind of hybrid footwear, part shoe and part sneaker, that Maddie thought looked like an experiment gone terribly wrong.

"Isn't that her?" Maddie whispered.

"Quick! Find me a mop!" Beryl said. "If I pretend I'm a cleaning lady she'll never see me."

"Meryl!" the redheaded woman said in a loud, raspy voice. "I hope you're signing up for public relations again."

"No habla inglés," Beryl answered.

Confused, Ruth hesitated but quickly recovered. "You crack me up, Meryl."

"It's *Beryl*," Beryl corrected, "not *Meryl*. And I don't know *what* I'm signing up for yet. Have you met Marilyn?"

Maddie just shook her head like a mother who knows she should be exasperated by her precocious youngster. "It's *Madalyn*," she said, extending her hand. "Call me Maddie."

Ruth shook her hand and suggested Maddie and Beryl both sign up for the public relations committee. The two friends looked at each other.

"I will if you will," Maddie said.

"I will if Maddie can be committee chair." Beryl smiled. "Did you know she's a lawyer?"

"I don't think I *want* to be chair, Beryl."

"Of course you do," Beryl said. "Don't you know how much power you'll wield in this town as chairperson of the North Applewood Elementary PTA public relations committee? Besides, I'm sure Ruth doesn't want to be chair two years in a row." Beryl had turned her back to Ruth, excluding her from the conversation.

Ruth tried to wedge her way in. "Actually—" she began.

"C'mon, Maddie," Beryl interrupted, "think of the glory."

"Not if Ruth feels uncomfortable about it."

Beryl looked at Ruth.

"You're putting me on the spot," Ruth said.

Beryl turned to her friend. "What do you say, Maddie?"

"I say why don't *you* be chair? At least you've been on this committee before." Now I've done it, Maddie thought. This woman is going to hate both of us. She couldn't look Ruth in the eye.

"Okay," Beryl said, "I accept."

"Wait a minute," Ruth said, seething, "you can't just *decide* you're going to chair the committee."

Beryl put her handbag down and stepped toward Ruth. "Why not?" she said. "That's how you got appointed last year, isn't it?"

Furious, Ruth grabbed the public relations committee sign-up sheet and stormed off in the direction of Suzanne Podobinski. Beryl and Maddie watched her walk away, rubber soles squeaking on the polished floor all the way to the front of the room.

"Maybe we should beat it," Beryl said, "before they bring in the tanks like Tiananmen Square."

Before Ruth could reach her friend, Suzanne was already at the microphone, calling the meeting to order. Undeterred, Ruth remained at the front of the room, arms crossed, as Suzanne welcomed the attendees and introduced the officers of the PTA.

Preliminary business out of the way, Suzanne addressed

the issue that had been a main focus of this PTA for the past five years: raising enough funds to build a small stadium on Field Four.

"Everything the PTA does is important," Suzanne said into the microphone, "but getting this outdoor arena built will make us the envy of every elementary school on Long Island. And think how great it will be for the *kids*. We won't have to use the one at the high school every time we want to have a big event. So please, do everything you can to support our fund-raising efforts. Thank you."

While the crowd applauded, Beryl leaned in to Maddie. "Figure out a way to get that stadium built," she said, "and you'll be the biggest star this town has seen since Billy Joel stopped in the Seven-Eleven for a Slurpee."

The offices of Bruce's business, Long Island Chiropractic, were in a medical building just a few miles from Applewood. Bruce had moved there only two years ago, but that was before he added a second associate, and they were already outgrowing it. In another year, he promised Maddie, he would probably have enough patients to move to a bigger place and hire a third chiropractor. Then he'd have enough income from his employees to cut back on his own hours.

Sure, thought Maddie, I'll believe it when I see it.

Bruce's receptionist, Franny, an even-tempered woman in her late sixties, had an irritating habit of stating the obvious. Sometimes this amused Maddie, like when, after being asked if she had sent in those claim forms to Blue Cross yet, Franny responded, "Yes, I sent them today. In an envelope."

Other times Maddie was less than amused. Like when

she stopped by the office because Bruce had asked her to make a bank deposit for him. Before releasing the pile of checks and cash to Maddie, Franny held them out of her reach and said, "This is important, dear. *Don't* lose it." That's when the former attorney-at-law wanted to push the old pigeon out of her chair.

"Is he free?" Maddie asked.

"Yes, he's doing paperwork in his office."

"Thanks." Maddie headed past Franny toward Bruce's office.

"You can go right in," Franny added.

"Got it."

Maddie pushed open the door to Bruce's office. "Were you planning on going without me?" she said as she tossed the wedding invitation on top of the file Bruce was reviewing.

"What?" He looked down at their names written in calligraphy on the envelope and his face reddened. "No, honey, no. Of course not. I just forgot to tell you, that's all."

Maddie paused to take this in. "You forgot to tell me you sent it in, or you forgot to tell me you changed your mind?"

"Both, I guess."

Maddie was almost afraid to ask the next question. "What made you change your mind?"

"I spoke to my parents and they told me Jenna was going and I thought it would be fun."

Maddie cringed.

"I thought you'd be happy," he said. "You *like* Jenna."

"Not as much as *you* like her."

"What is that supposed to mean?"

"It means I won't be forced into going to this wedding."

Bruce's expression hardened at this. "Fine. Don't go. I'll go myself."

Maddie paused and looked at the man who once told her that the smell of her neck alone was enough to make him want to spend the rest of his life with her. She searched his eyes for any sign of softness, but he was resolute. That's what he really wants, she thought, he wants to go without me.

"Go to hell," she said and paused for a response.

Bruce picked up the invitation and slipped it into the top drawer of his desk. She had pushed his anger button, the one that turned off his sympathy for her like an engine gone cold. "Is there anything else?" he asked, closing the drawer. "I have patients waiting."

Maddie narrowed her eyes, turned and walked out. As she passed Franny's desk, the flighty old pest asked if she was leaving. Maddie just sighed and let the door shut behind her.

"Have a nice day!" she heard the cheery voice yell through the door. Maddie pulled the pin on an imaginary hand grenade and tossed it over her shoulder.

That night, Bruce apologized and told her he really wanted her to come. She knew it took a lot for him to come to her like this. Still, she needed more. She wanted him to say he wouldn't go without her.

"Will you come?" he asked. "Please?"

"What happens if I say no?" She looked at Bruce and thought, C'mon, honey, say it. Say you wouldn't dream of going without me. "What happens then?"

Bruce sighed. "Then I'll miss you."

Chapter Two

It was close to noon the next day when Maddie hurried into Bloomingdale's not thinking about why she was bothering to shop for a dress to wear to an out-of-town wedding she didn't want to attend for a person she barely knew with a husband who might ignore her when she got there. She thought about all that yesterday and came up with no good answer. She focused, instead, on whether she should make a quick dash to the bathroom before trying on dresses or just wait until she was on her way out. She eyed the escalator to the second floor, considering the logistics of her options, when she heard a man's voice call her name. Or rather the nickname "Shoeshine," which only one person in the world called her.

It was her old friend Jack Rose, who had stopped calling her "Mel" when she married Bruce and went from being Madalyn Sue Melman to Madalyn Sue Schein, which he thought sounded too much like Shoeshine to ever call her anything else. Jack occupied the slippery sliver of space in her heart between love and hate, and she hadn't spoken to him since the fight they had over two years ago. He was often an unkind friend, but she forgave him again and again, accepting his selfishness as one of the quirks that made him an Interesting Man.

For Jack, canceling plans to get together without offering an apology, and, in fact, acting as if an apology would compromise the integrity of a true free spirit, was nothing unusual. But at the time of the big fight he was doing it more frequently than ever. Over the phone, she told him that she thought his attitude was bullshit. And he told her that she was nagging him like a blood-sucking wife and should "back the fuck off." She hung up the phone and hoped he would call back, but he never did.

Now she had a decision to make. How should she greet him? Coolly? Contemptuously? With physical violence?

"Mel." He cocked his head to the side and put his arms out for an embrace.

He called me "Mel," she thought, as her resolve liquefied and her arms wrapped around him. But when he said, "I'm glad you don't hate me," the frustration of the argument she'd had with her husband the day before burned into the still-raw wound of her fight with Jack. She punched the center of his back with the hand she was using to hug him.

"Or maybe you do," he said.

"You are *such* an asshole."

"I know."

Maddie and Jack had been friends since college, where they met while waiting for a bus between campuses on a frigid Buffalo morning. He had worn an enormous down jacket tufted to look like a pile of tires. Like a lot of girls, she was egregiously underdressed, choosing the slim profile of a suede jacket over the warmth and comfort of a big coat. They had stood side by side, alternately peering down the road to look for the bus, when Maddie announced to the bulky stranger that she was freezing.

"Well, sure, when you're dressed like an *idiot*," he'd said.

"Better than looking like a Michelin display," she shot back.

He had laughed, and a friendship was sealed.

Jack was one of the few people Maddie was acerbic with. She had met him at a time in her life when she was figuring out the kind of person she wanted to be. Since she enjoyed his sarcasm, which made her feel included in a very private club because it implied that she was well liked enough for it to be ironic and smart enough to get the joke, she decided to try it herself. She was good enough at it to earn Jack's admiration, which she coveted, so it became an integral part of their relationship. But, with an irony that wasn't lost on Maddie, it disqualified her as a romantic interest for Jack.

It was fairly early on in their friendship that Maddie realized this. She was out to dinner with a raucous group of friends that included Jack and his love interest of the moment, a petite brunette named Abby. Maddie couldn't help but notice that the girl, who barely spoke, laughed only at Jack's jokes. Slowly, while she stared at Abby's adorably lopped profile, a sort of gravitational force pulled together fragments of thought that had been floating around in her mind. She realized, with surprisingly little dismay, that she and Jack would never date. Ever. So she closed off the part of herself that felt an attraction and looked at him like a brother from that moment on. It was easy for Maddie to go cool when there was no heat from him because, like a lot of women, what drew her most to a man was his desire for her. Besides, she reasoned, he could never be faithful to one woman. And that was a trait she simply couldn't live with.

In the years that followed, their relationship became so familial that when she was occasionally reminded that she had once been attracted to him she was surprised that she could ever have had such an incestuous thought.

Now, in the middle of Bloomingdale's, between the beckoning scents of the cosmetic counters and the sober call of the escalator to designer dresses, Maddie scanned Jack's face for clues on how to feel. She noticed that the skin around his eyes looked thin and dark, and she wondered if he'd just had the flu, or if it was simply the two years that she hadn't seen him.

He folded his arms as if he were waiting for her to say something. When she didn't, he announced, "We should have lunch."

"Now?"

"Why not? We can talk about what happened. I'll let you call me all sorts of names."

It was a tempting offer. Maddie looked at her watch. If she timed it right, she could manage to buy a dress, grab a quick lunch, and be home in time to get the kids off the bus. She knew she should tell him to get lost, since he would probably just wind up hurting her again if she let him back in her life. But on the other hand, the heady fun of her friendship with Jack might be just what she needed at this point.

So she agreed, and they arranged to meet at a restaurant in the mall an hour later.

"But if you're not there," Maddie warned, "I'll hunt you down and shoot you like a dog."

She found a dress she liked right away. Though on sale for fifty percent off, it was still expensive, and she knew

Bruce would balk. But if she was to be forced into going to a wedding, she was damn well going to wear what she wanted.

Maddie stared into the dressing room mirror, pleased at how lithe she looked in the pricey dress. But she couldn't help picturing herself standing alone at the wedding in this lovely outfit, sipping a cocktail and trying not to look miserable while Bruce and Jenna huddled together talking and laughing, as if no one else existed. She remembered the time her husband walked away from her in mid-conversation because he saw Jenna come into the room. Granted, it was after Jenna's mother died and he could have simply been trying to console her, but when Maddie approached the two of them and tried to get in on the discussion by putting her hand on Bruce's shoulder, which was nearly touching Jenna's, he was unyielding, and Maddie felt worse than ignored. She felt rejected.

"Are you crazy? She's my *cousin*!" he said later, when she confronted him with her suspicions.

Yeah, *right,* she thought. A second cousin who's *adopted.* You two could get married and have a hundred babies and not one of them would have the tail of a pig.

"That doesn't mean you can't have a crush on her."

"Her mother *died,* Maddie," he spat. "I refuse to have this conversation."

And then he went silent, ignoring her for the rest of that night and the entire next day while they sat shivah, paying their respects at Jenna's father's house. Maddie, who couldn't help wondering if he was using his righteous anger as an excuse to focus all his attention on Jenna, filled the day thinking about what her life would be like if they got divorced. During the car ride home she let it all out and cried bitterly, telling Bruce between sobs that this was

not what she wanted from a marriage. She expected him
to wrap her in assurances, but his anger was too potent for
her pain to penetrate. This made her even more distraught,
as Maddie blamed herself for pushing him so far that no
amount of tears could yield the sympathy she craved. She
sank further into despair.

Maddie approached the door to the restaurant and decided
that if Jack wasn't inside she would give him exactly five
minutes before heading for her car. She'd be damned if she
was going to wait around forever for a guy who was per-
petually late. When he bothered showing up at all.

Once, when they were both doing their graduate work
in New York, he told her he wanted to fix her up with a
medical-school buddy of his. So they decided she'd bring
a girlfriend for Jack, and the four of them would hook up
at a restaurant uptown to accommodate his busy schedule.
But Jack never showed up.

"Where *were* you?" she asked him the next morning.

"You know that girl Leeza, from my anatomy lab?"

"Oh, *please*." Maddie never bought the conventional
wisdom among her circle of friends that Jack's sexual appetite was of historic proportions.

"What was I supposed to do?" he said.

"Keep it in your pants. For once. You know what *I* was
doing while you were fucking your brains out?"

"You didn't like Eugene?" He sounded hurt. She was
glad.

"Don't ever do that to me again."

"What, fix you up?"

"*Stand* me up."

"I can't promise that," he said, and she knew he meant it.

Now here she was scanning the booths along the back wall of O'Rourke's, A Place Where Good Friends and Good Food Meet, hoping, at least this one time, he had the sense to show up. To her great relief, Jack's big wave caught her eye.

"So how's Deb?" Maddie asked as she settled herself in. For over seven years, Jack had been living with a woman she and Bruce usually referred to as Deb the ditz. Maddie wondered how someone so obviously bright—she was, after all, a veterinarian—could act so stupid. Maddie suspected it was an act.

"Gone," Jack responded. "How's Bruce?"

"What do you mean *gone*?"

"Gone. Like I'm-sick-of-waiting-for-you-to-decide-whether-or-not-you're-going-to-marry-me gone."

"When?"

"About two months ago."

"Are you okay?"

He shrugged. "It was inevitable."

She knew she shouldn't press the issue, as Jack despised the subject of marriage, at least as it pertained to him, beyond all reason. On the few occasions she'd brought it up in the past he became incensed, accusing her of being obsessed with the subject and of having the same judgmental, hypocritical value system he deplored in his parents. But she wasn't going to dance around his sensitivities. Not now, after the way he'd treated her.

"Why didn't you, Jack? Marry her, I mean."

"What for?"

"Because you loved her and wanted to spend the rest of your life with her?"

"Don't start on me, okay?"

"Now you're going to tell me I sound like your mother and we're going to get into a fight again."

"I've turned over a new leaf. No more fighting with the people I love. How's Bruce?"

Expressing his love for her in a brotherly way was nothing new for Jack. And in fact, it was now a bit of a sore point for Maddie, who had begun to see it as part of his arsenal of defenses for why she should never be mad at him no matter how badly he treated her. *I know I didn't call or come see you when you were hospitalized with double pneumonia, Shoeshine, but we're above all that, aren't we? You know I love you.*

"Apparently, Bruce *hasn't* turned over a new leaf," she said.

"That bad?"

Unexpectedly, her eyes filled with tears. "Damn it," she said.

"Do you want to talk about it?"

"No." Embarrassed to be crying, Maddie didn't look up.

He reached across the table and pushed a strand of hair out of her eyes. This surprised her, as there was rarely even the mildest hint of physical tenderness between them.

"Oh, Mel," he said gently, "I don't know why you and me never got together."

She stopped crying. "You and me? When was *that* ever an issue?"

"When was it not?"

She looked hard at his face for traces of sarcasm but could find none. "Is this a joke?"

He looked down at his hands. "I'm serious," he said.

She looked at his hands, too. He still bit his nails. A nervous habit, she thought, that belied his laid-back façade.

She felt a chill and realized that she was sitting under an air-conditioning vent. Could she have been so wrong all this time? she wondered. Could she have missed the signs that he was attracted to her?

"We've been friends for twenty years, Jack. You've never even *flirted* with me."

"Didn't you ever wonder why?"

"I assumed I wasn't your type."

"What's my type?"

Maddie dumped the artificial sweetener packets out of their plastic container, straightened them out like a deck of cards, and put them back in again. "C'mon, Jack. You know you usually dated girls with IQs below room temperature."

He smiled. "True enough. It doesn't mean I found you unattractive. Is that what you thought? Jeez. If you knew how many times I've fucked you in my mind."

She put her hands over her ears. "Oh, God, Jack!"

He grabbed her hands and pulled them away from her face. "I think we should talk about this," he said.

I think I should go, Maddie thought about saying, but instead muttered, "I think we should look at the menus. I don't have much time."

The following week, Maddie burned her thumb taking a pizza out of the oven for the kids. "Mother shit *fuck*!" she whispered.

"Mothershitfuck?" came a small voice from the table. "Mommy, did you say 'mothershitfuck'?" It was Hannah, her five-year-old.

"No! I mean, yes, I did. But those are bad words. Don't say those words."

Maddie was behind schedule trying to get out of the

house for Meet the Teacher night in Russell's classroom. She had gone out at the last minute to get the refreshments she'd promised she'd bring, and the errand cost her precious time. Bruce, who was coming home early to watch the kids, would be there any minute and Maddie wasn't ready. She went to the sink and ran cold water over the throbbing burn on her thumb.

"Russell!" Hannah shouted. "Mommy said 'mother-shitfuck'!"

"Stop it, Hannah," Maddie said as the phone rang, "that's not polite." She picked up the telephone and wedged it under her chin. "Hello?"

"Hi, honey," Bruce said, "I'm sorry but I'm tied up here for a while. An emergency came in."

"Can't Marc or Ravi take it?" she asked, referring to his associates.

Truth be told, Maddie didn't really believe in chiropractic emergencies. If someone was in that much pain, she reasoned, they belonged in a hospital. In fact, she thought that most of Bruce's patients suffered more from psychological problems than physical ones. But she kept that to herself.

"Ravi has a patient and Marc's off on Tuesdays, you *know* that."

"But you knew I needed you. Couldn't you have asked him to come in tonight?"

"Well, what do you want me to do about it now, Maddie? I've got somebody in *pain* here."

Maddie pulled her thumb out of the water and shut it off. "You've got somebody in pain here, too."

"Don't go all melodramatic on me."

She sighed, exasperated. "What am I supposed to do?"

"I don't know. Take the kids with you?"

"I *can't*. They specifically say."

"Do you really need to be there?"

Maddie wanted to slam down the receiver, but it was a cordless phone, so all she could do was push the off button as angrily as she could. Unfortunately for Maddie, she did it with the thumb she had just burned, and now was in worse pain than before. She called Beryl and asked if she could drop her kids there for an hour or so.

"No problem," Beryl said, "we just opened up a bottle of Absolut. I've got plenty to go around."

After dropping off the kids at Beryl's house, Maddie sped to the school, her mind wandering, as it had all week, to the things Jack had said to her over lunch. He couldn't stop thinking about sleeping with her, he had said, and wanted to know what she thought about that.

"What do I *think* about that?" she answered. "I think you want to know if I'll have an affair with you but can't even commit to *asking* me."

"Okay," he said, reaching his hand under the table and putting it on her thigh. "I'm asking you."

His warm touch felt too good, awakening a surge of longing. She remembered that rush, that promise-of-a-new-partner tease that pulled her in the direction of abandon. This is why people have affairs, she thought, this very feeling. She pulled his hand off her leg.

"Jack," she said, in a voice that suggested she was putting an end to the discussion.

"Just think about it, okay?" he said.

"How come you never said anything before?"

He was drinking beer from an amber bottle. When he pulled it away from his mouth the suction broke with a pop.

"Didn't you ever like someone so much it scared you?"

he asked. "Like if you let yourself go you'd lose yourself completely?"

She looked straight into his eyes, expecting him to say something to clarify his point, to explain that he wasn't talking about his feelings for her, not really. But he just stared, unblinking, waiting for an answer.

She looked down. "No. I've always liked abandoning myself to love."

The screech of brakes shocked Maddie, who hadn't realized that she'd run a red light. She looked in horror at the car approaching and had just enough time to swerve out of the way so that it only grazed her rear bumper. Maddie sat for a moment, trembling. Then she took stock and realized it was a relatively minor accident and that she was okay. She exchanged information with the other driver and got back in her car, thinking that she was lucky not to have suffered a broken bone or other temporary handicap. After all, who would get the kids to soccer, dance, karate, gymnastics, swimming, piano lessons, and playdates? How on earth would she do two loads of laundry each and every day? Who would make their lunches and run to the school to drop off the homework they had accidentally left behind?

She was still running through the list in her mind when she arrived at the school almost twenty minutes late. The heavy soda bottles were threatening to break through the bottom of the shopping bag they were in, so she had to cradle them in her arm while balancing a platter of cookies on the other hand. Her handbag strap was over her shoulder, and she had to lean to the left so it wouldn't slide down her arm and pull on the hand holding the cookies. As she rushed through the lobby doing the best speed-walk she could under the circumstances, a beaming Ruth Moss ran up to her, flushed with excitement.

"Maddie! I have to tell you something."

"Not now, Ruth, I'm late."

With that, Maddie's handbag slid down her arm, jerking the hand with the cookie platter. She dove to the right to keep the cookies level and found herself losing balance, so she jerked herself in the other direction and tumbled to the floor in a thud.

"Are you okay?" Ruth asked.

"I think so," Maddie said, though her left ankle and hand hurt more than she wanted to admit. She stood up and retrieved the bottles of soda, which had broken out of the bag and were rolling away.

"Let me help you," Ruth said, picking up the platter of cookies, which, remarkably, remained unscathed.

"Thanks," Maddie said, thinking Ruth meant she would carry the tray to the classroom for her. But Ruth placed the platter on Maddie's hand, which was upturned because she was inspecting it for damage.

"Can you come to my house Wednesday morning for a committee meeting?" Ruth asked, smiling.

"I'll have to check my schedule," Maddie said. "I'll tell Beryl to check hers, too."

Ruth's expression changed to serious. "Um, Beryl," she said slowly, as if considering how to respond.

Maddie squinted at her. "There a problem?"

"No, no problem. But tell Beryl I'll call her. There's something we need to discuss."

Maddie figured it was some nonsense about chairing the committee and shrugged. Beryl, she knew, could handle herself just fine. "What's the meeting about, anyway?"

Ruth's grin reappeared. "Big news!" she said. "I'll tell you more on Wednesday."

Maddie nodded and limped away, wondering what on earth could have befallen the North Applewood Elementary PTA public relations committee that could warrant that kind of excitement.

Later, when Maddie arrived at Beryl's house to pick up her kids, Russell and Hannah were drinking Pepsi and snacking on a pile of Oreo cookie sandwiches, only they had licked out the cream and replaced it with chunks of squashed, chocolate-covered doughnuts.

"I would have preferred the Absolut," Maddie said to Beryl. "They're going to be bouncing off the walls."

"Not to worry." Beryl winked. "I spiked the soda."

Beryl walked Maddie outside as she limped to her minivan and loaded her kids inside.

"Were they good?" Maddie asked, worried that Hannah might have tried to impress Beryl with the multisyllabic word she had learned from her mother that evening.

"As gold."

Maddie was relieved. Not just because Hannah had got past her fascination with cursing, but because she knew Beryl would be so amused she'd sink her teeth into it and rattle it in Maddie's face.

Beryl noticed Maddie's limp. "What happened to *you*? You're walking funny."

"I fell. It's nothing. If you want something to get excited about, talk to Ruth Moss. Apparently she has some big news for the public relations committee. And something extra special she wants to talk to *you* about."

"Wuh-oh. I tried to usurp her crown. I'm probably scheduled for beheading."

"Wear something nice."

"Nicer than this?" Beryl said, pulling on her Bruce Springsteen T-shirt. "Listen, the truth is, I was just busting Ruth's chops. I really don't give a damn about being the chairperson of the public relations committee."

"So what are you going to say when Ruth calls you?"

"One word."

Maddie closed the back door to her car. "What's that?"

"Mothershitfuck."

Chapter Three

Painkillers helped Maddie fall asleep that night. But at two o'clock in the morning, the throbbing in her ankle woke her. Even in the dark she could see how badly swollen it was.

"Bruce, wake up," she whispered.

"What is it?"

She showed him her leg and explained how she had fallen. He clicked on the lamp next to him and carefully examined her ankle, holding her foot gently in his hands.

"Why didn't you tell me?" he asked.

"I thought it was nothing."

"You were wrong."

They called a neighbor to come over and watch the kids while Bruce took Maddie to the hospital.

"I don't want to go to North Shore," Maddie said as Bruce helped her into the car. She was referring to the large local hospital that employed Dr. Jack Rose as its chief of orthopedic surgery.

"Don't be childish," Bruce said. "It's a great facility and

I have some friends there. Besides, it's time you and Jack made up."

"We already did."

Bruce looked at her, surprised.

"I ran into him at the mall," she explained.

"Oh," he said, as if that answered the question about why she never bothered to tell him. "If he's not on duty I'm going to ask them to call him in."

Maddie tsked in protest but said nothing.

"Well," Jack boomed as he parted the curtain around the emergency room bed where Maddie was sitting, "I hear there's an amputee candidate in here."

"Orthopedist humor," Maddie said, shaking her head.

Jack made eye contact with her for a brief second before shaking hands heartily with Bruce.

"How many orthopedists does it take to change a light bulb?" Jack asked as he slapped Maddie's X-rays onto a box on the wall and flipped a switch. The screen flickered on.

"I give up," Bruce offered.

"Two," Jack said, "but they do it *jointly.*"

Bruce laughed, and Maddie wondered if this forced joviality was a normal part of Jack's bedside manner or if he was trying to deflect any current of sexual tension Bruce might sense.

As she watched her old friend point out her fracture and discuss it with her husband, Maddie made a quick comparison between the two men. She realized that objectively, Bruce was clearly the more desirable one, with his broad shoulders and V waist. Jack, always lean, had gotten even thinner, and she knew that beneath his white coat his backside was practically concave. But he desired her. And that alone made her feel feverish at the thought of him cradling her ankle in his warm hands the way Bruce had done only an hour before.

Jack explained that he would splint the ankle first, to allow for swelling, and then cast it two days later. "Normally I would have one of my residents do the splint," he added, "but in this case I think I'll do it myself. I could use the practice." He cracked his knuckles to emphasize the joke.

Thank God he's not casting it now, Maddie thought. If I had to lie here letting him touch me for as long as it took to smooth on a cast—with Bruce standing *right here*—I just couldn't take it.

But Maddie couldn't get that image out of her mind, and she suddenly felt as if her lungs wouldn't take in enough air. Deep breaths, she said to herself, deep breaths.

Bruce looked at Maddie and his expression changed in a way she didn't understand. "Are you okay?" He sounded alarmed.

"I'm fine. Why?"

Bruce and Jack looked at each other. It was then Maddie realized her fingers were tingling and the room was going gray. This can't happen, she thought. I can't faint. I *can't*.

"You're white as a ghost," Bruce said, and they both rushed to her.

The darkness increased. "I don't feel so good at all," she admitted. Jack quickly lowered the back of the bed so that she was reclining. He took her pulse. She tried to breathe evenly. This is normal, she told herself as the darkness faded. It reveals nothing. People get faint in hospitals all the time. She looked at Bruce. All she saw was concern. She glanced at Jack, who seemed to be concentrating on her pulse.

"Are you feeling a little better?" Jack asked as he strapped a blood pressure cuff on her arm.

"I think so," she said.

Jack pumped the cuff and Maddie turned to Bruce. "I don't know why that happened," she said.

"It's nothing," he said, taking her other hand. "You probably just got a little scared."

"I think I feel better now." She tried to sit up.

"You're fine." Jack gently pushed her back down by her shoulder. "But do me a favor and just lie there until your blood pressure comes back up a little." He ripped the Velcro cuff off her arm and told her he would be back to splint her ankle. Meanwhile, he would see if he could find a nurse to bring her some orange juice.

"This is embarrassing," Maddie said to Bruce after Jack left.

Bruce kissed her on the forehead. "It's a normal reaction, honey. It happens all the time. Don't worry, okay? I promise I'll stay right here with you."

But he didn't. When Jack came back to splint her leg, Bruce said he wanted to give Jack room to work, and left to get a cup of coffee. Maddie told him to call home and make sure everything was okay.

"You know," Jack said as he lifted Maddie's leg and placed it gently in a stirrup, "you could have just called and said you wanted to see me."

"Don't," Maddie said, "this is humiliating enough."

Jack took his hands off her leg. "Would you prefer if I had someone else do this?"

Lying helpless on the table with her leg in a stirrup while Jack peered down on her made Maddie feel acutely vulnerable. But she was afraid that if she sent Jack away and had a resident treat her she would never hear the end of it from Bruce. He would argue the stupidity of having a rookie care for her when the chief of orthopedic surgery was at her disposal.

"No, that's fine. I assume you know what you're doing."

"Anytime you want to find out . . ." He gently stroked the inside of her thigh.

Maddie looked straight at him. "Oh, nurse," she said in a voice so soft no nurse could possibly hear, "isn't there someone I can report this inappropriate behavior to?"

"There is," Jack said, nodding in the direction Bruce went, "but he's busy calling the babysitter."

She laughed in spite of herself and he gave her such a charming smile that she wondered how she could have spent so many years not wanting him. As he opened the sterile packaging on the splint his expression changed. He's put his doctor hat back on, Maddie thought, and wondered if he was as engrossed in his work as he seemed. After all, they were in an overtly sexual position, with him standing between her spread legs. And she could still feel his delicate touch on her thigh.

In the car on the way home, Bruce asked Maddie if everything was okay with Jack, as far as she knew.

"He broke up with Deb," she said.

"Yeah, I heard."

"You heard?"

He looked at her and then turned back to the road. "Hospital staffs love to gossip, especially about doctors."

"What else did you hear?"

He thought for a second. "Nothing, really."

"You going in to work today?" she asked.

"I have to, honey. But I'll help you get the kids off to school, first."

Maddie sighed and thought about the pile of laundry

that needed to be folded, the larger pile that had to be washed, and all the phone calls she would have to make within the next few hours to make sure her kids had transportation to their various extracurricular activities. Beryl, she knew, would be able to fill in if she wasn't shuttling Devin somewhere or on deadline with some copywriting project.

Two days later, when Maddie had an appointment to get the splint exchanged for a plaster cast, Bruce held open the car door for his wife and helped her get in without putting weight on her ankle. She was touched by his tenderness, and remembered how much she cherished it in the early days of their relationship. Maddie had met Bruce Schein while she was in law school and he was finishing his degree in chiropractic medicine. From the start, Bruce adored Maddie for all the right reasons, and told her so often. She reveled in his devotion, realizing that this was the kind of love she needed, the kind that wrapped around you like an oversized comforter and kept you warm and happy forever.

After they married, Maddie got pregnant and Bruce put his energies into building his practice, which went from being simply Bruce Schein, D.C., to *Long Island Chiropractic.* By the time they had two children, Bruce was so consumed by work he rarely found occasions to remind Maddie of the reasons he loved her.

Today, as she and Bruce drove to Jack's office to get her cast, she tried to fight off her dark impulses.

"I wonder if it will be off by the wedding," Bruce said as he merged onto the highway.

She stared down at her ankle and tried to imagine how she would look with one foot in a delicate high-heeled shoe and the other in plaster. It would mean she wouldn't be able to dance, and might spend the entire evening stuck in a chair watching Bruce have fun on the dance floor with Jenna.

"Well, whatever." She sighed. "I guess it isn't the end of the world if I have to go in a cast."

Bruce looked at her and then back at the road. Silence.

"What," she demanded. "You don't think I should go?"

Bruce shrugged. "See what Jack thinks."

"What are you talking about? I'm not going to be an invalid. I'll just have a *cast* on my leg."

"Don't get in a huff. If Jack says you can go, fine, you'll go."

"I don't believe this," she said. "You don't want me to go. You really don't want me to go."

"Are we back on this?" he complained.

"We never left it."

"I don't even want to have this conversation."

"Fine," she said, and they rode the rest of the way listening to Joe Walsh's sarcastic lyrics about the adolescent troubles of a spoiled rock star.

After they found Jack's office and Maddie checked in with the receptionist, Bruce announced that he had to go to his office to see a patient and would be back for her in an hour.

"You're not *staying*?" She leaned hard on her crutches for support.

"Honey, all I'd be doing is sitting out here in the waiting room."

Maddie looked around at the empty upholstered chairs. "So what?"

His face hardened to that mask she dreaded. "So I guess I can't do anything right," he said sarcastically.

"You're not even *trying!*" Maddie said. "Don't you think it's important, once in a while, to at least *pretend* you care about me?"

"I think it's important to work every hour I can so I can pay for that four-hundred-dollar dress you bought!"

The receptionist looked up. This was getting interesting.

"You know what? If we can't afford the dress, maybe we should *both* stay home from the wedding. How does that sound?"

Bruce opened the door to leave. "I'll see you in an hour." He let the door go behind him. The safety hinge made it shut with a hiss and a gentle click that Maddie found completely infuriating. "Don't do me any favors," she said through clenched teeth to no one. She leaned her crutches against the wall and eased into an upholstered cube-shaped chair. She looked briefly at the magazines fanned out on the table next to her but was too agitated to concentrate.

She thought about how much things had changed for them over the years. She remembered the time, back before he opened his own practice, that they were invited to an office Christmas party by the chiropractor he worked for. They were engaged and had just moved in together. The morning of the party, Maddie awoke with a pounding headache and a weakness in her legs she couldn't quite identify. She went back to bed and fell into a fitful sleep for several more hours. When she finally lifted her head, her stomach cramped and a wave of nausea gripped her like a ferocious undertow. She was barely able to make it to the toilet, where she began vomiting copiously. Bruce, in the kitchen filling up a water bottle to take with him on a jog, heard her retching and came running in. Without saying a word, he came up behind her and held her long hair back so it wouldn't be in the way. When she finally came up for air he asked if there was anything he could do for her.

"Do you have a bullet?" she said, easing her behind onto the hard bathroom floor.

He ran some cool water from the tap and filled a paper cup. "Have a small sip," he said, holding it out to her.

"I can't."

"Just a tiny sip. You don't want to get dehydrated." He held it to her lips and she drank. It felt good. She took another small sip and then felt an angry rumbling in her stomach. She put her head in the bowl and heaved violently, bringing up a flush of milky water followed by a yellow bile that burned her throat.

"I might have to kill you now," she said, when the vomiting subsided. He wet a washcloth and wiped down her face.

"I'll call Ron and tell him we're not coming tonight," he said, referring to his boss.

"No, you go. I'll be okay."

"I'm not leaving you like this."

She insisted, explaining that she would probably finish throwing up in a few hours' time and then, provided she was still alive, would just get in bed and sleep, and there would truly be nothing he could do for her. "Besides, it's important for you to show up at these things. You've said so yourself."

He kissed Maddie on her forehead. "Honey, nothing could possibly be more important than being here with you."

So he stayed. And while he couldn't do anything for her intestinal virus, his presence had a profound effect on Maddie, who realized, with her head in the toilet after a particularly spastic convulsion, that there might not be another woman on the planet more loved than she.

Why do I crave this kind of over-the-moon love? Maddie wondered as she picked up one of her crutches and bounced the rubber bumper tip against the firm jute carpeting of Jack's waiting room floor. She had read enough pop psychology books to know that, on a subconscious level, she was probably attempting to re-create her relationship with her father. Why then, when she met Bruce, did it feel like she had found the antidote to her father's conditional love? That he knew and loved the *real* Maddie, completely and unconditionally? Did *I* do this? she wondered. Am I pushing Bruce away so I can play out my relationship with my father again?

"Mrs. Schein?" It was Jack's receptionist. "Please come in."

Maddie picked up her crutches while the receptionist held the door for her.

When they reached the examining room, the woman pulled out a step stool so Maddie could get herself onto the paper-lined table. "Dr. Rose will be right with you. Would you like a magazine?"

"No, thanks," Maddie said, but regretted her decision when the receptionist left and closed the door behind her. Jack, she thought, might very well keep her waiting a long time, and the magazines were out of her reach. She eased herself off the table and carefully limped over to the magazine rack. She pulled out an issue that faced backward, thinking it might be something newsy. When she saw that it was *People,* her instinct was to put it right back, but the cover caught her attention. It was a smoldering black-and-white photograph of George Clooney, exuding such powerful masculine handsomeness she nearly lost her breath. No wonder Beryl has such a crazy crush on this man, she thought.

Maddie heard two quick knocks on the door. Jack entered.

"Don't tell me you actually found something worth reading," he said.

"Nah," she answered, embarrassed. She dropped the magazine back into the rack and hopped over to the table, wishing she had just slipped it into her bag before Jack came in. Something about that photograph made her want to possess it.

Jack carefully unwrapped the splint and examined Maddie's ankle. She laid her head back against the crinkly paper of the table. "It looks good," he said. "I'm going to have to ask my assistant to come in here and help me cast it."

Maddie thought he made it sound like a question. "That's fine," she said, but Jack didn't respond.

"Is something wrong?" she asked.

"I need to talk to you."

"So talk."

"Not here," he said. "Can we make a date to have lunch again?"

Though she got the sense that there was something serious he needed to tell her, the thought of meeting her old friend Jack for a sandwich suddenly felt dangerous.

"I don't know if that's such a good idea," she said.

Jack took her hand in his. "I understand," he said, and kissed it.

Then he called in his assistant, who held Maddie's leg while Jack pulled damp gauzy strips from an unrolled silver foil wrapper. While he worked, he occasionally glanced up at Maddie with the same masculine seriousness George

Clooney wore on the cover of the magazine. He's trying to tell me something, Maddie thought.

As she dressed to get ready to go out with her friend Beryl, Maddie drank deep from the cup of indulgent self-pity. And why not? She was getting her period and felt as bloated as a cow. Her most slimming pants—the straight-legged black ones—caught on her cast as she tried to pull them on. She gave them a hard yank and heard the fabric rip.

"Damn!" she said as she threw them into the corner of her bedroom. Maddie looked in her closet and disgustedly pulled out the long, dark skirt she had already worn twice that week.

A quick coat of nail polish, she thought, and I am *outta* here. She chose deep plum, a color she almost never wore. Maddie had just finished applying it carefully to both hands when the unthinkable happened: her leg started itching beneath her cast.

Jack had promised that wouldn't happen, and she felt somehow betrayed. She looked around to find something to scratch with, and spotted a pencil sticking out of a book on her nightstand. She grabbed it carefully between her fingertips without damaging her wet nail polish. Thinking the ridged metal clamp on the eraser would make an adequate scratching tool, Maddie held the pencil by the point and slowly inserted it inside her cast, anticipating the masochistic delight of assaulting the insufferable itch. But as the pencil reached as far as it could go while still held securely between her fingertips, she realized she would need something longer. Just as she was carefully extracting the tool and thinking about what else might work, the phone rang and startled Maddie, causing her to lose her grip and drop the pencil into her cast.

"Mother shit *fuck*!"

She lay down on the bed and held her leg straight in the air to try to get the pencil to fall out, but it didn't. The phone rang again.

"Bruce!" she shouted. "Can you get that?" She listened for an "okay" but didn't hear anything. "BRUCE!"

The phone rang again.

Maddie angrily picked up the phone, still trying not to damage her nails. "Hello," she demanded. She shook her leg over her head to get the pencil out. Still nothing.

"Hey, Maddie. How're you doing?"

She knew that voice. It was Jenna, Bruce's cousin. Why now? Maddie thought. But she didn't want to add fuel to the fire with Bruce, and readied herself to give Jenna an extra-friendly hello to make up for the angry way she answered the phone. Before she could say anything, though, she dropped the cordless phone off the side of the bed. It came flying out of her hand in an arc and crash-landed on the hardwood floor, sending the battery compartment skidding across the room.

"Mother shit fuck fuck *fuck*!" She swung her legs to the floor, put her weight on her good foot, and stood up quickly, feeling a rush to her head. *"Bruce!"* she screeched. She went to the top of the stairs and yelled his name again, as loud as she could. "BRUCE!"

"What is it, for God's sake?" he shouted.

"Pick up the phone, it's Jenna."

Maddie hobbled back to her bedroom and noticed that three of her nails were smudged. Beryl would be there any minute to pick her up, so she went into the bathroom and removed the ruined polish as quickly as she could, damaging another nail in the process. She opened the plum polish and deftly repaired her manicure. As she blew quickly on her fingertips to dry them, a car horn honked. Maddie carefully grabbed her pocketbook and pulled the strap over her shoulder. Then she looked at her crutches in the corner of the bedroom and realized there was no way she could grip her hands around them without damaging ten out of ten nails. Exasperated, she went back into the bathroom and removed all the polish with a saturated cotton ball. The car horn honked again. "I'm *coming*," she muttered through gritted teeth, trying to remove some of the deep purple rings now embedded in her cuticles. The horn honked more angrily. "Okay, *okay.*" She grabbed her crutches and left.

As she got to the bottom of the stairs and opened the front door, Bruce approached her looking furious. "There is *no excuse* for how rude you just were to my cousin," he said angrily.

"What?"

"You didn't even say hello. You just slammed down the phone as soon as you heard her voice!"

"No, no," Maddie pleaded. "It wasn't *like* that."

"I mean, what utter childishness, Maddie. Really."

"Bruce, listen to me."

The car horn honked again.

"No, go have fun celebrating your friend's birthday. I don't even want to *look* at you."

"Bruce . . ."

Beryl appeared at the door. "Everything okay here?" she asked.

"Hello, Beryl," Bruce enunciated in a slow, syrupy voice.

"How nice to *see* you." He shot Maddie a dirty look and stormed out of the room.

"Bruce, wait! Bruce! I dropped the phone! I *dropped* it!"

"I don't think he can hear you," Beryl said.

Maddie considered running after him to explain everything, but decided that since he was acting like such an idiot he didn't deserve a chance to redeem himself. Let him be a fool, she thought. He'll feel that much worse when the truth comes out.

Maddie gripped her crutches. "C'mon. Let's go."

At the restaurant, preoccupied thinking about her fight with Bruce, Maddie was on her second vodka gimlet when she remembered Beryl's birthday present. She reached into her handbag and took out a rectangular package dressed in cobalt-blue wrapping paper.

"Happy birthday," she said, handing it to her friend.

Beryl greedily tore away the wrapping paper, revealing a framed picture of Beryl and her portly husband, Jonathan, in Maddie's backyard. But where Jonathan's visage should have been, a tiny cutout of George Clooney's face had been pasted over.

Beryl spoke to the picture. "George, baby, come to Mama!" She held the picture to her breast and looked at her friend. "Thank you, from the bottom of my heart. But next year? Make it the real thing. I promise you I will ravage him to within an inch of his life. Now, tell me about Jack."

Maddie swallowed the last gulp of her vodka gimlet and held the empty glass in the waitress's view to indicate that she wanted another. "Jack," Maddie said to her friend, "wants to do to *me* what you want to do to George Clooney."

"Jack wants to rappel into your bedroom dressed like Catwoman?"

Maddie choked on a sip of her vodka. "Something along those lines."

"First he sets your bones, then he jumps them." Beryl stirred her piña colada. "Are you going to?"

"Of course not."

"Do you *want* to?"

"Not relevant."

The waitress set Maddie's drink down in front of her. She took a big gulp. "Jack fucked every girl in Buffalo except me," she said.

"I think you're getting kind of looped."

"Maybe we should order while I can still read the menu."

After the women scanned the menu and placed their orders, Maddie remembered the pencil in her cast, and leaned forward to try to fish it out with her fingertips. She couldn't locate it, and tried to reach deeper inside her cast. "You gonna come with me to that PR committee meeting tomorrow?" she asked.

"Is there free food?" Beryl looked curiously at Maddie's bent-over position. "What *are* you doing?"

"There's a pencil in my cast."

"I've got a pen in my bag. Does that help you out any?"

"Joke all you want. I can't get it out."

"Maybe you should call your orthopedist." Beryl put her hand to the side of her face as if she were talking into a phone and affected a sultry voice. "Hello, Jack? It's Maddie. I have a problem. But it's deep inside. Deep, *deep* inside."

Maddie smiled and gave up on her quest for the pencil. She sat up and took another swallow of her drink. "Somehow it's bothering me less and less."

The waitress brought their food and Maddie ordered another refill of her drink. She picked at her dinner, but the alcohol had killed her appetite. After taking a few small nibbles, she lost interest in it entirely and went back to her drink.

"So what are you going to do about you and Bruce?" Beryl asked, chewing.

"What *can* I do? He doesn't love me anymore."

"Of course he does."

Maddie started crying. "No he doesn't. He's in love with Jenna."

"He's in love with his cousin?"

"His cousin with a big fat ass."

"Hey, watch what you say about big fat asses."

"I gotta piss." Maddie stood and held on to the table to steady herself. She grabbed her crutches and limped carefully to the bathroom, nearly losing her balance on the way there.

"Hah. I get to use the handicapped stall," Maddie said to no one as she pushed open the door. She leaned her crutches against the wall and tried to put the strap of her handbag over a hook. She missed and tried again. "Gotcha!" she said proudly as the strap looped the hook. Maddie pulled out yards of toilet paper and lined the seat before sitting down. As she urinated, she got the drunken idea that it wouldn't be any big deal for Jack to cut off her cast, remove the pencil, and then put the cast back on again. She leaned over and grabbed her cell phone out of her pocketbook. After a few blinks the keypad came into focus and she carefully punched in Jack's home number. His machine picked up.

"Hey, you! It's Maddie. I dropped a cast in my pencil and I need my help. What did I just say? I mean, a pencil in my cast. I don't know what I'm saying. It was itching. You said it wouldn't itch. Maybe you can scratch it for me. Wouldn't that be nice, Jack? Maybe I'll come over there to- night. Fuck Bruce. You and me, baby. It's about time, don't you think?"

"Shoeshine?" Jack's voice.

"You're there."

"I just walked in. What's going on?"

"I don't want to wait until I'm an eighty-year-old widow, Jack. I want to sleep with you now."

"Are you drunk?"

"That a problem? You're not developing a conscience all of a sudden, are we?"

Jack laughed. "Hell, no. I'd take you right now if I wasn't on my way out."

"You just got in."

"I'm going out again. Let's meet tomorrow for lunch."

"And take it from there?"

"Sounds like a plan."

Chapter Four

RUTH

"Let's fuck. Can we fuck? I want to fuck."

Ruth pulled her sleeve down over her hand and used it to wipe the saliva off her husband's chin. "Not now, honey, I have to give you a bath."

She hadn't heard him say that for months. Maybe longer. Not that she missed it. After the stroke he had three years ago that left him brain damaged and sexually uninhibited, Keith Moss asked his wife for intercourse every time he saw her. Then his requests became less frequent. Ruth thought he had started to realize he was impotent, and wondered if he would ever acknowledge that the left side of his body was almost completely paralyzed.

She figured he asked her now because his nakedness reminded him of sex. Then another thought occurred to her. His nurse, who doubled as their housekeeper, had been bathing him. He had probably been asking Marta, a religious Catholic grandmother from El Salvador, to fuck him.

Normally Ruth would have felt at least a little chagrined about that. But right now she was too mad at Marta to have much sympathy. Marta forgot to tell Ruth until the very last minute that she couldn't work today. And Ruth had been unable to find someone to cover for her.

Now she was left to care for him herself on the day she had
arranged to have the Applewood PTA public relations
committee meeting at her house.

"C'mon, honey, let's get you into the bath," Ruth said.

She supported him on his paralyzed side, while she
helped him put his good leg into the tub.

"When are we gonna fuck?"

"Now hold on to the bar and bend your knee. Lower
yourself down."

Still holding his arm around her neck, she put his left
leg into the tub and helped ease him down into the warm
water.

"I hope you don't talk that way to Marta," she said.

"Marta has a stick up her ass."

Ruth was in a sweat from the effort of getting him into
the tub. She'd need to shower and blow-dry her hair be-
fore the committee arrived. She looked at her watch.
They'd be there in an hour. *Shit.* And where the hell was
Carmen, her cleaning lady? If she didn't show up soon
Ruth would have to do the breakfast dishes, as well.

She heard a key in the lock and the door open. It was a
big house, but the ceiling over the entrance foyer was
vaulted, and the sound carried like a concert hall.

"Carmen? Is that you? You're late."

"I sorry."

"I left the breakfast dishes. Start on the kitchen."

Ruth leaned over the tub to wash her husband. As she
reached across him for the soap, a harsh pain in her shoulder reminded her that she had been meaning to make an
appointment to get that looked at.

It had been aching for some time. But the real damage,
she knew, had come during her last tennis game with
Suzanne Podobinski. Suzanne was a great player and

fiercely competitive. They were pretty well matched. Suzanne had better form, but Ruth had something else. Something subhuman. Like a trapped animal driven to gnaw off its own foot, Ruth stopped at nothing for a point. She knew it was only a matter of time before one of her injuries was serious.

They played every other Monday morning at their private indoor tennis club. Last week, Suzanne had won the first set six–four. Damn stupid mistakes, Ruth thought, going into their second set, and promised herself she'd trounce her opponent this time.

But she didn't. Suzanne was up four games to three and it was Ruth's serve. With the score at forty–thirty, she needed this point to win the game and tie up the set. As she slammed the ball over the net and saw it sail past Suzanne, she felt a searing pain in her shoulder. But it didn't matter. The ball was in and the game was hers. The set was tied four all.

She saw Suzanne look at her watch. Oh, shit, Ruth thought, is our court time up? After losing the first set, Ruth couldn't face leaving the second set at a tie. She needed a win.

"Want to play a tiebreaker?" Ruth asked. They both knew the official tennis rule, which was that you didn't play a tiebreaker unless the score was six all. But with only an hour of court time, they often ad-libbed.

Suzanne shrugged. "Sure."

The score was at fifteen all when the service passed to Ruth. But oh, her shoulder! She tried to work it around to ease out some of the pain. I can do this, she thought. She bounced the ball twice to check for life. Someone coughed. Ruth looked up to notice that a crowd of women had gathered to watch the game. How long had they been there?

Focus. Ruth threw the ball up and brought her racket down on it with graceful force. It looked like an ace, but no. The spectators were shaking their heads. It was out.

Now her shoulder was the enemy, but she would defeat it. She would conquer this serve.

Again she tossed the ball in the air and brought her wrath upon it. It was fast and it was in. The crowd cheered politely and Ruth winced in pain.

She was up thirty–fifteen. The sting in her shoulder intensified her focus and she knew she would not let Suzanne get the next point. She was right.

Suzanne's serve again. Ruth needed this next point for the game. *Net, net, net,* she thought in silent prayer. But her opponent's serve whizzed over the net, looking a lot like her last ace. Ruth had to dive to contact the ball with the tip of her racket, and just managed to make it.

This took Suzanne by surprise. She ran to the ball and hit it back with a lob. Ruth backed up and knew she had it. Wait, she said to herself as the ball descended to perfect position. Just wait. And then, *whack*! Ruth slammed it with an overhead shot that made the racket fall from her grip and won her the game.

The small crowd erupted in ladylike applause. Ruth asked if somebody could get her some ice.

Suzanne congratulated Ruth and rushed for the locker room, despite the fact that one of the spectators was obviously trying to get her attention. With Suzanne gone, the woman timidly motioned to Ruth, who approached her.

"Are you Ruth Moss?" The woman had a small but interesting voice. Practically falsetto. Ruth wondered if she sang.

"Yes."

"I'm Lisa Slotnick. Can I talk to you about something?"

So *that's* Lisa Slotnick, Ruth thought. She'd seen the

woman around but had never connected her with the name. People spoke of her as an unfashionable little woman married to some computer nerd who made *millions*. Here, she wore clean tennis whites and didn't particularly stand out from the crowd. Only her meekness set her apart. Compared to this dainty little woman, Ruth felt almost masculine in her own energy.

One of the blue-shirted staff members handed Ruth an ice pack. She thanked him and put it on her shoulder as she turned back to Lisa. "What can I do for you?" Ruth asked.

"I spoke to Paul Capobianco and he said I should talk to you or Suzanne," Lisa said.

Paul Capobianco. Just hearing the name made Ruth almost unable to contain herself. He was the superintendent of their school district and a widower. Ruth had a terrible crush on him and often thought, When I'm ready to have an affair, he's the one. She shifted her weight from one foot to the other.

"It's about using the elementary school as a movie location," Lisa continued. She went on to explain that her husband's sister was a location scout who scoured Long Island for homes that fit the profile for specific television commercials and film projects. Sometimes she sought grand mansions, other times rundown dumps. In this case, there was a movie studio that needed a school, and North Applewood might be perfect. Of course, the school would get a fee. First, though, she would have to take some photographs to show the movie people.

"If I give you her number, can you call her and set it up?" Lisa asked. "Paul Capobianco said it's fine with him."

This is too good to be true, Ruth thought. A windfall for the PTA. An *in* with Paul Capobianco. And the project was hers. All hers. What luck that Suzanne, the snotty bitch, had made a beeline for the locker room before this woman could get to her!

Ruth told Lisa she'd be happy to take care of it, and graciously accepted a business card with the phone number of the location scout. They said their good-byes, but Ruth stopped Lisa before she walked away.

"Are you on any PTA committees?" Ruth asked.

"The ones I wanted were filled."

"Why don't you join public relations?" Ruth knew she'd have to boot either Maddie or Beryl to make room for this woman, but that was fine with her.

"Can I think about it?"

"Sure. Give me your phone number and I'll call, talk you into it."

Lisa released a small laugh. "Okay," she said, and wrote her phone number on the back of her sister-in-law's business card.

After showering and changing, Ruth and Suzanne went out to lunch at a diner Ruth had suggested.

"Listen," Ruth said as they walked in, "about the public relations committee."

"Oh, don't sweat it. The committee is yours. I already put you down as chair." Suzanne looked at the hostess and held up two fingers to indicate how many people they were. "But that little Beryl creep is *your* problem."

Ruth reminded Suzanne that the executive board had proposed the idea of starting a PTA newsletter committee this year.

"Well, then let's make Beryl the chair of that one," Suzanne said, as if she had thought of it.

"Great idea."

Ruth smiled, confident she could handle Beryl as well as she had handled Suzanne. She'd simply explain that as chair of the newsletter committee, Beryl would have open access to attend and report on virtually any PTA meeting she wanted. In a town fueled by gossip, a job like that had horsepower.

They were seated at a square table in the center of the noisy dining room. Ruth occasionally glanced up from her menu to look at the door. She knew that this was one of Paul Capobianco's favorite places for lunch and was hoping he would walk in. Sure enough, the waitress hadn't even taken their order yet when she saw his tall form come through the glass door.

"Look," she said, leaning in to Suzanne, "there's Paul."

Suzanne gasped. "Paul!" she shouted, waving.

Paul Capobianco acknowledged the women with a small half-smile that made Ruth feel almost goofy with delight. His posture was stooped, as if he'd spent his life ducking low ceilings, but his blue eyes and dark hair made Ruth think he had almost movie-star good looks. A reed-like Alec Baldwin with sad eyes and dimples.

He approached their table. "Hello, ladies."

"I hope you're going to join us for lunch, Paul." Suzanne flashed her perfect white teeth.

"I was just going to grab a quick bite."

"We can't let you eat *alone*," Suzanne insisted.

"If you're sure it's okay." That smile again. This time at Ruth.

She smiled back. "Pull up a chair."

Ruth glanced at Suzanne, who was arching her back and sucking in her cheeks. That flirty little bitch, Ruth thought. She has this gorgeous, healthy jock of a husband who probably can't keep his hands off her, and she has to try to upstage me with Paul? Ruth seethed. Suzanne knew full well that she was trapped in a life without sex, without intimacy, without a companion to share joy or heartache. Didn't she think Ruth deserved a break?

Fine, Ruth thought, if she wants competition, I'll give it to her.

Ruth smirked then, confident she knew exactly how to play it. She'd let Suzanne flirt her little heart out, and wait for just the right moment to score her best shot.

The waitress came over to take their order. She looked at Suzanne first, who pressed her hand flat against her abdomen as she scanned the menu. "I'll just have the house salad with dressing on the side."

"Is that it?" the waitress asked.

"Please. If I gain another ounce I'll kill myself." Suzanne looked around the table as if expecting an argument.

She's trying to impress Paul with her delicate appetite, Ruth thought. How predictable.

"I'll have the turkey club, no mayo," Ruth said. She glanced at Suzanne, who looked smugly satisfied that her own choice was more feminine. But Ruth had overheard Paul ordering lunch on more than one occasion, and was pretty sure what would happen next.

Paul looked at Ruth and then said to the waitress, "I'll have the same thing as her." He pointed at Ruth with his thumb.

"That's my favorite lunch," Paul said to Ruth after the waitress walked away. "I have it almost every day."

Ruth smiled at him, and then at Suzanne, who offered a stiff grin. Ruth noticed that her friend's posture had deflated to a more normal position.

"So what's new with the PTA?" Paul asked.

Suzanne straightened up, back in the game. "We're going to have a great year. I think we're going to break the fund-raising record." She flipped her hair back with a toss of her head.

"Are you chairing the public relations committee again?" he asked Ruth.

"We were just *talking* about that," Suzanne gushed, as if it were a startling coincidence. "I was just telling Ruth that I made her chair again. She did *such* a good job last year."

Paul looked straight at Ruth. "Do you know a woman named Lisa Slotnick?"

Ruth fixed on Paul's eyes and decided they were more indigo than blue. She might just have to write a song about them when she got home. "I spoke to her on the tennis court just before we got here. She gave me her sister-in-law's business card. I'll call her and set something up."

Paul put his hand on Ruth's arm. "Thanks for taking care of that. Keep me posted."

"I will."

"Is this something I should know about?" Suzanne asked.

"Remember that woman who was trying to get your attention after the game?" Ruth asked her. "That was Lisa Slotnick." Ruth related the details of their conversation, and Paul chimed in that when he was contacted originally, he thought it would be appropriate for the PTA to get involved.

Suzanne nodded thoughtfully and tsked. "But the public relations committee? I don't know."

"C'mon, Suzanne," Ruth said. "What are you going to do, give it to the cupcake committee?"

"*Bake sale* committee," Suzanne corrected, straightening her silverware.

"Look, it'll be fine," Ruth said. "I have a lawyer on my

committee, which could come in very handy with something like this. Plus, Lisa Slotnick just signed up. She's very interested in public relations." Ruth folded her arms across her chest, confident she could turn the small lie into a near-truth with one phone call.

"That sounds great," Paul said. "Did the waitress forget to take our drink order? I need coffee."

Later that day, Ruth phoned Jill Slotnick-Weiss, the location scout interested in North Applewood Elementary School. They set up an early-morning appointment to meet at the school, and Ruth nervously called the superintendent's office. She was hoping Paul Capobianco would want to attend. He answered his own phone.

"Hi, Paul. It's Ruth Moss."

"Hello, Ruth."

She told him she had set up a meeting with the location scout for early Tuesday morning, and asked him if he would like to attend. He checked his calendar and said he'd be delighted.

"That's great," Ruth said. "I'll see you there."

He hesitated. "Okay."

She sensed that he wasn't quite ready to end the conversation. She sat down on a kitchen chair. "Is there something else?"

"I hope you don't think this is out of line, but . . ." He paused.

"What is it, Paul?"

"I guess you've heard that I took care of my wife over a long illness."

"I did. I'm so sorry."

"I just . . . I wanted to tell you that I heard about your husband and I know what you're going through. So if you ever need to talk . . ."

Ruth closed her eyes and let her head roll back. When she opened them, she was looking at clouds through the skylight in her kitchen ceiling. They were moving across the sun, and Ruth could see a clearing in the distance. Any minute, her kitchen would be bathed in sunlight. "That's so kind of you, Paul. I might just take you up on that one day."

When Ruth wasn't busy with her kids or her tennis or the PTA, she shut the door of her room and took out her guitar. It was her one secret pleasure. She wrote songs. Lots of them. Her music had a Joni Mitchell quality, which didn't suit her raspy voice at all. She had no illusions about this, and liked to think that one day she would find someone with a crystal-clear voice to put her songs on tape. Then, she might even send them in someplace to see if she could sell them. In the meantime, they kept her mind so occupied that she had little time to dwell on the tragedy of her husband's ruined life.

Before his stroke, Keith had been a partner in an aggressive New York City law firm. He was a workaholic who took little care of his health, and largely ignored his diabetes until one day he awoke unable to move his left side. Keith knew that having a stroke was one of the rare but possible side effects of his condition, and told Ruth to call an ambulance. When he got to the hospital, he demanded the new clot-busting medication he had read about in the newspaper.

A neurologist was brought in, and explained to Keith that the medication might be contraindicated in his case. It could lead to a brain hemorrhage, which could make his stroke far worse, causing brain damage or even death.

Keith fumed. The article he had read said the drug had to be administered within the first three hours, and he'd be damned if he was going to let the opportunity slip by. More doctors were brought in to consult with the angry lawyer. But Keith railed and raged and threatened to litigate. Ultimately, the hospital decided it was in their best interest to give the patient what he wanted, and administered the medicine.

Ruth worried about the decision. Were the doctors simply browbeaten by her intractable husband, or was this medication what he truly needed? A few hours later she got her answer. Keith's brain hemorrhaged and he slipped into a coma.

She spent the next forty-eight hours at his bedside, occasionally dozing in the vinyl side chair. She wanted to be the first face he saw when he awoke. A nurse tried to persuade her to go home and get a good night's sleep. She said he wouldn't wake up all at once anyway, and would hover in a fog for some time. Someone, the nurse promised, would call her if there was any change.

So Ruth dragged herself home, determined to spend some time with her children. As she read *Green Eggs and Ham* to her daughter, Morgan, who was only five at the time, the phone rang. Keith was coming out of his coma. He was talking.

When she got back to the hospital, Ruth pressed the doctor to tell her what Keith's first words were. He hemmed and hawed and looked embarrassed, and said coma patients don't always know what they're saying at first.

"Just *tell* me," Ruth insisted.

The doctor hesitated. "Do you . . . do you know anyone named Sue?"

"Sue?"

"That was his first word," the doctor said. "He asked for Sue."

Ruth smiled. "That's great."

"Great?" The young doctor was confused.

"Sue," Ruth explained, "is not a name, it's a verb. He wants *to sue*." She paused. "My husband is back."

Of course, he wasn't back. Not fully. But lawsuits filed on his behalf against the hospital and three different doctors resulted in legal settlements totaling over five million dollars. That money, together with disability insurance and his interest in his law firm's partnership, afforded the Mosses the affluent lifestyle to which they had always aspired. And just before they sold their house in Applewood and moved up to a newly built mansion in Applewood Estates, Ruth wrote a song she called "Be Careful What You Wish For."

The appointment with the location scout was scheduled for 7:45 in the morning, early enough to be over before the first buses rolled into the school parking lot. Ruth wanted to be sure she wasn't late, and had arranged for Marta to give her children breakfast and get them ready for school.

Morgan, Ruth's nine-year-old daughter, wanted to come with Ruth for the photo shoot. But Ruth insisted that it was too early for her and would be boring for a child.

What Ruth didn't mention to her daughter was that she felt lonely and sexually starved, and saw this meeting as an opportunity to move closer to a relationship with Paul Capobianco. Three years was long enough to go without sex, she had decided. She never stopped missing it, not for a second, and guessed her involvement with the movie project had something to do with making her realize it was time to take action. It was as if the part of her that realized she was still important, still mattered in this world, had awakened from a long sleep. Besides, Paul was one of the most desirable men she had met in years. Everything about him—from his sinewy hands to the black sorrow he wore like a veil—made her ache with hunger.

Ruth left her house in a beautiful mood. She loved the morning, as it suggested nothing but possibilities for the day ahead. And this day in particular held so much promise. The weather was cool enough to smell like fall, but mild enough to forgo a jacket. She knew that all she had to do was give Paul a green light and everything else would fall into place. But when Ruth approached the back door where she had told Paul and the location scout to meet her, someone else was there. Suzanne. *Damn.*

"Hi," Ruth said stiffly. "I didn't know you were coming to this meeting."

"I thought it was important for me to be here, Ruth. Even if *you* didn't. I'm still the president of the PTA."

Ruth had never told Suzanne that the meeting was scheduled for this morning. She wondered how Suzanne had found out, but thought it prudent to let that go.

"Don't be so touchy. I just didn't think it was necessary for both of us to be out at this crazy hour. All we're doing is taking pictures."

Suzanne, who was dressed in a simple sweat jacket and jeans with her hair pulled back in a ponytail, dismissed the issue with a wave of her hand. She looked splendid, and Ruth's mood fell like a rock. Suzanne's slender presence changed everything. Besides spoiling her opportunity to give Paul a signal, it made Ruth feel matronly and overdressed.

While Ruth knew that every woman thought her own

figure problem was the worst in the world, she believed
hers truly was. Unless you're as skinny as a stick, she
thought, breasts as big as mine do nothing but make you
look fat. And it had been years since she'd felt that thin.
Plus, she didn't have the hips to balance it out, and
thought almost nothing fit her well. Blouses were out, as
they tended to gap between the buttons at her chest. If
she got one big enough for her breasts, it was ludicrously
large everywhere else. Clingy tops attracted way too
much attention, and loose-fitting ones hung from her bust
like a tablecloth, making her look almost fat enough to be
pregnant.

So she chose her black cashmere sweater with bugle
beads around the neckline. It seemed a touch too dressy
when she put it on, but she thought she could get away
with it. If only she had known Suzanne was coming.

"That must be Jill," Ruth said when she saw a tall blond
woman with a camera approaching.

They introduced themselves and chatted for several
minutes while waiting for Paul Capobianco to arrive.
When he did, Ruth noted with relief that he was wearing
a dark suit and crisp white shirt. Her decision to wear the
black sweater seemed appropriate again.

Together, the foursome walked around the perimeter of
the school. Jill Slotnick-Weiss shot pictures from every
possible angle. When they got to the area called "Field
One," the location scout asked about a single boulder that
jutted out from the grass and a large rectangular sign that
was next to it.

"That's Applewood Rock," Paul explained. "When the
land that is now Applewood township was bought from the
Algonquin Indians in 1648, the deed was signed at that
very spot."

Jill took a few pictures of the field, the rock itself, and the group moved on.

"This is Field Four," Suzanne said when they reached the area on the south side of the school building. "This is where we hope to build a stadium one day."

Jill looked shocked. "A *stadium*? You're kidding me!"

The threesome from Applewood exchanged confused looks. "Why would I be kidding you?" Suzanne asked.

"Because the movie is about a divorced father who gets involved in coaching his son's softball team," Jill said. "And the production people are looking for a school field where they can *build* a stadium!"

"A *real* stadium?" Paul asked.

"Usually they just build the parts of it they need for their shots."

"That's too bad," Ruth said.

"Well, I don't know," Jill said. "Maybe if you waive the fee they'll build a stadium you can really use."

"I wonder if we could work something out," Paul said, looking into the distance. Ruth got the impression he was considering his position of negotiation.

"The first step," Jill explained as she packed up her camera, "is for me to show them the photos I took today. Then, if they're interested in the property, they'll send a team of their people out to take a look. I'll keep you posted." She shook their hands and walked away.

"Wait a minute!" Ruth shouted after her. "Who's in this movie? Anybody famous?"

Jill didn't break stride. "You may have heard of the guy who plays the father," she yelled with her back to them. Then she turned around and smiled. "George Clooney."

Chapter Five

George Clooney?" said Beryl Berman, newly appointed chairperson of the North Applewood PTA newsletter committee. "You're kidding me!"

It was the year's first official meeting of the public relations committee, and Beryl was exercising her right to attend. She and Maddie sat in overstuffed chairs in Ruth Moss's decorator living room. Maddie's broken ankle rested on an upholstered ottoman that matched not only her chair but the balloon draperies on the windows.

"I *love* George Clooney." Beryl turned to her friend. "Don't I love George Clooney, Maddie?" She looked back at Ruth. "Maddie gave me a picture of George Clooney last night for my birthday."

"Can you talk a little softer, please," Maddie said, her hand shielding her eyes like a visor.

Beryl turned to Ruth. "We went out drinking last night. She's a little hungover."

"Shh!" Maddie pleaded.

"I just thought of a great title for my newsletter article,"

Beryl said, painting across the horizon with her hand. "'Applewood welcomes George Clooney with open arms.' Or should I say 'legs'?"

"Hang on a minute," Ruth said. "It's not a done deal. Jill is still waiting for final word from the production people about whether or not they like our school yard for the scenes."

"What's not to like!" Beryl shouted.

Maddie grabbed her head and moaned. "I think you're trying to kill me."

"She's just mad because we finally found a subject she doesn't know anything about."

Maddie looked at Beryl through barely opened eyes and smiled for the first time that day. "Try me."

"What famous person is he related to?"

"Rosemary Clooney is his aunt, not his mother like a lot of people think. He's also related to Jose Ferrer. He was born in Lexington, Kentucky, in 1961. Before leaving for Hollywood, he tried out for the Cincinnati Reds but didn't make it. Any other questions?"

"So are you like a closet George Clooney fanatic?" Beryl asked. "Is there a room in your house where you have thousands of pictures of him taped to the walls?"

"I just have sticky fingers," Maddie admitted. "I stole a copy of *People* from Jack's office the other day."

Ruth excused herself and went into the kitchen. She came back carrying a tray of steaming china teacups, trimmed in heavy gold leaf. "Our new committee member should be here any minute," she said.

Beryl looked at the fancy cup Ruth handed her. "Who is she, the first lady?"

Funny, Ruth thought, and smiled. "She's the sister-in-law of the location scout I told you about. Her name is Lisa Slotnick."

Beryl blew on her hot coffee. *"Slotnick?"* she said. "What was it before she changed it?"

"Am I the only one hearing bells?" Maddie asked.

"Oh!" Ruth said. "The front door! It must be her."

She ran to the foyer and saw Lisa Slotnick, already inside, looking pale and stricken. Next to her, grinning broadly as he leaned on his aluminum walker, was Keith.

"Oh, dear. What did you say to her, Keith?"

He smiled and shrugged.

Lisa swallowed hard, and then, in a barely audible voice, said, "He asked me to fuck him."

Ruth pointed down the hallway. "Keith! Go to your room and stay there like I told you to!" She turned to Lisa. "I'm so sorry. His nurse didn't show up today and . . ." She sighed, exasperated. "Can I get you anything, Lisa?"

Keith maneuvered around and started toward his room. "I bet her pussy's tighter than yours, you old cow!"

Ruth closed her eyes and shook her head. She put her hand on Lisa's back. "Come, I'll introduce you to Maddie and Beryl."

Lisa tucked her hair behind her ear. "I feel kind of funny about this whole thing. Didn't Beryl get pushed off the committee to make room for me?"

"Please. She couldn't care less—especially since she's chairing the newsletter committee now."

They walked into the living room where Ruth made the introductions. "Beryl," she said, "you don't have any hard feelings about how the whole committee business worked out, do you?"

"Heavens, no," she said. "Just because meeting George

Clooney is the dream that occupies virtually every waking and sleeping thought, doesn't mean I feel compelled to be on the committee that makes it happen. But let me ask you this, if Lisa should meet an untimely death, do I get her slot?"

Lisa blanched and Beryl touched her arm gently. "I'm kidding, dear," she said, her tone turning serious. "But promise me you'll make this happen."

"I promise," Lisa said.

Beryl turned to her friend. "Maddie?"

"I promise."

"What about you?" Beryl said to Ruth.

"You think you're the only one who wants to *shtup* George Clooney? Let's get this meeting started."

That evening, as Ruth helped her daughter, Morgan, with her homework, she wondered if she could find any time to work on a song that had been rattling around in her brain. Ben would be home from his karate class any minute, and would want to cook dinner for the family. Marta had been teaching him how to make *pupusas,* a Salvadoran dish Ben insisted they would like. If he didn't need her help, maybe she could steal a few minutes to herself while he cooked. It was unusually warm for September, and Ruth thought it would be lovely to sit outside on the porch with her guitar as the sun set.

She was still in Morgan's bedroom when she heard the double honk of a car horn, a signal from the carpool mom that Ben was being dropped off. Ruth heard him open the door and come in.

"Mom?" His voice sounded thin and unsure. Something was wrong. Ruth hurried down the stairs.

"What's the matter?"

"I don't feel so good."

She put her hand to her son's forehead. "You're warm," she said. "What hurts?"

He touched his neck. "My throat, a little."

Ruth walked her adolescent son upstairs to his bedroom. He was taller than her already, and she was glad he still needed her. She made him change into his pajamas and get into bed while she got him a glass of water and some Advil. She sat on the edge of his bed and brushed the hair off his forehead like she used to do when he was small.

"Think I should make those papooses?" she asked. "I hate to let the ingredients go to waste."

Ben managed to laugh. "Don't, Mom. And they're *pupusas.*"

Ruth laughed, too. "What did *I* say?"

"Papooses. Like what Native Americans used to carry their babies in."

"I thought that's what they called the last car in a train." She was kidding and he knew it. It was a game they sometimes played.

"Those are *cabooses.*" He thought for a second. "But you probably thought that's what they call people named after a short French artist."

Ruth played that back in her mind and then got it. "Toulouses! You're getting too good at this, Benny."

Ben smiled, and Ruth thought, Yes, be proud of yourself.

"I guess I'll order in Chinese," she said.

He chuckled. "Good idea, Mom."

He was making fun of her reputation as a terrible cook and she laughed. There was a sweetness about him. Even when he teased, he did it gently. Ruth looked at her handsome son and wondered how much credit she could take for how smart and kind he was growing up to be.

"I'll order you some soup."

After calling the Chinese takeout restaurant and checking Morgan's homework, Ruth went outside with her guitar. She sat on the front porch so she wouldn't miss the deliveryman, and started tinkering with the melody. She leaned back in the chair and played single notes at first, to be sure the tune worked, and then added chords. She found a rock rhythm and bluesy sound that felt warm and sensual. The drama of the melody overtook her and she closed her eyes and started to sing.

> *Something so sad and something so wise*
> *Something so real in those indigo eyes, indigo eyes*
> *When you soar over mountains of heartache and shame*
> *Find plateaus of pathos and rivers of pain*
> *When you travel away can you take me along*
> *To the place where they play your lost lover song*
> *Something so sad and something so wise*
> *Something so real in those indigo eyes, indigo eyes*

Ruth kept playing and hummed the melody while she tried to think of more lyrics. Though her eyes were closed she felt a presence near her. Still strumming, she opened them and gasped. A tall figure stood silhouetted against the setting sun. Her music fell silent.

"Paul! What are you doing here?"

"I hope I'm not bothering you. I was on my way home from work and thought I'd drop off the land survey you

said the movie production people need to make their decision." He held up what looked like an old blueprint.

"Thanks, I . . . How long have you been standing
there?" Ruth felt her face flush.

"Just a minute. I heard you playing and I didn't want to
bother you. It sounded nice. But unfamiliar, I think.
Would I have heard it before?"

She laughed shyly. "No, you wouldn't have. Do you
want to sit down?"

"Thanks." He sat on a wooden bench across from the
Adirondack chair she was on. "You have a nice voice."

She felt hot, like she had caught Ben's fever, and ab-
sently touched her cheek with the back of her hand.
"Me? No. It's all raspy with no range. My songs sound so
beautiful in my head and so disappointing when I sing
them."

"You *write* songs?"

"Sometimes." She looked down, unable to meet his
eyes. How much had he heard? She didn't think he knew
it was about him, but how could she be sure? "I never play
them for anyone."

"You should, Ruth. It's a gift from God. Did you write
that one you were playing?"

She nodded and looked back up at him. There was
nothing in his eyes that indicated he knew the song was
about him. She saw the sadness she sang about, and the
wisdom, too. But also something she hadn't noticed before.
Innocence.

"Thanks for bringing that by." She indicated the folded
page he held. "It was nice of you."

He handed it to her and shrugged. "It was on my way
home."

She looked at the red sun on the horizon and imagined him making the decision to drive to her house rather than simply ask his secretary to mail her the survey. He must have wanted to see her.

"Would you like to stay for dinner?" she asked. "We ordered Chinese food."

"Thanks, but no, not tonight." He hesitated. "Maybe another time?"

He wants to go out with me, Ruth thought, her heart pounding. Is he afraid to be more direct because I'm married?

"That would be lovely," she said. "I've been thinking about taking you up on that offer to talk. Just you and me."

He mumbled something she didn't hear.

"Excuse me?" she said.

"I said I like to cook."

She smiled and thought of Ben. "That makes one of us."

He smiled back. "Would you like to come over for dinner one night?"

The sky was darkening, and Ruth thought she saw a star in the distance behind where Paul was sitting. She made a quick wish as she took the guitar off her lap and rested it on the floor. Then she leaned into Paul and fixed on his eyes.

"I'd love to," she said.

Ruth picked up a potted chrysanthemum and turned it around. "What do you think?" she said, showing it to Maddie. "A plant or cut flowers?"

They were in a local garden store shopping for a token of appreciation for Jill Slotnick-Weiss. She'd been working hard to get the production studio to approve their school for the movie, and Ruth thought it would be nice to show their gratitude while they waited for the final word.

"I don't know," Maddie said, and tapped Lisa, whose back was to them as she inspected plants on another table.

Lisa suggested an African violet, and the three of them sorted through a counter filled with different varieties, looking for the lushest plant.

They were momentarily distracted when a hush fell over the store as a striking blond woman with regal posture and fashion-magazine features crossed the floor and approached the cash register. Every head followed her path.

"Who *is* that?" Maddie whispered.

Ruth glanced up and then back down at the table. She picked up a plant with purple blooms and arranged the leaves. "You don't know Regina Dewitt?"

"She's president of Applewood South's PTA," Lisa explained. "Tennis player, too."

"Everyone is staring at her," Maddie said.

Lisa looked at the woman and then back at Maddie. "I think she's used to it."

Ruth put down the plant. "Just you wait," she said. "We get this stadium built and everyone will talk about *us* when we enter a room. We'll be Applewood celebrities forever."

Lisa looked worried. "Celebrities?"

"Don't you want to be a star?"

Lisa shook her head.

A bell jangled as Regina Dewitt left the building and the door closed behind her. The atmosphere in the store shifted as the shoppers let out a collective breath and attention turned back to other living things. Even the plants seemed to sense the change in CO_2 levels.

"How about a hero?" Maddie asked Lisa. "It'd be nice to be the town heroes, wouldn't it?"

At that, they all smiled, and a robust African violet in the middle of the display caught Ruth's attention. The others agreed it was perfect, and they picked out a lovely hand-painted planter to go with it. As they pushed the shopping cart toward the register to pay, Ruth's cell phone rang.

It was Jill Slotnick-Weiss. Ruth spoke to her for a few moments and then snapped her phone shut.

"Was that Jill?" Lisa asked.

"What did she say?" Maddie gushed. "Did they approve our school? Are we in?"

"Celebrities," Ruth said, putting an arm around each friend. "You'd better get used to it."

A few days later, Ruth and her daughter, Morgan, were strolling through the local mall when they glanced into a sneaker store and saw Lisa Slotnick and her family. Lisa waved them inside. Apparently, the daughters knew each other from school, because as soon as they were near enough, the girls squealed and folded in on each other, gushing about which sneakers they liked.

Lisa introduced Ruth to her husband, Adam, who was crouched down on the floor tying shoes on their smallest son, while the twin five-year-old boys kept each other busy running between the aisles.

"Remember when there used to be salespeople in shoe stores?" Adam asked Ruth as he stood. He shook her hand warmly and then looked back down at the toddler's feet. "Walk to the mirror, Simon," he said, and watched intently as the boy did so.

Adam furrowed his brow and announced that he thought they looked too big. "In the heel, I mean. What do you think, Ruth?"

Ruth thought it was utterly touching that Adam was so serious about his son's sneakers. She remembered the time she and Keith went shopping together for Ben's very first pair of shoes. She had picked up the sweetest-looking blue buckskin walkers, imported from Italy. But when Ruth saw the price, she put them down and moved on. They were counting every penny at that point, as Keith hadn't yet made partner and they had just applied for their first home mortgage.

She found a shoe in soft white leather that looked like a serviceable first walker. "These are cute," she said to Keith.

"What about those others?" he asked, pointing to the Italian shoes.

"Too expensive," Ruth said.

Keith, who had Ben balanced in one arm, picked up one of the blue shoes and inspected it.

Ruth took the baby from him and said that they didn't need to spend that much.

Keith nodded, but Ruth could tell he wasn't agreeing but buying time while he thought about how they could swing the expense. She knew her husband well enough to know he was mentally analyzing their budget, deciding where they could cut to make up for this extravagance.

"Really, Keith," she had said, "these white ones are fine."

"He's our *son*," Keith said, as if explaining something she didn't know. Ruth smiled, because she understood exactly how fierce his love was for this child. Ben, she thought at the time, was a boy who would grow up with a daddy who would do anything for him. It was exactly what she wanted for her sweet baby. And then, as now, she swallowed against a lump in her throat.

"You want them a little big," Ruth said to Adam. "They grow so fast."

• • •

Paul lived in Quaker Bay, an old village on the north shore that hugged the Long Island Sound. While his house was not on the water, it sat on a lovely block of large Victorian homes, squeezed close together as if bracing for a cold wind. There was no bell, so Ruth used the brass knocker. The door swung open quickly, and Paul stood there wearing his half-smile. She smiled back, hardly believing that he had really called and invited her for dinner.

"Hi," he said. "Come in."

She noticed immediately that a fire burned in the hearth and a wonderful smell came from the kitchen. He told her dinner would be ready soon and showed her to the living room where she sat in an overstuffed love seat in front of the fireplace. He told her he'd be right back, and returned holding two glasses of wine.

He sat down next to her on the love seat. Ruth, just a little nervous, felt compelled to make small talk. She asked him about his neighborhood and complimented him on his lovely home. He told her he had lived in it sixteen years. She knew his wife hadn't been gone more than five.

"It must hold a lot of memories for you," she said.

"It does. After Cynthia died, people said I should sell it. Like I should erase as much of her as I could. But that didn't feel right. I thought, 'she's my wife, I'm *supposed* to grieve.' You know what I mean?"

Before she could respond, a buzzer sounded, and Paul said, "That's the rice." She accompanied him to the kitchen and sat on a counter stool watching him cook.

"Tell me about Keith," he said as he seasoned the fish with his back to her. "How bad is his condition?"

"He's paralyzed on the left side of his body, but he can move around pretty well with a walker. And despite the stroke and the diabetes, he's pretty healthy."

"What about mentally?"

Ruth studied a small round dish on the counter filled with a gloppy whitish substance. She had an urge to stick her pinky into it so she could taste it, but not knowing his tolerance for food touching, she refrained.

"It's weird," she said. "He's Keith but he's not. Like, he still reads the paper and rails against idiot politicians. And sometimes, when he does that, I try to look at him from his right side and remember what it was like before the stroke. But it's hard. His circuits are all jumbled and some things just don't register. He doesn't know he's paralyzed and says strange, inappropriate things."

"Like what?"

She frowned. "I don't know if I should tell you."

"Why?"

" 'Cause they're sexual."

There was a pause. "Oh," he said quietly. She couldn't see his face and found his body language difficult to read. Was it her imagination, or did his back go rigid?

"And he has no idea he's impotent." There. She'd said it. Now he'd know she got no sex.

Paul turned to face her. "Oh, Ruth," he said sympathetically.

She looked at the expression on his face and suddenly saw the tragedy of her life through the window of his eyes. A flood of memories of Keith before his stroke pushed down on her. More than anything, she saw him on the day he was promoted to partner and smiled so big his gums showed. That image of pride and promise released a torrent of emotion that took her by surprise. She started to weep.

Paul walked around the peninsula-shaped counter and put his arms around her. "I'm so sorry, Ruth," he whispered.

Her body shook as her tears turned to great heaves. She tried to talk but couldn't. She wanted to apologize for crying like this. He rubbed her back.

"It's okay," he said softly. "It's okay."

He was giving her permission to cry, which she needed. She let go, and only then was able to regain some control.

"I'm sorry," she said. "I didn't mean to cry like this."

He wiped a tear from her face with a warm finger. "I know."

She took a paper napkin from the counter and wiped the mascara that had dripped under her eyes.

"Can we talk about something else?" she said.

"Sure."

She pointed to the bowl of glop. "What *is* that?"

"Tartar sauce. Homemade. Want a taste?"

"Sure."

He dipped his finger in and brought it to her mouth. When he touched it to her tongue, she closed her lips around his finger while looking straight into his eyes. He pulled his finger away slowly and the tanginess of the silky tartar sauce lingered in her mouth. He leaned his face into hers and gently kissed her on the lips. They looked at each other.

"I should put up the fish," he said, but didn't move. His hand was on her knee and she ached for him to move it higher. She saw him look at her breasts.

"If that's what you want," she said.

He took his hand off her knee and straightened. "I'd better make dinner."

"Where are we eating?" she asked. She didn't see a table set.

He pointed to the counter where she sat. "I know it doesn't look like much," he said, "but watch." He threw a dark green tablecloth over it, and then a piece of ivory lace over that. She helped him set their places with some beautiful china she imagined Cynthia had picked out. When he turned around for a second, she lifted a plate to see what was stamped on the bottom. Wedgwood.

They ate by candlelight, and Paul told Ruth about Cynthia. He explained that before the girls were born, she was an interior decorator who painted as a hobby. After becoming a mother, she stopped working but painted more. He said a lot of her paintings were hanging in the house and he would show them to her after dinner. Ruth asked to see a picture of Cynthia, and Paul handed her a silver-framed photograph of the two of them in bathing suits smiling into the sun. They were young, and she was lovely, with a long face and olive complexion.

"That was right after Christina was born," he said. "It's one of my favorite pictures of her because she's smiling. She didn't like the way she looked when she smiled, so she looks very serious in most of her pictures."

"She has a beautiful smile." Ruth handed back the photograph.

"I know." He looked at it one more time and then put it down.

"Tell me about your girls," Ruth said.

Paul talked about his grown daughters as they finished dinner, and then Ruth excused herself to the bathroom. She wanted to freshen up but also to do a little snooping. She knew there had to be a bathroom on the first floor, but she was eager to peek into his bedroom so she went directly upstairs. She went to the bathroom first, so he would hear the water running and not wonder what she was doing up there. Then she took a quick look around for the master bedroom. She wanted to know what she was up against. If there were pictures of Cynthia everywhere, it could be a problem. Who wants to compete with a dead wife?

But what she found was worse. There, in his room, on an expansive beige wall behind his king-sized bed, hung one solitary object: a wooden cross.

Chapter Six

Ruth and Paul had dessert in the living room by the fire. He brought out coffee and a creamy cherry cheesecake that Ruth ate in tiny nibbles. As they talked, she waited for him to make a move, trying to give him every signal that she was ready. She sat as close to him as possible, and touched him frequently during their conversation. But he did nothing. That cross, she thought, is really in my way.

Paul looked at his watch and announced that it was getting late. Ruth wasn't ready to give up without a fight.

"Paul," she breathed, stroking his bicep. "I really don't want to leave. Not yet."

He closed his eyes and slowly opened them, then took a long, deep breath. "Ruth," he finally said, "I want to make love to you. Very, *very* much. But I can't." He took her hand off his arm. "It isn't right."

She leaned in to his neck and kissed him there. "It's very right," she whispered, rubbing his chest.

He kissed her hard on the mouth and she welcomed his tongue.

"You're married," he said. "It's a sin."

She put her hand on his crotch and smiled. "I know!"

She pulled him down to the floor. He fumbled with his belt buckle and she pulled off her sweater.

"This is wrong," he said, unclasping her bra.

She grabbed his hard penis. "So wrong."

He put his lips on her nipple and she moaned. He sucked forcefully and then bit hard enough for her to cry out. He looked up at her. "Is that okay?" he asked.

Ruth grinned. "Oh, baby!"

In her college days, Ruth was a wild girl. With her strawberry-blond hair, enormous breasts, and loud clothes, she was a recognizable campus figure. Almost all the guys wanted to sleep with her. And she rarely let an opportunity go by. Now, here with Paul, she remembered one particular thing she had learned. It wasn't the boisterous, beer-drinking, obnoxious boys who were ferocious in bed. It was the quiet, religious types. The repressed ones. Released from their cages, these guys became animals, rough and insatiable.

That was Paul. Ruth was transported.

Afterward, when she was dressed and ready to leave, Ruth noticed a painting hanging on the wall near the front door.

"Is this Cynthia's?" she asked.

"Yes. One of her favorites."

Ruth didn't know a lot about art, but she knew what she liked. And she didn't like this. It was a landscape with a small cottage in the foreground, all shuttered and closed. The technique, she guessed, was okay. But the colors were hideous. They were dark and muddy, and everything seemed a little off. Even the blue sky had a tinge of green.

Splashes of light colors appeared here and there, like an af-
terthought. She imagined the artist thought they added
brightness and cheer. But the effect was ghoulish.

"Was she already sick when she painted it?"

"Oh, no," he said. "She did this years ago. When the
girls were small."

Then Ruth knew that the reason Cynthia never smiled
in photographs had more to do with her disposition than
her vanity. She was one dark lady.

Paul kissed Ruth on the lips. "I'll call you," he said.

Ruth floated around in a giddy dream for the next several
days. She was even happy to see Suzanne at their next tennis game.

"How's the shoulder?" Suzanne asked.

"Better, I think. I don't know. I made an appointment
with Dr. Rose, that orthopedist everyone sees."

"You sure you want to play?"

Ruth smiled. "Yes!"

So they played. But Ruth quickly realized she was in too
much pain to go on. They were tied one game all when
she knew she had to throw in the towel. But first, one
more game to break the tie.

The pain was excruciating, but she scored the point, and
then told Suzanne she couldn't go on. Suzanne's reaction
was frosty but civil.

In the locker room, Ruth rested in a chair, icing her
shoulder. After several minutes, Suzanne approached, fully
dressed with a Prada bag over her shoulder and her car keys
in her hand.

"I have to tell you something," Suzanne said.

Ruth didn't like her tone. She sounded all bristly, like

she was ready for a fight. Was she mad that Ruth had quit the game while in the lead? Hell, Suzanne had done the same thing to Ruth only a few months ago when a sore throat got the better of her right after she scored.

"What is it?" Ruth asked, already annoyed.

"I decided that we need a special committee to handle the George Clooney project. I'm taking it away from public relations."

"What? You can't do that!"

"Don't tell me what I can't do. I'm president of the PTA."

"Suzanne," Ruth reasoned, "I already have a relationship with the location scout and the production studio. It doesn't make sense to start from scratch with a new committee. Who's going to chair?"

"You think you're the only one who can handle this, don't you?"

Ruth stared at Suzanne and then threw her ice pack on the floor. "You! You want the project for yourself!"

"You're not the only one who wants to meet George Clooney, Ruth."

"Is *that* what this is about? You want to *shtup* George Clooney?"

"I don't know *what* you're talking about," Suzanne snapped.

"Oh, I'm sorry, I forgot," said Ruth sarcastically. "You don't speak Yiddish. You're one of the *Mayflower* Jews."

"Huh?"

"*Shtup*. It's Yiddish for 'fuck,' honey."

"Go to hell." Suzanne sneered at her and stormed away.

"*Shtup* you!"

• • •

When Ruth got home she paced angrily, trying to decide who she could call to blow off steam. She thought of Paul first. Maybe he would even step in and try to help. But would it be appropriate for the superintendent to get involved in PTA business?

She picked up her guitar and strummed a few angry chords, but was too agitated to concentrate. She opened the refrigerator door and slammed it shut. Some half-dead flowers in a vase on the kitchen table caught her eye and she threw them out. Then she spilled out the dirty water and washed the vase.

She snapped off the blue rubber gloves and threw them under the sink. An image of Suzanne, tossing her hair back as she shared a laugh with George Clooney, made Ruth kick the cupboard closed in anger. She grabbed the phone and punched in some numbers.

Lisa answered on the third ring.

"You're not going to believe what happened!" Ruth blurted.

"Ruth?"

"Yeah, yeah," she said, as if she could barely be bothered with the interruption. "That bitch Suzanne pulled the rug out from under us. She's forming a separate committee to handle the movie project."

"What!"

"And guess who's going to be chair? Her!"

"We can't let her do that!" Lisa said. "Why don't you call a committee meeting for tonight? We'll put our heads together and come up with something."

Ruth agreed as she raised the window blind over her kitchen sink and looked out over the yard. "Hey, Lisa," she added, "think if I run for PTA president next year I could win?"

"You *want* to be PTA president?"

"God, no. I just want to beat Suzanne."

Lisa laughed. "You've got *my* vote."

That night Maddie and Lisa came to Ruth's house. Ruth held a pad on her knee and a pen in her hand as she told the women what had happened with Suzanne that afternoon.

"Now," Ruth said, pointing to the pad, "I need some suggestions on what we can do about this. I came up with a few of my own, but, well, you might not think they're very good."

"Try us," Maddie said.

"Okay, here goes. One, slash Suzanne's tires."

Maddie nodded thoughtfully. "That's not bad," she said. "But I think we can do better. How about if we steal all her Manolo Blahnik pumps and replace them with sensible shoes."

"From Payless!" Lisa added.

There was a momentary pause as Ruth and Maddie processed the idea of quiet Lisa offering a suggestion, let alone a funny one. Then they burst into fits of laughter.

"What did you put in this coffee?" Maddie asked.

"You know," said Lisa, "I actually do have a real idea."

Ruth and Maddie turned to face her.

"Um." She tucked her hair behind her ear. "What if I tell my sister-in-law to insist on dealing only with Ruth?" No one reacted immediately. "You know, like threaten to walk away if she has to deal with Suzanne? Do you think that's a stupid idea?"

"No!" Ruth blurted. "Not at all! I think it's a great idea. Do you think she'll do it?"

Lisa bit her lip and repressed a laugh. "She's *met* Suzanne."

Ruth drove her Lincoln Navigator down the long bumpy driveway toward Lisa Slotnick's house in a historic section of Applewood Estates. It was a heavily wooded area, where pre-Depression-era mansions, built by blueblood families with old money, were still standing. They were set back from the road, hidden by trees and wrought-iron fences. So even for Ruth, who lived in Applewood Estates, it was a treat to ride down one of those long driveways and glimpse the part of the world once known as the Gold Coast.

This was Gatsby's Long Island, and she imagined the people who had built these homes had done a lot of entertaining. How else would they have seen their neighbors? But that was then. And while some of the estates had been restored to grandeur, few retained their original acreage. At some point, the value of the real estate between the front door and the roadway became too tempting. So owners sold land, and developers created multiacre subplots with ranch homes and colonials for Long Island's postwar nouveaux riches. Eventually, even these quickly constructed dwellings became some of the most sought-after homes on Long Island. So today, some of Applewood Estates's wealthiest residents shared a driveway with their neighbors.

Lisa and Adam Slotnick lived at the end of one of those long, shared driveways. Their home had been the original manor, though it stood neither proud nor stately on its remaining acreage. Wearing a dull coat of paint and shutters in need of repair, it looked defeated, resigned to sharing its entry with the uninspired architecture of ordinary suburbia.

Yet the wooded landscape and insistent history of the place gave Ruth a feeling of tranquility she didn't get from her part of Applewood Estates, where the trees had been felled to clear the way for grand expanses of lawn. Ruth pushed the intercom buzzer on the front door and heard Lisa's pleasant voice crackle through and ask who was there. Ruth announced herself and then glanced through the sidelight window to see Lisa hurrying across the nearly empty great room to get to the front door.

"I'm sorry," she said, slightly winded, when she opened it. "I was in the back doing laundry. Come in."

Ruth followed Lisa through the vast empty room, past another large room lined with toys. Finally, they entered the kitchen, where Lisa invited Ruth to sit down and offered her coffee.

Ruth noticed a thick manila envelope on the kitchen table. "The contracts?" she asked.

Lisa nodded.

That morning, Suzanne had called Lisa to tell her she was coming by to pick up the contracts from the movie studio, so that she could handle the project herself. Ruth was determined not to let that happen.

The voice of Lisa's youngest son came through a monitor on the counter. "Ee baba wah."

"That's Simon," Lisa said, putting a cup of coffee in front of Ruth. "He's up from his nap. I'll be right back."

Lisa left the monitor on and Ruth heard her enter Simon's room. She couldn't resist listening in, even though she knew Lisa forgot about the monitor and was oblivious to being overheard.

"Hey, sweetie. How was your nap? Did you have a good nap?"

"Wee bee ah toe."

"Are you wet? Let Mommy change you."

The baby started to fuss and cry.

"Shh," Lisa said. "It's okay. Mommy will sing to you. Do you want Mommy to sing to you?"

The little boy's cries subsided as Lisa began to sing the Carly Simon–James Taylor version of "Mockingbird."

Ruth closed her eyes and listened as Lisa's voice flowed like a stream down a mountain, clear and pure and perfect. The little boy started to coo and almost sing along. Ruth could tell from Lisa's voice that she was smiling. Ruth smiled, too. I knew it, she thought. I knew she could sing!

When Lisa came back in the room leading Simon by the hand, Ruth grinned at her.

"You left the monitor on."

Lisa's face reddened. "I didn't realize."

"I know."

"This is embarrassing," Lisa said as she lifted Simon into a booster seat at the kitchen table. She took a sippy cup out of the refrigerator and placed it in front of him.

"Honey, if I had a voice like that I'd be singing in front of something with a lot more range than a baby monitor."

"I don't sing in front of people."

Ruth leaned her chin on her hand. "So you've said."

Lisa put a piece of American cheese and some Cheerios on a plastic plate and placed it in front of Simon. "Can I get you anything?" she said to Ruth.

Ruth laughed. "You can change the subject if you like, but resistance is futile. I'm going to get you to sing on tape for me, Lisa."

A short time later the doorbell rang, and the women went together to answer it, Simon riding on Lisa's hip. It was Suzanne.

"I came for the contracts," she said.

Ruth noticed that Suzanne was dressed in a meticulously tailored gabardine suit, and wondered how much time she had spent picking out the perfect power outfit to wear for this confrontation.

"I'm sorry," Lisa said, hiking Simon up higher on her hip. "There's a problem with that."

Suzanne folded her arms. "What's the problem?"

"Jill told me not to give them to you. She said if she can't deal with Ruth, the whole thing is off."

Suzanne's eyes narrowed. "What do you mean?"

"She means take a hike, Suzanne," Ruth said. "Either she deals with me or she deals with no one."

Suzanne paused to take this in, her gaunt face hardening. "Fine," she finally said. "She deals with no one."

"You can't mean that," Lisa said.

"Oh, I mean it," Suzanne said. "If I can't have those contracts, the deal is *off*. We'll find a way to build that stadium without them." She pivoted on her tasteful black pumps and walked toward her car.

Ruth felt a knot in her stomach, and wanted to kick herself for not seeing this coming. Despite what Suzanne said, this had little to do with getting the stadium built, and almost everything to do with trumping Ruth. There was simply no way she would let her opponent win. Unless, of course, there was another rival Suzanne wanted to trounce even more. Ruth knew exactly what she had to do.

"Lucky Regina Dewitt," she muttered.

Suzanne stopped in her tracks. "What?" she said, her back to them.

"No one told you?" Ruth asked. "Jill said the field at Applewood *South* would do just as well, and Regina's been trying to woo her ever since."

Suzanne whirled around, and Ruth saw the fierce fire of combat in her eyes. This was almost too easy. Regina Dewitt was the one woman Suzanne felt truly diminished by. A former model and star of the Applewood tennis circuit, Regina Dewitt was local royalty. As if being the head of the PTA at their rival elementary school, Applewood South, weren't bad enough.

Suzanne put her hands on her hips. "South?" she spat. "Over my dead body."

Ruth poked her head into the superintendent's office. "Mind if I come in?"

Paul looked up from the page he was studying on his desk. "Not at all."

Ruth entered and closed the door behind her. "I have good news," she said, sliding a side chair as close to him as possible and sitting down in it. "My committee is still in charge of the movie project."

"How did you get Suzanne to change her mind?"

"I had to play a little poker," Ruth said. "But it all worked out." Ruth sat back in her chair and grinned.

Paul smiled but shook his head. "You're proud of yourself, aren't you?"

"Yeah, why? You think it's wrong to bluff a little when you have to?"

"I think it would have been more . . ."—he paused to find the right word—"more *honorable* to have reasoned with Suzanne."

"Please. There *is* no reasoning with Suzanne. Anyway,

it's done. Maddie Schein is looking over the contracts as we speak. She'll coordinate between the school district's lawyers and the production studio."

"That's fine."

Ruth leaned forward. "You want to have lunch with me today?"

"I can't. I have a meeting."

"Too bad." She put her hand on Paul's thigh.

"Ruth," he said without removing her hand, "we have to talk about this. About us."

She snorted. "Again?"

After that first Friday night at Paul's house, they had had two more sexual encounters. The last time, they actually wound up in his bed, rather than on the floor in front of the fireplace. But each time, Paul expressed his conflict about the morality of their trysts. "We shouldn't be doing this" was becoming a familiar refrain in their lovemaking.

Paul pushed his chair from his desk and swiveled to face Ruth directly. "I spoke to my priest."

Ruth leaned back and exhaled, deflated. "You *didn't*."

"We can't keep doing this, Ruth. It isn't right."

"Why not?"

"You took a covenant before God. Keith is your husband, for better or worse, in sickness and in health."

"Tell me something I *don't* know!" Ruth stood, growing agitated. "Do you see me abandoning him? Am I walking out the door? No. I'm staying. I'm staying to take care of a man who will never be healthy. Will never be normal. Will never be a real husband to me. I deserve *something,* Paul." She started to cry. "So don't give me this sanctimonious crap, okay? Because your wife *died.* You're free. I'm stuck. This is my forever." She dissolved into sobs.

Paul's eyes filled with tears. He stood and embraced her.

As she wept, he smoothed her hair and whispered, "Shh, shh, it's okay."

"I'm sorry," she said into his shoulder. "That was terrible."

He pulled his head back and looked at her face. He started kissing her tears and wound up with his lips on hers. They both started breathing heavily. She kissed his neck.

"I think we're getting in over our heads," he breathed.

"Did you say you want me to give you head?" She smiled, feeling a tightness in her face where the tears had dried. She opened his zipper.

He put his hand on her breast. "We shouldn't be doing this."

"I know."

He kissed her lips. "I'm drunk on you."

She pushed him back into his chair and got down on her knees. She pulled his hard penis out of his pants and put it as far into her mouth as she could. His head rolled back and he moaned at the ceiling.

The phone on his desk rang.

"God, oh, God," he said. "Stop."

She didn't.

"Ruth!"

"Ignore it," she said, and went back to what she was doing. When the phone stopped ringing, she got up and unbuttoned her top. Then she unfastened the front clasp on her bra and released her breasts. He put his hands on them as she wriggled out of her panties. She climbed onto him and eased him inside her.

"You're so wet!" he breathed.

She held on to the arms of his chair and slid herself up and down on him, while he held her backside with his large hands. "I need you, Paul. I need you!" she cried.

He picked up his hips and thrust hard into her. She cried out in pain.

"Too rough?" he asked.

"A little," she said.

"Sorry, baby. Sorry."

They had just worked into a comfortable rhythm when the phone rang again.

"Someone's trying to reach me," he said.

"No, no, no!"

"I have to get that."

"Don't!"

He held on to her with one hand and grabbed the phone with the other.

"Hello?" he said. "Yes. Yes, I know who you are, Maddie. What? Why? What did you tell them? I don't know. Can I call you back later? That's all right, I can find your number. Bye." He hung up the phone.

"That was Maddie Schein," he said.

"I figured." She could feel his erection starting to shrivel inside her.

"She said the production company wants to build the stadium on Field One."

"Field One? Why?"

"Something about the angle of the school building in the background. They like the visual."

"What about Applewood Rock?"

Paul shook his head and sighed. "They want to move it."

"What if we say no?" she asked.

"It's a deal breaker."

She laid her head down on his chest. "Damn."

Chapter Seven

LISA

A few days later, Lisa pushed open the door of her pet project—an empty white ranch house—and tried to view the interior as if she were seeing it for the first time. The periwinkle-blue walls of the living room were clean and cool, with a chalky matte finish that looked as appealingly lickable as the Necco wafers she remembered from her childhood. She breathed in the lingering scent of fresh paint and tried to recall the distinctive smell of those odd little candies. Was it mint? Licorice?

She walked diagonally across the room listening to the echo of her footsteps as they bounced off the bare wood floors and blank walls. It was the sound of emptiness. The sound of peace.

Lisa and her husband, Adam, lived in the big, noisy house next door. The house where her four children ran, laughed, coughed, fought, watched TV, chatted, chewed, snored, whined, yawned, babbled, stomped, burped, vomited, wheezed, sneezed, farted, sang, and played with an array of shrill electronic toys. She loved the volume of the house. But like a favorite song played in an endless loop, she also delighted in the silence of its abrupt interruption.

So she had made the empty house next door her pet hobby. When her husband insisted on buying it a year ago, "for privacy," she thought it was an extravagant waste of money. She knew their bank accounts were swelling, but still. People didn't just go around buying houses they didn't need. He was adamant, though, and one night, after the children had gone to bed, he took her by the hand and brought her to see the empty house.

"But what do you want to *do* with it?" she asked, examining the terrible wallpaper and stained carpeting the elderly Essermans had left behind.

"I don't know," he said. "Maybe raze it one day. Build a big new house for us. But for now, nothing."

"Can I have it?"

"What?" He laughed. Clearly, this odd request amused him. "Why?"

"I don't know. I think I'd like to see what I could do with it." She tapped on a wall that she assumed was not part of the original structure. Without it, the front door would open to a normal-sized living room with glass doors to the backyard, instead of a tight little windowless space.

He shrugged. "Knock yourself out."

And so she did, starting with that insulting wall. She went to Home Depot, bought herself a sledgehammer and went to work. It was gratifying, pounding away at the plasterboard and creating huge holes she could see right through. She liked the way the material cracked and crumbled, and enjoyed pulling off large chunks and letting them drop to the floor in a satisfying thud that forced her to back up to avoid inhaling too much dust.

Soon, she realized she would need to ask someone the

best way to remove the wood beams that had been hiding beneath. So she made another trip to Home Depot, driving what would soon become the most familiar route in her life. Though shy about talking to strangers, Lisa got used to approaching people in orange aprons for help. Occasionally, she received unsolicited advice from contractors, men with large hands and honest dirt on their clothes, shopping for items that seemed utterly mysterious to her. But she listened, and little by little, Lisa received an education in demolition and restoration.

As she worked, she piled the rubbish in a corner of the living room. Eventually, the mass of torn-down plasterboard, split two-by-fours, ripped-up carpeting, wallpaper shreds, bent nails, and other debris got too large to ignore. So she rented a Dumpster to keep in front of the house until the demolition phase was finished. This was her husband's first visible sign that she was actually doing something inside, and it made him laugh.

"Just don't rip out any load-bearing walls, okay? I don't mind if the house falls down, but I don't want you buried in it."

Lisa didn't laugh. "The house won't come down," she said.

Back home that evening, hours after finishing her work at the white ranch house, Lisa kneeled beside the bathtub, washing Simon's silky two-year-old skin. The twins, Austin and Henry, ran in and out of the room shouting something about Pokémon trainer battles.

"Get naked, you guys, you're next," she said to her five-year-olds.

Austin ran back into the bathroom, dropped a handful of dismembered action figures into the tub with a splash, and dashed back out again.

"Ugh!" Lisa complained. "What did you do *that* for? Now I'm all wet." She plucked a figure out of the tub and made a face as she examined it. "These things are *filthy.*"

"They're for Simon," Austin shouted. "I don't want them anymore."

"Super." Lisa lifted Simon up out of the tub and dried him off. He was holding a headless blue and yellow man in his chubby fist. She wrapped him in a towel and leaned over the bathtub to open the drain. She scooped the plastic figures out of the water and laid them on a towel like the aftermath of some horrific war.

Simon held his headless, muscle-bound toy in Lisa's face. "Dada!"

"Dada? Did you say 'Dada'?"

"Dada," Simon repeated.

"Yes!" Lisa said excitedly. "That's a man, like Daddy. See? A man. Only Daddy has a head."

"But I've been known to lose mine, too." Adam's voice startled Lisa, who turned around to see him standing by the bathroom door.

"Where did you come from?"

"Side door. I stopped to help Sarah with her homework."

"Did you hear him?" she asked. "He said Dada."

"I heard him." Adam crouched down and Simon came running into his arms. "That's my little man," Adam said as he hugged his son. "Now tell Mommy not to worry so much. Tell her Einstein didn't talk until he was four."

Adam stood and gave his wife a kiss. She was about to ask him how his day was when the phone rang. Adam said he'd take Simon and Lisa went to answer it.

It was her sister-in-law, following up on her e-mail. She wanted to set a time to meet with the committee so she could discuss her idea for how they could convince everyone to let them build a stadium on Field One. Since the very thought of moving Applewood Rock had sent a ripple of angry gossip through the community, Lisa wasn't confident the town could be swayed. But the committee wanted desperately to save this project, so she set up a date.

Thus, the following Wednesday morning found Lisa making coffee and arranging a platter of bagels for the members of the public relations committee. Before anyone arrived, Beryl called from her cell phone.

"Have you seen what's going on out here?" Beryl asked.

Lisa heard something in the background that sounded like shouting. "Out where? What do you mean?"

"The end of your driveway. I got an anonymous tip that there was something going on here that I might want to put in the newsletter. I think you'd better come out and have a look."

Lisa hung up the phone, grabbed a sweater, and went outside. She couldn't see the end of her driveway from her front door, and had to walk past her beloved white ranch house and the homes of her closest neighbors to get to the street. As she approached, hugging her sweater around herself, she heard female voices chanting and saw a group of women she thought she knew from the PTA holding up large, hand-lettered signs. When she got closer she saw that the signs said SAVE APPLEWOOD ROCK and that Suzanne Podobinski was among the protesters. Lisa listened carefully to the chant, and finally made out what they were saying: "I-don't-care-what-people-say! Applewood-Rock-is-here-to-stay!"

The women were blocking the road, and Beryl sat in her

car trying to pass. She honked her horn and screamed out the window, "Protest on the side of the road, you dimwits! You're blocking traffic!"

The women continued chanting and marching in a circle.

"What should I do?" Lisa shouted over them.

"Tell them you're calling the police!" Beryl answered. "If they get arrested, it'll make great copy for my newsletter."

Lisa froze, not knowing what to do. Beryl yelled at the protestors, "Children are starving! The rain forests are being destroyed! You're protesting a goddamned *rock*!"

Just then, Lisa saw another car pull up behind Beryl's. Maddie Schein got out, sliding a single crutch after her. She put it under her arm and limped slightly as she approached Beryl's window. The two women chatted for several minutes, and then Maddie limped confidently toward Suzanne Podobinski. They had a conversation that included a lot of pointing at the roadway. Maddie swung her crutch like the pencil arm of a compass, drawing imaginary arcs. Finally, Suzanne nodded, and Maddie went back to her car, giving Beryl the thumbs-up on the way. Suzanne ushered her protesters to the side of the road and let the vehicles pass.

"Hop in," Beryl said to Lisa, "I'll drive you back to your house."

"What did Maddie say to them?" Lisa asked. "I couldn't hear."

"Lawyer stuff. She explained that they were free to protest as long as they didn't block the entrance. Said she would be forced to call the police if they didn't move. All without threatening to clobber anyone with her crutch."

Lisa invited Beryl to sit in on the committee meeting,

and after Maddie pulled up, the three of them went inside. As Lisa escorted them through the long, nearly empty great room toward the kitchen, Beryl let out a low whistle.

"Where do you keep the bowling pins?" she asked.

"You could throw a huge party in here," Maddie added.

Lisa sighed. "This is all Adam," she said apologetically. "He can never have enough space for some reason. And I refuse to furnish it until the kids are bigger."

The intercom buzzed just as they reached the kitchen. It was Ruth. Lisa told Beryl and Maddie to help themselves to coffee and bagels, and ran back through the two long rooms to get to the front door.

"Bitch," Ruth said, when Lisa swung it open.

"Excuse me?"

"Podobinski," Ruth explained. "You think she really gives a shit about Applewood Rock? This is personal."

When she got to the kitchen, Ruth told the others there was no way she'd let Suzanne win this one. "We're building this stadium if I have to move that rock myself!"

"They think they're so clever with their stupid chant," Beryl seethed.

"We need our own," Maddie said. "Something stronger than theirs."

"Something with muscle," Ruth added.

Beryl started to sing in a deep voice, "We will, we will ROCK YOU!" She pounded the kitchen table with her fists, shaking the coffee cups.

Ruth laughed and joined in. "We will, we will ROCK YOU!"

"We should make some signs and stage a counter-protest," Maddie said, her eyes twinkling.

"You serious?" Beryl asked.

The four women exchanged glances and started to laugh. It was settled. Lisa produced some posterboard and heavy black markers left over from one of Sarah's science fair projects. Then she ran to the Dumpster next door to find some pieces of wood that would make good signposts. While carrying them back to the house, Lisa saw her sister-in-law's BMW pull up. Jill, briefcase in hand, got out of the car and looked at the pieces of wood Lisa was holding.

"I hope you're planning to use those to beat the shit out of those PTA mothers from hell."

"More or less," Lisa said, leading Jill into the house.

While Jill explained the idea she thought would win over the school board as well as the Applewood Town Council, the others drew large signs that said KIDS, YES! on one side and ROCK, NO! on the other. They listened carefully to Jill as they toiled, interrupting her occasionally with pointed questions.

"God, that sounds perfect," Beryl said. "I hope you gals will let me help."

"Of course," Ruth said. "I could use your skills in all this." She then asked Jill to please keep her idea a secret for now, and told her they would be in touch when they needed her.

After Jill thanked them and left, the four women gathered their signs and went outside.

Suzanne's nostrils flared when she saw the group approaching, four abreast. Maddie, walking with a crutch, wore her sign like a sandwich board. The other three held theirs aloft on posts. They chanted, "WE WILL, WE WILL ROCK YOU!" and then pounded their sticks twice on the ground in unison before repeating the refrain. Lisa glanced over at Ruth, who looked as fiercely determined as a warrior. Then she looked back at Suzanne, who seemed stunned by the imposing demonstration.

"What do you think you're *doing!*" Suzanne shrieked at Ruth.

Ruth signaled her group to stop chanting. They halted in their tracks.

"Counterdemonstrating," Ruth said.

"If you think you're going to sway *anybody,* forget about it. The whole PTA is against moving that rock, so why don't you just go crawl under one."

"Easy there, girl," Beryl said. "Another attempt at wit and you might strain yourself."

Suzanne glared at Beryl.

"Is this what you want?" Ruth asked Suzanne. "You want Jill to give this movie project to Regina Dewitt? You want Applewood South to get the stadium?"

"Ha." Suzanne sneered. "Fool me once."

Ruth looked stymied, but only for a second. "Did you take a vote?" she asked.

Suzanne wrinkled her brow. "What?"

"Did you take a vote? To see how many members of the PTA are on your side."

Suzanne snickered. "You want me to take a *vote?* Sure, I'll take a vote. Like you have a *chance* of winning." She glanced back at her followers for support, but most of them had laid down their signs and were chatting distractedly.

Ruth signaled her friends to pick up their signs and resume chanting. They continued their march.

"C'mon," Suzanne said to her group. "We're going. I need to schedule a meeting for the entire PTA. We're taking a vote."

Lisa hugged herself against the brisk wind as she glanced down the street hoping to spot her children's school bus.

At last, she saw lights flashing at the top of the hill, which meant that Haley and Jake Fishbein were being dropped off. She'd only have to wait another minute or so.

Sarah, Austin, and Henry got off the bus all noise and energy, arms, legs, and backpacks rolling down the steps with more momentum than control. Lisa smiled, watching her happy children make the transition from one environment to another, brimming with joyous excitement. These were the most difficult moments of a child's day, Lisa knew, as they hadn't yet developed the maturity to cope calmly with sudden change.

It delighted Lisa to let them spend their energy naturally. The boys, as usual, raced each other to the house, and Lisa imagined sitting in the bleachers of the new stadium watching them try to outrun a soccer ball to the goal. Or maybe squinting against the sun as one of them adjusted a batting helmet two sizes too big as he waited for an underhand pitch. She loved the idea of having an arena for the children to play in—contained, safe, and happy—as their parents sat and watched, sharing thermoses of coffee, their cups running over with pride.

Sarah walked backward in front of Lisa, animatedly relating a story about her class's pet iguana, which had been found dead in its cage after recess.

That night, Lisa cooked dinner for the children as Sarah sat at the kitchen table working on her spelling homework.

"I want to call Emily," Sarah said, referring to a friend from her class. "Can I call Emily? Can I?"

"After dinner," Lisa said. "Now finish your homework."

Later, when the phone rang, Sarah jumped up.

"Sit," Lisa admonished, but felt torn when she saw the look of disappointment on her daughter's face. "You can call her later, I promise."

Sarah sighed and sat down. Lisa picked up the phone expecting a small nine-year-old voice, but heard her mother's familiar lilt.

"Hi, baby."

Lisa sighed. "What's going on, Mom?"

"I'm on the wagon."

Over the years, Lisa should have grown inured to Nancy's declarations of sobriety and the inevitable backslide into the abyss of alcoholism. Yet every time her mother swore up and down that this was different, a small part of Lisa felt ignited by hope. And how could it be otherwise? Lisa was a mother who loved her children fiercely, and had to believe in a certain rightness to the world. She wanted so much for them.

"Good for you," she said without enthusiasm.

"But I'm in a jam. A really bad jam."

"Money?"

"I lost the apartment."

"What do you mean you lost the apartment?" Lisa leaned against the kitchen counter and looked out at the empty birdhouse in the backyard.

"I was a little behind on the rent. They kicked me out."

For as long as Lisa could remember, her mother had been a struggling singer who blamed her lack of success on "shit luck" and "sleazy creeps who won't give you a break unless you suck their little dicks." The last part was usually said with her pinky wiggling to emphasize the point. But Lisa knew it was alcohol that made her mother a failure.

"What happened to the money we sent you?" Lisa asked.

Since Nancy had lost her part-time receptionist job nearly a year ago, she called her daughter every few months asking for money. Lisa suspected the singing gigs had dried up completely and she was Nancy's only source of income. So she wired the money quickly. This increasingly infuriated Adam, who wanted to send the money directly to the landlord, insisting Nancy would only spend it on booze. Lisa knew he was right, but still. Infantilizing her own mother was more than she could take.

"It wasn't enough," Nancy said.

"Did you use it to pay your rent?"

"I don't care for your implications."

A buzzer sounded in the kitchen. Lisa picked up a pot of boiling pasta and poured it through a colander in the sink, leaning back to avoid the steam.

"So where are you staying?" Lisa asked, the phone tucked under her chin.

"With LuAnn, my AA sponsor. But she says I have to find a place of my own and I'm completely strapped."

Lisa imagined how Adam would react if she wired her mother money yet again. But now there was no landlord to contact. Still, maybe she could verify the story.

"Can I talk to her?" Lisa asked.

"Talk to her?"

"This LuAnn person." Lisa picked up the colander with two hands and shook it against the sink to drain any excess water. Then she dumped the entire contents into a large bowl.

"She isn't here now."

"Well, give me the phone number there and I'll call her later."

"Why do you want to talk to her?"

Lisa took a breath and closed her eyes. "I want to know that you're really on the wagon before I send any more money," she said quickly.

"I'm really on the wagon, baby."

"Fine. Just give me the number there."

"I don't know it," Nancy said quickly.

"You don't know the number you're calling from?" Lisa stirred a simmering pot of tomato sauce and then blew across the spoon before tasting it carefully with her tongue.

"It isn't written anywhere."

"Then tell LuAnn to call *me*."

"I really don't see why."

"Adam put his foot down." Lisa felt ashamed of herself. Why blame Adam? Why not just say she didn't believe her?

"Okay, I'll have her call you. But can you wire me just a little bit right now? I don't even have money for a cup of coffee."

"I gotta run, Mom. Have LuAnn call me."

There was no response. Lisa heard the metallic sound of change falling through the mechanism of a pay phone.

"Mom? Are you there? Mom?"

There was no answer. The connection was severed.

Not that it was ever that strong to begin with. Lisa remembered being sick with the flu when she was ten years old. Her mother was out at one of her gigs, and Lisa lay in bed drifting in and out of sleep, imagining her illness eliciting feelings of tenderness in her mother. Her babysitter that night was her mother's friend John, who for years Lisa thought was named John Thaveri, because her mother always referred to him as "John the fairy" when he wasn't around.

Though she was thirsty enough to feel parched, Lisa repeatedly turned down John's offers to get her a glass of water or anything else. She wanted to be truly suffering when her mother got home. Surely the sight of her beloved daughter in such distress would tap some inner reserve of motherly love.

Lisa lay still in bed when she heard her mother come in, waiting until John was paid and out the door before weakly crying out.

"Mom? Mom?"

"What is it, baby?" Nancy called from the living room.

"I don't feel so good."

"You have the flu, baby."

"Can I have some water?"

"Water? Sure. Just a minute."

It was a small Greenwich Village apartment, and Lisa was able to hear the *clunk clunk* of her mother's shoes dropping off her feet, and then the long *pffff* of the zipper on her dress coming down. The glittery red one, Lisa thought. She always took it off as soon as she walked in the door because it had sequins and couldn't even be dry-cleaned.

Lisa heard her mother pad her way to the tiny kitchen, and listened for the sound of the tap. Instead, she heard the freezer open and then the clink of ice cubes in a glass. She was about to call out, "I don't want ice," when she heard the thick sound of the cupboard opening and realized it wasn't for her. Nancy was pouring herself a drink. Probably scotch. She had forgotten about Lisa's water.

At that exact moment, a young girl with a sore throat and lips cracked from fever decided that she would grow up to be an entirely different kind of mother. And as she drifted to sleep, still thirsty, she imagined flitting around her own ailing daughter, ministering to her needs with love more tender than the velvety softness of a good-night kiss.

Chapter Eight

When Lisa was three, her father disappeared, leaving sixty-five dollars cash and a note that said he wouldn't be back. So she and her mother existed on what her mother earned from her kitschy, ironic singing act, and whatever money she could get from her parents by begging and pleading. Occasionally, Nancy was forced to take a "real job" as an office temp, which embarrassed her greatly. Lisa suspected that Nancy feared her friends would find out that she had completed Katharine Gibbs and could type like a fiend. When she was sober, anyway. How Lisa adored those months when they were so strapped for cash that her mother was forced to wake up early each day and go out into the world dressed like a regular person!

When it came time to apply to college, Lisa felt certain she would get into her first-choice school, MIT, where she knew she had the least chance of meeting people like Nancy and her entourage. "My little accountant," Nancy said derisively to her bohemian friends when the letter of acceptance came. "She'll probably wind up supporting *me*

one day." It was, Lisa knew, an insult wrapped in a compliment. Calling someone an accountant was Nancy's way of
accusing them of an unforgivable sin: being uncreative.

Lisa's grandparents, who were delighted to see her becoming the antithesis of her mother, gladly paid for her
education. So Lisa went off in pursuit of a degree in eco-
nomics, and met a wonderful boy with two feet on the
ground and a genius for computers.

After school they got married, and Lisa worked for several years as a researcher for a New York City investment
bank. She enjoyed her job, but when she got pregnant with
Sarah, she happily gave it up to devote herself to an ordinary life as wife and mother.

The pregnancy ushered Lisa into a hormonally induced
state of oblivion. Not blissful, but blessedly removed from
worrying about the big things, like whether her baby
would be healthy or what kind of mother she would be.
Instead, she fixated on the minutiae, magnifying the significance of every small decision. Choosing the baby's layette
nearly sent her into a panic. How can you make those de-
cisions, she asked a heavily made-up saleswoman at the
baby clothes store, when you don't know the sex of the
baby? "Calm down," the lady said when Lisa's eyes filled
with tears. "You'll pick out two different layettes, one for a
boy and one for a girl, and leave them both here. After the
baby is born, someone can come by and pick up whichever
one you need."

"Someone comes while I'm in the hospital and picks it
up for me?" Lisa was incredulous. She couldn't imagine
how it could possibly work so simply.

"Yes, dear. Most women ask their mother to do it."

Lisa practically snorted. Her mother, sure. Like that

would ever happen. She'd have to ask someone from Adam's side of the family.

As it turned out, Nancy, who was in one of her sober phases and actually dating a man with a car, was eager for the job.

"Let me and Naldo pick it up for you. It'll be a hoot."

"Mom, there's going to be a very small window of time to get this done. You'll have to drive out here from the city after I have the baby but before I go home. What if Naldo is working?"

"He'll swoop down in his helicopter!" Nancy joked. Naldo Reagan was a traffic reporter for a local radio station and often broadcast from one thousand feet above the Long Island Expressway. The last time they spoke, Nancy confessed to Lisa that Naldo wasn't his real name. He had changed it from Ronald because he was sick of the wisecracks about sharing a name with a former president. But Lisa thought an Irish guy called Naldo was a lot funnier than a traffic reporter named Ronald Reagan.

"Seriously, Mom. I'm going to need all this stuff when I get home with the baby."

"Not another word, okay? I want to do this. I was a shitty mother, but I think I can be a good granny."

Lisa sighed. "Okay," she said, and worried about how difficult it would be to ask someone else to help out at the last minute if her mother didn't come through.

"It's a girl!" the doctor said as she pulled Sarah's slithery pink body from Lisa. She quickly suctioned the baby's nose and mouth and held her up for Lisa and Adam to see. "Your daughter!"

A gulp of wind hit Lisa's throat. She looked at the living, breathing, wailing creature and was slapped with a reality as new to her as oxygen to the baby's lungs. She was stunned. Not by the baby's gender, but its very existence. There she was, facing the very moment she had spent so many months preparing for, and yet she felt as surprised as if she had opened her eyes to discover the world in color for the first time.

She inhaled with a deep shudder. "We have a baby," she said to Adam. "A baby!" She saw tears on Adam's face and realized she was crying, too.

"We have a baby!" Adam echoed, and laughed. "Our little girl."

Later, when the new mother was wheeled to her room and the baby was taken to the nursery, Adam told Lisa she should get some rest.

"Do you want me to call everyone?" he asked before he left.

"Yes," she said, trying to get comfortable on the flat hospital pillow, "and don't forget to tell my mother to pick up the layette."

Lisa fell into a deep, dreamless sleep for several hours. She awoke to a pulsating pain in her crotch and looked up to see Adam back in her room. He sat on a chair holding his new daughter.

"Are we calling her Sarah?" Adam asked.

"Sarah Elizabeth," Lisa pronounced.

"Sarah," Adam said, looking at the baby. "You're Sarah."

Lisa shifted in the bed, trying to get comfortable. "Did you call my mother? When is she picking up the layette?"

"Tomorrow."

"I'll probably be *dis*charged tomorrow."

"She's coming first thing."

Lisa pushed the control button on her bed. The motor whirred as the back of the mattress moved up, helping Lisa into a sitting position.

"Let me hold Sarah," she said.

That night, after her visitors left and Adam had gone home, Lisa complained to a kind nurse named Maureen about her discomfort. She gave Lisa a fresh ice pack to put on her episiotomy, and asked the new mother if she wanted her to take the baby to the nursery for a few hours.

"So you can get some sleep," Maureen said.

Lisa bit her lip. "I don't know. I'm breast-feeding."

"It's okay. I'll bring her back in a few hours."

Lisa nodded. She was as tired as she'd ever felt and was glad to be relieved of the responsibility for a few hours. As she listened to the sound of her baby's bassinet being wheeled toward the nursery, Lisa fell into a deep sleep.

There began a dream. Adam telling her about some new software he had created. A wonderful, glorious, revolutionary product. He was excited to show it to her in action, and led her toward a building where a company was using it to multiply profits beyond imagining. But on the way there she lost sight of him. She came upon a factory and went inside to see if Adam was there. She found him and the dream changed. The thing that he wanted to show her now was a beautiful melody coming from the walls of the baby's room. Or was it the baby singing? As she followed him toward the song, the dream was interrupted by a woman's voice.

"Mrs. Slotnick? Do you want to nurse your baby now?"

Lisa didn't want to open her eyes. She wanted to drift back into the dream and find the source of the beautiful melody. She let her eyelids flutter open so that she could tell the woman to go away and let her sleep.

"I need more sleep," she planned to say, but stopped. At the sight of her infant something deep in the animal region of her brain produced a tidal force of maternal longing that drowned her intention. "I need . . . my baby," she said, reaching for the tiny package. And as she cradled her daughter in her arms, she took a deep inhale off the top of the newborn's head and discovered the savage, feral power of motherhood. Lisa fell in love.

She kept the baby with her the rest of the night, refusing offers to have her taken back to the nursery. My baby, she thought, *my* baby, and wondered if her mother had ever felt this way. Not that it mattered anymore. Her love for Sarah, she thought, had eclipsed her need for her own mother's love.

Which made it all the more frustrating that she was dependent on her now. Lisa looked at the clock. Five A.M. What time would they discharge her? What if they sent her home first thing in the morning? No way her mother could pick up the layette that early. She guessed she could send Adam out for it, but that meant she'd be alone in the house with her brand-new baby. What if something happened?

Lisa placed Sarah in the bassinet and dozed off again. She was awakened at seven-thirty when an orderly came in with breakfast trays for her and her roommate in the next bed. Lisa glanced over at Sarah and then peeked under the plastic lid covering the plate on her tray, expecting steam to escape. But no. The scrambled eggs were cold as death. Ugh. She pushed the tray aside, picked up the phone next to her bed, and called her mother.

"Hello?" Nancy's voice sounded gravelly with sleep.

"Hi, Mom."

"Hey, baby. How are you feeling? What time is it?"

"Seven-thirty. I'm fine. Sarah's fine, too."

"Can't wait to see her." She yawned.

"What time are you coming? I'm going to need that layette."

Nancy yawned again. "Naldo said he'd call me first thing." Her voice was clearing.

"They're discharging me today."

"That's great."

"But I mean it could be early. I have no idea what time. And there are so many things in that layette I'm going to need when I get home. I don't even have a sheet for the bassinet."

"Relax, baby. You're not getting out of there that early."

"Mo-om," Lisa whined. She knew she sounded like a child. *Damn* her mother for reducing her to this. And damn herself for relying on the old swillpot for something important.

"First thing. I promise. Okay?"

Back then, Lisa and Adam had still lived in the tiny split-level they bought when they got married, and it was close to noon when they walked through the door with their new baby and no layette. Lisa wanted to cry. She felt shaky and exhausted, overwhelmed by worry for the new life in her arms, and sick with disappointment over her mother's failure to come through when she needed her most.

Still wearing her coat and holding little Sarah, Lisa sat down on the sofa. "What do we do now?" she asked her husband. "I need the layette."

"You want me to go get it?"

"No. I want you to stay with me. Can you call Jill?"

"I'll call the store first. Maybe your mother is already there."

Lisa nodded. She transferred Sarah from one arm to the other while she shook off her coat. Adam telephoned the store and then reported to Lisa that her mother had picked up the layette over an hour ago.

"So where is she?" Lisa demanded. "It's only ten minutes away. What did she do—go out for lunch? Knock back a few highballs?"

The telephone rang and Lisa rushed to answer it.

"Jeez, they kicked you out of here in a hurry," Nancy said.

"Mom? What are you talking about? Where are you?"

"I'm at the hospital. I got all your baby girl stuff."

"Why did you go to the *hospital*?"

"I thought you'd be here."

Adam walked over to Lisa and silently offered to take the baby from her. She shook her head. "I'm home, Mom. Can you come straight here?"

"I don't know if I can get all this stuff into a cab."

"A cab? Isn't Naldo with you?"

"He had to work. A last-minute thing."

"How did you get out to Long Island?"

"I took the train and a cab. Then somebody who worked at the store gave me a lift to the hospital. But she had one of those big Jeep things. I'm not sure I can get these boxes into the trunk of a car."

"Mom, aren't there *bags* inside the boxes?"

"Let me check. Oh, yeah, there are. So you want me to just ditch the boxes and load all these bags into a cab?"

Lisa sighed, exasperated. "Hold on a second." She put her hand over the mouthpiece and asked Adam if he could pick her mother up at the hospital.

Alone with the baby, Lisa wasn't as nervous as she thought she would be. Still holding Sarah, she went into the kitchen and poured herself a tall glass of water. She returned to the living room, where she sat back down on the sofa and began to nurse her baby. Her breasts were swollen and hard, and it hurt when the baby latched on. But after a minute, her nipple got numb, and she released herself into the pleasure of watching the tiny newborn suckle.

She sat, sipping water and singing softly to her baby, when she became aware of her throbbing bottom again. As she shifted her position, Lisa felt a rush of bloody discharge. Her sanitary napkin was overflowing. She took the baby off her breast and looked around, trying to decide where to put her down while she went to the bathroom. The bassinet was parked in the middle of the living room but had no sheet. She went to the linen closet to retrieve a clean towel to lay down, cursing her mother for her ineptitude.

Worse still was how her mother managed to never be at fault when she screwed up. Either she was too drunk to be held accountable, or so overwhelmed by life without alcohol that you were supposed to excuse her stupidity. And be *grateful* she was sober. And *grateful* she went through all the trouble of taking a train out to Long Island. Well, who the hell asked her to take the train? Why didn't she just call so they could have made other arrangements? Drunk or not, it was just so like her to run around bumping into walls.

By the time Adam and Nancy arrived, Lisa was all buttoned up and in no mood to overlook her mother's incompetence. She coolly thanked her for picking up the layette, and nodded in the direction of the bassinet, indicating that Nancy could take a look if she liked.

Nancy peered inside at the sleeping newborn. "Looks kind of raisiny," she said, cocking her head.

Lisa gritted her teeth. "Jeez, Mom, she just spent *nine months* in amniotic fluid."

"Okay, okay. Don't get huffy."

"It's just, you know, she's your first grandchild. I'd think you might have something *nice* to say."

"I'm not a baby person. You know that."

Lisa rolled her eyes. "You want a soda or something?"

Nancy nodded and followed Lisa into the kitchen. She looked up at the stencil that ringed the top of the walls. "Pretty," she said.

Lisa opened the refrigerator and pulled out a can of Diet Coke. "But your granddaughter looks like a raisin."

"Oh, would you stop." Nancy took the soda from Lisa and sat down at the kitchen table.

"You said you wanted to be a good grandmother. You're not off to an auspicious start." Lisa put on rubber gloves that were hanging over the side of the sink and began washing some dishes Adam had left.

"I guess I can't do anything right," Nancy said.

Lisa heard the baby making tiny sounds and pulled off her gloves. She went into the living room and gently picked her up. Nancy followed behind and watched as Lisa unswaddled the newborn, changed her diaper, and then wrapped her up again.

As Lisa held the baby against her shoulder, gently patting her back and soothing her with cooing sounds, Nancy sidled up close and said, "You're a lucky baby, little Sarah. You have a good mama. Better than me, that's for damn sure."

And that would have meant a lot to Lisa if she hadn't caught a distinct whiff of alcohol on her mother's breath.

Adam worked as a corporate computer consultant then, traveling from client to client, installing systems and tinkering with software. At home, in his spare time, he worked on writing a computer program for inventory tracking that he was sure would make them rich. When he was ready, he borrowed money from Lisa's grandparents, took out a bank loan, and set to work building his business. He rented an office and hired a staff. The ambition of it all terrified Lisa. She didn't want to shake his confidence, so she tried to keep her feelings to herself. At night, she tossed and turned and worried about their future. But then things started to happen. Quickly. Night after night, Adam came home wildly excited about the deals he was making. Businesses were buying his software, and within a year of start-up, he was in the black.

By the time she was pregnant with the twins, they had more money than they could spend. That's when he started making comments about moving. One day, he came home from work and cooed to little Sarah as he picked her up, "Would you like Daddy to buy you a big, new house? A house for a princess?"

"There's nothing wrong with *this* house," Lisa said, looking at the kitchen's stencil border her mother had admired. She had done it herself before Sarah was born and suddenly felt that the delicate cherries and curved leaves were her only anchor in a roiling current. How could she ever leave?

"Honey, we could buy a house three times this size tomorrow. And pretty soon, we'll be able to afford any house we want."

Lisa sighed. "Maybe we should wait. Make sure things are really stable with your business."

Adam smiled like he had a wonderful secret to share. "Leelee?" He stuck his hands deep into the pockets of his worn jeans and beamed. "I'm going public."

"What?" Lisa said, but knew exactly what he meant. He meant he was going to sell stock in his company. And she knew what happened when people did that with successful high tech businesses. They became rich. Unimaginably rich. She started to cry and he embraced her.

"I know," he whispered, "I'm happy, too."

And that's when it struck her that it wasn't the idea of failure that she found so terrifying. It was success.

After the twins were born they started to look for a home in the most exclusive areas. Lisa and Adam didn't know what kind of house they wanted, so they had a hard time explaining their preferences to the real estate broker. But after seeing several showy new homes with grand entrances and towering ceilings—houses they later found out were sometimes derisively called "McMansions"—they knew what they didn't want.

Then the Realtor took them to an old estate at the end of a long driveway on Deepdale Road. A house with history and wainscoting. "This place goes on forever," Adam said, walking from room to room, opening and closing doors. The Realtor explained how rare it was for a house like this to come on the market, and told them how lucky they were to get the opportunity to see it.

Lisa could sense Adam's excitement, and knew he would want to put in a bid. His searing intelligence was often masked by the bright hues of a childlike intensity, and today he shone like neon. So she walked around the oversized house trying to find something about it to love. She settled on the kitchen. The cabinets were terrible and needed to be replaced, but the back of the room opened into a breakfast nook that was surrounded on all sides by tall old windows. Outside, just to the left, was a dogwood tree in need of pruning. But she could imagine hanging a bird feeder from it and looking out as the children ate breakfast. Just to the right, where weeds grew, she could put a wooden bench and plant a small garden. Maybe get one of those clay turtles.

Adam walked up behind her and gently kissed the back of her neck. "What do you think?" he said, turning her around to face him. His eyes twinkled in anticipation.

Lisa smiled. "I love it."

Chapter Nine

She tried to walk away, but George Clooney grabbed the delicate blonde in his arms and kissed her passionately on the mouth.

Lisa leaned in toward Ruth and whispered, "I'm not sure this is a great movie for kids."

It was a Sunday matinee. The two women had taken their nine-year-old daughters to see the new George Clooney movie. Afterward, they dropped the girls off at a birthday party in a town several miles away. Since they would have to pick them up again in only an hour and a half, it didn't pay to go home, so Ruth and Lisa decided to go someplace local for a cup of coffee.

"But where?" Lisa asked Ruth, who was driving. "I don't know a single place in this area. I'm not sure I've ever even been to Quaker Bay before, have you?"

"Uh, a couple of times," Ruth said. "I know this quiet little café that's kind of nice. I've been there once or twice with a friend."

After settling into the booth at the tiny eatery, Ruth told

Lisa that if she was in the mood for soup, this was the place. The pea soup especially, she said, was delicious. But Lisa wasn't that hungry, and they decided to order coffee and split a slice of pecan pie.

"Are you nervous about that PTA vote?" Lisa asked. "Suzanne seems so confident everyone will side with her about not moving that stupid rock."

"Not nervous at all," Ruth said. "I have a plan that starts with Jill's suggestions about the stadium and ends with George Clooney as the imaginary lover of every horny housewife in Applewood."

Lisa beamed. "Tell me!"

"I will," Ruth said, "later." A sly grin crossed her face and she leaned in toward Lisa. "So, what do you think he's really like?"

"Who? George Clooney?"

Ruth nodded, and Lisa fell silent. There was no way she could tell her friend what she really thought about the handsome celebrity. It was too embarrassing. Ridiculous, even. She hated to admit that she was one of those horny housewives who fantasized about him. But it was true. She sometimes had imaginary conversations where he told her he knew she was special the minute he saw her, even though she was surrounded by women who were practiced at attracting attention, like Jill and Ruth. And when she would ask, "Why me?," the sensitive star would whisper something poignant like "still waters run deep," only much more clever. Nor could she ever admit that he was there with her, sometimes, in the empty white ranch house, complimenting her on her work. She even went so far as to imagine that he would want to live in that house while he was shooting the movie. And as to her sexual fantasies, well, Lisa blushed and stuck her fork into the pecan pie. "I hear he has a great sense of humor," she said.

Ruth laughed. "Oh, c'mon, Lisa. That's not what I meant and you know it. What do you think he's like *in bed*?"

Lisa laughed, but then felt sad for her friend. Poor Ruth. She probably had no sex life and needed these kinds of fantasies more than Lisa did. "Slow," she said seriously. "Slow and gentle."

"Really?" Ruth pierced the pecan pie with her fork and picked up a big gob of whipped cream with it. "I think he loses himself in it like an animal. I think he's the kind of guy you have to remind to slow down. And . . ." Ruth stuck the fork into her mouth. "I think he's very oro."

"Very *what*?"

Ruth swallowed. "Very oral."

Lisa laughed. "No question about that!"

Ruth's eyes opened wide. "Lisa Slotnick," she teased. "You've given this some thought!" Ruth pointed the fork at her. "Okay, how big?" she asked, ignoring the flush rising up in Lisa's face.

"Ru-uth!"

"C'mon. How big do you think?" Just then a handsome young waiter was walking by, and Ruth stopped him. "Excuse me. Do you have those foot-long hot dogs?" She held her hands wide apart in demonstration.

Embarrassed, Lisa covered her eyes with her hands.

"No, ma'am," said the waiter, nearly laughing. "No hot dogs. Can I get you something else?"

The two women were still giggling like girls when Lisa looked up and saw someone she thought she knew at the takeout counter. "Ruth," she said, "isn't that Paul Capobianco?"

"What?" Ruth turned around to look.

"Paul Capobianco. The superintendent?"

"That's him," Ruth said, running her fingers through her hair. She called out, "Hello, Paul!"

Paul looked up, and Lisa noticed that he seemed momentarily frozen. Then he waved and finished paying the cashier for his takeout package before approaching their table.

"Hello, ladies."

"Our daughters are at a birthday party up the block," Ruth said. "We just popped in here to kill some time. You know, instead of going all the way home just to come back again."

Lisa thought it odd that Ruth launched into an explanation for their presence. It almost sounded like she thought they needed an excuse for being there.

"I hope you enjoy it," said Paul. "I just came in for some takeout." He held up the brown paper bag. "They make great homemade soup here."

"No kidding?" said Ruth. "Well, we just ordered the pecan pie."

Lisa wondered why Ruth didn't own up to knowing about the soup. Then, a thought struck her. A huge thought. But was she right? She mentally backtracked, connecting the dots. She looked at Paul. She looked at Ruth.

"The pie's good, too," Paul said.

"Delicious," Lisa added.

"Well, we won't keep you," Ruth said to Paul. "I'm sure you don't want your soup to get cold."

When Paul left, Lisa thought she caught Ruth scrutinizing her face for any signs of awareness. It would be easy to pretend she didn't know, but that felt so dishonest, and Ruth was her friend.

"He's nice," Lisa said tentatively.

"Yeah, very nice." Ruth glanced back toward the door and then picked up her fork, moving it between her fingers. "I heard he lives around here."

"You two are . . . pretty friendly?"

Ruth looked up and offered Lisa a small grin that erased any doubt. Lisa noticed the lovely greenness of her friend's eyes. Paul, she thought, probably tells her she has beautiful eyes.

"What gave it away?" Ruth finally said.

"The soup. You acted like you didn't know about the soup."

Ruth smiled. "Done in by soup."

"It's okay, Ruth. I wouldn't, you know, say a word to anyone."

"I know. Thanks."

Later, when they rose to leave, Ruth reached into her purse and pulled out a cassette tape. "I want you to listen to this when you get a chance," she said, pushing it into Lisa's hand. "It's my songs. I think some of them are pretty good, but you have to promise not to focus on my shitty voice."

"You just want me to listen?"

"Yeah, for now. I'll bug you later about singing them for me on a demo tape."

"Ruth."

"I know, I'm obnoxious. Lovable, but obnoxious. But take it, okay? Just listen when you get a chance."

Lisa climbed down from the stepladder one final time and surveyed the work she had done in the dining room of the empty white ranch house. Two more days, at most, and she'd be finished with the wallpaper. But for now, it was time to clean up and get ready for the children.

First, though, she pushed the power button on her portable stereo and turned on the radio. Lisa always waited until it was cleanup time before listening to music. The work, she had decided, should be done in silence. Otherwise, it lost its meditative quality. But as she cleaned brushes and buckets and took out the trash, she enjoyed a few minutes of music.

She had the radio tuned to an oldies station, and they were playing "Love Me Tender." Lisa considered turning the dial. She had nothing against Elvis Presley, but the song had been part of her mother's repertoire for years, and she couldn't bear hearing it. Once, when she was just five years old, Lisa had entertained a group of her mother's drunken friends by imitating the songstress's emotional rendering of the tune. It was the first and last time Lisa ever did anything like that. The friends squealed in delight at the small child's characterization, but afterward, when the party was over, her mother attempted to slap her across the face. She was drunk enough to mostly miss, her fingernail scratching Lisa's cornea.

"Make fun of me again, you little shit, you'll find yourself living with Phillip and Rosalie," Nancy said, referring to her parents.

"You got my eye!" Lisa cried.

"Oh, boo-hoo. I'm going to sleep." Nancy retreated to her bedroom and came out a few minutes later dressed for bed. She didn't so much as glance Lisa's way as she shuffled to the bathroom and shut the door. When she emerged, Lisa was still crying in the living room. Nancy handed her daughter a cold, wet washcloth and told her to put it on her eye.

"Thanks." Lisa sniffed, putting it carefully against her eye. It felt good, but the morsel of compassion only whetted Lisa's appetite for more. She squinted hungrily at her mother with the other eye.

Nancy tsked and shook her head. "You'll live, kiddo." She kneeled down by the couch and put her hand on her daughter's back. Lisa leaned into it like a desperate kitten and breathed in the familiar scent of metabolized alcohol leaking from her mother's pores. Nancy put her mouth to Lisa's ear and whispered throatily, "You like singing?"

Lisa shrugged, not sure what answer her mother was after. She wanted so badly to get it right. She wanted her mother to keep whispering like that in her ear.

"Well, don't bank on it, baby. You sing like a squashed cat." Nancy patted her daughter on the head and went to her bedroom.

Lisa turned her attention back to the music and suddenly remembered the cassette Ruth had given her. She put it in the tape player and, despite her promise, the first thing that caught her attention was Ruth's voice. It was raspy, to be sure, but that wasn't the main problem. Ruth's range was so limited that she strained hard to reach the high notes. And even the low notes, which Lisa expected Ruth to hit with ease, were below her register, and she struggled with a guttural sound that was hard to control and went flat. Lisa couldn't help but imagine how the plaintive, bluesy melody would sound in a clear, beautiful voice. A voice like her mother's. Or hers.

Lisa knew she didn't sing like a squashed cat. If she did, doing it in front of people wouldn't be so hard. It was the loveliness of her voice that embarrassed her. It felt like showing off, letting people hear how sweet and smooth she could sing, gliding effortlessly from alto to soprano. Unlike

Nancy, who wore her glitter on the outside, Lisa wrapped hers under cozy layers of anonymity. As a child, it had helped keep the peace with her mother. As an adult, it defined her place in the world. Lisa listened to one song after another as she washed off her supplies, swept up, and organized everything into neat piles. The music wasn't half bad, and there were even a few songs she rather liked. One, in particular, she suspected was about Paul Capobianco. But she wasn't going to sing for Ruth or anyone else. The problem was finding a way to say no to her pushy new friend.

The next day, Adam took off from work to accompany Lisa and Simon to the Long Island Center for Speech and Language. They were taking their young son for an evaluation to determine the reason for his speech delay. Adam hadn't wanted to go, insisting the kid was just fine. But Lisa reasoned that it couldn't hurt just to get him *evaluated,* and had been told that this was the best place to go.

Adam put his signal on and merged onto the Long Island Expressway. Simon, in the back seat, fussed a little, and Lisa reached behind to hand him a small container of Cheerios. It seemed to be what he wanted.

"I got a call from that LuAnn person," Lisa said to her husband.

"And?" Adam glanced in his mirrors and changed lanes to pass a slow-moving Volvo.

"My mother wasn't exactly telling the truth. One, LuAnn is not her AA sponsor."

"And two?"

"My mother isn't even staying with her. She's in a homeless shelter. LuAnn is her social worker."

"Oh, jeez." Adam merged back to the right.

"The good news is that she was telling the truth about being on the wagon. She hasn't had a drink for days. But LuAnn said she needs to get into a rehab program."

"And that's where we come in, right?" Adam glanced over at his wife. "Listen, Leelee," he said, "if she's serious about this, I'll foot the bill, no problem."

"It's more complicated than that. She can't go right into rehab. She has to do a partial hospitalization program first, which means she'll need someplace to stay for about three months. And LuAnn doesn't think the shelter is the best place for her."

"Let me guess. She wants to stay at our house."

Lisa sighed. "I can't do it, Adam. I can't live in the same house as her. And I don't want her around the children."

"What are the alternatives?" The road narrowed to two lanes for construction. Adam tsked and merged left again.

"I don't know." Lisa looked out her window as a man in a hardhat picked up some orange cones that had fallen over. "And I think I'm finally at the point where I just don't care."

Adam drove on in silence. When he got off the expressway, Lisa rolled down her window a few inches. They reached the Long Island Center for Speech and Language and Adam pulled into a parking space. He hesitated before getting out of the car.

"You're only kidding yourself, Lisa. There's no way you're turning your back on your mother."

Lisa took a deep breath and exhaled. She made a face. "I think Simon pooped."

Inside the building, Lisa took her small son to the ladies' room to change his diaper. She laid him down on a plastic, fold-down changing table.

"Hey, buddy," she said as she removed his diaper and cleaned his bottom with Wetwipes. "Did you make a poop? Tell Mommy you made a poop. Say 'Mommy, change me, please. I made poop.'"

"Tirtee wan wa-wa pee," Simon said.

Lisa gasped. "Did you say 'Thirsty, want water please'? Is that what you said?"

"Wa-wa pee."

"I'll get you water, sweetheart, one second." Lisa cleaned her hands with a wipe and then frantically dug into the diaper bag. She pulled out a sippy cup that had a small amount of orange juice inside. "Stay there," she said, leaving Simon on the changing table and running over to the sink. She rushed back to him, sat him up, and handed him the cup.

"Here's water, Simon. Is this what you wanted? Water?"

Simon took the cup in his two hands and drank. Lisa started to cry. "They're going to think I'm crazy," she said, "and maybe I am." Simon handed her back the empty cup and she hugged him.

"Did you really say that, sweetheart? Did you really ask for water?" She looked into his eyes, which were crystal blue like Adam's. He smiled at her and she smiled back. She kissed his cheeks, his nose, his chin, and got the same drugged feeling she always got when she consumed her children. It made her grow roots into the ground, like a huge happy oak tree anchored to the earth.

"I love you up, down, and sideways," she said. "Come, let's go play some games with the grown-ups."

When they emerged from the bathroom, she thought about telling Adam what Simon had said. Or what she thought he said. But she stopped herself. The timing seemed too coincidental. Adam would assume she had imagined it. And maybe she had.

Then the three of them were led to the audiology department, where Simon was scheduled for a hearing test. The coordinator had explained to Lisa that even though it seemed unnecessary, they had to rule out hearing problems before psychological or neurological assessments.

His hearing checked out fine, and afterward, Lisa's mouth went dry as they were ushered into the office of the neurologist, Dr. Alexandra Graf, a bone-thin woman smartly dressed in an expensive suit. Under it, she wore a white blouse open to the top of her bra, which Lisa could see when the doctor bent forward. After shaking hands with Lisa and Adam, the doctor introduced a young resident named Peter Hwang.

There was a child-sized table in the room, where Simon sat with Dr. Hwang, playing an imitation game with small blocks. While Dr. Graf observed, taking notes, she peppered Lisa and Adam with questions they had already answered on a ten-page form that had been sent to them before the evaluation. The doctor asked when Simon had reached developmental milestones, like turning over, sitting up, crawling, and walking. Then she wanted to know how he asked for things. Did he point? Use jargon? Lisa knew these were the important questions, the ones that would determine neurological deficits, and she felt herself getting anxious about giving the right answers. Yes, she thought, picturing a finger extended from his chubby fist, he points. He points! Tell me my baby is okay. Tell me to go home and stop being a nervous mother.

After the questioning, Dr. Graf leaned in to the young resident to confer in a soft tone. Lisa could see ridges of bone beneath the thin skin on the woman's chest as she strained to hear their conversation. She heard mostly mumbles that didn't make sense, but after a few seconds she made out a word that Dr. Hwang uttered. It made her go cold. Autism. Lisa felt the blood drain from her body and the room suddenly seemed too bright and far away. She leaned back in the chair and tried to breathe deeply. She rubbed her hands on her legs to make sure she could still feel. Adam reached over and grabbed her cold hand. She looked into her husband's eyes and blinked back tears.

"I heard them say 'autism,'" she whispered.

Adam let this register for a second. "Excuse me," he said to the doctor in a voice that jarred Lisa. "You're not thinking it's autism, are you?"

"We don't see any factors that point to it," Dr. Graf said.

"But it's a difficult diagnosis to make," Dr. Hwang added.

Lisa suddenly hated Dr. Hwang. Loathed him. The stupid creep. The jackass. That's my child, you son of a bitch! Don't go throwing out a line like that to pump yourself up. To make your day more *interesting*.

"Still," Dr. Graf interjected, "his eye contact is good and he seems quite related."

"Does he line things up?" Dr. Hwang asked. "You know, like train cars?"

Lisa looked at Adam and then back at Dr. Hwang. "Aren't children *supposed* to line up train cars?"

"Not the way autistic children do it."

God, Lisa thought. This guy is just dying to make a diagnosis of autism. "Well, he doesn't line things up." There, that did it. They were safe.

Dr. Graf told the anxious parents that Simon had a speech delay, and that he would probably do very well in a language-based preschool. She gave them a list of schools to call, and said that she thought Simon would probably catch up by kindergarten.

Lisa felt emboldened and wanted to hug Dr. Graf. Instead she said, "Just a little while ago, I was changing him in the bathroom, and I think he asked for water. It sounded like he said: Thirsty, want water please." She looked hopefully from Dr. Graf to her husband.

Dr. Hwang chuckled condescendingly and shook his head. "It was probably just jargon."

Lisa looked at Dr. Hwang sitting in the tiny child-sized chair and thought how easy it would be to tip him over with one swift kick.

Dr. Graf smiled. "It's hard to say, but I'm optimistic about his progress." She extended her hand and told Lisa and Adam it was nice to meet them.

Dr. Hwang extended his hand, too, but Lisa ignored him and lifted Simon up from his little chair. It stuck to his bottom, and Lisa had to shake it free. It fell, very nicely, on Dr. Hwang's foot.

In the car on the way home, Lisa and Adam were giddy, relieved to have the experience behind them. They laughed about the chair falling on Dr. Hwang's foot. Simon laughed, too.

Adam glanced at Lisa. "He's going to be fine, you know."

"I know," she said.

Lisa relaxed and closed her eyes. She suddenly felt sleepy.

"Leelee?" Adam said.

"Hmm?"

"How about if we let your mother stay in the empty white ranch house?"

Lisa didn't open her eyes. "Over my dead body."

Chapter Ten

MADDIE

Maddie drove west through the interminable stretch between exits 40 and 39 of the Long Island Expressway. Traffic sometimes got so bad in that spot the truckers called it "Death Valley." Today, it moved pretty close to the speed limit, and Maddie figured she would make it through without too much trouble. A good thing, because she still had the remnants of a headache, despite the three Advils she swallowed before getting in the car.

She knew she shouldn't have had so much to drink when she went out with Beryl last night. Those vodka gimlets got her so plastered she had called Jack and made a date for a tryst. She was on her way there now to tell him she had changed her mind. She wasn't going to cheat on Bruce. Not with him, not with anybody.

Maddie wished she could get as worked up about the whole movie business as the others did. Not that she wasn't invested in making it happen; she loved the idea of seeing Beryl get to meet George Clooney at last, and she even thought it would be great to be one of the town heroes for getting the stadium built. But it was hard to focus on anything without thinking of it in terms of what it would mean for her relationship with Bruce. The vibrations of her troubled marriage created a hum over her life that made distractions all but impossible. Even during those fleeting moments when she forgot about her problems with Bruce—like when she first awoke and the world wasn't yet in focus—there was this murmur reminding her that all wasn't well, that there was something big to worry about. Then, in a second, the disquiet went from vague to distinct. *He doesn't love you anymore,* it seemed to say. Right, she thought, it could happen any time. She pictured him coming home from work, throwing his keys on the hall table, and saying, "We have to talk." Then he'd tell her he was leaving.

Occasionally, Maddie asked herself why she stayed if she felt so miserable and unloved. "Maybe *I'll* leave," she said to herself. "To hell with him—lots of women start over." But it was a phony thought. Maddie loved Bruce fiercely and didn't want to spend her life without him. Besides, she still felt like there was something temporary about the troubles they were having. The solution was out there, if only she could figure it out.

She sometimes wondered if going back to work would help. A lot of women she knew did it to regain some self-respect. Maddie's goal was different, though. She was more interested in bolstering her image in Bruce's eyes. As a working lawyer, she'd go back to being his bright, professional wife, instead of a mindless hausfrau, consumed with the minutiae of motherhood and housework. But Maddie hated to leave the children. Every time she saw a kid in a supermarket with a nanny it broke her heart. What kind of way is that to grow up? she thought. That kid should be with someone who loves him.

At one point, she thought the perfect solution would be to return to work part-time. But when she discussed it with Bruce, they concluded it wasn't worth the trouble. With all the money she would need to spend on clothes, dry-cleaning, and commuting, they wouldn't come out ahead. Bruce had said it would be like running in place.

Now she realized that money wasn't the issue. If it could save their marriage, she would do it anyway. She wondered if there was some way she could ease back into legal work to see if it had any effect on Bruce. Maybe, to start, she could handle the contracts between the school and the movie production company. Of course, the district would want their own counsel involved. Still, there had to be a role she could play.

Maddie pictured herself reviewing a boilerplate contract, making notes as she went along. She would write an insightful rider, terse and flawless, and insist on attaching it. The school's lawyers would be impressed with her skill and offer her a job. Part-time, of course. Bruce would be impressed that they were impressed. Then she'd have it all: kids, career, a husband who loved her.

Maddie reached the next exit and got off the expressway. Then she got back on in the opposite direction, heading home. She dug into her handbag for her cell phone. She would call Jack and tell him she wasn't coming. No reason she had to do it in person. Why flirt with danger?

But her phone was dead. She had meant to recharge the battery last night, but was too drunk to remember. *Damn.*

I'm not turning around, she thought. To hell with him. He's stood me up plenty of times. I'll just go straight home. Eventually, he'll figure out I'm not coming.

But was she being fair to Jack? He really hadn't done anything wrong. And he had taken time off from work to meet her. Maddie pictured him standing in the park with a picnic basket he had prepared for her. If she knew Jack, he had probably brought a bottle of wine and real glasses. Standing him up without even calling just seemed too cruel. Maddie decided the right thing to do was to turn around again and face him. But she was back in Death Valley and had to go miles before the next exit. Maddie sighed, exasperated.

When she finally pulled into a parking space at Clark Gardens, where they had scheduled to meet, Maddie cut the engine and put her head down on the steering wheel. Why am I so nervous? she wondered. Am I worried that he'll seduce me? The thought of kissing Jack made Maddie shudder. She could almost feel his hands on her. I should leave, she thought, still gripping the wheel. A tapping on the glass next to her jolted Maddie. She looked up to see Jack's bright smile.

"Hey," he said through the window. "I didn't think you were going to make it."

Jack helped Maddie with her crutches and led her to a private area away from the picnic tables. He pulled a blanket out of one of the bags he was carrying and spread it out on the grass. Maddie figured this was one of his more popular seduction approaches. A romantic picnic outdoors. Some kissing and groping. Then a quick trip in his Porsche to his condo nearby. Tell him now, she said to herself. Tell him *now.*

"Jack," she began.

"Sit," he said, taking her crutches. He helped her ease herself down onto the blanket.

"Last night, when I called you?"

"You were drunk." He moved one of his canvas bags from the grass onto the blanket.

"I was drunk."

"You didn't know what you were saying."

"Right."

He unzipped the rectangular bag and looked inside. "You want a sandwich?"

Maddie ripped a handful of grass from the ground and sprinkled it back down. "I'm not going to sleep with you, Jack."

"Sure you are."

"No I'm not."

"Not today. But I'll wear you down, eventually." He offered her his most generous smile. Then he opened a sandwich wrapped in white deli paper, put it on a plate, and handed it to her. "You like chicken salad, right?"

She took it. "I love you, Jack, but I'm pretty sure I can resist you."

"See, that's where you're wrong." He pulled a bottle of Pellegrino water out of the bag, uncapped it, and filled two plastic cups. "What should we drink to?"

Maddie took her cup and looked into it. She looked back at Jack. "Health? Long life?"

Jack grunted. "Fuck that. Let's drink to us."

"I'm trying to make my marriage work. I can't drink to *us*."

"To your marriage, then."

"You're trying to get in my pants and you're toasting my *marriage*?"

"That doesn't work for you?"

Maddie smiled and shook her head. "To my marriage," she said.

They tipped cups and drank. "I'm not a home wrecker," Jack said after draining his glass. "I just think it would be good for both of us to act on this passion we've been suppressing so long. It'll probably *help* your marriage."

"Please."

"I mean it, Mel. Life is too short to ignore the things that mean the most to you." He refilled his cup.

"Why does this mean so much to you?"

"Because you have always been one of the hottest women I know."

"Bullshit," she said. "I bet there are ten gorgeous nurses in your hospital right now who would sleep with you in a second."

"Some of them are doctors," he said. "But I'll forgive the sexism."

"I'm thinking it's *because* I'm married, not in *spite* of it. It takes commitment out of the picture."

"Wrong. It's twenty years of longing I can't ignore anymore. It's me waking up from a self-induced coma." He finished the water in his cup and then crushed it. "I should have told you I love you a long time ago."

"You've told me you love me plenty of times."

"Yeah," he said, "but I pretended it didn't mean anything."

"What *does* it mean?"

Jack made a sound of exasperation. "You think *way* too much." He leaned in to Maddie and kissed her on the lips. She meant to resist, but he moved in closer and, as if in a dream, she found herself reclining beneath him without knowing how she got there. He touched her nipple lightly with his thumb and she sighed. He moved his face into her neck.

Maddie put her hands on his shoulders and tried to push him away. "No," she said, nearly crying. "No, no. *Please.*"

He rubbed her thigh. "I want to be inside you," he whispered.

"Get off me."

"You sure?"

"Get *off* me!"

"Okay, okay," he said, picking himself up.

Maddie sat up and felt a distinct wetness in her panties. She put her face in her hands. *"God,"* she said.

"Are you all right?"

She kept her face covered. "My husband makes me feel like shit and you make me feel beautiful and sexy and *loved,* you asshole, and I have a pencil in my cast and my marriage is a wreck and no matter how much I want to sleep with you I don't want to sleep with you. So no, I am *not* okay."

"You have a *pencil* in your cast?"

Maddie uncovered her face, which was wet with tears. "Can you help me?"

"With the pencil?"

"That would be a start."

Maddie watched him peer inside her cast to find the pencil. He's too thin, she thought, and wondered if he had been eating well since Deb left and there was no one to cook for him.

He slid his hand into her cast to try to reach for the pencil. "I'm an orthopedist," he said. "This should *not* be getting me horny."

Maddie smiled. "Shut up. Just get it out."

"I'm thinking." He bit his lower lip and looked around. "Do you have any gum?"

"In my bag."

"Give me a piece."

"What do you want gum for?" she asked as she rummaged for it.

"You'll see."

She handed him a piece of Trident, which he unwrapped and put in his mouth. As he chewed, he asked her for another pencil, which she also found in her handbag. He took the sticky gum from his mouth and molded it over the eraser. "Now watch this," he said. Jack stuck the gummy end of the pencil deep into her cast. "Hold still, I think I got it." Slowly, he extracted his instrument. It emerged with the point of the other pencil trailing behind it.

"You did it!" She laughed.

"A successful pencilectomy," he said, handing her the original culprit. "I think I'll publish a paper." He dug the gummed pencil into the ground like a stake.

"Hey, Jack," she said, taking a bite of her sandwich. "Was there something else you wanted to tell me?"

"I changed my mind."

"Was it important?"

"Don't sweat it. I'll tell you another time." He moved closer to her. "Now what does Dr. Jack get for his services?"

She pulled the gummy-ended pencil from the ground and held it toward him like a weapon. "File a claim."

That night, in a renewed effort to shore up her marriage, Maddie made love with her husband. Soon after they began, his touch became Jack's, and her flesh responded in shivers. She moved his hand to witness her slippery wetness and he reacted with a slow moan. He entered her and whispered, "Oh, Maddie."

"Bruce," she cried as he thrusted. "Bruce! Bruce! Bruce!" Yet when she neared climax in the darkness, she imagined Jack's eyes on her naked body and shuddered in silent spasms.

Over the next few weeks, Maddie felt her resolve tested daily. Each slight from Bruce—late nights home, good-bye kisses missed—rubbed her raw. Yet she acted insistently cheerful toward him, swallowing rebukes and quashing nags. She began tuning in to a radio advice show hosted by a woman whose Christian conservative views on gays and abortion had made her the punch line to many jokes among Maddie's circle of friends. Still, the woman's articulate views on devotion to home and family struck a chord with Maddie, and she listened. Feelings follow actions, the radio woman said. If you want to feel more loving toward someone, act more loving, and it will happen. Maddie wasn't sure she believed that, but thought, at the very least, it would soften Bruce. And if he responded in kind, well, what more could she want?

On Saturday, Maddie awoke at five-thirty and tiptoed downstairs. Ruth Moss had given her the contracts from the movie studio for her review, and Maddie wanted to capture a few solid hours in which to spread out her papers on the dining room table before the rest of the family got up. She pored over the pages, taking notes, and got so engrossed she didn't hear Bruce come down the stairs and walk up behind her. He kissed her softly on the neck.

"Good morning," he said. "What are you up to?"

"I'm working on those contracts between the school district and the production studio."

"Wasn't there a problem with that? Something to do with moving that rock?"

"Ruth is confident we can work that out. I hope she's right."

He yawned. "That's great. Can I make you a cup of coffee?"

He padded to the kitchen and she heard him get busy with the coffeemaker. "Hey, Maddie," he called out, "they paying you for this?"

Maddie felt her blood pressure rise, but took a deep breath. Do not get into a fight with him about money, she told herself. Do *not*.

"Of course not," she said. "It's for the pee-tee-*ay*."

"Oh, yeah. Right."

Maddie exhaled and went back to reviewing the contract. A few minutes later Bruce came in with her coffee. She took a sip and told him it was good, then she asked him to sit with her a minute.

"I'm thinking about going back to work part-time," she said. "I know we talked about it, and it doesn't make much sense financially, but I think I need to do it. You know, keep one foot in the water."

"If that's what you want to do, hon, I think it's great."

"You do?"

"Sure. Did you think I wouldn't be supportive?"

Maddie took off her glasses and put them on the table. "Sometimes I don't know *what* to expect from you, Bruce. You're just—"

"I know."

"I've been trying so hard to get things back on track for us. I wish . . . I don't know. I wish you would try, too. I can't do this alone."

"I *am* trying."

"You are?" she asked.

He laughed. "You didn't notice?"

Maddie smiled and shook her head. "I guess. I don't know."

"Come here," he said, and hugged her. "Oh, Maddie. I want you to be happy. Tell me what I can do."

"See, that's what I'm talking about," she said. "I didn't know. I didn't know you wanted me to be happy. I thought you didn't *care*."

"God," he said, "are you kidding?" He put his hands on her shoulders and looked at her. "Maddie, you are *everything*." He put his hand on her chin and moved her face toward his. "Look at me," he said. "You are everything, the sun, the moon, the stars. Don't you know that?"

"I forget sometimes, if you don't remind me."

"I'll try to be better about reminding you. Okay?"

She sighed. "Okay."

The following week, after the run-in with Suzanne and her band of protesters outside Lisa Slotnick's house, the public relations committee met at Ruth's to discuss their strategy. They were preparing for a vote by the entire PTA on the issue of letting the film company move Applewood Rock in order to build a stadium.

Ruth invited Maddie and Lisa into her living room. While they sipped coffee, she set up an easel behind her and placed an enormous picture of a shirtless George Clooney on it. It was the same smoldering shot Maddie had seen on the cover of *People* magazine, only this one was larger than life, and that much more alluring.

"Tomorrow," Ruth began, "after Podobinski gives her spiel about the history of that stupid rock, I'm going to launch into a speech about the *real* history of Applewood and how we can build a stadium and honor the past at the same time."

"Wait a minute," Maddie interrupted. "What's with the picture of George Clooney?"

Ruth smirked. "You like that?" she asked.

"Like it?" Maddie said. "I want to have its children. I can barely concentrate on what you're saying."

"That's more or less the idea. I mean, I think we make a

pretty strong case for letting them move the rock and use our school for their film. But this"—she spread her fingers over George Clooney's face—"is insurance."

"By the time you get to the pièce de résistance," Maddie agreed, "there's gonna be enough wet panties in the room to mop all of Applewood."

The next morning, as Suzanne Podobinski addressed the standing-room-only crowd of stay-at-home moms in the cafeteria of North Applewood Elementary, the audience shifted restlessly. She read into the mike from notes, educating these women about their town's history. She mentioned settlers whose names they recognized from streets and hamlets throughout the area. She talked about the spot where the deed to the town was signed, listing the Indian chiefs and Quakers in attendance. Suzanne's voice rose to be heard over the din of private conversations that were bubbling up throughout the room. "And I *promise* you this PTA will eventually earn enough money to build the kind of stadium we need . . . without defiling history by moving a nearly sacred stone that has been untouched for over three hundred and fifty years!"

There was a smattering of applause as she stepped down and handed the microphone to Ruth. Maddie and Lisa hurried up to the front of the room and set up an easel with the oversized photograph of George Clooney. The room quieted almost immediately, and then burst into a cacophony of whispers and giggles, as the women responded to the picture with jokes to their friends about the desirability of the exquisite movie star.

Ruth called the group to order and, after several pleas for quiet, got their full attention.

"Thank you, Suzanne," she began, "for the enlightening history lesson. I agree that we must respect and honor our past. And I think it's important to teach our children to do the same. But I am here to tell you that we can preserve this important slice of Applewood history *and* get the stadium our children deserve *and* get to meet George Clooney in the process!"

The members of the public relations committee responded with enthusiastic applause, prompting a portion of the audience to join in. Ruth continued, "There is an important historical fact, however, that Suzanne omitted from her presentation. And that is: *the rock was not there when the settlers signed the deed to Applewood.* It was placed there as a marker nearly seventy years later when the apple tree that grew in that spot succumbed to old age and the elements of nature. It is the place, not the rock, that has historical significance. I am proposing, therefore, that we erect a *new* marker. Something that will commemorate the event with more meaning than a simple rock ever could. Something that will honor our past as well as our future. Something that will celebrate our history *and* meet the needs of Applewood's precious children. Parents and faculty, I give you *Applewood Rock Stadium!*"

With that, Lisa removed the photograph of George Clooney to reveal an artist's rendering of the proposed stadium, complete with a sign, almost as large as the building itself, that said *APPLEWOOD ROCK STADIUM.* As the crowd applauded wildly, Ruth took the poster in her two hands and held it overhead. She walked around the room in that triumphant posture so that everyone could get a closer view of the picture. Maddie glanced over at Beryl, who gave her the thumbs-up. Victory was at hand.

After Ruth finished her march, Mary Molinari, recording secretary for the PTA, took the mike and called the room to order. She announced that the vote would be taken by a show of hands, and recapped the two choices.

"Now," she said, "all in favor of preserving the current status of Applewood Rock and rejecting the proposal to build a stadium in its place, please raise your hand."

Maddie glanced around the room and saw only Suzanne and three of her friends raise their hands. Ruth, she noticed, stood at the back of the room wearing a beatific smile.

The recording secretary counted the raised hands and made a notation on her clipboard. "All in favor of accepting the proposal to move Applewood Rock and build a stadium in its place, please raise your hand."

A few hands went up, but most of the women simply cheered and applauded, causing Mary Molinari to lose her composure. "Please!" she pleaded. "I need a show of hands. For the record! I need a count—I need *hands*!"

But the audience was out of control. Beryl rushed to the front of the room, grabbed the picture of George Clooney, and held it over her head. "Cloo-ney! Cloo-ney! Cloo-ney!" she chanted, and the crowd joined in. Just then, the loud sound of the double doors to the cafeteria opening and slamming shut stilled the mob, who turned in unison to see Paul Capobianco looking frantic. Beryl put the poster down and the crowd quieted.

Maddie broke the silence. "What's the matter?" she said into the mike.

"It's gone," Paul answered, his deep voice penetrating the atmosphere like a meteor. "Someone stole Applewood Rock."

Chapter Eleven

By the time the public relations committee convened several days later to discuss the latest turn of events, the town buzzed with theories about who had stolen Applewood Rock and why. The general consensus was that it had to be Ruth Moss, abetted by her notorious band of outlaws. Who else, wagged the lively tongues of Applewood, had the motive? They figured Ruth had hired someone to steal the rock as insurance. This way, even if she lost the vote, there would be nothing standing in the way of building a stadium on Field One, and welcoming George Clooney into her wily clutches.

And there were other rumors making the rounds. People were saying that when Suzanne and her group showed up at Lisa's house to protest, Ruth had tried to run them down with her SUV.

"If only I had!" Ruth seethed, assuming Suzanne was the source of the accusations. "That bitch is ground zero."

Beryl, amused by the drama, produced a child's glove she insisted was found at the scene of the crime. She printed a picture of it in her newsletter, under the headline IF IT DOESN'T FIT, YOU MUST ACQUIT!

The members of the committee were more circumspect and met to discuss their concerns about the vote being overturned as a result of the mounting ill will.

"We have to do *something*," Maddie said. "These rumors are getting toxic."

Lisa chimed in. "Jill said this is the kind of thing that can scare a production company away. They're not going to want to deal with a hostile community."

Ruth snorted at that, then turned to Maddie. "Have the police made any progress?"

They were all aware that an investigation was under way, the one key piece of evidence being a license plate number belonging to a Ryder truck that had been parked near the school field. A savvy student had taken down the number.

"I'm not sure the recovery of a rock is their top priority," Maddie said.

"Could we hire a private investigator?" Lisa asked.

Maddie sipped her coffee. "It's expensive."

"Screw it," Ruth said to her. "*I'll* fund it. Just tell me what I need to do."

"I made dinner reservations at Spencer's," Bruce said, referring to a trendy new restaurant. "For your birthday."

Maddie was stunned. Bruce never took the initiative to make reservations. Even during their courtship, he had left these types of details to Maddie.

What had changed significantly over the years was the gift-giving. He no longer spent weeks digging for clues on what would bring a smile to her face. He simply asked what she wanted or told her to go shopping and pick something out for herself.

Last year, she had hoped things would be different. She was in a desperate state of neediness and felt headed for a crash. So rather than leave things to chance, she scattered catalogs around the house with items of jewelry circled in red. Maddie was even careful not to go overboard and select anything too expensive. It wasn't, after all, about money, but where she ranked in his life. Would he take the time to show her he cared? She circled simple gold pieces and ignored the items that sparkled with diamonds. Occasionally, just for the heck of it, she drew an arrow next to something unusual with a semiprecious stone, and imagined how they'd laugh when she opened the box and feigned surprise.

On the day of her birthday, a bouquet of roses from Bruce arrived at the door. She called him at work to tell him they were lovely. Silently, she hoped there was something more to follow. Dialing for flowers was easy. He could have even had his receptionist do it. Maddie pictured stupid Franny placing the call: "I'd like to order a bouquet of long-stemmed roses. You know, with petals and everything."

That night, when they went out for dinner, she kept hoping he would reach into his breast pocket and extract a tiny box. But it never happened. And when they went to bed that night, she wept, the disappointment washing over her in suffocating waves.

"*What* is wrong?" he asked. Not a hint of tenderness.

"You didn't get me anything for my birthday," she blurted into the darkness.

"What are you talking about? I sent you flowers. I took you out to dinner. I paid for a babysitter."

"Fuck you. Leave me alone."

"You're turning into a real princess, you know that?"

She cried off and on for days, hoping Bruce would try to make it up to her by coming home one day with a present. But he didn't, and in fact barely spoke to her all week. Eventually, life distracted her enough to lift Maddie from the depths of her funk, but her disappointment in Bruce lingered.

So his announcement that this year he had made dinner reservations—at one of the hottest restaurants around—surprised and delighted Maddie. He had to have made the plans weeks ago. Be happy with that, Maddie coached herself. He's trying, he's thinking of you. It's enough.

In the spirit of the occasion, Maddie went out that day to get her hair done and have a professional manicure. She put on her long, silky cranberry dress, which she knew was sexy and thought maybe, just maybe, didn't look too ridiculous with a cast.

As Maddie gave the babysitter instructions on bedtimes, the phone rang and Bruce answered. Maddie half listened to his conversation as the babysitter asked questions. She caught enough of the discussion for her heart to sink.

"You're not going to believe it," Bruce said when he got off the phone.

Maddie looked at him. "Don't tell me."

"I'm sorry, honey. I have to go in. It shouldn't take long."

"But the reservations."

"Why don't you go on ahead and I'll meet you there. So we don't lose the table."

Maddie grabbed the car keys. "You have half an hour," she said, and stormed out the door.

As Maddie nursed her second drink, she saw a man at the bar notice her. She looked toward the door, hoping to make it clear she was waiting for someone. Aware of her own appeal, Maddie let her mind drift to Jack. She imagined him finding her crazy sexy in her slinky dress, and wanting to press himself against her. He would pull her close and caress the naked skin of her back. He'd slip the strap of her dress down over her shoulder and whisper that they should go someplace private.

Maddie picked up her cell phone and rubbed the buttons thoughtfully with her thumb. I could do that, she thought. I could call Jack. Then I could call Bruce and tell him not to come, I've made other plans. Or better yet, let him come. Let him walk in and see me with Jack. Open his eyes a little.

Yeah, *right,* she chided herself, putting the phone down. Like I would ever have the nerve to do that.

Maddie saw the man at the bar glance at her again and look away quickly. Just then, she felt a hand on her shoulder. She looked up to see Bruce standing behind her. "I'm so sorry, baby," he said, kissing her. "Can you forgive me?"

"I don't know," she said, tears welling. "It's getting harder and harder."

"Maybe this will help." He put a small, velvet-covered square in front of her and sat down. Maddie stared at it dumbly. Then it registered: this is a jewelry box. She touched it lightly and, in spite of herself, noticed how feminine her manicure looked against it. "Go on," he said, "open it."

Maddie looked at Bruce and saw an eagerness in his face that touched her heart. It was the Bruce who loved her. She looked back down at the little box and suppressed an urge to rub her cheek against the lovely, soft fabric. She wanted the moment to linger, and considered asking Bruce if he would mind if she opened it after dinner. But curios-

ity got the better of her. Was it a pair of gold hoop ear-
rings? About a month ago she lost one of hers. Perhaps
he'd bought her a replacement pair. Then she thought of
the delicate pieces she had circled in last year's catalogs.
Was it one of those?

Slowly, she lifted the hinged cover until it sprang open.
Maddie looked inside and gasped. She had never seen anything quite like it. Hanging from a simple gold chain was a
dazzling pendant. A heart, studded with diamonds. Dozens
of diamonds. Brilliant diamonds. Diamonds that captured
the restaurant's pin dot lights and reflected them back in
luminous prisms of color.

Maddie put her fingertips between the heart and the
satin beneath it. She tipped the pendant from side to side,
mesmerized by the sparkling play of colors. Bruce, she
thought, bought me this beautiful thing. Bruce, who worried constantly about money. He put all that aside. For me.

"Bruce, I . . . oh, my God."

"Do you like it?"

"Can we *afford* this?"

"Maddie," he chided.

"I know, I'm an idiot. Sorry. *Thank* you. It's the most
beautiful thing I've ever seen." Bruce smiled. Maddie rose
from her chair and leaned in to kiss him. "Put it on me?"

The next morning, Maddie put the necklace back on after her shower. She touched it frequently as she woke the
children, cooked them breakfast, made their lunches, and
sent them off to school. She touched it after she made the
beds and before she threw in a load of laundry. She fin-
gered it while she made her morning phone calls to schedule playdates, arrange carpooling, and check in with Jerry,
the private investigator she had retained for the committee.

She cleaned the toilets upstairs and touched the heart

after she snapped off her rubber gloves. Her hand rested on it as she turned on the computer and waited for it to boot. She rarely went online, and didn't even have her own e-mail address. But Russell's soccer coach had e-mailed the schedule and she needed the information. She logged in under Bruce's screen name and clicked on the mail button.

A list of new e-mail messages appeared on the screen, including the one she was looking for from the coach. But another subject line caught her eye. It said "Just between us?" and was from Jenna442. Bruce's cousin.

Maddie sat back in her chair and tried to decide whether or not to open the e-mail. I shouldn't, she thought. It's none of my business and Bruce would be furious. But that subject line. What does it *mean*? And why should these two be sharing secrets? Maddie leaned forward, clicked on it, and read:

b-

yes, i am very very sure i am doing the right thing. if you love me (and i know you do!) you'll be happy for me that I finally met someone I want to spend my life with.

i know you think you should tell Maddie everything, and if that's your decision, fine. but could you do me a favor and wait until after lenore's wedding? i'm not sure how she'll react, and i'd just as soon avoid a scene. for now, anyway.

meanwhile, please don't get all weird on me about this, okay? you are and always will be one of my favorite people in the whole wide world, and i still need your friendship. love, j

Maddie clicked the print button and read the message four more times, her heart pounding. Did it mean what she thought it meant? She searched the words for clues that proved her right. Or wrong. Could this possibly be anything *other* than a post-breakup letter? Why else would he get "all weird" over the news of Jenna's new love? And then there was the bit about keeping it from her. No, it could only mean one thing. Right? She needed to think about this. Show it to someone, maybe. "It's obvious," she could almost hear Beryl saying, "they had an affair and she broke up with him because she found someone else. Now that it's over, he wants to tell you. Clear his conscience. Make a fresh start."

No, no, no! Maddie thought. To hell with trying to put a positive spin on this! Even the necklace, she reasoned, was connected to his deceit. Of course! Why else would Bruce do something so uncharacteristically generous? He's laying the groundwork for his confession. He'll probably even lie and say *he* broke it off with *her.*

And the wedding. Now it made sense. They were still involved when the invitation arrived. That's why he wanted to go as soon as he found out Jenna would be there. No wonder he was less than enthusiastic about Maddie coming with him!

Jenna. Fat-assed Jenna. Aren't-I-such-an-individual Jenna, with her twinkly eyes and hippie clothes. Maddie always knew he was enamored of her, but thought it was just a crush, not a full-blown affair. How silly it seemed now, to be jealous of an innocent, puppy-dog sort of attachment. Betrayal is a whole different animal, with claws and fangs. A stalking beast, ready to devour her family, her life.

I'm hyperventilating, Maddie thought. Breathe, she told

herself, breathe. But she couldn't control it and struggled for air. She remembered that you were supposed to breathe into a paper bag when this happened. There wasn't one nearby, so she cupped her hands together and covered her nose and mouth. It worked. Her breathing slowed and the crisis passed. But she felt as if her brain circuitry were temporarily jammed. The synapses weren't making connections. She couldn't think.

Maddie shut off the computer and went into her bedroom, where she took off the necklace and dropped it into her jewelry box. Then she folded the printed e-mail and stuffed it into the pocket of her jeans.

Maddie decided to go on about her day as if nothing had happened. She'd think about this later, when the fog lifted.

She involved herself in housework, trying to remember exactly what it was she was supposed to do. She folded the laundry, rehung a picture that had fallen off the wall in Hannah's room, and cleaned out the refrigerator. While wiping down a sticky jar of jam she accidentally dropped it on the floor, shattering the glass and creating a gooey blackish puddle filled with dangerously sharp splinters. She stared blankly. "How does one go about cleaning a mess of this sort?" she asked herself, in those actual words, as if hyperarticulating her confusion would restore some order to her thinking. Finally, she grabbed yards of paper towels to protect her fingers from the shards of glass, and managed to get it cleaned up.

Maddie then moved on to Russell's closet. He had dropped sand-filled sneakers in there yesterday and everything on the floor had to be cleaned before she could vacuum. She pulled out the offending shoes and was banging them over the garbage to knock out the excess sand when she heard the doorbell ring.

As she hurried down the stairs, being careful not to put too much weight on her cast, Maddie reflexively touched the spot on her neck where the heart had been. Just as reflexively, an alarm went off. Gone? Oh, right, she thought, her brief second of panic giving way to the full, terrible memory of why she took it off.

Maddie inhaled deeply and flung the door open. The face she saw was out of context, and took a second to register.

"Jack?" she said, surprised.

"Good morning."

"What are you doing here?"

He held up a wrapped package and smiled. "Your present. Can I come in?"

"Present?"

"As in birthday?"

"Oh, yeah," she said, and pointed to her head. "Scrambled eggs." She motioned him in and meant to lead him to the kitchen table. But Jack plopped down on the living room sofa, putting the gift on the cocktail table in front of him.

"Can I get you something?" she asked. "A cup of coffee?"

"No, thanks, I'm fine."

"Did you have breakfast? Lunch? What time is it?"

"Maddie, I'm fine. Come sit down and open this."

She made an effort to focus. "You look thin," she said as she sat down. "I've been meaning to tell you. Are you so busy you're forgetting to eat?"

"I lost a little weight, but I'll put it back. Here." He handed her the present.

"You didn't have to do this," she said, and he flashed her his beautiful smile. She touched the hollow of her neck again and took a deep breath. "Okay," she said, "let's see what this is."

Through the paper, Maddie could tell it was a book, but couldn't venture a guess as to which one. She tore off the wrapping and stared, speechless, at the title stamped into the antique hardcover. It was *Mio, My Son,* by Astrid Lindgren, a book she had loved desperately as a child. It was a sweet, magical fairy tale, and she remembered the story as if she had read it yesterday. But she hadn't seen it for years. It was out of print, and all her efforts to locate it had failed. How had he found it? And how did he know she wanted it?

Maddie opened her mouth to speak, but couldn't find a single word. She made a few sounds like a motor that couldn't turn over and Jack laughed.

"You like it?" he asked.

"I . . . uh." She turned the book over as if surprised it had three dimensions. "I can't believe this."

"Are you *crying*?"

She sniffled. "This is the nicest thing anyone's ever done for me. How did you know? How did you *find* it? I don't even remember talking to you about this."

"It was back in college. We were in my room, studying. I think I was helping you with statistics."

"I can't believe you remember all this."

Jack put his head down and laughed as if recalling a private joke. "It's not something I could forget," he said, his tone changing to serious. "You were so . . . passionate. And there I was, with this amazing girl in my room. This brilliant, beautiful girl who smelled like, I don't know, gardenias. And then you started talking about this book you read as a kid, and your *eyes.* You looked at me and told me the whole story from start to finish. For a minute, I got as excited about it as you were, like we were both eight-year-olds experiencing this fairy tale for the first time. I wanted you so badly just then. And I don't mean just to fuck you, though I did want to fuck you. But I wanted to lock the door and seal us in there forever, laughing and fucking and studying statistics. It scared the shit out of me, no joke. So I told you I had to get up early for chem and asked you to leave."

Maddie looked down, as if speaking to the book. "I remember. Not the part about telling you the story, but when you asked me to leave. I was confused. First I thought you liked me. And I was interested, *really* interested. Then you asked me to leave and I thought, does he really have to get up early? The next day I saw you with that girl. What was her name? As dimwitted as a bar of soap. I thought, I'm not his type. Forget about him. Go have a crush on somebody else. And I did."

"Abby Milkowski."

"Huh?"

"Her name. Abby Milkowski. A nursing major. I called her right after you left. She came over and I banged her all night, trying to put you out of my mind."

Maddie shook her head. "I bet she married a doctor."

"Steve Finkelstein, an anesthesiologist."

"Oh, don't tell me," she said, laughing.

"Works at my hospital. The husband, I mean. Calls me 'Jacko.' Thinks I'm a stitch. Keeps inviting me over for a barbecue."

"I'm guessing he doesn't know you boffed his wife, *Jacko.*"

He smiled. She smiled back and he kissed her gently on the mouth.

"I had no clue," she said, looking directly at his eyes. "In college. Thought I was just your funny pal. You know, one of the guys. You even told me about the girls, sometimes."

"In graphic detail, right? Yikes, what an ugly thing to do. That's what fear looks like, I guess." He put his arm around her and she relaxed against him. "Remember when we first met?" he said. "At that bus stop? I thought, 'God, what a great girl,' and I couldn't wait to see you again, to get close to you. I thought a lot about, well . . . about being inside you. What you would feel like, what your face would look like just then. I wanted to make you fall in love with me. Of course, it was my fantasy, so I was studly enough to pull this off with my superhuman lovemaking abilities." He smiled at this and laughed a little, but Maddie stayed serious. He pulled his arm from behind her and took her hand. "But then, that time in my room, I got so scared, because it was me that was falling in love."

"And now?"

"It's all the same feelings, Maddie. Except the fear is gone."

"Completely?"

"There's maybe this much left," he said, showing her a tiny space between his thumb and index finger. "But I can't let fear rule my life anymore." He kissed her. "Are *you* scared?"

"I'm so short-circuited right now I'm not feeling anything. Kiss me again."

He did, and she released herself into it completely. "Feel anything now?" he asked.

"Again," she demanded, and he complied, searching her mouth with his tongue over and over. When he finally surfaced for air, her face was wet with tears.

"Are you okay?" he asked. She nodded, and he softly licked the tears from her face. Then he held her for several minutes, still and silent.

"I want to do this," she finally said.

"Are you sure?"

"I'm sure."

Jack pulled her shirt off and unhooked her bra. She wriggled out of it and he grabbed both her breasts at once. "Oh, Maddie." He sighed. "Maddie!" He kissed her neck, worked his way down her chest. He sucked on one nipple and then the other as she moaned.

He sat up and unbuttoned his shirt. She reached for his belt and unbuckled it. Jack stood and stepped out of his pants, while Maddie pulled hers over her cast and slid them to the foot of the couch. As he got on top of her the phone rang.

"Shit," he said.

"Don't worry," she assured him, "I'm not answering it." But they slowed to listen as her outgoing message finished and the caller's voice came on:

"Hello, Maddie? It's Mother. Your father's had a heart attack."

Chapter Twelve

In her haste, Maddie left her crutches at home, forgetting how long a walk it was from the parking lot to the main building, and then through the hospital's endless corridors. By the time she pushed through the double doors to the intensive care unit and saw her mother standing in the hallway, she felt weary and uncomfortable, her ankle aching from the walk.

"Mom," Maddie said, limping toward her mother. "How is he?"

Her mother hugged her. "Stable," she answered, wiping her nose with a well-worn tissue. "We'll know more to-morrow. Where are your crutches?"

"Home. Can I see him?"

"He's sedated, but come. I'll show you his room."

Her mother led her down the hall, filling Maddie in on all the details of the event, from his collapse at the high school where he taught, to the terrifying scene in the ER where they had to revive him twice.

"He wasn't feeling well before he left." Her mother sniffed. "I never should have let him go in today."

Maddie rubbed her mother's back, and looked through the large window into the room where her father lay like a lump of human tissue, his mouth open around a tube pumping oxygen into his lungs. A nurse was at the foot of his bed, glancing at the monitors and writing on a chart. She looked efficient, competent, but Maddie wondered if she realized there was a whole person in that bed. Look at him, she willed the busy woman. Just once, glance his way. Touch his hand. Something. But the nurse finished taking her readings and hung his chart on the foot of the bed.

Maddie stopped her as she left the room. "He's a teacher," she said. "Did you know he's a teacher?"

"Are you the daughter?"

Maddie nodded. "They wanted him to be principal but he turned it down."

"We're doing everything we can for him," the nurse assured her.

"When he likes a product? He writes the president of the company a letter. Like they care how he grades the flavor-tight packaging on their cream cheese, you know?"

The nurse nodded. "Can I get you anything?"

Maddie shook her head and the nurse left. Her mother went to get a cup of coffee and Maddie went into the room alone. She stood next to her father's bed watching his chest rise and fall. Alive, she thought. She looked around at the putty-colored walls and felt that his mortality was outside him somehow, yet here, in this room, watching her. She took a seat beside his bed.

"Daddy," she said, lightly touching his arm just above the milky tape holding the IV needle in place. He made a muffled noise. "You don't have to wake up. I just want you to know I'm here."

Maddie put her hands in her lap and looked around the room, breathing in the scent of disinfectant and something else, something familiar. Sterile packaging? That was it. Like the wrapper from a Band-Aid.

"You have interesting timing, Dad, I'll give you that." She paused and sighed. "But maybe that was the point. Maybe you were watching over me, making me stop before I did anything stupid." She sniffed and ran her finger under her nose. "You know, you could've just called."

Maddie glanced over at the EKG machine noisily recording the rhythm of his heart. Pages of zigzag lines were spilling out of it, self-folding into a tray on the floor. Maddie cocked her head sideways to look at it, as if she could discern something from the pattern. It looked pretty normal, as far as she could tell. She leaned into him and whispered, "You're gonna be okay, Dad. You have to be, Mom needs you." She took a breath and exhaled hard. "I need you, too. Things aren't going so well for me right now." Maddie grabbed a tissue from the box near his bed and wiped her nose. "I could use a little unconditional love right now. Although . . ." Maddie stopped and looked at him. She noticed saliva dripping out of her father's mouth and down the side of his face. She pulled a fresh tissue from the box and wiped him off. "I'm probably in the wrong room for that. Huh, Dad? You always made me work for it."

Maddie studied the constellation of age spots on her father's hand. "Remember that time you punished me for not knowing Bolivia is in South America?" She balled up the tissue and threw it in the wastebasket. "I was *seven*.

Seven! I was so mad at you I purposely failed my spelling test the next day. Can you imagine that? It was the worst thing I could think of doing to you. No wonder I'm such a mess. Even now, I feel like I'm not good enough. Like if I could just be a little smarter. If I could be a little smarter . . ." Maddie grabbed another tissue and blew her nose. "You would really love me." The hurt rushed toward her like a wave she couldn't outswim. "This is not how it's supposed to be! Love is not a final exam. You're just supposed to *love* me." Maddie cried out and surrendered to the pain, letting it pull her under. She put her head down and wept, great heaves of sadness washing over her. Someone walked into the room and put a hand on her shoulder.

"You okay?" Bruce's voice.

Maddie shook his hand off her. "No!" she wailed. "I'm not okay."

"Maddie, honey. Try to calm down. His chances get better every hour. I just spoke to the doctor."

"Leave me *alone*."

Bruce crouched beside her to get close to her face. "What is it, honey? Is something else wrong?" She didn't respond. He touched her arm. "Talk to me, Maddie. I love you."

"*Do* you?" she spat.

"Of course. Of course, I love you."

Maddie's mother and brother entered the room and Bruce stood to greet them.

"Everything okay?" the older woman asked.

"Yes," Bruce answered.

"No," Maddie countered.

"She's just upset," Bruce explained. "A little hysterical, actually."

Maddie stood. "Why *shouldn't* I be hysterical? My father's had a heart attack and my husband . . . my husband . . ." She trailed off into sobs.

"I love you, Maddie." He tried to hug her.

"I don't believe you."

Bruce turned to the mother and brother. "She doesn't know what she's saying." He turned back to his wife. "Maddie, what's going on? Don't you remember last night? The restaurant? The necklace? Honey, you *know* I love you."

"Fuck you and fuck the necklace!"

"Maddie!" her mother gasped.

"Whoa," the brother said, "she's *lost* it."

Maddie grabbed her purse and limped out of the room, yanking her elbow away from Bruce as he tried to grab her. He followed her into the hallway.

"I'd like to know exactly *what* is going on," he demanded.

Maddie waved him away and kept walking.

She got in her car and drove off, not conscious of where she was going or who she needed, but eventually found herself standing before Beryl's house with her finger on the doorbell.

"Who is it?" Beryl shouted through the thick door.

"It's Maddie. Open up."

"Maddie?"

"Open the door!"

Beryl opened it a few inches, blocking Maddie's entrance with her body. "What's shakin'?" she asked.

Maddie tried to see past her. "Are you hiding something? Why aren't you letting me in?"

"I'm kind of busy. Do you need something?"

"Don't be an ass. Let me in."

Beryl sighed and backed away. Maddie stepped into the

living room and saw Ruth and Lisa sitting on the sofa. Lisa looked down, embarrassed, but Ruth wore a huge grin. "Hey, Maddie," she said. "What's going on?"

Maddie narrowed her eyes. "I should be asking *you* that," she hissed. "Looks like you're having some kind of PTA meeting. Did someone forget to tell me?" She put her hands on her hips for emphasis.

Ruth looked at Beryl. "Let's just do this now."

"Where is he?" Beryl asked.

"We sent him to the kitchen."

"What are you guys talking about?" Maddie asked.

"We have a little birthday present for you," Beryl explained, smiling. "We were sitting here planning it—auditioning someone, actually—when you so rudely interrupted. We were going to surprise you with this tomorrow, but we may as well do it now."

Maddie shook her head. "This is not a good time for me. I'm a walking train wreck."

"Maybe we *should* do it another time," Lisa said. "If this isn't good for her."

"It's fine," Beryl said, and then turned to Maddie. "Sit," she commanded, pushing her friend into a large easy chair. "This'll cheer you up."

Maddie fell back into the seat and sighed, too distraught to put up a fight. She saw Ruth march out of the kitchen with a young man behind her. Okay, she thought. Let's just get this over with.

"Hit it," Beryl said.

The young man parked himself in front of Maddie with his legs planted apart and his pelvis thrust forward. "I'm Alec," he said.

He put the stereo down on the coffee table and pressed a

button. The Bonnie Tyler song, "Holding Out for a
Hero," burst through the speakers.

Maddie looked from Alec's crotch to his face, and
thought his cheekbones and dark lashes didn't quite com-
pensate for his crooked nose and uneven eyes, leaving him
a little shy of handsome. He locked his fingers behind his
head and started to dance, swaying his hips from side to side
at Maddie's eye level. She glanced over at Beryl and rolled
her eyes. "I'm going to *kill* you," she mouthed. Alec shimmied and gyrated, then turned around and bent over at the
waist to shake his posterior in Maddie's direction. He
stood and turned to face her again, unbuttoning his shirt.
Then he leaned back and moved his midsection side to side
to demonstrate the washboard ripples of his abdomen.

"Take it off!" Ruth yelled. "Woo-hoo!"

The young man took off his shirt and threw it Ruth's
way. She twirled it over her head and shouted, "The pants!
We want the pants!"

Alec moved closer to Maddie and thrust his pelvis
toward her. He licked his thumb and ran it down the middle of his body until it reached the top of his pants. He
pointed to his belt buckle, indicating that she should open
it, but Maddie shook her head.

Beryl put her hand to the side of her mouth and called,
"Party pooper!"

"Come to Mama, baby," Ruth said. "I can help you get
those off."

The young man moved toward Ruth and she pulled
open his belt buckle. "Anything else you need help with,"
she said, "you let me know."

Alec took his pants off to reveal a skimpy, leopard-print
G-string beneath. He shook his package at Maddie and

then grabbed her hands in an effort to get her to her feet to dance with him. "I'm a little incapacitated," she shouted over the music, pointing to her cast. "But I think big mama over there would love to."

Alec turned to face Ruth, who got to her feet and shimmied at the young man. He went around behind her and rubbed himself against her body. Ruth threw her head back and laughed. Maddie couldn't get into the spirit of the fun. An image of Jenna and Bruce forced itself before her, and her eyes started to sting. She dabbed at them surreptitiously, but noticed Lisa staring straight at her. Then Lisa looked at her so pityingly that a lump rose in Maddie's throat and she had to blink away tears.

Lisa stood and walked to the stereo. She pushed a button and the music stopped. Ruth, Beryl, and Alec turned to her, surprised.

"I think Maddie's had enough," she announced.

The group turned to look at Maddie, who buried her face in her hands and wept.

After Beryl paid the young man and sent him on his way, she approached Maddie, who had moved to the sofa between Lisa and Ruth. "Maddie, honey, what's the matter?" she asked, crouching in front of her friend.

Maddie looked down and sniffed. "My father had a heart attack."

"Oh, Maddie." Beryl hugged her. "Is he going to be all right?"

"I think. I don't know."

"Poor baby. Sorry I subjected you to that." Beryl pointed to the door the young man just departed through. "Can I get you anything?"

Maddie sighed and shook her head. "There's something else."

Beryl looked at Ruth, who shrugged.

"What is it, sweetie?" Ruth asked. "What else?"

Maddie reached into the pocket of her jeans and extracted the folded page she had put in there earlier. She handed it to Beryl. "I found it on the computer this morning. It's an e-mail to Bruce from his cousin Jenna. Read it out loud."

Beryl read: " 'B, Yes, I am very very sure I am doing the right thing. If you love me, and I know you do,' exclamation . . ."—Beryl looked up, as if to confirm that they understood it didn't actually say "exclamation," and then continued—"you'll be happy for me that I finally met someone I want to spend my life with. I know you think you should tell Maddie everything, and if that's your decision, fine. But could you do me a favor and wait until after Lenore's wedding? I'm not sure how she'll react, and I'd just as soon avoid a scene. For now, anyway. Meanwhile, please don't get all weird on me about this, okay? You are and always will be one of my favorite people in the whole wide world, and I still need your friendship. Love, J.' " Beryl folded the page and looked from Maddie to Ruth to Lisa. "What does it mean?" she said, handing it back to Maddie.

"What do *you* think it means?" Maddie stuffed it back into her pocket.

"Look," Ruth said, "it doesn't *necessarily* mean he was having an affair with this woman. Maybe she's in love with someone he doesn't approve of."

"Does he know you have it?" Beryl asked.

"No."

"You should ask him," Lisa said. "Ask him what it means."

"I'm not going to do that," Maddie said. "Not right now."

"Why?" Ruth asked. "There could be an innocent explanation. And if not, well, you need to deal with that."

"First of all," Maddie said, "if there *is* an innocent explanation, can you imagine how pissed he'll be that I read this? I think it's best not to tip my hand, especially since he's planning on telling me anyway. I'll wait until after the wedding. Give him a chance to come clean on his own. Besides . . ." She paused and looked up at Beryl. Then she looked down at her hands and got busy with a cuticle.

"What?" Ruth asked impatiently. *"What?"*

"I need time to decide what I'm going to do. I mean, say he *did* cheat on me, do I forgive him? Maybe I want out of the marriage, anyway. Even if he didn't."

"Are you *serious*?" Beryl asked.

Maddie started to cry. "I don't know. I just don't know."

"Wait," Beryl said, "does this have anything to do with . . ." She glanced pointedly at Maddie's cast.

"Jack." Maddie sniffed. "He came over right after I found the e-mail and brought me the sweetest present and, well, we wound up naked on the couch."

"Jeez," Beryl said.

Lisa emitted a small gasp.

"But nothing happened," Maddie said. "The phone rang before we did anything."

"Saved by the bell," Beryl said.

"You think it would have been a mistake?"

"Christ, Maddie. You've got to be kidding me."

Maddie put her head on Beryl's shoulder and started to cry. "The thing is," she said, "I think I'm in love with him."

Beryl sighed. "You *are* an idiot," she said, hugging her friend.

"But you love me anyway."

"I do," Beryl said.

"We all do," Ruth added.

• • •

Maddie could think of no other recourse than to put everything out of her mind until after the wedding. For now, there simply was no e-mail, no husband-who-maybe-cheated. And no Jack-who-she-almost-slept-with.

She put the necklace back on and apologized to Bruce for the way she had behaved at the hospital, saying she was so upset about her father she went a little crazy. "A little?" Bruce laughed, and gave her a hug. All was forgiven.

That night, when the children were in bed and Maddie was finishing the last of the dishes, the phone rang and Bruce answered it. Whoever it was must have asked about her father, because she heard Bruce explain what they knew: that the breathing tube had been removed and that he was alert and feeling fine. If all went well, he would probably be moved out of the ICU later tomorrow. Maddie was dumping the slop-filled drain basket into the garbage when Bruce held out the phone.

"It's Jack," he said. "He heard about your father."

Maddie casually finished what she was doing and dried her hands before taking the phone.

"Hello?" she said.

"Hey, baby. You miss me?"

"Hi, Jack."

"I've been thinking about you all day," he said.

"Uh-huh."

"I'm incorrigible, right?"

"You bet." Maddie looked over at Bruce, who was going through the day's mail.

"And I didn't even *start* talking dirty yet."

"Don't."

He laughed. "This is way too much fun. I'm picturing you standing there all red in the face with Bruce right next to you. Of course, I'm envisioning you completely naked—"

"So Bruce filled you in on my dad?" she interrupted.

"Okay, I'll stop. Yeah, he filled me in. I think he'll be fine, Maddie, I really do."

"Me, too."

"When can I see you again?" he asked.

"When I get my cast off."

"You're not serious."

"I am."

There was a pause. "Do we need to talk?" he asked.

"I guess so."

"Can I come by tomorrow? I have some time in the morning."

"No, don't. I'll call you, okay?"

The next day, Maddie got the kids off to school, straightened the house, and sat down to make her morning phone calls, putting Jack's name on the bottom of the list. The first person she called was Jerry Murphy, a private investigator her old law firm had used several times. Maddie had hired him to work on the case of the missing rock, and needed to check in on his progress. She got his machine and left a perky message for him to call her back. The last time they spoke, he had mentioned that no one treats private investigators "like people," and she wanted to be sure she didn't hurt his feelings. She also remembered that one of the associates at her old firm used to refer to him as "Jerry Murphy, the hypersensitive private investigator guy," like he was a character from a *Saturday Night Live* sketch.

After finishing all her other calls, Maddie finally dialed Jack's number. She wanted to talk to him, but a part of her dreaded the call and hoped his machine would pick up. He answered on the first ring.

Maddie quickly explained that she couldn't see him for a while, that she needed some time to think. He asked if this had anything to do with her father's heart attack.

"No. I don't know. Maybe. I'm all fucked up, Jack. I need a little space. A little time."

"I want you so bad, Maddie."

She sighed. "I want you, too."

"How much time?"

Maddie picked up the wooden napkin holder from the kitchen table and scraped off some dried food with her thumbnail. "You need specifics?"

"Days? Months? I mean, you never know when someone's going to jump the divider."

Maddie got his reference. A college friend of theirs had died on her way home from work one day when a driver traveling in the opposite direction had a heart attack at the wheel. The other car jumped the divider and crashed head-on with hers, killing her instantly. The police said she didn't even hit the brakes, which meant she never saw it coming. Dead. Just like that.

"Weeks," she said. "I promise. No more than a few weeks."

"I love you, Mel."

She swallowed hard. "I love you, too."

Seconds after she hung up the phone it rang again. She thought he was calling back with more to say, but it was Jerry, the private investigator. She wanted to cut to the chase and ask him if he had made any progress on the case, but thought better of it.

"So how *are* you?" she asked.

"Better," he said. "Thanks for asking. It wasn't as bad as I thought."

Better? What on earth was he talking about? Did he mention some malady in their last conversation she had forgotten about? "Well, I'm glad to hear that, Jerry. I, uh . . . know how those things can be."

"Did you ever have it?"

Oh, shit. Maddie thought. *Now* what do I say? "Excuse me?"

"Root canal. Did you ever have it?"

Phew. "Oh, no. But you know, I've heard it can be bad. Glad you're feeling okay." Maddie took a deep breath. "So, anything cooking with the case?"

"Yes," he said slowly, dragging the word out. She could hear the smile in his voice. "The Ryder truck? I'm working on finding out who rented it."

"Good work, Sherlock!"

There was a pause. Jerry made a sound like he was sucking air through his teeth. Uh-oh. Had she said something wrong?

"I appreciate the compliment, Maddie. I really do. But I would prefer if you didn't call me 'Sherlock.' People are always calling private investigators 'Sherlock.' Like we're not real people or something."

"Sorry, Jerry."

"That's okay. Normally I wouldn't even say anything. But you're such a nice person and all."

Maddie tried to follow the logic of that and failed. "Well, thanks," she said. "That's kind of you to say."

"Some of my clients aren't pleasant at all. I have this one, a stockbroker who thinks his wife is cheating on him. I'm not going to mention any names, of course. But this guy.

Sheesh! Calls me up and barks questions into the phone and then hangs up without even saying good-bye. Like I'm not a person or something. Like I have no *feelings*."

"Do you have a lot of clients like that? I don't mean nasty, I mean who think their spouse may be cheating on them?"

"Bulk of my business."

"Hmm. That's interesting."

"How so?"

"Well, I was just wondering. Let's say someone thinks their spouse isn't *currently* cheating on them, but may have cheated on them in the past. Would you have any way of verifying that?"

"It depends. If the affair was a long time ago and the spouse was very careful, it can be hard to find evidence. But usually, if there was an affair, I can find *something*."

"I see."

"Maddie? Is there something of a personal nature you'd like to discuss with me?"

Maddie's busy day kept her from dwelling on her concerns about Bruce. It was Jack who kept popping into her mind. Whether she was driving to the hospital to see her father or filling in for an hour at the PTA book fair, she would find herself imagining him there with her, adoring her for every small thing she did or said. It sneaked into her self-image, insidiously brightening her mood. Making her feel like a woman worthy of love.

That night, she got into bed beside her husband and abandoned herself to thoughts of Jack. Over and over, she heard him tell her how much he loved her. "I love you, too," she said.

She looked at the clock. One forty-eight, and sleep was

as far away as the stars. She listened to the steady breathing of deep slumber on the other side of the bed and sat up. She stared into the darkness for a moment and then put her slippers on and tiptoed downstairs. She picked up the phone and dialed Jack's number.

"Hello?" he said, his voice vague and gravelly.

"Hey. Sorry to wake you," she whispered.

"Maddie?"

"I couldn't sleep. I need to tell you something."

"What is it, baby?"

"I changed my mind. I want to see you. Soon. Like tomorrow."

"Mmm. That's good news. Only I can't tomorrow. I'm going to a conference in San Francisco. I'll be back in a week. Can we meet a week from Friday?"

"It's a date."

Chapter Thirteen

RUTH

Ruth adjusted her wipers to the fastest speed and turned on the seat warmers. Not so much for her as for Ben. She was on her way to pick him up from his private tennis lesson at a local indoor court and thought he might be waiting outside under the awning catching a chill.

She honked when she saw him and pulled as close to the building as she could. He dashed into the car.

"How was your lesson?"

"Awesome."

She smiled, delighted he was enjoying tennis so much. He was a natural at the sport, and she looked forward to seeing him get good enough to beat her. She glanced at his rangy, boyish arms, knowing they would soon thicken with muscles and he'd be able to put more force on the ball than she could handle. She wondered if he would have the temerity to trounce her once he could.

"Did you shower?"

He swiped his hand across his hair, flicking water at Ruth to indicate how wet it was. "What do *you* think?"

"Yuk. I think you're bratty enough to have stood out in

the rain to get your hair wet just so I would *think* you showered."

"Okay, smell." He leaned in to her so that his head was right under her nose. She closed her eyes for a second and inhaled. It was the same clean, soapy smell she remembered from when he was small and she toweled him off after his bath.

"Rainwater," she said. "Definitely rainwater."

"Funny." He clicked on the radio.

"I have to stop for bananas."

"Can we go to Green Earth?" he asked, sounding like a child. It was an upscale local market specializing in wholesome gourmet foods and exotic imports, and one of his favorite stores now that he liked to cook. "So I can pick out something to make for dinner?"

"Sure," she said, "why not."

When they reached the store, they rushed inside and Ruth banged the water off her umbrella. Since they only needed a few things, they decided not to grab a shopping cart. Ben took the wet umbrella with him to the butcher department at the back of the store, while Ruth strolled the produce section. After getting bananas, she saw the Fuji apples Keith liked and dropped four of them into a bag. She grabbed some grapes for herself, and then remembered that she also needed carrots. She was low on skim milk, too. Ruth looked around for a shopping basket, but didn't see one. Her arms full, she walked to the bakery department, where she met up with Ben.

"What'd you get?" she asked.

"Leg of lamb," he said, holding up a clear plastic bag that held a triangular slab wrapped in white butcher's paper. "I want to get some really good olive oil to make a marinade."

His mother told him to pick out some bread, first. He

pointed to a crusty baguette, and the woman behind the counter slipped it into a long bag and handed it to him. They went to the aisle where elegant bottles of golden olive oil in different shapes and sizes stood side by side like proud Mediterranean beauties. He picked a tall, thin jewel from Spain and carried it by the neck like he planned to take a swig.

On their way to the cashier, he grabbed a jar of imported mustard and then spotted some pignoli nuts.

"Can we get these?" he asked, putting the wrapped lamb between his knees and picking up the bottle.

"Nine dollars for a jar of nuts?" she said, looking at the sticker.

"Please," he whined. "They're *so* good."

She relented, but wondered aloud how they would carry the jar. Their arms were completely full.

Ben tried to put the packaged baguette under his chin to free a hand but Ruth stopped him. "Just stick the nuts in my bag," she said, and he did.

They unloaded their arms onto the conveyer belt at the checkout. After paying and grabbing their bags of groceries, Ruth remembered the nuts in her pocketbook.

"Oh, shoot," she said, stopping in her tracks.

Just then, she felt a hand on her shoulder—her injured shoulder—and looked up to see a security guard dressed in a forest-green uniform that matched the décor of the store. He couldn't have been much older than Ben.

"Aren't you forgetting something?" the guard asked.

"Huh?"

He pointed to her handbag.

"I meant to pay for them," she said, putting her bags down and retrieving the jar of nuts. "I just forgot."

"Yeah, *right,*" a female voice behind her said. Ruth

turned to see Donna Fishbein, a woman she knew from the PTA. "Don't believe her," Donna said to the security guard. "A woman who would steal a town's historic rock would have no trouble shoplifting!"

Shoppers stopped to watch the scene and Ruth froze, mortified.

"And she involves her son, no less!" Donna said to the onlookers. Then she turned to Ruth. "You *disgust* me."

"But I—" Ruth looked at the guard. "You have to believe me. I never meant to steal these."

"Come with me, miss," the guard said, and led Ruth and Ben through the aisles to the manager's office in the back of the store. Like criminals on a perp walk, they hung their heads as all eyes focused on them. Ruth wanted to disappear.

The manager, a doughy man with smart brown eyes, listened thoughtfully as Ruth and Ben explained how full their arms were and that they had meant to pay for the nuts. The man apparently believed them. He apologized for the embarrassment at the checkout and even offered to let them have the pignoli nuts for free, but Ruth refused, insisting on paying for them, and gave the manager the money right there in his office. It was a matter of pride, though it did little to salve the deeps wounds of humiliation.

Leaving the store was torture. People pointed and whispered. An old lady in a stained sweatshirt scolded Ruth. "You ought to be ashamed!"

"Get a life, you old bag," Ruth said, scowling. "And while you're at it, check out aisle three. They have a new thing you can buy. It's called *detergent*."

Ruth glanced over at Ben, who looked damaged. "It's

all right, baby," she said, tousling his still damp hair. "*We* know we didn't do anything wrong."

Ruth supposed that Ben was just as humiliated by her brashness as he was by the scene at the door. He was in the midst of that adolescent learning curve where social behavior was a novel that revealed its layers as you went along. Kids his age thought they grasped it all, when really, they were barely past the prologue—the part about keeping a low profile in public. Unbeknownst to them, their parents had finished the book, tossed it aside, and decided for themselves which chapters were worth heeding. This was inconceivable to teenagers, who thought the only excuse for their parents' behavior was that they didn't even know the book existed. Unlike other kids his age, though, Ben was too kind to chastise his mother for embarrassing him. He simply sucked up the pain. Ruth hated to see him suffer, and meant to curb her confrontational style when he was around. Usually, she got too caught up in the moment to remember.

As they got into their car, Ruth saw Donna Fishbein heading for her Mercedes, and remembered that she was the woman whose husband had been indicted for stock fraud. Ruth thought about letting the moment pass. But as she stuck the key in the ignition, an image of Donna telling Suzanne Podobinski about the alleged shoplifting played out before her in vivid detail. She imagined Suzanne maliciously spreading the lie throughout the tennis club, the PTA, everywhere. "I'll give them something to talk about," she said out loud.

"What?" Ben asked.

"Give me the nuts," she demanded.

"Why?" he asked, looking into a grocery bag.

"Just give them to me."

Ruth dashed out of the car into the rain, carrying a jar of nine-dollar nuts and no umbrella. Soaking wet, she approached Donna's car and knocked on the glass.

"What is it?" Donna said angrily.

"Open your window!"

Donna rolled her eyes and complied. "Whatever you're selling, I'm not buying."

"Oh, I'm not selling anything. In fact, I have a present for you." The greed light flickered in Donna's eyes as she heard the word "present," but she recovered quickly, affecting an expression of hard incredulity.

"You might need these," Ruth said, opening the jar and tossing the contents at Donna, "in case your husband loses his *nuts* in prison!"

Donna ducked, and it was only then that Ruth realized someone was sitting in the passenger seat. The nuts flew by Donna and hit the unsuspecting woman square in the face. Wet from the rain, most of them stuck there, making it look like her skin had erupted in hideous boils.

"You bitch!" shouted the woman.

Ruth stared for a moment and then threw her head back and laughed, unable to contain her glee over her good fortune. The woman who took the hit—and who now looked ridiculous trying to shake off the nuts like a wet dog—was Suzanne Podobinski.

Before she walked away, Ruth stuck her head into the car and smiled. "Now *that's* what I call an ace!"

Sunday morning, with Ben and Morgan at friends' houses, Ruth arranged her living room for a meeting of the public relations committee. It was early enough for breakfast, so she put out bagels and coffee, and set Keith up in the den with a remote control and his favorite snacks. Maddie arrived first, and was still chatting with Ruth in the foyer when Lisa arrived with a paper-thin older woman wearing leggings, high heels, and a skimpy top with no bra. Except for the conspicuous lack of makeup, Ruth thought she looked like a streetwalker.

"I'd like you to meet my mother, Nancy," Lisa said. "She's staying with us for a while so I thought I'd bring her along. I hope you don't mind."

"What she really means," Nancy said, "is that she doesn't trust me alone in the house. Thinks I'll raid the liquor cabinet or something. Apparently, I'm a liar and a drunk."

"Mom, please," Lisa said.

Ruth invited everyone into the living room, and expressed concern about how uninteresting all their committee business might be for Nancy.

"My husband's watching TV in the other room," she said. "Do you want to join him? I have the feeling you two would really hit it off."

"He likes ex-drunks?"

Ruth smiled. "Come, I'll introduce you."

When Ruth got back to the living room, she assured Lisa that her mother would be fine with Keith. "They're watching TV, and the only liquor we have is in a locked cabinet in this room."

Lisa sat down and sighed. "Thanks. Sorry I had to bring her."

Ruth patted Lisa on the back and then turned to Maddie. "Now, please tell me the private investigator is close to solving this missing rock thing. Because I don't think I can take the accusations another day."

Maddie picked up half a bagel and put it on a plate. "He's getting there," she said, smearing low-fat cream cheese on it. "He found out the truck was rented in the city and is working on getting us a name."

"Tell him to work fast," Ruth said, "or I may be forced to commit *real* criminal activity. Like murder one. As it stands, I'm wondering if I could do time for attacking Suzanne Podobinski with a jar of nuts."

Maddie sat down. "Any jury would believe that was self-defense."

"Not that I even care anymore, but when the town yentas get a hold of this one, it'll mean more bad PR for the PR committee."

Lisa poured herself a cup of coffee. "They already did."

"What?"

"They already got a hold of it. I heard about it yesterday, at Yogurt 'n' Such." She turned to Ruth. "Did you really tell Donna Fishbein you would cut off her husband's nuts?"

Ruth sat down heavily. "I have to move."

"To hell with them," Maddie said.

Ruth sighed. "It's not just my reputation I'm worried about. All this angry gossip about the rock being stolen could send the movie studio running. They don't need this crap. Plenty of PTAs would kill to have a movie made in their school yards."

"I can't see how the movie people would hear any of the gossip," Lisa said.

"They will if Podobinski has anything to say about it," Ruth answered.

Maddie said, "Then we'll just have to keep her out of the loop."

Ruth sighed. "Jill and I are meeting the executive producer at the school yard next week. We're doing it early in the morning so no one will be around, but one of Suzanne's minions lives right over the back of the field and watches over it like a hawk. If she spots us there, she'll make a call no matter *what* time it is."

"Terrible," Lisa said, and rubbed Ruth's back reassuringly.

"How are things with you?" Ruth asked Lisa. "It must be tough having your mother there."

Lisa shrugged. "I have no choice. She's in treatment and has no place else to stay."

"I wonder what she and Keith are up to," Maddie said.

Lisa stood. "I think I should check on her."

Ruth rose to accompany her and Maddie followed behind.

Lisa was the first to view the scene in the den, which caused her to let out a shriek as all the color drained from her face.

"My God!" Ruth said.

Maddie's jaw simply dropped.

Keith was seated on the couch where Ruth had left him. But instead of staring at the TV, he looked at Nancy, who stood in front of him, completely naked. His grin was idiotic.

"Mother!" Lisa howled.

Nancy picked up her clothes. "He *asked* me," she said, in a voice that implied such a request left her no choice. "Poor guy hasn't seen a titty in years."

Lisa covered her eyes with her hand. "Get dressed. I'm taking you home."

"I did ask her," Keith said in her defense.

As Nancy pulled on her clothes, Ruth chastised Keith and Lisa apologized to everyone for her mother's behavior.

Lisa was literally dragging Nancy to the door when Keith hoisted himself up on his walker.

"It was nice meeting you, Nancy," he said.

"Bye, baby!" she shouted to him from the door. "Call me."

After the others left, Ruth scolded her husband and made him promise to never do anything like that again. Then she quickly went about cleaning the living room. Marta, she knew, would be there any minute to look after Keith, freeing her to run a few errands. She needed to buy ballet tights for Morgan, and planned on going to a store in Quaker Bay, giving her an excuse to drop in on Paul. She hadn't slept with him in nearly two weeks and was feeling overlooked. She picked up the phone and called to see if he was available, but the line was busy. Still, before she left she went upstairs and changed from her regular panties to a thong, just in case.

Ruth called from the car on her way up there and got a busy signal again. Annoyed that he was so stubbornly old-fashioned that he refused to get call waiting like everyone else, Ruth decided she would just pop in on him after her errands even though he had told her to always call first.

When Ruth reached Paul's house, she noticed a blue Toyota in the spot where she usually parked. She pulled up in front of the car and debated for only a second or two about whether or not she should go in.

She tapped three times with the brass knocker and Paul came to the door.

"Ruth," he said, surprised. "I didn't know you were coming."

"I tried calling, I—" She looked past him and saw someone sitting on the sofa. It looked like a dowdy older woman wearing a wool suit and sensible shoes. No contest. Ruth sucked in her stomach. "You have company. I'm sorry."

"It's okay. That's Margie, from my church. She's in my Widow and Widowers group. Would you like me to introduce you?"

Widow and Widowers group? Yikes, Ruth thought, bad sign, given how drawn he is to suffering. She peered inside again to get a better look.

"I don't want to interrupt anything."

"Ruth," Paul whispered, "Margie and I are just friends. Why don't you come in."

She squeezed his hand and, apparently by accident, brushed her breast against his arm. "Thanks, I believe I will."

She released his hand and followed him inside, where he introduced her to his little Margie. On closer inspection, Ruth realized that his church friend wasn't as old as she seemed. In fact, she wasn't much older than Ruth. Not only that, but her suit wasn't even that bad. The shoes, however, were another story entirely. Ruth looked at her own feet, cradled in three-hundred-dollar crocodile-skin ankle boots with stiletto heels, and then back at Margie's thick-soled, lace-up vinyl horrors. Why, Ruth wondered, would any woman do that to herself?

"Ruth heads up one of the PTA committees," Paul explained to Margie. "She's handling that movie project I told you about."

Ruth shifted uneasily from one foot to the other. He was making excuses for her presence. Apparently, he didn't want Margie to know there was anything between them. She understood discretion, but this seemed more aggressive than necessary.

Ruth noted that Margie was seated on the sofa, not the

love seat. At least there's that, she thought. But it remained to be seen where Paul would choose to park himself now that Ruth was there. Would he sit beside Margie, as he had obviously been doing before she arrived? It would force Ruth into the straight-backed armchair facing the couch, like a formal guest. Or would he take the chair for himself, and let Ruth sit beside Margie on the sofa? Ruth stood, waiting for Paul to make a move.

"Please," he said, "sit." He pointed to the side chair as he seated himself on the sofa next to Margie.

So this is how it is, she thought. Fine. She looked at Margie's legs, knees together, feet neatly crossed at the ankles. Ruth crossed her legs at the thighs, twisting her body to the side so that the half of her rump facing Paul was lifted off the chair. She contemplated Margie's sex appeal, or lack thereof, and couldn't imagine Paul sleeping with her. Especially given his preference for rough play. Would Margie enjoy having her nipple chewed or her ass slapped? Doubtful.

Besides, Paul couldn't possibly be attracted to this woman, could he? She was plain to begin with, and made no attempt at attractiveness. Except for some sheer pink lipstick, she wore no makeup at all. And that hair. Was there a special old-lady beauty parlor in Barrett where time stood still?

"Margie's husband was a teacher," Paul said.

Why is he telling me this? Ruth wondered. Is this supposed to be something we have in common? Like, Margie was *married* to a teacher, you *know* teachers. You two must have tons to talk about.

"Social studies," Margie added. "He died in eighty-nine."

For a second, Ruth thought she meant *eighteen* eighty-nine, and pictured a stagecoach accident. Must have been the term "social studies" that drew her mind to history.

"I'm so sorry," Ruth said. "Was he very ill?"

Paul put his hand on Margie's arm. "Clem had an accident," he said, as if trying to spare her the pain of having to utter the words herself.

Margie grabbed a tissue from the box on the side table as if she were preparing to cry. "Fell off the roof."

Well, what was he doing on the roof, for heaven's sake? Ruth wanted to ask.

"He was fixing the TV antenna," Margie said, as if she heard her. "Wanted to watch a rerun of *Columbo*."

Columbo? He died for a rerun of *Columbo?*

"It *was* a good show," Ruth comforted.

"He lost his footing because of the rain," Margie explained.

It was *raining*?

She continued. "And we think the lightning may have startled him."

"And the thunder," Paul added.

Thunder? Lightning? "He must have really loved *Columbo*," Ruth offered.

"Now he doesn't get to watch anything," Margie said as she shook her head sadly.

"He's in a better place," Paul consoled, gently patting her on the knee.

Keith's idea of heaven, Ruth thought, would be a place where the TV was tuned to the Playboy channel twenty-four/seven. She imagined Margie's husband sitting in an easy chair, breaking wind and watching Peter Falk solve crimes for all eternity.

"It must be very hard for you," Ruth said.

Margie nodded, apparently too lost in emotion to speak.

Paul leaned in to the unhappy widow. "Can I get you a glass of water?" he asked. She shook her head no.

Ruth studied Paul's face and noticed something that alarmed her. Low down on his cheek, about an inch to the left of his mouth, was a pink smudge. Ruth looked at Margie's lipstick and determined that it was the same color. Of course, she could have just kissed him hello, but even the chance that the two of them might have been starting to neck when she knocked on the door gave Ruth the same feeling she got when someone returned a serve she thought she had aced. Oh, no you don't, said her inner voice. This point is mine. And I know just how to play it.

Ruth rubbed her forehead as if she had a headache.

"Something wrong?" Paul asked.

"I'm fine. Just had a rough weekend. But I don't want to take any more of your time." She stood and extended her hand. "It was nice meeting you, Margie."

"You don't have to leave," Paul said.

"Thank you, but I don't want to intrude. I'll talk to you another time."

He stood. "At least let me walk you to the door."

Paul stepped outside with Ruth and asked her what was wrong.

"It's sort of a long story," she said, looking down at the ground.

"What is it?" he asked. "Did something happen?"

"Yesterday." She sniffed. "At Green Earth . . . oh, it was terrible!"

"Tell me."

She filled him in on the public humiliation surrounding the pignoli nuts, leaving out the part where she threw them into Suzanne Podobinski's face.

"Oh, you poor thing!" he said, hugging her.

"It gets worse."

"Worse?"

"Today, Keith did something even more embarrassing. In front of my friends. But I don't want to talk about it now. You have company."

"Wait here," he said, and left the door ajar while he went back inside to chat with Margie. Ruth peered in and watched them speaking in hushed tones. Margie nodded and picked up her handbag, as well as an avocado-colored something that looked like a hand-knitted poncho Ruth assumed was completed sometime in the mid-seventies.

"Good-bye, dear," Margie said as she sidled past Ruth out the door.

"Good-bye, Margie," Ruth said. "Cute poncho."

Chapter Fourteen

When Ruth pulled into the parking lot of North Applewood Elementary School, it was deserted except for one other car. She parked right next to it and peered inside. Sure enough, it was Jill Slotnick-Weiss.

Jill motioned for Ruth to come inside her car, which she did.

"Cold today," Ruth said as she slammed the door. "Are they here yet?"

Ruth and Jill were scheduled to meet the movie producer and set designer at the school so they could see the location for themselves. It was the producer's idea to meet at the ungodly hour of six A.M.

"Still waiting," Jill said, looking at her watch.

"What's he like? The producer?"

"I've only spoken to his secretary, but she said to be forewarned."

"What does *that* mean?" Ruth asked.

Just then, the women heard a screech and saw a yellow sports car veer into the parking lot so fast a lesser vehicle wouldn't have made it on all four wheels. The driver pulled up sideways in front of Jill's car and came to an abrupt stop. The door opened from the bottom like the hatch on a spaceship.

A man emerged. Not tall, but he loomed like a giant compared to the flat profile of his foreign sports car. He was tan with thinning blond hair, and wore a black knit shirt with short sleeves that hugged his meticulously pumped biceps. Vanity, Ruth thought. He'd rather freeze than hide his muscles under a jacket. Probably works out with a personal trainer every day. In his own gym. Bet he's got his own tanning booth, too. And that microfiber T-shirt. Any sleeker and it would be liquid. Could this guy *be* more L.A.? Ruth wondered if he paid someone to airlift his Lamborghini from the Coast so he wouldn't have to drive a rental.

The women got out of the car and approached. Jill extended her hand and introduced herself.

"Rod Martin," he said as he gruffly shook her hand. "Where the fuck is my set designer?"

"Uh, not here yet," Jill stammered. "This is Ruth Moss. She's our school liaison."

Rod Martin grunted at Ruth and shook her hand. "I told that little shit to be early so I wouldn't have to stand around waiting for him." He reached into his pants pocket and extracted the tiniest cell phone Ruth had ever seen. As he punched in numbers, Ruth studied his face and tried to figure out why he looked familiar. Did she know him from somewhere? Maybe he wasn't a Californian after all.

"Where the fuck are you?" he barked into the phone. "Yeah? Well, tell him to hurry. I'm not going to wait around all day. I have to be back in the city at nine for a meeting."

He shut his miniature phone and said to no one in particular, "Little prick is taking a limo out here. Spends my money like he's a fucking star."

"You're from L.A.?" Ruth asked.

He made a noise that sounded like *puh,* followed by, "Unfortunately."

Ruth shrugged. She guessed she didn't know him after all. Probably just his alpha-maleness that seemed so familiar. She knew the type.

"You want to wait in my car until he gets here?" Jill asked. "It's pretty cold to wait outside."

Rod Martin pointed to the school. "Can't we wait in there?"

"It's not open."

"Why the hell not?"

"It's six o'clock in the morning," Jill said. "The custodians aren't even in yet."

He turned to Ruth. "You couldn't get a key, Miss School Liaison?"

She could have, of course, but that would have meant letting Suzanne know about this meeting, and she just didn't want to risk having Podobinski show up here and scare the producer away.

"First of all," Ruth said to Rod Martin, "it's *Mrs.* School Liaison." She looked at his face to see if she elicited a smile, but his focus had already wandered. He was looking from his watch to the road leading up to the parking lot. "And second of all . . ." She paused, waiting for his attention. "Second of all, I didn't think it was necessary, since you're not using the interior of the building. But if you need to take a piss, there's a wooded area out back."

Surprised by her cheek, he looked at her and folded his arms. Something like a smile tugged at his tight mouth, but he caught it in time and furrowed his brow. She crossed her arms, too, as if to say, you don't scare *me,* you nasty bastard. I've known guys like you before. Hell, I was married to one before his brain hemorrhaged.

"All right, ladies. Show me where I'm building a stadium for your precious progeny."

"Actually," Jill said, leading the way to Field One, "I'm not one of the parents here. I'm the location scout working with your production team."

"Well, bully for you," he said. "I'll send out a press release."

Ruth stopped in her tracks and stood in Rod Martin's path with her hands on her hips.

He rolled his eyes. "What," he said, "you gonna tell me off?"

"You know what?" she said. "We get it. You're rich and powerful and can be as much of an asshole as you want. But we don't need your money that badly. We can build our own stadium, thank you very much. So if you want to make your movie here, drop the attitude."

"Ooh, look at you, Norma Rae. Okay, Red, I'll be a good boy, I promise."

"It's *Ruth,*" she said, softening her tone.

"You have nice breasts, Ruth."

"Go to hell."

"It was a compliment." He took out his phone again. "I'm going to make some calls while we wait for his royal highness to show up."

While Rod Martin talked on the phone, Jill whispered to Ruth, "Who is he *calling* at six o'clock in the morning?"

"Please," Ruth said, "you think a guy like that cares if he wakes people up?"

After several minutes, Ruth saw a Town Car pull into

the parking lot. "I think your little friend is here," she said to the producer.

Rod turned around and they all watched as a young man with jet-black hair scurried toward them, his long trench coat flapping in the breeze.

"Sorry I'm late," he panted.

"About time," Rod muttered.

Jill introduced herself and Ruth. The young man extended his hand. "Chet Eng," he said. "Nice to meet you."

Rod Martin pulled Chet Eng by the sleeve, and the two of them marched around the perimeter of the field, leaving Ruth and Jill under the building's awning.

"Mr. Personality," Jill said when they were out of earshot.

"Did you notice?" Ruth teased. "No wedding ring."

"If I ever get that desperate, shoot me." Jill squinted in the direction of the parking lot. "Who's that?" she asked.

Ruth turned and saw a slender female figure approaching. "It's Podobinski," she moaned. "She must have gotten a call that we were meeting with someone driving a three-hundred-thousand-dollar sports car and hightailed it over here."

"Do you think she'll say anything about the rock and all that?" Jill asked.

"I think she's more interested in rubbing elbows with all that glamour and money than screwing with us, but you never know with her. Let's hope she gets too distracted flirting to even remember how much she hates me."

"Flirting?" Jill said. "With Mr. Personality?"

Ruth smirked. "She doesn't have to know that."

The women looked at each other, a conspiratorial buzz passing between them.

"This ought to be fun," Jill said. Ruth rubbed her hands together.

"Hi," Suzanne said when she reached them. "Are those the movie people?" She nodded in the direction of the two men in the distance.

"Wait till you get a load of the producer," Jill said.

"Adorable," Ruth added. "And sweet as sugar."

"Really?" Suzanne sucked her cheeks in and arched her back.

"Said he wants to meet you." Ruth turned up her collar against the cold. "You being the president of the PTA and all."

Suzanne shook out one of her pant legs until it fell perfectly over her shoe. "That makes sense."

The three women stood in the cold, stamping their feet to keep warm as they waited for the men to return.

When they did, Chet announced that they had got what they needed and could start making plans.

"Fucking frigid northeast," Rod said. "Let's go."

"Wait," Jill said, "Rod Martin, I'd like to introduce you to Suzanne Podobinski."

Rod glanced at her quickly and then said to Ruth, "Who the fuck is *she*?"

"Head of the PTA," Ruth said. "A VIP around here."

Suzanne grabbed his hand and shook it. "It's so nice to meet you, Mr. Martin. Is that your Lamborghini parked out front?"

Ruth wasn't sure, but she could have sworn Suzanne actually batted her eyelashes at the handsome producer.

Rod Martin pulled his hand away from the effusive Suzanne. "Shouldn't you be home wiping someone's ass?"

Suzanne's mouth opened and emitted three clearly un-

intentional squeaks. "What the—" She turned to Ruth.
"You *bitch*."

"What'd *I* do?" Ruth said innocently.

Suzanne grabbed her handbag and slammed it into
Ruth's injured shoulder.

"Ay!" Ruth screamed in pain as she doubled over.

"She's a liar and a thief!" Suzanne said to Rod Martin.
"She stole Applewood Rock and now the whole town
hates her!"

Rod turned to Chet. "Why is this woman talking to
me? Make her go away."

Chet spoke softly to Suzanne in a conciliatory tone as
he tried to pull her aside.

"Oh, get off me," she snapped. "I'm leaving anyway."
She stormed off.

"You okay?" Jill asked Ruth.

Ruth stood and tried to recover. "I'm going to kill that
woman, so help me, God."

The foursome walked to the parking lot and Rod Martin grabbed Ruth's hand when they reached his car. He
pressed something into her palm and quickly whispered,
"Take care of that shoulder, hot stuff," before sinking into
his vehicle and vrooming off, burnt rubber marking his
departure.

"God Martin, we call him," Chet explained. "He's a
trip." He told the women it was nice meeting them and
got into his waiting limousine.

Ruth looked down at the slip of paper in her hand.

"What's *that*?" Jill asked.

"His phone number," Ruth said, crumpling it into a
ball. "Can you imagine?"

• • •

The following Saturday felt like a gift, mild and sunny. Ruth had the hatch of the SUV open as she went back and forth from the house to the car, loading it with everything she'd need for Morgan's soccer game, including Keith's wheelchair. Since he couldn't navigate the rough terrain of the field in his walker, she had to push him herself through the grass.

People could never manage to be subtle about staring at the wheelchair. Wives poked husbands, children tugged at parents' sleeves and pointed. But none of that bothered Ruth. It was watching the other families act so normally and take it all for granted that made these outings so difficult. A father stopping to pick up his son's sweatshirt could make her eyes sting. A wife badgering her husband for forgetting to pack the water bottles might start her sniffling. A girl running from the field into her daddy's arms and getting tossed in the air made her want to wail and tantrum at the unfairness of it all.

Today, as she pushed the wheelchair through the massive expanse of lawn surrounding North Applewood Elementary School, she glanced from Morgan to Ben and wanted to tell them how sorry she was. They were supposed to have perfect lives, her children. This was never part of the plan.

At nine years old, Morgan was already taking on a maternal role with her father, rubbing his back and asking if she could get him anything. Sometimes wiping his face with a napkin and reminding him to take his vitamins. And Ben tried to look after his mother, the woman with a husband but no man.

Ah, but there *was* a man. There was Paul. Thank God for Paul, who made her feel whole. She loved that this good, smart, sensitive man was insane with desire for her.

So powerful was his passion that it won the battle of his conscience every time. Ruth hated to admit it, but what a thrill! If she could conquer that cross over his bed, she could conquer anything.

It was thoughts of Paul that got her out of bed in the morning and thoughts of Paul that lulled her to sleep at night. She couldn't even remember how she had managed to get through her day before he was in her life.

"Do you want me to push for a while, Mom?" Ben threw the straps of the collapsed field chairs over his shoulder to illustrate that he could manage both. Sweet, sweet Ben.

When they reached the sidelines, they found the Slotnick family already there, set up with folding chairs, blankets, and coolers. Ruth noticed that the whole gang was in attendance, including Lisa's mother and her boyfriend. Nancy broke away from the pack and rushed up to them.

"Hey, sweetie!" she said to Keith.

"Lookin' good, Nance," he answered back.

Nancy invited Keith to sit with her and Chris, her boyfriend, which was fine with Ruth. He had so few friends left since the stroke, and she thought it was healthy for him to have people in his life besides her and the kids.

Ruth approached Lisa, and Ben immediately made it his job to entertain Lisa's little one, Simon, who played on the grass with a sealed juice box.

"Any news yet on the rock?" Lisa asked Ruth.

"Not yet," Ruth said. "And Podobinski nearly blew it for us with the producer."

Lisa shook her head and tsked. "I'm worried. A day like today, I can't help thinking how perfect it would be to have our own stadium, you know? I can picture us all there, sitting together, cheering the kids on."

"I know," Ruth said, suddenly aware that her shoulder

was throbbing in pain. She winced and rubbed it with her other hand.

"How bad is your shoulder?" Lisa asked.

Ruth opened up her folding chair with her good arm and sat down. "Bad enough to need surgery if I ever intend to play tennis again."

"I can't *believe* that."

"Believe it," Ruth said. "Believe it."

"Oh, no," came Ben's voice from behind. "Now I have that 'I'm a Believer' song in my head. From *Shrek.*"

"It's not from *Shrek,* dear," his mother said. "It's a wonderful old Monkees song."

"Wherever it's from, it's moved into my brain and won't leave."

"'I thought love was only true in fairy tales!'" Ruth sang. "'Meant for someone else but not for me.'"

"Stop!" Ben pleaded.

"'Love was out to get me.'"

"Someone help!"

"'That's the way it seemed. Disappointment haunted all my dreams.' Sing with me, Ben . . ."

At that point, Nancy joined in, and together, they sang the song to the end, at which point Ben moaned, "Now I'll *never* get that song out of my head."

Keith, who had been listening and smiling during the performance, said, "Give the song to Daddy. I'll store it away in my brain's dead spot. Nothing ever escapes."

The group fell silent. No one knew quite how to react to Keith's public acknowledgment of his neurological condition. Ruth wasn't surprised. She'd heard him make remarks like that before. What struck her was the poetry of his statement, "Give the song to Daddy." She said it over and over again in her head, until it had a tempo and a melody. The line took on a life of its own, sounding so emotional, so hauntingly beautiful that it gave Ruth a chill. She could hardly wait to get her hands on her guitar and work out the rest of it.

The ref blew the whistle and the game began, diverting everyone's attention to the field.

"Lisa," she said, "did you ever listen to that tape of my songs?"

"I did. You're a wonderful songwriter, Ruth." Lisa brushed some grass off her knee. "But I can't record those songs for you. I can't. I'm . . . I'm not a singer."

"I've heard you sing, Lisa. I *know* you can knock those songs out of the park."

Lisa shifted in her seat uncomfortably and looked out at the soccer field, avoiding Ruth's eyes. She shook her head. "I'm sorry," she said softly.

"I'll do it," came a loud voice from behind. Ruth and Lisa both turned their heads to see Nancy standing over them.

"What?" asked Ruth.

"I'll sing. Record your songs. Whatever it is you need."

"Mother!"

"Don't *Mother* me. Why shouldn't I do it? You'll never have the guts to."

"You're putting Ruth on the spot."

"What?" Nancy asked. "You think I lost my voice?"

"Of course not."

"'Cause I may not have the range I used to, but I can still sing better than—" Nancy stopped herself as if editing her own words. "Better than half those losers on MTV." She turned to Ruth. "Give me a shot. I can knock *anything* out of the park."

Ruth looked at Lisa for a clue. Was this okay with her?

"Whatever," Lisa said, getting the message. "As long as it doesn't interfere with her treatment."

Despite the fact that the community was still abuzz with gossip that she had stolen the rock, Ruth felt happy. Her week was starting out great. She took a swig from her water bottle and turned the treadmill up to six and a half miles an hour. She had weighed herself before running and was down three pounds. Three pounds! She'd go out and buy herself a sexy new teddy today. Something naughty that would throw Paul into a frenzy of guilty lust, driving the Catholic schoolboy in him into paroxysms of desire.

Plus, the tape she had made with Nancy came out better than she expected. When she first heard the older woman sing, she was a little concerned, as her voice showed signs of age and hard living. In her head, Ruth had been hearing Lisa's silky voice dress her melodies in yards of glorious color. But once she adjusted her expectations, she was pleased with Nancy's polished performance. The professional songstress learned the tunes easily and was quick to understand even the subtlest emotional components. The result, Ruth thought, was a simple recording that illustrated the potential of her music. She'd be proud to play it for anyone who would listen.

Finding someone who would was the tricky part. So one day last week she smoothed out the paper Rod Martin had written his phone number on and called him. She knew it was a long shot, but figured it worth a try.

"Who is this?" he barked into the phone.

"Ruth Moss. From Applewood. Remember me?"

"Hot stuff. Is this a booty call?"

She was prepared for that and took a deep breath. "Not

exactly," she said, and went on to explain about the tape and her songwriting, hoping that he might want to grab the opportunity to strut his power by connecting her with someone in the music business.

He cut her off. "Going into a meeting now, Red. I'll have someone contact you." He hung up without saying good-bye.

She figured he was either blowing her off completely, or at least until he could find a way to parlay it into a reciprocal arrangement, trading sex for a favor. She mentally crossed him off her list, deciding she'd need to find someone else to help her out.

Ruth slowed the treadmill to start her cooldown. She grabbed a towel and wiped the sweat from her face as she walked the last five minutes of her circuit, her heart rate decreasing. She moved her shoulder around to check if the injury had changed any, hoping for some miraculous, spontaneous recovery that would enable her to cancel the surgery. But no. The pain was still there. She comforted herself with the thought that her surgeon had a stellar reputation, and was largely considered one of the best orthopedists in the country.

The operation was scheduled for right after the Christmas break so it wouldn't interfere with vacation plans. Every year, she took the kids down to Florida to visit her parents. Keith hated to travel so he stayed home. It worked out fine, because his parents made it their business to come stay with him, giving her a guilt-free respite and affording them some quality time with their son. As usual, they would stay on a few extra days when Ruth got home so they'd get to enjoy their grandkids, as well.

While she was in Florida, Ruth's parents always encouraged her to take a few days for herself. In the past, she took the opportunity to go down to the Keys and spend some relaxing time on the beach. This year, she would head west for Marco Island, where Paul had a town house and spent nearly all his time off. The only problem was that she hadn't yet told him her plans. She would wait until the last minute, perhaps springing it on him in the throes of passion when he wouldn't possibly turn her down. In the meantime, she'd drop lots of hints and hope he would ask her to come before she had to invite herself.

Ruth turned off the treadmill, and stretched for a few minutes before heading upstairs for a shower. When she passed through the kitchen, Marta stopped her to say she needed to run out for eggs.

"I was just going to pop into the shower," Ruth said. "What is he doing?"

"He's fine," Marta said. "He's reading the paper."

"All right. I'll see you later."

Ruth found Keith in the den with his *New York Times* and *Wall Street Journal*. She kissed the top of his head and told him she'd be upstairs showering. "Holler if you need anything, okay, sweetheart?"

"Okay."

Ruth was just pulling off her sticky workout clothes when the phone rang. It was Jill.

"What's going on?" Ruth asked.

"I was just meeting with a woman here from Rod Martin's office. She's on her way to the airport, but said Rod told her to swing by your house and pick up some tape before she goes. I gave her directions."

"What?"

"She should be there in ten minutes."

"Huh? Shit. I don't even have a copy made."

"Well, you'd better hurry."

"Thanks," Ruth said, and quickly hung up the phone. She got dressed and ran downstairs to the den, where she kept the stereo equipment. She inserted the recorded tape into one slot and a new blank tape in the other. "Hurry, hurry," she whispered to the machine.

"What are you doing?" Keith asked.

"Making a copy of that demo tape. I've got someone coming by for it in about ten minutes."

"Ah, Nancy." Keith smiled. He knew she had recorded the songs for his wife, and got a goofy look on his face every time he thought of her. "Can we fuck soon? I want to fuck."

"Shut up, Keith."

Keith shrugged and went back to his paper, grumbling something about the news and crooked politicians.

The phone rang and Ruth ran for the kitchen to get it, thinking it might be Jill again. "Don't touch that," she said to Keith, indicating the audio system.

Ruth heard what sounded like an alarm ringing loudly on the other end of the phone line. A woman's voice said, "I have a code. Dey set be hobe."

"What? Who is this?"

"It's Nancy. I have a code. They set be hobe."

"Nancy? I can't hear you? What's all that noise?"

"It's the alarb."

"The alarm?"

"She never showed me how to shut it off."

"Who, Lisa? Where is she?"

"She's not hobe."

"She's not home?"

"I went to da treatment center, but they set me hobe. I have a code."

"You have a cold?"

"I can't shut off the alarb. The police are coming."

"Goddamn."

"Can you cub over? Right dow?"

"Jeez, Nancy."

"What?"

"I said . . . never mind. Where's the housekeeper?"

"I don't know."

Ruth sighed, exasperated. "Shit. Okay. I'll be right there."

She ran back into the den and looked at the tape, which was just finishing. She hit the eject button and pulled it out, quickly scribbling something onto the label.

"Listen, Keith," she said as she wrote. "I need you to do something very important for me."

"What's that?"

"There's a woman coming to the house for this tape." She held it up. "She'll be here any minute. I have to run out. Your friend Nancy is in a jam."

Keith smiled. "Nancy?"

"When the woman comes, you have to give this to her. Can you do that?"

"Of course I can do that. I'm not an idiot."

"I know you're not an idiot, honey. But listen"—she bent down to look him straight in the eye—"no funny business, okay? Just give her the tape and tell her I had to run out for an emergency. Don't say anything else. You understand?"

"I understand."

Ruth rushed to Lisa's house, expecting to see Nancy in handcuffs being led away by the police. But as it turned out, Lisa reached the house just seconds before Ruth, turning off the alarm. The police arrived moments later, and left soon after questioning Lisa about what had happened, but not before instructing her to make sure her mother knew how to work the alarm system in the future.

Lisa thanked Ruth for her trouble and she sped home, hoping she would make it there before the woman from the studio, though she knew she had little chance of that. The roads between her house and Lisa's were too narrow and winding to make the trip quickly.

When she finally pulled into her driveway, Marta's car was already there, and Ruth ran into the house. She found Marta in the kitchen.

"Did someone come by while I was gone?" Ruth asked.

"I just this second got in," Marta answered.

Ruth went into the den, where Keith sat watching TV. "Did she get here?" Ruth asked. "Did you give her the tape?"

He didn't look up from the television.

"Keith! I'm talking to you!"

Keith held out the tape for her with his good arm. "She didn't want it."

"What do you mean she didn't want it!" Ruth shrieked.

"I tried to give it to her but she just left."

"Keith, did you say something to her? Something you shouldn't have?"

"I hardly said a word. Besides, I wouldn't have fucked that bitch with someone else's dick. An ass like a truck."

Ruth buried her face in her hands and fell into a chair. "Oh, Keith, you didn't. I told you not to say anything to her. I *told* you."

The phone rang and Ruth picked it up, hoping it might be Jill calling to say she'd heard from the woman and everything was fine and Ruth would get a second chance to give her the tape. But it was her orthopedist's office. The doctor—the one who inspired such confidence in her—was undergoing chemotherapy and would have to cancel her surgery. Would she, they'd like to know, care to take down the names of some other orthopedists in the area?

Ruth hung up the phone and wept. She thought about calling Paul, but she had already left three messages for him over the past two days and didn't want to call again.

The phone rang again. What now? Ruth figured she'd let the machine get it. By the third ring, though, she changed her mind. What else could go wrong today?

"Hello?"

"Hello, Ruth? It's Paul. We have to talk."

Chapter Fifteen

Oh, my God, they have *MTV* on!"

Ruth and her children had just walked into an electronics store to shop for a DVD player for Keith's birthday, and nine-year-old Morgan exploded into a preteen frenzy. Her favorite girl pop singer of the moment was fluffing her hair and pouting into the camera on a whole wall full of televisions. Morgan asked if she could please, please, please stay there and watch.

"And I promise not to move from this spot," she added, anticipating her mother's one condition.

Ruth agreed, and went off with Ben to explore the equipment, all of which, she thought, looked like undifferentiated black boxes. She read the cards listing the features, and thought how ironic it was that despite his mental impairment, Keith still had more of a knack for technical gadgets than she did. It was as if that part of his brain were untouchable.

"What about this one, Ben?" she asked. "It has a VCR,

too. Does that mean you can make copies of the DVDs? I think Dad would like that."

Ben grunted.

"Is that a yes?"

He shrugged.

He's been so moody today, Ruth thought. Quieter than usual. "Is something wrong?"

Another shrug. He picked up a remote control from one of the DVD players, pretending to examine it.

"Please talk to me, Ben. Maybe I can help."

Ben gently shook the remote control, as if checking its weight. He opened the battery compartment and looked inside. "It's Dad."

Normally, she might have quipped, "He's inside the remote control?" but she knew this was serious. "What about Dad?"

Ben put down the remote control and looked toward the back of the store. "I think we should get him one of those cell phones that let you take pictures."

"Look at me, Ben," Ruth said. "If there's something bothering you, I want to know."

He looked down at the floor and then met her gaze, taking a deep breath. "Dad told me something he doesn't want you to know, but I think you should." He paused and swallowed. "He told me he might kill himself."

"What?" Ruth felt something like panic.

"He said if he kills himself someday I shouldn't think it was my fault, that one day he might just decide it's not worth going on."

"When did he tell you this?" She was trying so hard to understand. Keith wanted to kill himself? How could she not know that? There were quiet moments when his face went blank, but she never imagined there was anything introspective going on. She thought he was having little seizures. Coma flashbacks, she'd been calling them.

"About two weeks ago. He told Morgan, too."

"He told *Morgan*?" She put her arms around him and held him close. "Oh, Ben!"

At that moment, Ruth felt no sympathy for Keith, only fury. How dare he! How dare he do this to these darling children! To *her*. After all she'd done for him. She didn't even believe he was truly depressed. It's arrogance, she thought. That's what it is. Like he thinks this disabled life might be okay for somebody else, but not for a king of the alpha dogs like him.

Ruth thought of the one person she knew who had committed suicide. Steven Alvarez, a half-Cuban boy from college. He had dark lashes and pretty teeth, and couldn't have been more different from Keith. In fact, it was his timidity that attracted her to him. Most of the boys she dated were full of bravado in one way or another. There were a few quiet ones, but Steven seemed different, right from the start. It wasn't like she was in love with him or anything. She just thought it would be . . . *interesting* to sleep with such an odd, intense boy. Just like she thought it would be interesting to sleep with her French professor. Or the black guy from her psych class. Or the Persian boy with a gold tooth who directed all his comments to her breasts. Of course, most of the time, the ones she thought would be interesting were the most boring in bed. Not Steven, though. He wept while he was coming, and Ruth thought that was about the weirdest thing she had ever seen.

"Are you okay?" she had asked him.

"I'm fine."

"You're crying."

"Yes."

Ah, she thought, no wonder he was so disappointed when she wouldn't let him do it from behind—he didn't want her to see him crying. But she had never been able to get him to open up to her, and eventually became frustrated enough to move on. Shortly after that, she started seeing him around campus with a reclusive girl named Christina who everyone said was a lesbian. They were always walking together and speaking in hushed tones. Well, good for her, Ruth had thought. She got him to talk. The next thing she knew, though, she was awoken from a deep sleep by her roommate, who plopped down on her bed and announced that Steven Alvarez was dead. "Slit his wrists in the shower. Cops are all over the hallway if you want to see."

"Huh? What?"

Her roommate repeated the speech, but Ruth still had trouble processing what she heard. Steven Alvarez? Dead? She remembered kissing him. He had the sweetest breath. She put the pillow over her head and told her roommate to fuck off.

A few days later, Ruth saw an older woman in the hallway with striking green eyes rimmed in red. She looked at Ruth like she was trying to tell her something. Something terrible. For a second, Ruth felt the weight of the burden she bore and understood. Of course. It was Steven Alvarez's mother. She had come to collect his things.

Ruth gave Ben a tight squeeze and fought back tears. She wanted to cry. Not for Keith or even for the strange boy who killed himself, but for his mother. For Steven Alvarez's mother, who was expected to go on living in a world that had swallowed her son whole.

Ruth wanted to go home and shut the door of her room and be alone with her pain and her fury. Instead, she let Ben pick out a camera cell phone for Keith, and took her children out for frozen yogurt so the bitterness of what they needed to discuss could go down a little easier.

Daddy, she assured the kids, wasn't going to kill himself. It was one of those short circuits in his brain that had caused him to say something so terrible. And just to be safe, she would take him to a doctor who would talk to Daddy about what was bothering him, make him feel better. Nothing is going to happen to Daddy, nothing. Did they understand?

Ben said he did. Morgan used the tip of her spoon to grab a Gummi Bear off her yogurt and deposited it between her back teeth. She chewed it thoughtfully.

"He's not like other dads," she said.

A twisted lock of red hair hung over Morgan's face and she accidentally flicked it with yogurt. Ruth leaned over and pushed it back behind her ear. "I know, baby."

"Maybe we should let him."

"What?"

"I mean, if that's what he *wants.*"

Oh, right, Ruth thought. At her age, it's all about desire. "But I *want* it," Morgan would sometimes explain when Ruth denied one of her requests, as if that were argument enough.

"Honey, it's not like wanting Gummi Bears or to stay up past your bedtime. When someone wants to kill themselves, it means there's something not right in their brain."

"I guess."

I guess. The Swiss army knife of comebacks. A thousand and one uses. A way for nine-year-olds to agree without really agreeing.

"You'll understand better when you're older," Ruth said. "You finished?"

That night, while Morgan slept and Ben studied quietly in his room, Ruth spoke to Keith about her conversation with the children. He was defensive at first, annoyed that the children had betrayed his confidence by telling her. Then she asked him the question at the heart of it all.

"Did you mean it, Keith? Do you really want to kill yourself?"

He picked up the remote control from the nightstand. But he wasn't pretending to examine it, the way Ben did in the store. He was, she could tell, eager for their conversation to be over so he could watch TV.

"Sometimes," he said quietly. "It comes and goes. Sometimes I wonder what the point is. You know?"

"I think everyone feels that way sometimes."

"But I was supposed to be taking care of my family. Not the other way around."

He was having an unusually lucid moment. She didn't know whether that was good or bad. Sometimes she thought it would be best if the part of him she loved stayed dead and buried so she could just mourn and move on.

She sat down next to him on the bed and kissed his forehead. "It sucks, I know. But the kids love you. And they need you. They really do."

"And what about you?"

Ruth sighed and looked at the remote control. Suddenly, turning on the television didn't seem like such a bad idea. She swallowed hard against a lump in her throat.

"I need you, too," she lied.

"Remember that white nightgown? The one you bought for Aruba?"

Even his memory was sharp tonight. And yes, of course she remembered that nightgown. It hung right in the middle of her closet, reminding her daily of the life she used to have. She bought it for a trip they took right before his stroke. She looked glorious in it, she knew, and he made her wear it every night of that vacation, only to tear it off minutes later.

"I remember," she said.

"Can you put it on for me?"

"Keith . . ."

"I just want to see you in it."

She wanted to say no, but he looked at her so beseechingly. So she made a deal. She told him she would put it on if he agreed to go see Dr. O'Neill, a psychiatrist they knew.

Ruth went into her walk-in closet, which doubled as a dressing room. She took off her clothes, slipped into the sheer white negligee, and stared at the full-length mirror. Her nipples and pubic hair were softly visible through the diaphanous fabric, and the effect was dramatic. Virgin-whore, she remembered thinking when she bought it. Only with her body, the emphasis seemed to be on the latter. Maybe if my chest was smaller, she thought, looking at herself from the side.

She flipped her hair over her head and teased it with her fingers. She flipped it back and walked out to give Keith a show.

When she emerged from the closet, though, Keith's eyes were focused directly on the TV screen, and his face had that slack-jawed expression of mindless absorption.

"Here I am," she announced.

He glanced up, and she saw his eyes darken and narrow.

The sex look, she used to call it. But something on the television quickly distracted him. Ruth stood there for a moment, but he didn't look back. She turned and left the room.

Downstairs, Ruth took out her guitar and started plucking notes. She tried to remember the feel of Keith's hands on her body the last time she wore the nightgown for him. But the memory was gone, vanished, as if his very touch were swallowed by the vortex of his diminished mind. In its place was a scene she recalled as vividly as the conversation they just had. It was from the early days of their relationship, maybe only their second or third date. They were having dinner at a lovely restaurant on the water. Her entrée arrived and she could tell by looking at it that no heat was rising from the dish. Not wanting to seem fussy to this adorable man she was quickly falling for, Ruth surreptitiously touched the fish with her pinky. It was indeed cold, but she stuck in her fork and began eating as if it were delicious. Somehow, Keith picked up on the truth.

"Is that hot?" he asked.

"Not exactly. But it's fine."

At that moment, a busboy was walking by the table and Keith stopped him. "Can you get our waiter, please? The lady's fish is cold."

What impressed her at that moment was that there wasn't a touch of bravado in the action. He was a man who would take care of her as naturally as a shoot growing toward the sun. If I marry him, she thought, I'll be happy forever.

Tears burned at her eyes and she felt as if she merged with Steven Alvarez's mother, the pain tearing at her like it was trying to escape her body. She was at once inside herself and outside herself, seeing grief-stricken green eyes rimmed in red. She knew then that she shared a terrible bond with the dead boy's mother. It was the sisterhood of a loss so profound as to leave the mourner hollowed.

The ache found its way to her fingertips, as they plucked the strings of her guitar, and note by note, droplets of pain connected one to the other and a melody emerged, sounding like an incessant stream of sorrow. She played and played, and found herself strumming hard as the music peaked toward a heartbreaking crescendo.

The phone rang. Ruth stopped playing and noticed her face was wet with tears. She wanted to let the answering machine pick up but was afraid the ringing would disturb the family. She sniffed hard and grabbed it on the second ring.

"Hello?"

"Ruth? It's Paul."

Paul. Since the "breakup" he'd been calling roughly ever other day to make sure she was okay. Ruth knew what it all meant. He was still utterly conflicted about seeing her. He meant to break up, but couldn't quite let go. Fine, Ruth had thought. I'll just sit tight, pretend it's over. Then one day we'll find ourselves alone together and his pent-up passion will explode. We'll be right back where we started.

"Hi," she said. "What's going on?"

"Just wanted to make sure you're okay. I heard the private investigator might have a lead on who stole the rock."

Maddie had been keeping him apprised. "Yeah, we're supposed to have a meeting about it."

"You don't sound so good."

Ruth knew there was no surer way to Paul's bed than to play on his sympathies, and had even planned on making it part of her strategy. But not now. Not this. She didn't want to tell Paul about Keith's shameful admission to the children. And she certainly didn't feel like sharing the story about Steven Alvarez, or his mother and their shared pain. Ruth caressed the smooth surface of her guitar. Her sadness, like her songs, belonged to her.

"I'm fine."

"No you're not. Tell me what's wrong."

Ruth sighed, exasperated. This insistent appetite for unhappiness could wear on her nerves.

"Nothing, really. I was just in the middle of something. Can I call you back?"

"When? Tonight?"

She tsked. "I don't know, Paul. Maybe."

"Oh . . . uh, okay. I guess I'll call you tomorrow if I don't hear from you tonight."

He sounded hurt, but she was in no mood to coddle. "Fine. Whatever," she said. "I'll talk to you." Then she hung up the phone without saying good-bye.

Ruth started fingering the strings of her guitar again, but the feeling was gone. Her irritation with Paul had severed the connection with her grief.

Sometime later, when both children were asleep and Keith had finally dozed off under the flickering glow of David Letterman, Ruth turned off the lights and got ready for bed. As she brushed the tangles from her hair that her finger-teasing had created, she thought she heard a car pull up on her driveway. She opened the blinds to peer out. Sure enough, there was a sedan in her driveway with its headlights on. Curious, she watched and waited for something to happen. Maybe it's just someone looking for an address, she thought. Finally, the door opened and a man got out. He shut the door and leaned back against his car, looking up toward her window. It was Paul. For heaven's sake.

• • •

Ruth went into her closet and reached for her bathrobe but it wasn't on the hook where she normally kept it. Right, she remembered, it's in the wash. She grabbed the white wrap that matched her negligee, slipping it on as she hurried down the stairs.

"Paul," she said as she opened the front door and tiptoed onto the cold driveway in bare feet. "What are you doing here?"

The wind pushed open her light robe and it flew back like a cape. She fought the breeze to find the fabric and quickly wrapped it around her body, but it was too late. Paul had taken in the full effect of her sheer white negligee—dramatized by her erect nipples and long hair blowing in the wind—and looked positively stricken. Like a man awoken in the night by a hungry succubus he was never meant to see.

"I . . . I was worried about you. You sounded upset before."

"I *was* upset."

"About me?"

She shrugged. "No." She felt justified in inflicting some pain back at him for breaking it off with her. Or meaning to, anyway.

"Oh." He looked down. "I just thought you might need someone to talk to."

Ruth sighed. She thought about telling him to get lost, leave her the hell alone, but the pull was too strong. She didn't want to hurt this gentle, tortured man. Not really. "You want to come in for a minute? I'm freezing out here."

Inside, they sat at the kitchen table and she made them each a cup of herbal tea.

"I'm sorry if I disturbed you," he said, carefully sipping

the hot liquid. "I know it's late, but you sounded like you were crying before. I didn't know what else to do."

"It's okay. I was just working on a song. A sad song. Got carried away, I guess."

"That's marvelous. That you have an outlet like that, I mean."

She had never heard him use that word before and it made her smile. "Yeah," she said. "I guess it is . . . *marvelous.*"

"Would you play it for me? I'd love to hear it."

She usually didn't like to play a song for someone until she had completed it. But something softened her—the late hour, the aroma of the tea, his eyes—and she felt the need for an intimate connection. Not sexual, just genuine. At that moment, the idea of opening herself sounded liberating.

She put both hands on the table. "Okay," she said, rising, "come."

She led him to the den, where her guitar rested against the leather sofa. They sat side by side, but when she picked up her guitar, Ruth turned her body to face him. She closed her eyes for a moment, remembering the melody and the feeling. It came back in a torrent and she started to play. The notes filled her, and though she kept her eyes shut, she knew the power of her song filled the room. She could feel it in every cell. As she reached the dramatic crescendo, which would become the song's refrain, the lyric became clear to her. "I'll stop the hurting. I'll take your pain," she heard in her head. "Give the song to Daddy, baby. Give the song to Daddy."

She played the chorus again. Yes, it worked. Amid all the sorrow, there was something about that part of the melody that offered hope. She shivered as she strummed the last chord and opened her eyes. Paul looked as if he'd been hit by a train.

"Ruth," he began, "I . . . I don't know what to say." He put his hand to his forehead and looked down at the carpet and then back up at her. "Yes I do. I think—and this might sound crazy to you—but I think that came straight from God. Really. I could feel Him, here, in this room, while you played."

She put down her guitar. "That doesn't sound crazy," she said softly. At that moment, she wanted nothing more in the world than to be hugged. Simply hugged. She looked at him, and knew that he got it. And in fact, she saw him make the tiniest move forward and pull himself back. He clasped his hands in his lap.

"Do you want to talk about it?" he asked.

She knew that he meant the emotions that triggered the song. She hesitated for a moment, and then made the decision.

"There was this boy," she began, and proceeded to tell him everything. The sex, the tears, the suicide, the stupid roommate. She told him about Steven Alvarez's mother and how her pain made a home in Ruth's heart and never left. She told him how she could see her own loss reflected back in the eyes of the dead boy's mother. She told him how much she missed the husband she had loved. By the time Ruth finished, she was wracked with tears, and noticed Paul crying, too.

"Oh, Ruth, I am so sorry. So sorry!" Finally, he wrapped his arms around her and she let go completely, sobbing until she couldn't catch her breath.

He stroked her hair and her back, telling her over and over it was okay.

"It's *not* okay," she whispered when she finally caught her breath. "It's not."

"I wish there were something I could do for you," he said.

"Just hold me."

He pulled her closer and she became aware of something. Paul had an erection. Is this how it's going to be? she wondered. Are we going to make love now? It hadn't been her intent. Not today. And she wasn't sure she wanted to.

She laid her head on his chest and closed her eyes. She suddenly felt tired, very tired.

"I might fall asleep on you," she said.

He stretched himself out so that he was fully reclined on the sofa, with her on top of him. "That's okay," he said, stroking her hair. "Fall asleep if you want."

She felt herself dozing, but he was touching her too much for her to go completely under. He stroked her shoulder and the side of her body, grazing her breast. His hand slid down her back until it rested on her bottom. She felt him push his hips up toward her.

"Paul," she said, "what's going on here?"

"I should leave, right?"

She didn't want to move from that spot. She wanted to lay her head down and let the sleepiness come back while she listened to the steady thump of his heart. "No," she said, "don't go."

There was a pause and then: "I love you, Ruth."

"You do?"

"I do."

At that moment, Ruth felt utterly liberated. She had opened herself to him completely, held nothing back, and now he professed his love. Oh, what a glorious moment!

Her grief was supplanted with the thought that she could
be loved again as she once was. Forget sleep, she wanted to
take him inside her and hold him there until the rest of the
world disappeared. She would mount him and ride him
and love him and nothing could stop them. Nothing!

He loves me, she thought, as she unbuttoned his shirt and
started kissing his chest. "I love you, too," she whimpered.

"Wait," he said, grabbing her wrists.

She looked at his face. "Wait?"

"I *told* you. We can't do this anymore."

"What do you mean?"

He sat up and buttoned his shirt. "Friends. I just want us
to be friends, like I said."

"You've got to be kidding me. You tell me you love me,
you grind your hips into me—with a lump the size of Applewood Rock in your pants—and then you say you want
to be *friends*?"

He looked down, ashamed.

She reacted with disgust. "Oh, grow *up.* This isn't
Catholic school. You can't play these kinds of childish
games with me."

"I'm sorry," he said. "I don't mean to play games. I just
can't have a sexual relationship with you, no matter how I
feel."

"But I suppose you can have one with *Margie,*" she spat.

Then he blurted something he would, no doubt, later
regret. "Margie's not married," he said.

Silence. She looked at him, and he put his hands to his
mouth as if trying to take it back. Too late. Ruth felt an
angry tingling that started in her toes and intensified as it
traveled up her body. She stood, accidentally knocking
down her guitar. It made a hideous sound as it hit the floor,
but she ignored it.

"Get out of my house," she said.

"Ruth," he said, reaching for her arm.

She held up both hands like stop signs. "Don't touch me. Don't speak. Just get out. *Now.*"

"Can't we talk about this?"

She glared at him.

"Okay," he said. "I'm going."

She didn't move from that spot as she heard him walk toward the front door and shut it after himself. She listened to the sound of his car start and drive away. Ruth glanced toward the window and watched as his taillights disappeared into the darkness.

Chapter Sixteen

LISA

A few days later, Lisa's alarm went off at 5:05 A.M. and she awoke with a vague sense of uneasiness. Something wasn't quite right in her world. Whatever it was, she wanted to ignore it, drift back into her lovely dream, where Simon jumped from surface to surface in the kitchen, floor to table to countertop, reciting poetry as he went along. "How do I love thee?" the toddler cried as he flew through the air. "Let me count the ways." There was nothing about it that didn't astound Lisa. What jumping! What speaking! And where did he learn those poems? Had he been able to talk like that all along? Good heavens! Lisa swelled with pride. She had to be a wonderful mother to produce a child so miraculous.

Then she remembered. Mother. That's what was wrong. Her mother. Nancy was staying in the guest bedroom of their home while she completed the three-month outpatient treatment for substance abuse at one of Long Island's large medical centers. Lisa hadn't wanted her mother to come, but what choice did she have? Nancy had stopped drinking and was willing to check herself in. If Lisa turned her away, she'd have no place to go, and would most likely end up drunk and homeless. Lisa pictured her sleeping in a cardboard box somewhere in Grand Central Station. Or worse, walking the streets of the West Side half-naked, selling her body to lonely truck drivers more tempted by a bargain than youthful flesh.

Adam had thought it would be fine to put Nancy up in the empty white ranch house, but Lisa refused. Anything but that, she had said. The house was an almost holy refuge for her, and she would not allow Nancy to desecrate it. Besides, at least here, under the same roof, Lisa could keep half an eye on her.

Lisa hit the snooze alarm and rolled onto her side. She didn't want to think about her mother now. If she couldn't recapture her dream about Simon, at least she could think about her plans for the ranch house. Last week she had sanded down the oak cabinets in the kitchen, but couldn't come up with a plan for the décor. The room needed *something*. Didn't she have an idea last night as she dozed off? She could swear she'd had an inspiration that got her excited, but damn if she could remember it.

She sat up groggily and switched off the alarm. Tired as she was, Lisa would get dressed and go over there to work. Maybe the idea would come back to her.

Rising early to get in some time at the empty house before the children awoke was part of Lisa's routine. Even when she was making a racket with a hammer or, heaven help her, a power tool, the work had a meditative quality, which Lisa felt she needed for her mental health. Now, especially, with her mother there, the therapy was essential.

She glanced over at Adam, locked in the steady breathing of deep sleep. She rose quietly so as not to wake him and slipped into her work clothes. She brushed her teeth, splashed water on her face, and padded quietly downstairs. A quick cup of coffee and she'd be out the door.

When she reached the kitchen, Lisa noticed a sheet of yellow paper propped up against her coffeemaker. She picked it up and saw Nancy's distinctive print, all capital letters written on a slant.

L-

OOPS! SPILLED COFFEE ON ONE OF THE SOFA PILLOWS. THREW IT IN THE WASH. SEE? STILL HAVE A DRINKING PROBLEM. HA HA!

Lisa crumpled the note and threw it in the trash. Fine. Whatever. It's just a pillow, right?

She grabbed a filter from the cabinet and pulled the basket out of her coffeemaker, only to discover it was full of Nancy's wet grounds from the night before. Accidentally spilled coffee was one thing, but not even bothering to throw out her own garbage was another. It was just so like her mother, Lisa thought, dumping out the wet mess and rinsing the cone-shaped plastic. After measuring out her coffee, she suddenly remembered that she had left a load of white clothes in the washing machine, planning to run it this morning. Had her mother thought to take out the clothes before tossing in the slipcover from the pillow?

On her way to the laundry room to survey the damage, Lisa glanced into the living room to see which throw pillow was missing. The red one. Damn.

She opened the white metal door of the washing machine and peered inside. Sure enough, her family's white clothes—now damp and pink—shared the space with the bright red fabric of the pillow. But there was something else going on inside that cold drum. Pieces of something crumbly and yellowish were littered everywhere. Lisa picked up one of the spongy morsels and squeezed it between her fingers. Then she realized what it was. In addition to the slipcover, her mother had put the pillow's synthetic foam body into the washing machine and it had disintegrated.

Lisa growled and stamped her foot. Those tiny shreds had probably clogged the drain, and she'd have to call in the plumber before running another wash. She poured some Clorox and a small amount of detergent into the slop sink and filled it with hot water. She would try to bleach out the clothes right away to see if she could get the pink out. She sighed heavily. So much for getting to the empty white ranch house this morning. It would take her the better part of an hour to clean up the mess her mother had created.

By the time she finally made it back to the kitchen, Nancy was sitting at the table drinking the coffee Lisa had made. Or so she thought. Lisa pulled out the carafe and poured herself a cup without saying good morning. She couldn't bring herself to look her mother in the face, let alone speak to her.

The coffee looked especially black in Lisa's cup, so she tipped in more than her usual amount of milk, but it didn't seem to lighten.

"Huh?" Lisa said. "Why is this so dark? I must have used too much."

"You didn't put in *enough*," Nancy said. "It was like dishwater. I spilled it out and made another pot."

"You spilled it . . ." Lisa stopped herself. She wanted to scream, stamp her feet, spill hot coffee on her mother's head, *something*. Instead, she closed her eyes and counted to ten. Then she slowly poured the muddy brew from her cup down the drain. She took a deep breath.

"Mother," she began. "I'm going to buy a second coffeepot today so we can each make our own from now on."

Nancy shrugged.

"But really, Mom, you could have just poured mine into a cup and left it for me. You didn't have to spill it out."

"It was undrinkable."

"To *you.*"

"So shoot me. I was just trying to help."

Lisa massaged the back of her own neck. "Do me a favor and don't do me any favors, okay? Thanks to you, all my white clothes turned *pink.*"

"What do you mean?"

"Never mind. I'm going into the shower." Lisa turned and left the room.

"How come you never let me do anything to help you?" Nancy shouted after her.

Lisa had a hectic morning schedule. After getting the children off to school, she needed to drive Nancy to the medical center before heading over to Maddie's house for a committee meeting. The private investigator had some big news to share and was meeting them there. Plus, Lisa was hoping she would have time to give Simon a quick bath before heading out. Adam was always after her to let Bonnie, the housekeeper, do such things. "That's what we pay her for," he had said. But Lisa insisted that she didn't have children just to let someone else raise them. She could bathe her own kids, thank you.

Lisa had a full head of lather going in the shower when the water turned tepid and the pressure went soft. "Idiot," she said, meaning her mother, who she figured must have gone into the shower at the same time, creating competition for hot water. Lisa turned the chrome lever closer to the red *H.* That worked for a few seconds, until her mother obviously turned *her* water hotter. Exasperated, Lisa finished rinsing her hair under the cold water, got out and toweled herself off.

Afterward, Lisa woke Sarah and the twins, made their lunches for school, and got breakfast started. She went back upstairs and admonished the twins, who were playing some sort of game that involved licking the bottom of their feet and kicking each other, instead of getting dressed.

She went to see if Simon was awake but when she checked his bed, it was empty.

"Simon!" she called. "Simon! Where are you?"

"Wobee ah bah," she heard, and suspected it was coming from the bathroom. When she walked into the room, she saw him, all alone, sitting in a tub of water. Nancy came rushing into the room with a bath towel.

"I'm giving him a bath," Nancy said.

"I can see that."

"I know you're mad at me for leaving him alone. But I just ran out for a second to find a towel."

No, she wanted to say, I'm mad at you for being an incompetent dolt without the sense to wait until a person's out of the shower before running the bath.

Lisa folded her arms. "Why didn't you just *ask* me?"

"You would have said no. You never let me help you."

"Because you screw everything up!"

"How can I screw up giving a kid a bath? No offense, but it's not exactly rocket science."

"Just go get dressed," Lisa said. "We have to leave soon."

Later, as she drove her mother to the medical center, Lisa was quiet, pretending to be in a pensive mood so she wouldn't have to get into a conversation that would only wind up irritating her more.

Nancy broke the silence. "They need another payment today," she said, referring to her treatment program. "Can I borrow your credit card again?"

"I'll just go in with you."

"Why? You let me borrow it last time."

Lisa glanced at the clock on the dashboard. "I have a few minutes today."

"You treat me like a child."

You act like one, Lisa thought, but kept it to herself. What good would it do to start an argument?

When she reached the building, Lisa parked and got out of the van with her mother. On their way inside, Nancy asked Lisa if she could pick her up later.

"Today? I thought Chris was getting you." Chris McNatt, Nancy's current beau, lived thirty minutes away in Queens, and drove out often to visit her.

"He was supposed to. His brother needs the car."

"He lets his brother borrow the car?" Lisa tried to picture Chris as the swell big brother, handing over the keys to his Camaro, but couldn't get an image.

"Other way around. It's his brother's car. Chris doesn't have one."

Ah, Lisa thought, now that makes sense. Nancy had claimed Chris was a "working studio musician," but he had told Lisa that he worked part-time at a Sam Ash music store, and she figured it was most likely his only source of income.

"What about that Honda you two tooled around in all weekend?"

"Rental. He does that sometimes on weekends. Says it's still cheaper than owning. So can you do it? Otherwise I need to take a cab."

"I'll work it into my schedule."

Lisa arrived at Maddie's house a few minutes late, but still ahead of Ruth. She was curious to hear what the private investigator had to say, and wanted to see for herself if he was really as hypersensitive as Maddie had claimed.

When introduced to Jerry Murphy in Maddie's living room, Lisa couldn't help smiling. Though toweringly tall, he bore a remarkable resemblance to Mark Hamill from *Star Wars*. This gave him the look of an overgrown boy who had sprouted like a marsh weed before puberty had a chance to catch up and slow him down. She imagined him skulking around the halls of his high school, head down, shoulders hunched, trying to ignore taunts about the weather up there. It was probably then that he started wearing his heart on his sleeve, so that the world would know that though as tall as a man, he was merely a suffering child. Ironically, he kept this boyish face so that now, as a man, it was his puckishness that set him apart. Lisa looked at the pained grimace he wore to illustrate his distress, and couldn't help feeling a bit of tenderness. He seemed too fragile for this unkind world.

"We'll wait for Ruth before getting started," Maddie announced.

"Can you give us just a little hint, Jerry?" Lisa asked. She said it lightly, but he responded with gravity.

"I'd prefer to give everyone the news at once," he said.

Like a movie detective, Lisa thought, but bit her tongue. She'd tread carefully.

The doorbell rang and Maddie went to answer it. Lisa heard Ruth's raspy voice bellow from the hallway, "I hope he has some good news. I could use it. I'm ready to bite someone's head off today."

"Jerry, I'd like to introduce you to someone," Maddie said as she entered the room trailing behind Ruth, who had quickly marched up behind him.

Jerry, whose back was still turned, took a step backward and landed his heel hard on Ruth's foot.

"Ow!" she cried. "Look where you're stepping!"

"I'm sorry. I didn't see you."

"Big oaf."

"I said I'm sorry."

Ruth looked up at his face. "Christ, I've been attacked by the Jolly Green Jedi."

"All right," Maddie said. "Take it easy, Ruth. It was an accident."

Ruth fell heavily into a chair and rubbed her foot. "Fine. An accident."

"You okay?" Lisa asked her.

Ruth slipped off her shoe and wiggled her toes. "I'll be okay when I find out who stole that damned rock. Let's just get on with it." She replaced her shoe.

"I'm not getting on with *anything*," Jerry said. "Not till she apologizes."

Ruth looked at him. *"Me?"*

"For the Jolly Green Giant remark."

"I said Jolly Green *Jedi*."

"And that makes it okay?"

"Well, you *do* look like him. And you are, you know, tall."

"Ruth . . ." Maddie chided.

"Okay, okay. I'm sorry. I'm sorry I called you the Jolly Green Jedi. Now can we find out who stole Applewood Rock?"

Jerry sat down opposite Ruth and scratched a crumb off his knee. "I don't think she meant it."

"Oh, for God's sake." Ruth rolled her eyes.

"I have feelings, you know," Jerry said. "You think it's easy walking around looking like this?" He stood up for illustration and then sat back down again, deflated.

"Oh, Jerry," Maddie offered consolingly, "don't say that. You're a very attractive man." She turned to the others. "Isn't he an attractive man?"

"And tall," Ruth added. "Very, very tall."

Maddie gave her a dirty look.

"What did I say?" Ruth complained. "Who wouldn't want to be tall? Tall is good."

Jerry sighed heavily. "Not when surveillance is part of your job. I don't exactly blend in."

"Nonsense," Ruth said. "If you were standing in a crowded room I probably wouldn't even notice you."

Maddie and Lisa exchanged looks, anticipating a bad reaction to their friend's last remark, but Jerry seemed comforted by it.

"Really? You wouldn't notice me?"

"Not for a second. Wouldn't even look your way."

"Gee, thanks."

"In fact, if someone pointed you out and said, 'Doesn't that tall guy look like—' "

"Okay," Maddie interrupted. "I think we get the picture. Let's move on. Who wants coffee?"

After taking orders, she left the room and Ruth leaned in toward Jerry. "You know," she said, "I know someone who literally *died* for *Columbo.*"

"That's interesting," he said dismissively.

"Really, this guy gave his life for a TV show."

"Maybe we should talk about something else," Lisa offered.

"Why?" Ruth asked. "This is a hilarious story. You'll love it."

"I just don't see what it has to do with *me,*" Jerry said.

"Columbo's a detective, *you're* a detective. Get it?"

"I'm a private investigator."

"Whatever. The point is, this guy wanted to watch *Columbo* so badly he climbed onto his roof to fix the antenna *in an electrical storm.* Can you imagine?"

Jerry shrugged.

"It wasn't the lightning that got him. He *fell* off the *roof!*" Ruth slapped her thigh and grinned hugely to facilitate a reaction.

Lisa smiled meekly.

"I don't think that's funny at all," Jerry said.

Ruth pouted. "You guys have no sense of humor."

Lisa rose and announced that she would go see if Maddie needed any help in the kitchen.

"I'm worried about Ruth," Lisa said as she helped Maddie load cups of steaming coffee onto a tray. "She's been so strange since . . . well . . ."

"Since Paul broke up with her," Maddie offered.

Lisa looked around the room. She had real concerns about Ruth, yet felt uncomfortable talking about her. She didn't want to betray her friend's trust.

"What else can I do here?" she asked.

Maddie gave Lisa a box of assorted cookies to arrange on a plate, while she opened and closed cabinet doors looking for sweetener.

"About Ruth," Lisa said. "You don't think . . . I mean, she just seems so testy with the private investigator. It makes me wonder . . ."

Maddie turned to face her. "You think Ruth stole Applewood Rock?"

Lisa admired Maddie's directness, and imagined that she

had probably been a very good lawyer. A certain fearless-ness, she thought, was essential in that profession.

"Crazy idea, right?"

Maddie shrugged. "I don't know. Why would she?"

"Maybe she thought people would assume it was Suzanne and it backfired on her."

Maddie took a deep breath and picked up the heavy tray. "Nothing would surprise me."

"Your ankle," Lisa reminded. "Let me carry that."

"I can manage," Maddie said. "Let's go find out about that rock."

"Why don't you have a seat?" Jerry said to Maddie after the coffees were distributed. "I'd like to get started."

Maddie sat on the sofa next to Lisa. Ruth remained in the adjacent armchair.

"First off," Jerry began, "I have a source at the second precinct who shared some key evidence."

The women collectively leaned forward.

"Do you mind if I open this window?" Jerry asked Maddie. "It's a little warm in here."

"It might not stay open, but go right ahead," Maddie told him.

"It seems," he continued as he pulled open the sash, "that there were wheel tracks leading across the field from the spot where the rock was to the very place the Ryder truck had been spotted. The tracks appeared to be those of a hand truck or dolly—just the type of thing someone would need to move the boulder. This suggests very strongly that the driver of the truck was involved in the theft."

"Cut to the chase, Sherlock," Ruth interrupted. "Whose truck was it?"

"You know," Jerry complained, "if you insist on being rude I'm not going to continue."

"Put a sock in it, Ruth," Maddie said before turning to the private investigator. "Go on, Jerry," Maddie said gently. "I promise Ruth won't interrupt again."

Lisa looked over at her friend in the side chair, sitting with her arms folded across her chest. Poor Ruth, she thought. If she had anything to do with this theft, things will go from bad to worse for her. News like this always finds a way to leak and spread. Her reputation, already shaky, will be shot. She'll get booted from the PTA. Suzanne would probably wind up heading the committee herself. And Paul. Paul would never speak to her again.

"I won't say another word," Ruth promised.

"Okay," Jerry continued. "The truck, as you know, was a rental." He patted the pockets of his sports jacket as if looking for something. "It's not easy to get a rental car company to release information, which is why it's taken me so long to get to this point. But I did find out whose credit card account the truck rental was charged to."

"You did?" Maddie said, excited. "You found out?"

Jerry's eyes smiled but his mouth stayed fixed. "I did," he said. "But you have to keep in mind that sometimes credit cards are used by persons other than the account holders. So just because I know who it was charged to, doesn't mean I know who the driver was. In fact, I interrogated the Ryder agent who rented out the truck, and he intimated that the driver was not the credit card holder."

"A stolen card?" Lisa asked.

"Perhaps," Jerry said. "But more likely it was borrowed. If it was stolen, the card would have been reported missing. It was not."

Lisa tried to read Ruth's expression. This did not look

good for her. If she had hired people to steal the rock, it's likely that she would have loaned them her credit card for the job. But what was that expression on Ruth's face? She looked just as eager for the information as the rest of them. Maybe she was wrong. Lisa crossed her fingers and hoped that she was.

Jerry Murphy extracted a folded sheet of paper from his breast pocket and opened it. "It was a Visa card account in the name of two individuals."

The room went graveyard quiet as the women sat stone-still, holding their breath for what he was about to reveal. A strong wind rustled the leaves of a tree just outside and then, *thwump*! The window behind him slammed shut, startling everyone. He opened it again and then turned to look at the group.

"It was a Visa card account in the name of two individuals," he repeated. "The Ryder van parked near the North Applewood Elementary School on the day the rock was reported stolen was rented on the account of Lisa and Adam Slotnick."

Chapter Seventeen

I was only trying to help!" Nancy screamed from the parking lot of the Plainview Residence Inn.

Lisa inched the van forward and considered ignoring her completely, but something inside her needed to get out. So she shifted into park and opened the door. Breathing through her nose in short bursts like an angry bull, she stepped out and stood facing her mother. But when she opened her mouth to speak, nothing emerged but a rumbling growl. She snorted twice more, stamped her foot, got back into the van, and drove away.

She had been no less furious when she left Maddie's house earlier in the day after learning that Applewood Rock was stolen by someone driving a Ryder truck rented on her credit card. Connecting the dots posed no challenge. Lisa realized the theft occurred on the same day Nancy's last payment was due for her treatment. Lisa had been in a hurry to get to the school for the PTA vote, and so had loaned her credit card to Nancy, who must have made prior arrangements to meet Chris and pass him the card so that he could carry out their idiotic plans.

What were they thinking! And why couldn't they just mind their own business? Well, one thing was for damn sure: it wasn't going to happen again. Lisa would get her mother the hell out of her house. And wouldn't waste a second doing it.

She drove straight home from the meeting and called a local hotel that specialized in extended stays. She made her mother a reservation for the duration of her treatment. Then she packed up Nancy's things and took them to the hotel. This way, she could pick her up after today's treatment, drop her off, and be done with her.

When she got into her van, Lisa slipped one of her Aretha Franklin CDs into the stereo and turned the volume up until the space filled with the glory and the power of the queen of soul asking for a little bit of R-E-S-P-E-C-T. Lisa wanted to sing along. She opened her mouth and drew a large breath, trying to fill her lungs with the kind of gusto she'd need to match Aretha's passion. But she didn't know how to find the place inside herself where such raw emotion dwelled, and exhaled, deflated. With Aretha, music came from somewhere so deep within that its release was, well, the only word Lisa could think of was "orgasmic." But it was way more intimate than sex. With sex, you could close your eyes and go away. To sing like Aretha, you had to put it all there on the outside. Lisa wondered if such liberation was even possible.

She was almost home and still listening to the CD when track nine came on. It was the song "Think," and as Aretha bellowed the word "freedom" louder and louder, Lisa felt compelled to do *something.* She pulled over to the side of

Deepdale Road. She wanted to sing along, but couldn't. She wanted to switch off the stereo, but wouldn't. She wanted to turn down that long driveway toward home, but thought she'd wind up doing something destructive if she did. Lisa felt utterly stuck, like she was locked in place by a parking brake and couldn't find the release lever. She looked out the passenger side window and stared at the YIELD sign she had seen a million times but never up close. That yellow, she thought, picturing the kitchen in the white ranch house, that's what I need. She pulled back onto the road and turned her car around. She drove straight to Home Depot, where she bought five gallons of Sundrenched Yellow in a gloss finish, which she knew was completely excessive. She didn't need such a blindingly bright color and she certainly didn't need five gallons. But it felt like freedom.

Lisa was so excited to get to work with the new paint she didn't even go home to change. She went straight to the empty white ranch house. She set one of the cans on the kitchen counter and pried off the lid with a screwdriver. She stared into the brilliant yellow liquid and smiled for the first time that day. She closed her eyes and could swear she remembered finger painting with just such a color. How old could she have been? Three? Two? It seemed like one of those primal, prelanguage memories. Or maybe it never even really happened. Maybe it was something her mind just invented. No matter. This was going to be more fun than finger painting ever was.

Lisa stirred the paint with the wooden stick Home Depot provides for free if you remember to ask for it. She pulled it out of the can and held it above, watching the paint slide from the stirrer to the can in a thin, elegant line. She wiped the stirrer off and set it down on the lid. Then she readied herself for what she thought was the most pleasurable part of any painting job: watching the color pour from the can into the paint tray. Every color looked luxurious as it pooled within the well for the first time, but this one had an especially sumptuous quality to it. Like Aretha's voice.

Lisa pushed her napped roller into the color, then back and forth along the ridged ramp. She went to work on the wall opposite the cabinets, not bothering to do any taping to protect the ceiling or the woodwork. What the hell, she thought, as she rolled right up the wall, past the crown molding and onto the ceiling, I'll do the whole damn room. And she did. She worked for hours, quickly and messily covering every inch of wall and ceiling, finishing one paint can and opening another. At one point, she accidentally dripped a small puddle of paint onto one of the oak cabinets, and decided she'd paint those yellow, too. She knew they should have been primed first, but didn't want anything to slow her down. She took out a large brush and stroked up and down, up and down, covering the cabinets in glossy yellow, inside and out.

By the time she paused to look at her watch, she realized she would have just enough time to go home and get cleaned up before getting the children off the bus. She threw the brushes and roller into the sink, then took a step toward the counter where the paint can rested. But she forgot that she had moved the tray to the floor when she was working on the baseboard molding, and accidentally stepped on it, tipping it over and spilling the dense liquid color all over the floor. What the hell, she thought. I'll paint the linoleum, too. She took the roller out of the sink and moved it back and forth across the puddle on the floor. She backed up as she painted, and didn't stop until she had reached the floor saddle that separated the kitchen from the living room. She stood, holding the roller in her hand, and surveyed her creation. Bright, blinding yellow everywhere, like looking into the sun. Just then, Lisa thought she heard the hiss of air brakes and glanced at her watch. The kids! She ran out the door and down the driveway, reaching the road just as their school bus pulled up.

Sarah was the first one off and stared at her mother, shocked. "Mom, what happened to you?"

Lisa looked down at her clothing and realized she was covered in yellow paint. Not only that, but she still held the dripping yellow roller. She slapped her own face in surprise.

"Now your *cheek* is all yellow," Sarah said.

"Hey, Big Bird!" a boy shouted from the bus window. "Can you tell me how to get to Sesame Street?" He squealed with laughter.

Sarah turned to face him. "Shut up, Brandon!" She turned back to Lisa, tilting her head back to look at her from beneath her too-long bangs. "Are you okay, Mom? How come you're all covered in paint?"

"I was working on the house. Lost track of the time."

Austin and Henry rushed past their mother, oblivious to her appearance.

"Did you get the big chocolate chips?" Henry shouted back to her, referring to his favorite after-school snack.

"Not yet."

"But you said."

Lisa shrugged. "Tomorrow. I promise."

By the time Lisa got Sarah started on her homework, made a snack for the twins, and checked in on Simon, she had only half an hour to shower, change, and get to the medical center to pick up her mother. As she quickly washed her hair and watched the yellowish water run down the drain, she paused and thought, why am I rushing? Let her wait for me.

So Lisa decided she'd take the time to condition her hair. As she worked the milky cream into her tresses, she pictured her mother standing at the curb muttering curses under her breath. When she finished showering, Lisa toweled herself off slowly, then carefully lotioned her body and clipped her toenails. As she dressed, she heard Simon stir and went in to comfort him.

"I'm here. I'll bring him down," she whispered into the monitor before shutting it off. She knew Bonnie listened for him in the kitchen, and didn't want her coming in and interrupting.

Lisa climbed into bed with Simon and wrapped him in her arms. She took a good, long sniff off the top of his head.

"You have a good nap, sweetie?"

He cooed, and Lisa thought she heard him make a "mm" sound, like he was going to say "mama."

"That's right, baby. Mommy's here. Can you say 'Mommy'? Mah-*mee*."

Simon opened his eyes wide and looked straight at her as he uttered a string of nonsense syllables intoned as if they were a perfectly understandable sentence.

"Well, okay then." Lisa smiled, pretending she understood.

The proximity to Simon very nearly lifted Lisa out of her funk. By the time she got back in her van and headed for the medical center, though, the anger was stronger than ever. What a mess her mother had created for her. What a goddamn mess. Pretty soon, everyone in the community would be talking about Lisa Slotnick, the quiet little woman who stole Applewood Rock. She had worked so hard to create the only kind of life she could feel comfortable with, the kind where she participated quietly from the sidelines, attracting as little attention to herself as she could. And now her meddling mother had pushed her right in front of the klieg lights with banners waving and trumpets blaring. Fool. Crazy, stupid, annoying, can't-mind-her-own-business *fool*.

If only I'd stuck to my guns and not let her stay with us, Lisa thought. She gripped her steering wheel hard and growled. At least one thing was for sure, she consoled herself. I'll never let her set foot in my house again. Never.

As Lisa drove into the circle where she knew her mother would be waiting for her, she noticed that the car in front of her was a taxi. Then she had a terrible thought. She was almost a half hour late. What if her mother had got tired of waiting and called a cab to pick her up? What if she had already been picked up and was speeding her way toward Lisa's house right now?

No! Lisa wanted to scream. She's not going back to my house. She's *not*. The taxi in front of her stopped, and Lisa saw her mother run out from beneath the awning toward it. Oh, she *did* call a cab! And it's right in front of me! Lisa smashed her fist into her horn to get her mother's attention, but the crazy old bird ignored her. She honked again as her mother opened the door of the cab. Frantic, Lisa pulled away from the curb as fast as she could, stopping short in front of the taxi. She opened the door and got out.

"Mother! What are you *doing*?"

Nancy stepped out of the cab. "I thought you weren't coming."

Lisa sighed. "Get in."

"Sorry," Nancy said to the cabdriver, leaning toward the window so he could see her cleavage. Probably her idea of compensating him for his trouble, Lisa thought. "My daughter." Nancy pointed at Lisa with her thumb.

"Why were you taking a cab?" Lisa asked as her mother belted herself in.

"Figured you forgot about me."

"Believe me," Lisa said, "that wasn't going to happen."

"Why are you so late?"

Lisa gritted her teeth and glared at her mother before turning her eyes back to the road. "Why do you insist on ruining my life?"

"Oh, jeez, what'd I do now? Use the wrong laundry detergent?"

Lisa paused before responding. She wanted to give her mother time to get nervous about the shoe she was about to drop. When she stopped at the traffic light, she turned to look at Nancy. "Make any unauthorized credit card charges lately?"

Nancy tsked, as if Lisa were merely bringing up another niggling complaint. "I can explain that. Chris had to pick up an amp some guy was giving him and we needed a truck. I figured you wouldn't mind. I meant to tell you."

"Uh-huh."

"I'm sorry. Chris said he'd pay you back. Honest."

"Oh, of course. I'd never *question* your honesty. You and Chris being such upstanding citizens and all."

"What are you getting at?" Nancy asked.

Lisa took her eyes off the road to look hard at Nancy, who seemed to be losing color as they spoke. She drove on in silence, passing right by the entrance to the highway she normally took home.

"Where are you going?" Nancy asked, looking back at the turn they missed. "Are we making a stop somewhere?"

Lisa said nothing.

"Baby?" Nancy said. "What's going on?"

Lisa cleared her throat. "Who stole Applewood Rock, Mom?"

Nancy put her head down against the dashboard. "Shit."

"Yeah. Shit."

Nancy sat back and looked up at the ceiling. "Do you know *why* we did it?"

"Oh, please enlighten me. Because for the life of me, I can't figure out why on earth you would do something so completely moronic."

"I was trying to help."

"God, here we go again."

"Really, baby. You gotta believe me. That whole movie thing and building the stadium seemed so important to you. And you were so worried that it would get voted down. So I got this great idea. I figured if somebody stole the rock, there'd be nothing standing in your way. And who would get hurt? No one, that's who. I thought it was a neat idea. Still do." Nancy folded her arms for emphasis. "Am I in trouble? I mean, with the police or anything?"

"Not yet. They don't even know it was you."

Nancy sighed, relieved. "Thank God."

"But they will. Unless . . ."

"Unless what?"

"Here's the deal. One, you're not staying with me anymore. I checked you into a hotel. All your stuff is there already. And two—"

"Wait," Nancy interrupted. "What do you mean you checked me into a hotel?"

"And two," Lisa continued, "you and Chris are going to

sneak in during the night and put the rock back. Otherwise, I'm going to the police. Got it?"

On Friday night, after a busy week for both of them, Lisa and Adam rented a DVD so the two of them could just relax on the couch and unwind after the children went to bed. An hour into the movie, though, Adam dozed off. Lisa watched the rest of it alone, happy to let her husband get some needed sleep, content just to have him near.

As the credits rolled, Lisa thought she heard a knock on the front door and looked at her watch. It was after eleven.

"Who is it?" she asked, pressing the intercom button.

"It's Mom," she heard, followed by a garbled sentence starting with "I need" and ending with "the rock." Apparently, her mother had let her finger slip off the button while she spoke. Lisa felt a tightening in her chest. Was her mother drunk, or was it just her normal ineptitude? She took a deep breath and opened the door.

"Hi, baby," Nancy said.

Lisa leaned in toward her mother and took a sniff. Nothing. She looked at her eyes. Clear as the moonlight. She sighed, relieved, then remembered that she was supposed to be angry. She had made it quite plain that her mother wasn't allowed back. "What are you doing here?"

"We're returning the rock tonight, but we need to borrow your van. Can't fit a big boulder like that in a little Camaro."

Lisa glanced past her mother, where the sports car was idling in the driveway. She noticed a silvery contraption tied to the roof.

"What is that?" Lisa said, pointing to it.

Nancy turned to see what she meant. "On top? It's Keith's walker."

"Keith? Keith Moss? Why do you have his walker?"

"Because I have Keith. He's in the car."

"Keith is in the car? Why?"

"We kind of have to steal the rock back from where Chris left it, and we thought it might be a good idea to have a lawyer along."

Lisa closed her eyes for a second, buying time to take that in. "What do you mean you have to steal the rock back?"

"After Chris took it, he didn't know what to do with it. So he just left it in someone's yard. They already had a rock garden with giant boulders, and he figured they wouldn't notice one more."

Lisa narrowed her eyes. "Where?"

"Near here."

Lisa pictured the ornate landscaping of her neighbors, Donna and Howie Fishbein. "How near?"

"Just up the road, I think."

Lisa rubbed the bridge of her nose. "And you thought Keith Moss could help you?"

"He's a lawyer. Might come in handy. You know, just in case."

"*Used* to be a lawyer," Lisa corrected. Now he can't even tie his own shoelaces, she wanted to add. She glanced at the Camaro again. "How did the three of you fit in that car?"

"I sat on Keith's lap."

"You sat on his lap? The man is half paralyzed, Mom."

"Right! He hardly knew I was there." She giggled. "He even told me I felt as light as a feather."

Lisa shook her head.

"So how about it?" Nancy continued. "Can I borrow

your keys? And that hand truck you keep at the ranch house?"

Lisa paused, trying to envision Nancy, Chris, and Keith pulling this off successfully. But the only picture she could get was that scene from the Three Stooges movie where the guy in the middle has a long two-by-four on his shoulder and keeps knocking everybody on the head as he turns from one side to the other.

"Let me get my shoes," she said. "I'll drive."

While Lisa sat behind the wheel waiting for Chris to load everything into the van—including Keith's walker, the hand truck, and some wood planks he said they'd use as a ramp—she asked Keith if she could borrow his cell phone, as she had forgotten hers.

"Who are you calling?" Nancy asked.

"Ruth," Lisa said as she punched in the numbers. "I think she should know what her husband is up to."

Nancy folded her arms and pouted. "God, it's like having your grandmother drive you to the prom."

"*Someone* has to be the grown-up here. Hello, Ruth?"

Lisa had expected Ruth to demand that they drop Keith off at home immediately. But when Lisa explained the purpose of their trip, Ruth insisted on coming along.

"Swing by and get me," she said. "I'm not letting you do this alone."

"I'm not alone."

"Of course not, you've got Moe, Larry, and Shep."

Lisa smiled. The more she knew this woman the more she loved her.

By the time they reached Ruth's, she was waiting outside for them. She opened the back door of the van and slid in behind Lisa, slamming it shut behind her.

"You need to pick up Maddie," she said.

"Maddie?"

"I called. She's expecting us. I figured it wouldn't hurt to have a lawyer along."

"*I'm* a lawyer," Keith protested.

"Yes, dear, but you'll probably be the first one arrested," his wife said affectionately.

Keith smiled proudly.

When they got to Maddie's house, they saw that she wasn't alone.

"Figured you wouldn't mind if Beryl came along," Maddie said as she scooted into the third row of seats.

"I wasn't going to miss all the fun," Beryl added, moving in beside her.

"Hey, Maddie," Keith said, "what do you call a thousand lawyers at the bottom of the ocean?"

"A good start," Beryl interrupted. "Now let's get moving. Where's that rock we need to pick up?"

"I left it on Deepdale Road," Chris said. "In someone's garden."

"Deepdale Road?" Ruth asked, alarmed.

"Guess whose house," Lisa said as she backed out of Maddie's driveway.

Ruth gasped. "Oh, don't tell me . . ."

Lisa shifted into drive. "Donna Fishbein," she said. "Can you believe it? We have to steal the rock back from Donna Fishbein."

As she approached the front of the Fishbeins' house, Lisa shut off the headlights and slowed the van to a quiet stop. The night was pitch-black, and she couldn't even make out the showy wrought-iron gate framing the driveway. She told Nancy to hand her the flashlight from the glove compartment.

"How heavy is the rock?" she asked Chris.

"Pretty damn heavy."

"Okay," she said. "Listen up. Mother and Keith, you two stay in the car as lookouts. The rest of us are going to get the rock and hoist it onto the hand truck."

"What about Maddie?" Nancy asked. "She's still in a cast. Shouldn't she stay in the car, too?"

"I'll be fine," Maddie said. "It's a walking cast. At this point, it barely cramps my style."

The Fishbeins' rock garden was close to the road and easy to find. But when Lisa shone her flashlight over the boulders, she found it impossible to tell which one was Applewood Rock.

"Chris," she whispered as he approached with the hand truck, "which one is it?"

He stared for a moment and scratched his chin. "That one," he said, pointing to the largest boulder.

"Are you sure?" Maddie asked. "That looks awfully big."

"I'm sure. I remember my friend Vin, I had my friend Vin with me, said it was the biggest rock here."

"On Vin's word then," Ruth said, "let's move that rock."

Chris took a small gardening shovel out of his back pocket and dug a trench around one side of the rock. "I have to be able to get the toe plate part of the hand truck underneath it," he explained as he worked. "Then you guys can push up on it while I tilt the truck back. That's the way I did it with Vin."

"Looks pretty heavy," Beryl said.

"Wasn't easy getting it here," Chris whispered. "There." He stood. "Now I'll try to wedge in the toe plate." He wheeled over the truck and pointed the front into the soil. He shimmied it from side to side, working it beneath the rock. "I think all of you should get on the other side and push on it while I tilt the truck back."

Ruth, Maddie, Lisa, and Beryl knelt before Applewood Rock like an altar.

"On three," Lisa said. "One, two, *three!*"

The women grunted in unison as they tried to move the rock, but it wouldn't budge.

"This thing is heavy," Ruth said.

"Are you sure you have the right rock?" Maddie asked.

"I'm sure," Chris said. "Let's move the smaller rocks in front out of the way and dig a trench all the way around."

The women got to work moving rocks out of the way while Chris nosed the pointy end of his shovel into the dirt and dug.

"Jeez," he said. "This thing is really wedged in."

"A flashlight!" Ruth gasped, pointing in the distance. "Run!"

They all stood and stepped in the direction of the van.

"Where are you going?" said the voice behind the flashlight. "It's me, Nancy."

"You scared the shit out of us, Nance," Chris said.

"Sorry," she whispered. "But I didn't want to shout out or anything. There's something you guys gotta see."

"What is it?" Ruth asked.

"Me and Keith got bored and took a walk around the property."

"Are you crazy!" Lisa admonished.

"Listen," Nancy continued, "you gotta come see this. They have an indoor pool surrounded by glass. If you stand behind the bushes you can see *everything* and they can't see you!"

"What is there to see?" Beryl asked. "Skinny-dipping?"

"*Somebody's* dipping *something,*" Nancy answered. "But I wouldn't call it skinny."

"I got to see this," Chris said.

"I think we should get this rock into the truck," Lisa reminded.

"Oh, c'mon, Lisa," Ruth pleaded. "Let's just take a break for a second."

"How often does an opportunity like this present itself?" Beryl asked.

"You guys go," Lisa said. "I'm staying here."

"Oh, no you don't," Ruth said, pulling her by the arm. "We're in this together."

The group followed Nancy over to the side of the house where Keith stood behind a bush, leaning on his walker and peering into the illuminated room, which housed a large, blue, in-ground pool. A naked woman with her back to them was bent over at the waist shaking out her wet hair. A man hoisted himself out of the water. He was completely naked and quite erect.

"That's Howie Fishbein," Ruth whispered. "Guess he's happy to be out of jail. *Very* happy."

"He was in jail?" Chris asked.

"Stock fraud," Maddie explained.

The naked man approached the naked woman from behind, moving in close as he grabbed her hips and rubbed up against her, effectively blocking their view of her.

"Move, you idiot," Keith whispered, obviously frustrated by his vantage point.

The woman stood and turned around, providing a full view of her face and body.

Lisa gasped, covering her mouth to prevent a shriek from escaping.

"Holy shit," Ruth said, giving voice to Lisa's thoughts. "That's not Donna Fishbein. That's Suzanne Podobinski!"

Chapter Eighteen

The group watched in stunned silence as Howie Fishbein led Suzanne Podobinski to a lounge by the side of the pool. She lay down and drew up her knees. He positioned himself between her legs and bent over to put his face into her crotch.

"Man oh man!" Keith squealed.

"My God," Ruth said. "I'd love to see the expression on Donna's face."

"You might get your chance," Beryl said. "Look!"

They were so busy watching the scene on the lounge chair that they had missed a door opening on the far side of the pool enclosure. Like the rest of the group, Lisa turned to look, and saw a gold-streaked blonde, standing regally with her body wrapped, sarong style, in a sunset-orange towel. It was Donna Fishbein herself.

"Oh, no!" Lisa whispered.

"They are so busted," said Chris.

Ruth grabbed Lisa's arm. "This is too good. It's just *too good*!"

Donna walked slowly across the room to where the busy lovers continued their act, unaware of her presence. Lisa closed her eyes. She couldn't look.

"Maybe we should get out of here," Maddie said. "There's going to be a major scene. Could get ugly enough for someone to call the police."

"Wait," Ruth said, "I'm not leaving yet."

Lisa opened her eyes for a moment and saw Donna standing at the edge of the lounge beside her busy husband. What she saw next utterly shocked her. Donna Fishbein pulled off her towel and dropped it to the floor. She was naked.

Howie Fishbein glanced up at his wife and smiled, then went back to work. She moved behind him and slid her hand from his backside downward to his scrotum.

"Rock and roll!" Chris said.

"Lucky prick," Keith muttered.

"I *knew* she wasn't a natural blonde," Beryl said.

Lisa took a step back. "I think we've seen enough."

"Hate to break up the party," Maddie added, "but Lisa's right. When they're through, Suzanne's going to leave. I think we want to be finished with our business before they're finished with theirs."

"Yeah," Beryl agreed. "It would be slightly less fun if *they* caught *us* in the act."

"I'm not moving," said Keith.

"Fine," Ruth said. "You and Nancy stay here. Let us know if anyone's coming."

Beryl smirked. "And the way you can tell is, she'll arch her back and moan."

They all laughed, some of them a little too loudly.

"Shh!" Lisa admonished. "They'll hear."

Sure enough, Donna turned around to face the window

where the group stood watching. She tapped Howie and said something, pointing to the window where they stood. Lisa froze.

"C'mon!" Ruth whispered, grabbing her by the sleeve. Before Lisa knew what was happening, everyone seemed to scatter and she found herself facedown in the dirt behind some hedges. She felt her heart pounding against the earth, and glanced up at the spot where Keith had been. Nothing. Where was he, and how had he gotten away so fast? Lisa heard a door open and saw Howie Fishbein emerge, the towel wrapped around his waist. He looked from left to right. She tried not to breathe.

Lisa heard a faint voice from inside the house say, "Get a flashlight."

"Fuck it," Howie said. "There's no one here."

"You sure?"

"I'm sure." He went back inside.

Lisa heard a gentle "Shh," from Ruth, who needn't have bothered. Lisa wasn't about to make a sound. Not yet. She lay there for several minutes, smelling the fragrant earth and listening to the sound of her own pulse. Just as she wondered if it was okay to rise, she heard Nancy's voice whisper, "All clear. They're back at it."

Lisa rose and saw the silhouettes of her friends emerge from the surrounding greenery.

"Help me get Keith up," Nancy whispered to Ruth.

She led them back to the spot where Keith had been standing. He was lying supine on the ground, his walker over him like a cage.

"He was brilliant," Nancy said, pulling the aluminum contraption off him. "Went down in a flash, pulling this thing right over him. I dove right on top. They never saw us."

Ruth and Nancy hoisted Keith back up.

"Are you okay?" Ruth asked.

"Fine," Keith said. "I could do this every night."

"Let's get back to work," Maddie said. "We should get out of here as fast as we can."

It took some work, but the group finally managed to get the boulder onto the dolly, up the makeshift ramp, and into Lisa's van.

Once everyone was settled in, Nancy glanced back at the cargo from her seat. "That thing sure is big," she said.

Lisa looked back at her, pretty sure she was talking about the rock. From the expressions on their faces, it was clear everyone had the same thought. Beryl, of course, beat them all to the punch.

"The rock's not too small, either," she quipped.

"I didn't expect it to be so hard," Maddie joined in.

"Or in so deep," Ruth added.

A ripple of titters washed over the giddy, tired group.

"Nothing like a good, hard rock," Nancy said.

Chris snorted several times, working hard to catch his breath. "I may need your help pulling it out," he said to Nancy, before exploding in an infectious burst of staccato giggles. Even Lisa found herself laughing.

But when they reached North Applewood Elementary, they had to get serious again and start the difficult task of completing the process in reverse. Together, Chris, Lisa, Ruth, Maddie, and Beryl moved the rock out of the van, across the field, and back to the spot where it sat for so many years.

Chris backed the hand truck into position over the deep depression that marked its former position.

"Okay," he said, "let's put this puppy back."

Lisa shone her flashlight from the hole to the rock and

back to the hole again. "Wait," she said, "something's not right."

Maddie knelt, putting her weight on her good leg, and looked at the ground. "Chris, are you *sure* we got the right rock? It looks nearly twice the size of this imprint."

"I thought I was sure, but . . ."

"But what?"

"It didn't seem so heavy last time."

"You idiot!" Ruth seethed. "This isn't Applewood Rock!"

"You think anyone'll know?" Beryl asked.

"Of course they'll know," Ruth snapped. "We have to go back."

"She's right," Lisa said. "We can't put back the wrong rock."

Maddie concurred. And so, tired, angry, frustrated, and cranky, the group moved the boulder back to the van and headed once again for Deepdale Road.

This time, Ruth instructed Keith and Nancy to stay in the van. "No one goes near that house, understand?"

When they reached the rock garden, Chris slapped his forehead. "Right, of course! Now I remember. I was going to put the rock on the right side of the garden but decided it would be much easier to put it up front. It's this one right here."

"Are you *sure*?" Ruth asked.

"I'm sure."

"One hundred percent?" Beryl asked.

"One hundred percent," Chris repeated.

Lisa shone her flashlight on the boulder. "This time I think he's right," she said. "See this pointy part over here? The hole in the ground matched that shape."

After examining the other large boulders in the garden,

the group decided that the one in front was indeed Apple-wood Rock. So they slid the larger boulder back into place and went to work digging a trench around the historic rock.

Lisa glanced toward the front door of the house. Did she hear a voice, or was it her imagination?

"Shh!" she alerted the group. "I think I hear something."

They quieted. The sound of a female voice drifted over the trees.

"It's Suzanne!" Ruth whispered. "Let's get out of here!"

She put her arm around Maddie to help her along and told Lisa to run and start the van. Beryl supported Maddie on the other side, and the three ran behind Lisa and Chris. Ruth was the last one to climb into the van. But just as she was about to shut the door Suzanne's nasal voice resonated directly behind her.

"Hey! Who's there? Ruth? Is that you?"

"Suzanne," Ruth said, stepping out of the van. "What are you doing here?"

"What are *you* doing here?" Suzanne asked.

"Uh . . . I'm with Lisa. Lisa Slotnick. We're looking for her dog."

"Lisa Slotnick has a dog?"

"They just got one. Uh . . . a rottweiler."

Suzanne put her hands on her hips and squinted dubi-ously. "What's its name?"

"Fluffy," Ruth blurted.

"Fluffy? A rottweiler named Fluffy?"

Lisa stepped out of the van. "The kids named it," she said.

Suzanne looked from Lisa to Ruth. "You two are up to something. What was that thing I saw by the rocks?"

The hand truck. They had left the hand truck.

"I don't know what you're talking about," Ruth said. "We've been driving around looking for Fluffy. We thought we saw him run into Donna's yard."

"I don't believe you. I should call the police."

"I don't think you want to do that," Ruth said.

"Oh, I think I do."

"Okay," Ruth said, "if you must, but I think the members of the PTA would be very interested to hear how *close* you are to Donna Fishbein . . . and her husband."

Suzanne's eyes widened. She looked stricken. "What?"

"You heard me."

"How do you . . . ? Who told . . . ?" Suzanne looked back at the house, glancing straight at the glass-enclosed pool area, where light shone through the trees. "Oh, my God!"

"Just leave, Suzanne. Leave quietly, and this stays between us."

Suzanne regained her composure "You know," she said through gritted teeth, "I think the PTA would be a lot more interested to hear about you and Paul Capobianco."

She's bluffing, Lisa thought. She might have her suspicions, but she doesn't know a thing. Hang in there, Ruth, Lisa tried to convey telepathically. Don't tip your hand.

"There's nothing going on between me and Paul Capobianco."

Lisa exhaled. Way to go, Ruth.

"Maybe, maybe not," Suzanne said. "But it wouldn't be hard to start a rumor. The superintendent and a married parent? Could ruin his whole career."

"You even *think* of starting a rumor and I'll tell everyone what I saw tonight."

"Your word against mine, sweetheart," Suzanne cooed.

"And mine," Lisa said, backing up her friend.

"And mine," came Beryl's voice from within the van.

"Mine, too," said Maddie.

Nancy, Chris, and Keith also piped up.

Suzanne gasped. "What the?"

Ruth smiled. "I suggest you get in your car and drive away."

Suzanne pointed a dainty, manicured nail in Ruth's face. "If you *ever* tell *anyone* . . ."

Ruth raised her hand and slowly pushed Suzanne's finger away from her face. "Good night, princess."

The return of Applewood Rock created a stir within the community. Even News 12 Long Island caught wind of the event and showed up at North Applewood Elementary with a camera crew to report the story. They followed it up at a local supermarket, where the reporter stuck a microphone in front of people coming out of the store for their reactions. One woman brushed her hair out of her face and said, "I think it was just some kids pulling a prank. But I'm glad they put it back. They did the right thing." As she spoke, a woman with an empty shopping cart passed in the background on her way into the store. The reporter stopped her for an opinion. It was Suzanne Podobinski.

"What do you think about the strange reappearance of Applewood Rock?" the interviewer asked.

"I agree with her," Suzanne said. "Probably just some kids."

And that was that. Within another day or two, local chatter had moved on to something else. Applewood was back to normal.

Lisa felt relieved, and thought she could return happily

to her routines. But even though the rock was back and her mother was gone, every day was a struggle. She couldn't face going back to the empty white ranch house and seeing the disaster she had created in the kitchen by slathering that screaming yellow paint everywhere. How could she have done such a thing? Had she completely lost her mind?

And her mother hounded her constantly, asking for permission to come back. Nancy had thought that returning the rock would redeem her in Lisa's eyes, and expressed surprise that her daughter was still resolute in her decision.

"But the rock is back, baby. And you know I'm never going to do anything like that again. Please. It's lonely here. And there's a bar just down the road. I have to pass it when I walk to the supermarket. It's a danger for me."

"Take some responsibility for yourself, Mother," Lisa said. "I can't look after you. I have four children to raise." Some people take motherhood seriously, she wanted to add, but couldn't see the point of starting an argument that would get her nowhere.

Lisa tried to immerse herself in taking care of her family. But without those early-morning hours she spent at the empty white ranch house, life felt imbalanced. Today, however, would be a good day. At the suggestion of Simon's speech therapist, who had been seeing him weekly since the evaluation, Lisa enrolled her small son in a morning preschool program.

"Today's your first day of school, sweetheart," she said to Simon as she pulled a royal blue sweatshirt over his head. "Remember the nice classroom we visited? Remember Miss Danielle?"

Simon smiled eagerly, and Lisa thought he understood. Together, they went down into the kitchen, and Lisa immediately noticed that two of the gas cooktop burners were on. She knew it had to be the twins, whom she had admonished repeatedly for playing with the knobs.

"Hey!" she shouted, turning off the flames. "Austin and Henry! Get in here this minute!"

Lisa demanded to know who was responsible, but they were mum. So she punished both of them, making TV off limits all week.

"This is very dangerous," she said. "Do you understand? Never ever ever do this again. If the whole house burns down, you'll be without TV for more than a week. Get it?"

The twins said they did, and Lisa got everyone fed and ready for school. She was about to leave for the bus stop when the phone rang, which gave her a jolt. Early-morning calls had a way of doing that to her. If it's something about Nancy, she told herself as she picked up the phone, it's not my fault.

But it was Jill.

"Quick question," her sister-in-law said. "Are you doing anything after you drop Simon at school today? I have a court and no partner."

She was talking about tennis. Jill was a terrific player, and Lisa loved getting the chance to go up against someone so much better than herself. So she quickly agreed, and they arranged to meet at the indoor court.

"Okay," she said to the kids after she hung up, "let's go to the bus stop. Wait, where's Henry?"

"He left," Austin said, pointing out the door. "Just now."

Lisa tsked. "Alone? C'mon, let's go catch up with him."

When she got out the front door, Lisa saw Henry's small form making a beeline for the empty white ranch house.

"Henry!" she called as she ran outside. "Stop!"

But he didn't listen, and before she could reach him he

slipped right through the door of the house, which she had inadvertently left unlocked.

Holding Simon by the hand, Lisa hurried to the house and went inside, with Sarah and Austin following behind.

"Henry," she said from the foyer, "get over here this instant. You're not allowed in here."

"The kitchen is yellow," he said from inside, his voice bouncing off the bare walls. "All yellow. Even the floor."

"Let me see," Sarah said, pushing her way past Lisa. Austin went, too. Even Simon pulled at Lisa's hand to get a better look.

"Yikes," Sarah said. "It looks weird in here. Like the inside of a crayon."

"Cool," Austin offered. "My feet are sticking to the floor."

Lisa approached and stood at the threshold of the kitchen. She touched the floor with her fingertips. The paint on the linoleum was tacky. It had refused to dry, as if realizing it didn't belong. She stood and took in the whole kitchen. Sarah was right. It looked like an explosion at a Crayola factory.

Lisa sighed. It was a monstrosity. Why had she thought she could take all the rage she felt at her mother and cover it up with a few gallons of Glidden Sundrenched Yellow?

As she walked the kids to the bus stop, her mind stayed in the empty white ranch house. It really wouldn't be so hard to fix that room, she realized. The walls could be repainted, the floor could be ripped up. Probably there was even hardwood underneath. And if she got to it soon while the paint was still fresh, it wouldn't be too hard to strip the cabinets with a chemical solvent.

I'll do it, Lisa thought. Maybe I'll even stop at Home Depot after tennis and pick up what I need.

Feeling lighter, Lisa smiled as the kids got on the school bus and waved good-bye. She turned to Simon, "Ready to go to school, buddy?"

Soon after Lisa and Jill started their game, two women showed up at the next court. Lisa glanced quickly over and realized one of them was Suzanne Podobinski. Right, Lisa remembered, this is the regular Monday-morning game she used to play with Ruth, who's out of commission due to a shoulder injury. And even if she wasn't, Lisa thought, there's no way those two would continue playing together after everything that's happened these past few weeks.

Now she wondered whether she should just continue playing and pretend she didn't notice her, or glance up and say hello. Jill made it a moot point by shouting "Hi, Suzanne!" from the other side of the court. Lisa turned and nodded, offering a barely audible greeting.

She tried to get back into the game, but missed two shots in a row and tapped the third one lamely over the net, giving Jill the chance to wallop it past her.

"Stop holding back," Jill said. "Pretend the ball is your mother."

Lisa didn't laugh, and returned the next ball with such force Jill's mouth dropped open.

"Now *that's* what I'm talking about. Hold on a minute, my cell phone is ringing."

While Jill stood on the far end of the court talking on the phone with her hand over her other ear to make it easier to hear, Lisa took a ball out of her pocket and bounced it on her racket. Anything to keep her from looking over at Suzanne. And after what they saw that night, Lisa could barely glance her way without turning red. Finally, Jill ended the torture by calling her over.

Lisa walked to the net. "What is it?"

"That was the movie people," she whispered, smiling.

"And?"

Jill leaned in and grabbed Lisa's hand. "We have a date! They're on schedule to start filming early April. Next month they'll send a crew over to start building the stadium. Isn't that fantastic?"

Lisa nodded enthusiastically.

Jill continued. "After the game we'll drop in on Ruth and tell her, okay? Maybe this will pick her spirits up."

So that's what they did. And since they came in separate cars, they drove over that way, with Jill following behind. At one point, Jill got stuck at a traffic light that Lisa had sailed through, so she was alone when she pulled into Ruth's driveway. She got out of her van and waited for Jill so they could go to the door and tell Ruth the good news together. As she leaned against the chassis peering down the road for Jill's red BMW, she heard the sound of a guitar coming from the corner window of the house. Ruth started to sing, and Lisa listened closely. The melody was so beautiful and haunting that Lisa felt a distinct chill. She tried to make out the lyrics, which sounded like "I'll stop the hurting. I'll take your pain." Then Ruth's voice rang out with an emotion as pure and raw and deep as Aretha's. "Give the song to Daddy, baby," she sang. "Give the song to Daddy." And Lisa could only get an image of a small frightened girl hovering in the corner as her angry drunken mother screamed that she wished she'd had an abortion so she wouldn't have to look at such a pitiful creature every time she came through the door.

"Are you okay?" Jill asked when she got out of her car and looked at Lisa's stinging eyes.

"Allergies," Lisa said dismissively. "Let's go give Ruth the good news."

Ruth was so excited about getting a start date she decided it called for a celebration. "Besides," she added, "I could really use a party about now."

"We can do it at my house," Lisa said.

Ruth smiled. "I was hoping you'd offer."

Chapter Nineteen

MADDIE

Maddie stared at the mirror and frowned. She knew she looked good in her black camisole top and short black skirt, but there was a problem. Before meeting Jack for a passionate encounter, she needed to visit Hannah's classroom and read the children a book. She was today's "secret reader," an honor both for the chosen child and the parent. How could Maddie dress sexy enough for a tryst, and yet wholesome enough for a classroom full of kindergarteners?

She pulled her light blue silk blouse out of the closet and slipped it on, buttoning it over the camisole. Perfect, she thought, tucking it in. The blouse could come right off between appointments. But there was still the problem of the shoes or, more accurately, shoe, as she still had her cast and could only wear one. A short skirt, she knew, needed a pair of killer heels to look truly sexy. But when she slid into her favorite strappy black sandal, she thought the look was far too slutty for her first stop. Then she remembered her tall boots. She found them in the closet and shimmied her right foot inside. Excellent, she thought, standing before the mirror. The height balanced out the cast on the other leg, and would even provide some protection from the elements. It was a cold, blustery day and she wasn't wearing pantyhose, since she'd have to cut off the left leg to wear them and she didn't feel like ruining a perfectly good pair. Besides, she reasoned, how sexy is a woman in bisected pantyhose?

As she pulled on her jacket, Maddie closed her eyes and imagined Jack's hot breath on her neck. She could feel his hand slipping up beneath her skirt. Then she remembered something he said just before they got off the phone when they arranged this date. "Don't wear underpants," he had whispered. Was that a joke? No matter, she'd do it anyway. Maddie slipped off her black panties and threw them into the hamper. Then she grabbed her purse and a copy of Dr. Seuss's *Fox in Socks* and was out the door.

Maddie found a parking space in the back of the elementary school's large lot. As she got out of the car, a strong gust of wind blew up under her skirt. Horrified, she dropped what she carried and fought the breeze to keep her skirt down over her bare bottom. "Idiot," she chided herself, thinking how much smarter it would have been to have simply taken off her panties later and balled them into her purse.

But it was when she got to the classroom that the stupidity of her decision really hit her. At first, she was mesmerized by Hannah's beaming visage, so sweet and perfect and brimming with joy at the sight of her mother. Maddie looked at the other children, who were all seated in a semicircle on the floor, quietly waiting. Then it hit her. Instead of a chair, the space they faced had nothing but a small square pillow for Maddie. She was meant to sit on the floor with them! How on earth could she manage to position herself in a short skirt without exposing *everything*? Under normal conditions, she might have been able to lower her-

self carefully and sit on her knees. But the cast made that
impossible. Maddie looked at the teacher beseechingly.

"Oh, dear, your cast," the teacher said, obviously sensing
Maddie's distress. "Would you be more comfortable in a
chair?"

Maddie exhaled. "Yes, please."

The teacher pulled one over for her and Maddie sat,
yanking her skirt tightly around her thighs and locking her
knees together like a clamp. She began to read the book
she brought, which started out simply enough, with lines
like "Socks on Knox and Knox in box," and graduated to
the most maddening tongue twisters, like "Luke Luck likes
lakes, Luke's duck likes lakes," which Maddie stumbled
and faulted over. She paused again and again to reread pas-
sages she messed up, as well as to swallow her own copious
saliva, which by now threatened to spill out of her mouth
and onto the floor.

On the way back to her car, she chastised herself in
Seussean verse:

> *Who made a really stupid choice*
> *Choosing Seuss instead of Joyce*
> *While drooling like a Droogeldroyce?*
> *And if it wasn't bad enough*
> *To struggle through such slippery stuff,*
> *Who took a cheap but childish chance*
> *And left home with no underpants?*

Slamming the car door and cursing her own judgment,
Maddie set off to meet Jack. At least I'm clear on one
thing, she thought. Having this affair is no mistake. After
all, Bruce has probably been sleeping with Jenna for years.
And this was something she desperately needed. It had

been so long since Maddie felt truly desired that the idea of being with Jack felt as natural as coming in from the cold.

They were meeting at a hotel because Maddie did not want to have their rendezvous at his condo, the site of so many of his conquests. So they arranged to meet at the clubby restaurant of a swank North Shore inn, where they would have lunch before going upstairs to the room he had reserved.

Maddie smiled as she imagined leaning across the table at lunch and telling him she wore no underpants. He would probably reach under the table for her thigh, and she would grab his hand and guide it up beneath her skirt so he would know she was telling the truth. This would get him so excited he would start to tear her clothes off before they could get inside the room. She felt herself getting wet at the thought.

She arrived at the restaurant five minutes late, but was unconcerned that he wasn't yet there. He had explained to her when they spoke nearly two weeks ago that he had made an exception to his schedule that morning for a special patient. She figured he was probably talking about some famous athlete. He had many as patients, and often worked around their busy schedules.

So he had said he would probably be able to make it by noon, but that she shouldn't worry if he was a little late. It just meant he was tied up with his patient. "I'll be there," he had said, "come hell or high water."

Maddie took a seat facing the door and ordered a glass of wine. She made up a little game to keep her from glancing at her watch too often. She could only check the time, she decided, whenever someone walked into the restaurant wearing a hat. But people kept trickling in without hats, and none of them was Jack. So she changed the rules. She could look at her watch if someone came in wearing blue.

A woman entered wearing a red dress. She was accompanied by a man in a dark suit, which Maddie figured may as well be blue. She glanced at her watch. He was thirty-five minutes late. Maddie took out her cell phone and called his office, but got the service. She left no message. She checked her answering machine at home. Nothing.

He wouldn't just stand me up this time, Maddie thought. He wouldn't. Then she got an idea. Maybe they got their wires crossed and he was waiting upstairs in their room. Agitated, she stayed another ten minutes and then paid for her wine and went to the front desk to ask if Dr. Jack Rose had checked in. He had not, the young clerk determined, but would she care to leave a message? No, she would not.

Maddie left the hotel more confused than angry. There had to be some sort of explanation, didn't there? But why didn't he call her cell phone? He'd better be lying dead someplace, she decided, or I'm never going to speak to him again.

One tiny detail kept coming back to Maddie, getting in the way of her righteous anger. She had an appointment with him at his office the very next morning to get her cast taken off. Why would he stand her up like this only to risk a nasty confrontation the very next morning? It didn't make sense.

When Maddie got home, she saw the message light flashing on her answering machine, meaning someone had just called. It must be him, she thought, and pushed the playback button. It was, surprisingly, the receptionist from his office, saying her appointment for the next morning was canceled. Dr. Rose, the voice said, would no longer be taking appointments, and provided the names and phone numbers of three other orthopedists.

Maddie was furious. Why couldn't that sniveling little rat dog pick up the phone himself? She lifted the coffee mug she had left on the table that morning and banged it hard against the kitchen counter. The ceramic handle came right off in her hand and she threw it hard into the sink, watching it shatter.

Maddie growled. To make matters worse, she and Bruce were leaving for Massachusetts tomorrow to attend his cousin's wedding. She had made a last-minute appointment to get her cast off because Jack had been away and it was the only time he could see her. Now she was up a creek.

Maddie replayed the message and scribbled down the numbers of the three orthopedists. She had to get in to see someone fast. The first one on the list couldn't take her until next Wednesday, and that was only because there was a cancelation that day. And no, there was no way they could squeeze her in tomorrow morning. Maddie called the other two doctors on the list and didn't fare any better.

"Mother shit *fuck*," she said, pacing her kitchen, all her anger focused on the need to get the cast off.

She remembered that Ruth had been seeing an orthopedist about her shoulder, and thought she may as well give another doctor a try. So she picked up the phone and dialed Ruth's number.

"You're not going to believe this," Maddie said, when her friend answered the phone. "I was supposed to get my cast off tomorrow but Jack canceled the appointment."

"Well, for heaven's sake," Ruth answered, "did you expect him to do it from a hospital bed?"

"Hospital bed? What are you talking about?"

"The bone marrow transplant."

"Huh?"

"The chemo didn't work. My new orthopedist is a friend of his and keeps me apprised."

"A friend of whose? Not Jack. Jack Rose." Maddie was getting more confused by the minute.

"Yes, Jack Rose."

"Jack doesn't have cancer."

"Lymphoma, Maddie. I thought you knew."

Maddie dropped into a kitchen chair. She felt all the blood drain from her face. "That can't be."

"He didn't tell you?"

Maddie leaned her elbows on the kitchen table and rubbed her brow, as if trying to knead in some understanding. "Since when?"

"A while, I guess. I think that was his second round of chemo."

"Jack has cancer?"

"Yes, honey. Jack has cancer."

Maddie opened and closed her fists, trying to get some feeling into her fingertips, which had gone numb. "Is he going to be okay?" she said, surprised that her voice came out sounding so choked.

"I don't know, Maddie."

God, oh, God, Maddie thought. Cancer. Jack. The two ideas seemed oppositional. His whole life was based on the philosophy that there were no real consequences to anything. To Jack, all mistakes were reversible, all actions inconsequential, all injuries fixable. He brushed off worries like crumbs from a collar.

Then something else occurred to her. Could this be why he wanted to sleep with her now, after all these years? Because it might be his last chance? Maddie saw a teardrop splatter on the kitchen table. She stared at it dumbly. She hadn't even been aware that she was crying.

"Oh, Ruth," she barely got out, "I don't want to lose him!"

The nurse made Maddie put on scrubs and a mask before going in to see Jack, explaining that he was very susceptible to infection now. To prepare for the implant, she went on, his bone marrow was being systematically destroyed, making even the most innocuous germs potential killers.

"I suppose you think this is a good excuse for standing me up," Maddie said as she entered his room. It was a rehearsed line she had prepared in the car on the way over, intended to lighten the mood.

"Was that today?" he responded seriously, pushing the button on his bed to raise himself into a sitting position. "I lost track of time."

"Don't worry about it."

"Sorry I didn't call."

She sat down next to his bed and took his hand, which seemed more fragile than she remembered it. This is why he's been looking so thin, she thought. She looked at the skin around his eyes, puffy and brown. I should have known, she chided herself.

"I'm glad you came," he said.

She was silent for a moment. "Why didn't you tell me?" she finally asked.

"I meant to, but . . ." He looked at the colorless view out the window and then back at Maddie. "I didn't want to spoil the fun, I guess."

Maddie swallowed hard against a lump in her gullet. "You're going to be okay, right?"

"Depends who you ask."

"What do you mean?"

"They got me on antibiotics here," he said, indicating the plastic bag of liquid hanging on a pole next to his bed. "Oncologists love this scientist shit. Microscopes and chemicals and lab results. Me? Give me some pins and saws and a busted leg and I'm as happy as a grease monkey."

"You didn't answer my question. About your prognosis."

Jack picked up the water pitcher from the arm of the tray that extended over his bed. He poured himself a glass a water and took a sip. "Warm," he said, making a face.

"Can I get you some ice?" she asked.

"Thanks." He handed her the pitcher. "Nurses' station."

When she returned, he was staring out the window, far into the grayness of the damp autumn afternoon.

"The thing is," he said, still gazing into the distance, "I want to live. They say that's key."

"You have to get well," she said. "There's a room waiting for us at the Claremont Hotel."

He picked up her hand and rubbed it against his cheek. "Shoeshine, I think we made a mistake about that."

Maddie shivered. "What do you mean?"

"He loves you."

She started to cry.

"I was being stupid," he said. "Stupid and selfish. You need to make your marriage work."

Maddie couldn't speak. Didn't he know she wanted to make her marriage work? Didn't he know she had tried and failed? Didn't he know that it was all her fault? That she just wasn't lovable enough? She choked on her sobs.

"Talk to me," he said.

"Bruce doesn't see me the way you do," she finally said.

"What do you mean?"

"I just . . . I don't know if I can make him love me again."

He stroked her hair. "I've seen the way he looks at you."

"Stop. It's not true."

"It *is* true."

She hesitated telling him the next part—should she really be burdening him with this? But she looked into his eyes and they still sparkled with confidence. Amazing. Even in a hospital bed fighting for his life, Jack was more confident than she.

"He was sleeping with someone else, I think," she finally said.

"You *think*?"

Maddie nodded.

"You know, Shoeshine, you always were given to paranoia and jealousy. Give him the benefit of the doubt, at least. Talk to him."

"I'll make you a deal," she said. "I'll make my marriage work if you make this work." Her hand swept past the IV bags and medical monitors.

Jack smiled and shook his head, amused. "You lawyers. Always negotiating."

The next morning, Maddie hobbled quickly from room to room, getting the children bathed, fed, and packed. Bruce went down to the basement to get out the big garment bag so they could both pack their evening clothes for the wedding. As Maddie pulled her dress from the closet and transferred it to a wire hanger for packing, Bruce looked at his watch.

"Don't you have an appointment with Jack this morning?"

Maddie hadn't told him yet and didn't realize why until that very second. She was afraid that if she couldn't get her cast off he would suggest that she stay home.

She sighed. "Jack's in the hospital, Bruce. He's getting a bone marrow transplant."

"Ah," he said, as if that made perfect sense.

"You knew? You knew he has cancer?"

"Hospital gossip."

"Why didn't you tell me?"

"I figured if he wanted you to know he would have told you. I didn't even think it was right that *I* knew."

Okay, Maddie thought, I'm not going to get mad at him for holding out on me. It's a doctor thing. Medical conditions are confidential.

Hannah dashed into the room. "Are we going yet?"

"Soon, sweetie," Maddie said.

"Hold on a second," Bruce said, picking Hannah up by the waist and placing her on the upholstered chair in their room. "Your shoelace is untied." He looked up at Maddie as his fingers worked. "But what about you? You planning on going to the wedding with that cast?"

Uh-oh, she thought. Here we go.

"Yeah," she said through gritted teeth. "I'm planning on going to the wedding with this cast. What choice do I have?"

"Well, *I* could take it off."

That stopped Maddie cold. "You can?" she asked, wondering why she hadn't thought of that.

Her shoelace tied, Hannah jumped out of the chair and ran from the room, yelling, "Thanks, Dad!"

"Sure," Bruce said. "After we drop the kids at Beryl's we can stop by my office. I'll take a quick X-ray, just to be safe, and then I'll cut it off. No problem."

Maddie grinned. "Honey!" She put her arms out and gave him a big hug. Maybe Jack was right. Maybe it was all her paranoia and this man still loved her with all his heart.

After dropping the children at Beryl's house and getting assurances that they would get at least two hours' sleep a night and she would only beat them where the marks wouldn't show, Maddie and Bruce headed for the door.

"You'll call if there's a problem?" Maddie said.

Beryl folded her arms. "I'll call."

"I'll keep my cell phone on."

"Go," Beryl said, literally pushing them out. "I promise I won't sell them into slavery. Child labor laws and all."

Maddie and Bruce drove to his office. Franny, the receptionist, greeted them when they entered.

"Still wearing your cast?" she asked.

Maddie looked down at her cast and then up at Franny, and wondered how Beryl would respond. "Still without a brain?" she'd probably ask.

Maddie sighed. "Not for much longer," she said.

In the examination room, Maddie held still, her body covered with a lead apron as Bruce stepped outside to push the button on the X-ray machine. She waited for the familiar buzz and click.

"Uh-oh," she heard Bruce say.

"What is it?" Maddie called.

Bruce poked his head in. "Just a second."

She heard him walk to the reception area and say to Franny, "Didn't we have the X-ray machine serviced?"

"Jason was here on Monday. He said he'd be back Tuesday with a columnation bulb."

"And what happened?"

"He never came back."

"Franny," Bruce said in his I'm-so-pissed-I'm-going-to-speak-as-calmly-as-I-can voice, "call Jason and tell him the X-ray machine is not going to fix itself."

"Okay."

"No, wait. Don't literally say that. Just call him and tell him to get here with that part as soon as he can."

"I'm sorry, honey," Bruce said when he walked back into the exam room. "The X-ray is broken."

Maddie pulled off the lead apron and Bruce took it from her. "No big deal," she said. "Just cut the cast off anyway."

"I can't do that."

"Why not?"

"Because there's always the chance the bone didn't set yet. It would be irresponsible of me to just remove your cast without an X-ray."

"I'm sure the fracture is healed. Seriously, Bruce, the X-ray is just a formality."

"It's not, Maddie. Let's just go. You'll get the cast off next week."

"If you're so sure then why—"

"Please," he interrupted, "forget it. Let's try to make the best of this."

Maddie swung her legs over the side of the exam table and pursed her lips. She knew the decision was hers. She could either be pissy and angry or just accept it and move on. Make the best of it, like he said. She looked at him, and knew it wasn't his fault. Before he knew the X-ray was broken he really did want to take her cast off. And he hadn't suggested that she cancel her plans and stay home.

"Okay," she said, "let's go."

As they passed the reception desk on their way out, Franny looked at Maddie's cast and said to Bruce, "You didn't take the cast off?"

Maddie, her back to Franny, gave Bruce a look that said, How on earth do you deal with someone this stupid?

Bruce put his arm around his wife. "See you Monday, Fran."

On the drive up to Massachusetts, they played a game of saying things Franny would say.

"Are you driving now?"

"Yes, the car."

"Don't forget to steer."

They got sillier and sillier. When they stopped at a restaurant for lunch and the waitress asked if they'd like to see a menu, Maddie said, "Is that where you list the different foods you have here?"

By the time they arrived at the hotel, their giddiness had reached a fever pitch and they could barely keep their composure as they checked in. Every question asked by the woman behind the desk seemed ripe for a stupid Franny response. And while they both bit their tongues, they seemed to be aware of the joke the other was thinking, and their bodies shook with suppressed giggles.

Up in the room, they released their energy on the king-sized bed, making love with more unrestrained passion than they had in a long, long time. Afterward, Maddie rested her head on Bruce's bare chest and smiled. The storm had passed and her marriage was still alive. And Jack, she knew, would keep his part of the bargain and be just fine.

Chapter Twenty

A gown would have been a better choice, Maddie thought, as she slipped on the short blue dress she had bought for the wedding. If only I had known I would be wearing a cast. But it's okay, she told herself as she turned sideways to glimpse her profile in the mirror. It's definitely okay.

When they arrived at the wedding, the ceremony hadn't yet begun, and the crowd was mingling in the open hall outside the sanctuary. Maddie and Bruce paid their respects to the bride's parents, who Bruce introduced as Aunt Shirley and Uncle Phil. Aunt Shirley's hands were constantly in motion, adjusting her guests' attire with quick little movements, straightening a tie here, moving a shoulder strap there.

"A little high-strung?" Maddie asked Bruce as they walked away.

"Everything has to be just so," he answered. "If she lives through this day it'll be a miracle."

Bruce's parents walked in and came over to exchange

warm greetings. Then Jenna approached with a group of cousins Maddie only vaguely remembered. Bruce held Maddie's hand as introductions were made and kisses traded. Jenna smiled warmly and Maddie remembered how easy it was to like her. Someone announced that the chapel was open and would everyone please take a seat.

"I have to dash to the bathroom," Maddie told Bruce. "I'll meet you inside."

Maddie walked into the ladies' room and let out a whistle. The door opened into a wallpapered parlor with a chintz-upholstered chaise longue against one wall and a mirrored vanity along the other. Fabric-lined baskets offered hairspray, hand lotion, tampons, small sewing kits, and other items. Aunt Shirley has really done it, Maddie thought. Everything is just so.

When she was in the stall, Maddie heard the rustle of taffeta and two young voices enter the lounge.

"It's gorgeous, okay? I'm not saying her gown's not gorgeous. But does she have to be so like 'aren't-I-the-center-of-the-universe-because-I'm-a-bride? Aren't-I-so-*beautiful*?' And I'm like, the dress may be pretty, honey, but you still have that *nose*. Like hello? You never heard of plastic *surgery*?"

Bitch, Maddie thought. Stupid little vacuous creep. She gave the toilet an angry flush to let the girls know she was there, and heard one of them shush the other as she emerged from the stall. She noticed that one was blond and the other brunette, and that they wore bridesmaid gowns, which only made her angrier.

"I don't care *who* hears," the brunette went on, looking straight into the mirror and yanking down her gown to show more cleavage. She used her finger to wipe mascara from under her eyes. "I always speak my mind."

"Such as it is," Maddie said.

The girl glanced over. "Huh?"

"See, this is why I favor gun control," Maddie explained. "If I had a weapon right now I couldn't be held responsible for my actions."

As she walked out the door she heard the girl say, "What's *her* problem?"

"Clomp, clomp, clomp," the blonde said, imitating the sound of Maddie's cast. "She sounds like a lame horse."

"Yeah, someone should shoot *her.*"

The girls screamed with giggles.

Maddie entered the chapel fuming and took the seat beside Bruce. She leaned in to share with him and Jenna the story of what had happened in the ladies' room.

"You know what you should do?" Jenna offered. "Stick your cast out just as she's walking down the aisle. Send her flat onto her face."

"I have a better idea," Maddie said as the ceremony began. The first bridesmaid to walk down the aisle was the blonde. Maddie caught her eye, and then deliberately picked a spot on her dress and stared at it quizzically, as if something were on it. There was nothing there, of course, but the girl's face turned red and she tried to brush the spot casually with her hand. When she got to the chuppah at the front of the room and thought no one was watching, she searched her dress for the imaginary stain and Maddie beamed. It was a small victory, but at least it was something.

Then came the brunette, the bitch, the one Maddie really wanted to torture. She had planned on using the same trick, but she couldn't catch the girl's eye. As Maddie watched her reach the front of the room, all smug and self-satisfied, a small part of her regretted not having taken Jenna's advice about tripping her.

By the cocktail hour, Maddie had forgotten all about it, aided, as she was, by a bartender who knew how to make truly dangerous vodka gimlets. Bruce stayed by her side as they sipped their drinks and ate hors d'oeuvres from tiny plates, chatting with this cousin and that. By the end of her second drink, Maddie was feeling light-headed.

At one point she was introduced to an awkward-looking twelve-year-old girl with a cast on her arm. Her name was Taylor.

"How'd you break your ankle?" Taylor asked.

"I fell at school," Maddie answered.

The girl's eyes lit up beneath her thick glasses. "Me, too!" she said excitedly, and Maddie knew this child would trail her for the rest of the night. She ordered another vodka gimlet.

Dinner was served in a large banquet hall, beautifully appointed with elegant settings and immense floral center-pieces. Maddie and Bruce were assigned to a table with Jenna and some other cousins whose names Maddie couldn't recall, even though she had been introduced just a short time earlier.

The band played some pop tune with a strong beat and most of the people from their table got up to dance. Only Maddie, Bruce, Jenna, and some woman with a funny name stayed behind. Maddie sipped her drink and tried to remember. Was it Clarabel? Cora Ann. That was it.

Maddie wanted to dance but knew she would feel like an idiot clomping around the dance floor in her cast. So she downed the last drop in her glass and ordered another instead.

Eventually she got drunk enough to not give a damn about the cast. The band launched into an oldies set and she felt the urge to move to the music and decided, what the hell, she'd get up on the floor. She figured Bruce would be just as eager.

She leaned into him. "I *know* you want to dance to this, honey," she began with a smile.

"You sure you don't mind?" he said.

"Huh?" Maddie was confused. Did he misunderstand her intention?

He turned to Jenna. "You want to dance?"

Jenna nodded, and he motioned for Cora Ann to come, too. It took a moment for Maddie to figure out what was going on. Bruce was getting up to dance, but not with her. He was dancing with Jenna and some other woman. Like that was supposed to allay any jealousy she might feel. Like if he was dancing with two women, it was innocent. If it was just him and Jenna . . . well, Maddie didn't even want to think about it.

Maddie sighed and took the lime from the side of her glass. She squeezed it then dropped it into the drink. She shook the glass gently and took a sip, closing her eyes and swaying to the beat of the music. When she opened them she became aware that her twelve-year-old friend, Taylor, had taken the seat next to her.

"What's the matter with your eyes?" Taylor asked.

Maddie stared into Taylor's glasses, which magnified her lashes to grotesque proportions, and wondered what the hell could be wrong with her own eyes. "What do you mean?"

"They're all red."

"Ah," she said, picking up her glass. "I'm drunk, sweetie. My eyes are red because I'm drunk." She downed the last drop in her glass and signaled the waiter for another.

"Then why are you still drinking?"

" 'Cause I'm not drunk enough."

After the waiter brought Maddie another drink, she asked Taylor if she would be dancing to this song if she didn't have the cast.

"Definitely," the girl answered. "You?"

"Me? Me, what?"

"Would you be dancing if you didn't have the cast?"

"Oh. Yeah, sure. Sure, I would. And you know what? I'm not even supposed to be wearing this cast right now. I had a . . . a . . . what do you call it when you're supposed to see the doctor?"

"An appointment?"

"Yeah, an appointment. I had an appointment yesterday to get it off. But my doctor got zick."

"Zick? You mean sick?"

"Yeah, sick. Very sick."

"I probably would have cut if off myself."

"What'd you say?" Maddie asked, taking a big gulp of her drink.

"I said I probably would have cut it off myself."

Maddie swallowed hard. "*That,* my dear, is a great idea."

"It is?"

Maddie picked up the dull knife that was in front of her. "I'll do it!"

"With a butter knife?" Taylor asked.

Maddie looked around the table, but all the silverware was the same as hers. Then she noticed that the waiter was setting down dinners at the mostly deserted table behind them. Each prime rib plate came with a serrated steak knife. Only one elderly couple sat at the table, and Maddie leaned over from her seat and grabbed the knife from the nearest vacant place setting.

"I'm just borrowing this," she slurred to the surprised couple, and tried to fit the knife into her tiny evening bag, which barely had room for her cell phone and one lipstick. "Fuck it," she said when she saw that the knife wouldn't fit in. The elderly couple stared, the shock registering heavily on their small, lined faces. Maddie, however, was oblivious. She left the purse dangling from her arm and got up holding the large knife in her hand.

"You coming?" she said to Taylor.

"Uh, I think I'll go back to my table. My mother is probably looking for me."

"Suit yourself," Maddie said, and then tried to wink as she bid her new friend adieu, but wound up closing both eyes, nearly causing herself to lose consciousness. She forced her eyes open and raised the knife triumphantly. "I'll be back!" she exclaimed.

Maddie exited to the lobby, where she crossed paths with the brown-haired bridesmaid she had so badly wanted to unsettle. Now was her chance.

"We meet again," Maddie said loudly to the girl. "Only this time"—she held up the knife and pointed it at her—"I have a weapon!"

The girl looked at the knife and gasped. She ran, tripping on her gown just as she entered the crowded banquet hall. Maddie heard a smattering of laughter from those who witnessed it, and felt vindicated.

"Sweet," she said to herself.

Inside the ladies' room, Maddie plopped onto the elegant chaise longue. She swung her left leg up onto it.

"Here I go," she said to no one. She angled the knife inside and began sawing downward. It was slow going, and created a surprising amount of dust that Maddie kept inhaling and then coughing out. When she had sawed down a few inches, she pulled off a chunk of the cast and dropped it onto the floor. She continued on in that manner, sawing, stopping, and dropping cracked pieces of plaster haphazardly onto the floor. She had gotten all the way down her leg and was starting on the area by her foot when the neurotic Aunt Shirley entered the room.

She looked at Maddie, the knife, the terrible mess on the elegant marble floor. "What the . . . ?"

Maddie smiled sweetly. "Hi, Aunt Shirley," she said, as if she were doing nothing out of the ordinary.

Aunt Shirley wheezed in shock and covered her heart with her hands. "My God!"

Maddie looked down, noticing the mess for the first time. "Oops."

"Are you crazy? What are you doing?"

"My orthopedist got cancer and then Bruce's X-ray machine broke and—" Maddie stopped, transfixed by the strange, faraway expression on Aunt Shirley's face. Her mouth was turned down in the most horrid grimace. Maddie stared, unable to identify the emotion it signified. Then the mouth opened and a strange, high-pitched sound came out. Finally, Maddie realized what it was. Aunt Shirley was crying.

"Don't cry. Please? I'll clean it up. I promise."

Aunt Shirley turned and ran from the room, bawling.

"I'll clean it up!" Maddie called after her. "You won't even know I was here!"

Maddie shrugged and went back to work. When the last of the cast fell to the floor, she wiggled her toes and felt satisfied, but only for a moment. She looked at her legs side by side and was stunned by the disparity. The cast leg had lost enough muscle tone to look positively shriveled. And it was a sickly white, especially compared to the other leg, which was encased in the beige pantyhose from which she had carefully amputated the left leg. Maddie looked from her right leg, flawless and tan, to her left, which looked like a stick. Like a skinny white stick. A skinny white stick with hair.

"Oh, shit," she said out loud.

Then she stood and realized something that hadn't occurred to her until that very moment. She had only one shoe.

"Mother shit *fuck*!"

Maddie was so addled that she forgot her promise to clean the bathroom. She took off her one shoe, grabbed her purse and the knife, and limped, barefoot, out of the room.

She padded back to the banquet hall, her left leg so weak with atrophy that she limped more heavily than she did with the cast on. As she passed the cloakroom, she heard a peal of familiar laughter and stopped. It sounded like Jenna. She put her ear to the closed door and heard breathy whispers she couldn't identify. Maddie shrugged, dismissing her own perception as nonsense, a figment of her drunken imagination.

She went into the banquet hall and noticed immediately that the band had taken a break and nearly everyone had returned to their seats for dinner. But Bruce's seat at their table was empty. So was Jenna's.

Maddie held on to the back of her chair, fighting back a wave of nausea. She had two ideas at that moment. One involved rushing to the bathroom, vomiting into the toilet, and then falling asleep on that comfortable chaise. The other involved pushing open the door to the cloakroom and seeing what was on the other side.

"You don't look so good," she heard a voice say. Maddie turned her head slowly, so as not to upset the god of motion sickness.

"Oh, Taylor!" she managed to utter.

"Can I get you anything?"

"Help me to the bathroom."

Taylor put her good arm around Maddie's waist and walked her back to the bathroom, where Maddie put her head over a toilet and let the spasms take over. When she finished, the girl handed her a Wetwipe, so graciously provided by their hosts, and then filled a paper cup with water.

Maddie rested on the chaise longue and wiped down her face and neck with cool astringent. She took the water from Taylor and sipped.

"You're a good kid, Taylor."

"I'm gonna get contact lenses."

"Yeah?"

"When I'm fourteen."

"Let me see how you look without glasses."

Taylor took off her glasses. There was no magical transformation from ugly duckling to beautiful swan. Her face looked vulnerable and unformed, like she needed the glasses for protection until she was ready to hatch. Maddie felt uncomfortable looking at her naked face, as if she were gazing at something she wasn't supposed to see. Like the perverse pornography of a medical textbook.

"Beautiful," Maddie said. "You're going to be a knockout."

Taylor put her glasses back on and smiled. "You feel better?"

"Yeah, thanks. Thanks for helping me. I think you should go back now. Your mother's probably looking for you."

"Aren't you coming?"

"There's something I need to do. I'll see you in a little while, okay?"

After Taylor left, Maddie found a tiny bottle of mouth-wash among the toiletries provided and swished some around in her mouth to get rid of the vomit taste. Then she looked at the dusty pile of plaster chunks she had dropped on the floor and thought she'd better do a little cleaning. Afraid that bending down to scoop them up would bring back the nausea, she used her newly freed left foot to kick as much of them as she could beneath the chaise longue.

"Enough stalling," she said out loud. "It's time."

Still dizzy from the alcohol but feeling some clarity of purpose, Maddie left the ladies' room and limped barefoot across the lobby to the cloakroom, staggering only slightly as she did so. She stood there for several minutes, quite sure that the moans she heard from within were Jenna's. She took a deep breath to fortify her resolve and pushed her way into the room with her shoulder.

Maddie gasped at the sight. Jenna, naked from the waist down, was perched on all fours on a table in the middle of the room, her bare, broad, cellulite-pocked backside facing Maddie. Jenna turned toward her, and immediately pulled down the fabric of her dress, which had been bunched around her waist. This covered the face of the person lying supine beneath her, whose head was buried in her crotch.

"What the—" came a muffled voice.

"Get up!" Jenna cried.

A person emerged from beneath the fabric of Jenna's dress and stood to face Maddie.

The information received by Maddie's brain made so little sense it took her a moment to realize what she had walked in on. The person having oral sex with Jenna was not Bruce.

It was Cora Ann.

"Maddie!" Jenna cried.

"I, uh . . . I thought . . . oh, my God." Maddie swayed as the room began to spin. She leaned against the door frame for support.

"I guess this would be a good time to come out of the closet," Jenna said, getting off the table and smoothing out her clothes.

A beam of light broke through the fog in Maddie's brain. This all made sense. This is what Jenna's e-mail was about, she thought, her relationship with Cora Ann. This is why she wanted Bruce to be happy for her, but didn't think Maddie should know. She wanted to avoid "a scene" at the wedding. Maddie looked from Jenna, all flushed from passion, to Cora Ann, face slick from cunnilingus, and wondered if this was the kind of "scene" she had in mind. Maddie tried to stifle a laugh, but it exploded in one cartoony "Ha!"

"You think this is funny?" Cora Ann asked.

"No, I . . . Jenna, I thought you were in here with Bruce. I thought—"

"There you are," came a voice from the hall behind Maddie. "I was looking all over for you."

It was Bruce. He stepped into the room and looked from Maddie to Jenna to Cora Ann and back to Maddie, focusing intently on her hands.

"What's going on here?" Bruce asked.

It was then that Maddie realized that she was still holding the steak knife, and that it was pointed at Jenna. She dropped it to the floor and started to cry.

"Bruce!" she said, throwing her arms around her husband and weeping into his shoulder. "I thought it was you. You weren't at the table and I heard Jenna's voice and I thought you were in here with her. I thought you were having an affair. And I was so scared. I love you! I love you so much! I've always loved you!"

"It's okay," he said, gently stroking her hair. "It's okay. I love you, too."

"Don't ever leave me, okay?"

"Of course not, sweetheart. How much have you had to drink, anyway?"

"A lot."

"Hey," Cora Ann interrupted. "What happened to her cast?"

Bruce released Maddie's embrace and looked down at her leg.

"Jeez," he said, "what happened?"

"I cut off my cast."

"Are you *crazy*?"

"Just drunk."

"For God's sake, Maddie. You could reinjure it. Here"— he pulled over a chair from the corner of the room—"sit down."

She did as he said.

"Now," he announced, "tell me what's going on. Really."

He looked straight into her eyes and Maddie knew he meant business. "Everything?" she asked.

"Everything."

"I'm so sorry, I didn't mean to snoop, but I was checking the e-mail and there was this one from Jenna and . . . God, Bruce! The things she said! I thought it meant you two were having an affair and that you were going to tell me after the wedding. I had no idea that it was about Jenna's . . . lifestyle choice."

"I'm so sorry," Jenna said. "I should have just told you."

"And that's another thing," Maddie said. "Why on earth did you think I couldn't handle it?"

"I don't know. You just always seemed so . . . so . . ."

"So straight?" Cora Ann offered.

"Yeah, so straight."

"But I'm so *cool*," Maddie whined.

Bruce smiled. "I know. You're the coolest minivan-driving soccer mom on Long Island."

"You mean housewife," Maddie said. She turned to Jenna and Cora Ann. "There's more to me than meets the PTA. Maybe not as much as there used to be, but I still have three dimensions. And I still understand love. I'm *happy* for you two."

"Thanks," Jenna said. "And what about you two? Are you going to be okay?"

Bruce put his arm around Maddie. "More than okay," he said.

And he meant it. The next day, he let Maddie sleep late, quietly ordering room service so she would have strong coffee and a good breakfast to fight off her hangover. Then he licked her fingers one by one, and nibbled his way up her arm and shoulder to the curve of her neck. It was Maddie's favorite place to be kissed, and as she let go—releasing herself to the pleasure of that spot—she started to weep. It was all her anxiety about their relationship spilling out in great waves.

"Are you okay?" he whispered.

She nodded and kissed him on the mouth, and it was as if everything she felt for this man were passing between them as their tongues met. Oh, how she loved him!

They both seemed to sense that this was a second beginning for them, and they explored each other like new lovers. Gone were the old patterns of where to touch and how fast to move. They teased and played and experimented. Bruce coaxed her to the precipice of orgasm again and again, making her buck and beg, only to stop before she climaxed. The result—when she finally released—was an orgasm that seized and shook her on and on. Even afterward, when they snuggled naked beneath the covers, she still shuddered in little seismic aftershocks.

"We can stay another night if you want to," he whispered.

"We can't," she said. "The children."

Bruce smiled and wiped a stray hair from her face. "I called Beryl and she said it's okay."

Maddie was deliriously happy. They showered together, had lunch in the room, and were about to make love again when her cell phone rang. Maddie answered it, expecting Beryl to be calling about the children, but it was Ruth, sounding terrible. Maddie received the news with a chill and hung up the phone.

"What is it?" Bruce asked.

"It's Jack," she said, the color draining from her face. "He's dying."

Chapter Twenty-one

Ruth stuffed a bulging cosmetics bag into her suitcase and glanced out the window. The car service would be there any minute to take them to the airport and she wasn't quite finished packing. It had been a hectic day. Keith's parents' flight arrived in the morning, and Ruth had driven to the airport to pick them up. Now she and the kids were getting ready for their annual trip to Florida.

Ruth ran down her mental checklist. All the necessities were packed and she still had room for a few more pairs of sandals. Normally this would have made her happy, but she had been so down since learning that Paul and Margie were involved that nothing could lift her out of her funk. She wedged the shoes into the suitcase and zipped it shut.

She glanced out the window again. Still no car. Should she have called to confirm the time? They'll be here, she told herself. Don't be so anxious.

She picked up the suitcase with her good arm and bumped it down the stairs, remembering another thing she was tense about—her shoulder surgery. It was scheduled for the day after her return so that her in-laws would be able to help with the kids while she was convalescing.

It was the flight, though, that had Ruth's stomach doing

loops. Not the flying part, but the confrontation. She had been a little sneaky and learned what flight Paul was taking for his trip to his Florida condo. He had once mentioned that though his place was on the Gulf Coast, he usually flew into Fort Lauderdale so he could stop and see some relatives. She finagled the flight information out of the travel agent they shared, and booked herself and the kids on the same plane. If she ran into him "accidentally," she thought, she might be able to stir him to realize that Margie was no match for him. It was a long shot, she knew, but she wasn't ready to give up on Paul. He was the only passion in her life and she needed him desperately.

"Ben," Ruth shouted down the stairs, "check and see if the car service is here!"

She heard the front door open.

"Not here yet, Mom," he yelled.

Ruth got to the bottom of the stairs and looked at her watch. They were late. Thank goodness she had built padding into their schedule. Otherwise they might miss their flight.

"Can I get you something to eat?" her mother-in-law asked when Ruth entered the kitchen. "You should eat. You got thin."

For Ruth, one happy side effect of her recent moodiness was a loss of appetite. Normally, she struggled with every pound. So though she knew her mother-in-law intended it as a gentle criticism, she took it as a compliment and kissed the top of her head.

"Thanks anyway, Beatrice."

"Shouldn't you be gone already?" her father-in-law asked, looking at his watch.

"They're usually so punctual," Ruth said, picking up the

phone. "I'm going to call to make sure they're on their way."

After being put on hold for several anxious minutes, during which Ruth kept peering out the front door, she finally spoke to the dispatcher who said that her car service had been canceled.

"What do you mean *canceled*?" she nearly shrieked.

"We called this morning to confirm and whoever answered the phone said that you arranged another ride."

"What!" She turned to Keith. "Did someone call this morning about my car service?"

"No."

"Are you *sure*?"

"Someone called about *a* car service. They said they wanted to confirm the time for the airport pickup and you had already left to get my parents. So I told them to forget it."

"Keith!" Ruth yelled. "You id—" She stopped herself. "That was the car service for *my* flight."

"Ma'am?" interrupted the dispatcher. "Do you want me to send another car?"

"How fast can you get someone here?"

"Twenty to twenty-five minutes."

"Twenty-five minutes!" she shrieked. This was getting way too close for comfort.

"I'll drive you," Keith's father piped in.

"Bless you!" Ruth said, and told the dispatcher she didn't need the car.

Ben loaded the suitcases, and Ruth hurried Morgan and her father-in-law into the SUV, announcing that she would drive, as she knew she had a heavier foot than the old man. She screeched out of the driveway and barreled through the winding streets of Applewood Estates, barely keeping all four tires on the ground. She made great time to the Long Island Expressway, but after about a mile the traffic came to a sudden and grinding halt. Ruth peered as far into the horizon as she could see, hoping to discover the cause of the slowdown. But all she could see was a long line of cars and brake lights, and no exit for miles. Ruth felt her last spark of joy extinguish. They'd never make the flight. She pictured Paul, sitting all alone, as the plane pulled away from the gate and taxied toward the runway. An opportunity missed. And it was all Keith's fault.

Damn him, she thought. *Damn* him! And before she knew it, it was happening again. A silent fury rose up in her as she remembered the day he awoke from his coma with a bitterness she could almost taste. If only he'd had the decency to just . . . She stopped herself and tried to push the thought away.

"Give me my cell phone!" she said through clenched teeth. But before her father-in-law could even react, she grabbed her handbag and pulled it out. Traffic was at such a standstill she had no problem making the calls she needed. By the time they began to inch forward, she had herself and the kids booked on a later flight. She had even been able to call her parents and give them the new flight information.

The flight was miserable. Morgan and Ben argued like they did when they were small, calling on her constantly for intervention.

"Mo-om!" Morgan whined. "Ben says I can't use the diving board in the big pool."

"Ben, leave her alone. She can use the diving board."

"But you have to be *ten,*" he argued.

"She's nine and a half. We'll bend the rules."

Ruth wanted to be alone with her thoughts, musing on what could have been if they had only made their flight. She would have found a way to sit next to Paul. They could have spent three whole hours just talking. By the end of the flight, he might have been more in love with her than ever.

The musing didn't help her mood at all, which got blacker by the minute. The children were driving her crazy and her shoulder was aching from shoving their jackets into the overhead bin. Plus, she thought she felt something sticky in her panties. Was she getting her period?

She got up and pushed her way down the aisle to the restroom. Sure enough, she was menstruating. Great. She rummaged through her bag for a tampon. No luck. So she balled up a wad of airline toilet paper and stuck it between her legs.

When she returned to her seat, the children were ready for her with a litany of complaints.

"He's being mean to me," Morgan complained.

"She thinks Florida's a *country,*" Ben explained.

"I do not!"

"Knock it off, Ben," Ruth admonished.

"She keeps bothering me," he said.

"Morgan, stop bothering him."

"He's hogging the armrest," Morgan whined.

"Ben, stop hogging the armrest."

Morgan stuck her tongue out at Ben.

"Mom," Ben protested, "she stuck out her tongue."

"Honest to God," Ruth said, "if you two don't stop I'm going to tell the pilot to turn the plane around and take us right back to New York."

By the time they got to Ruth's parents' house in Boca Raton it was past everyone's bedtime. Ruth's mother,

Anita, told her she looked tired, and suggested she go right to bed.

"I'll take care of the kids," she promised.

Ruth nodded and wheeled her suitcase across the long expanse of white tile to her bedroom at the far end of the expansive ranch house. She got ready for bed and dropped onto the mattress, which she hoped would swallow her whole. No such luck. She grabbed the remote control from the nightstand and clicked on the TV.

By two A.M., she was still awake, staring dumbly at the television, only her face was wet with tears. She had found a suitably sad movie and given herself over to it completely. When it ended, she thought hard about phoning Paul, wondering whether the depth of her despair justified a middle-of-the-night call. She was mulling this over when she was finally relieved of her sadness by the blessing of deep sleep.

She awoke the next morning to the sound of the children's voices down the hall, but didn't want to get up and face the day. She listened for a moment until she was sure she heard her mother's voice. Fine, she thought, they're taken care of, and drifted back to sleep.

Sometime later she heard a gentle knock on her door. It opened a crack and Ruth's mother stuck her head in.

"I'm taking the kids to the big pool. Are you okay?"

"Just tired."

"I'll see you later, then."

"Sunscreen," Ruth said, yawning. "Don't forget sunscreen." And she fell back asleep.

She drifted in and out for the next several hours. When she finally got to a point where she could no longer find the tail of a dream and ride it back into unconsciousness, she got out of bed and padded into the kitchen, dragging her body as if the force of gravity were almost too much for her.

Her father, who sat reading the newspaper and eating lunch, looked up. "You okay?"

"Why does everyone keep asking me that?"

"Because you slept for fourteen hours."

"Not really. I stayed up late watching some stupid movie."

Ruth pulled a box of raisin bran from the pantry and poured some into a bowl. She opened the refrigerator and found the skim milk.

"You're having *breakfast* now?" her father asked. "It's lunchtime."

It sounded to Ruth like a rebuke and she grunted. "Lay off, okay?"

"What did I say?"

"Nothing. Forget it."

She looked into the coffeemaker on the kitchen counter, but it was empty. She needed some caffeine to clear the cobwebs but didn't feel like making more. So she opened the refrigerator again and found a can of Diet Coke. She popped it open and put it down on the kitchen table.

"There," she snapped at her father. "I just made it lunch. You happy now?"

He shook his head. "Touchy."

Ruth swallowed a few spoonfuls and pushed the bowl away. She took her soda and shuffled to the overstuffed couch in the den, where she clicked on the television. She was still there several hours later when her mother returned with the children, who bounded into the house flushed and excited.

"You should have been there, Mom," Morgan said. "We saw the *fattest* man."

"He was bigger than Mr. Latham," Ben added, referring to his science teacher.

Ruth smiled weakly. "Sorry I missed it," she said, trying to fight her depression for the sake of the children. "Come give me a kiss."

"He jumped right into the pool," Morgan said. "I thought all the water would splash out."

"Sounds like quite a show."

Anita announced that she thought they should all go to Axle Alley for dinner. It was a local theme restaurant devoted to fast and unusual cars. They usually made it there at least once every trip and the kids loved it.

"Guess I should shower and get my act together," Ruth said without moving.

"Can I wear my purple pants?" Morgan asked her.

"If you want."

As if on cue, everyone but Ruth set off to get ready for dinner. She reacted to the flurry of activity by shutting off the TV, but couldn't find the motivation to get up from the couch. The misery of her life bore down on her. She pictured Keith, his face half-slack from paralysis, sitting in front of the television for hours on end. My fate, she thought morosely. My forever. If she'd had the energy she would have cried.

Finally, when Morgan ran into the room to proudly show her mom how the new purple Capri pants looked with her striped tank top, Ruth summoned all her strength and lifted herself from the couch.

"That looks great, sweetie."

"Hurry up, Mom. Get dressed."

Ruth stood in the shower, hoping the warm spray would wash away the blackness that was pulling her down. But it was no use. She turned off the water and wrapped herself in a terry robe. She went into her room and lay down in the middle of the queen-sized bed, waiting for something to happen that would give her the motivation to get dressed.

Overcome by emotional paralysis, she lay there, still and quiet, until her mother knocked on her door to ask how she was doing. Ruth took a deep breath and announced that she had cramps and they should go without her.

"Are you sure?" her mother asked. "You haven't been out of the house all day."

"I'm sure."

"I'll bring something back for you, okay? A turkey burger maybe?"

"That'll be great. Thanks, Mom."

Later, when they had all gone, Ruth tried to summon a sexual fantasy about Paul, but couldn't. She kept picturing him sitting on the couch with Margie and her ugly shoes, nodding sympathetically as she went on and on about her stupid dead husband.

Angry, she sat up in bed. That dull, support-hose-wearing twit did absolutely nothing to deserve Paul's affection except get lucky enough for her husband to fall off a roof and break his neck. Her rage felt luxurious. She got out of bed and began to pace the room. I'll call him, she thought. I'll call him and tell him what an asshole he is. I'll tell him to drop dead!

She picked up the phone and dialed his number in Marco Island, her breath quickening with every ring. Finally, he answered.

"Hello?" he said.

The sound of his voice brought back a rush of memories. His breath on her neck. The burning way he looked at her body. The words he said to her that day in her den: "I love you, Ruth."

She hung up the phone and cried.

The next day it rained. Ruth's father planned to take the children to the movies. Her mother wanted to go to the specialty shop where she bought custom-made bathing suits, and asked Ruth to come along.

"Please, honey," Anita said. "You know how I hate buying bathing suits alone. Besides, it'll do you good to get out of the house."

Though she wanted nothing more than to stay in bed with the covers pulled up over her head, Ruth relented. She knew another day in bed would alarm her parents to the point of suggesting professional help, and she just couldn't face that.

The woman who owned Isabella's greeted Ruth's mother with a warm hug. "I have the Daisy in metallic now," she gushed, obviously referring to a style of bathing suit her mother liked.

"Isabella," Anita said, "this is my daughter, Ruth."

The woman sized up Ruth's figure with her eyes. "I have a fabulous two-piece for you," she said.

"I'm not here to buy," Ruth said. "Besides, I haven't worn a two-piece in years."

"With that figure?" came a voice from behind them. Ruth turned and saw a heavyset woman with cottage-cheese thighs modeling a skirted swimsuit for her husband, who sat in a low easy chair that threatened to devour him.

Ruth also caught a glimpse of herself—it was hard not to in a store with so many mirrors—and was surprised by how thin she had gotten. But even if they are right, she thought, I'm in no mood for this.

"Thank you," Ruth said. "Maybe another time."

The heavyset woman raised her finger in the air. "You'd look great in a bikini," she practically sang. "Wouldn't she, Hal? Hal, look at her figure. Wouldn't she look great in a bikini?"

Hal turned to face Ruth. "Great," he said. "Great in a bikini."

Ruth thanked them for the compliment and went with Isabella and her mother into the back of the store. Ruth and Anita sat on an upholstered bench in the outer area of the dressing room while Isabella went to gather up some bathing suits. She came back with about half a dozen on hangers, explaining something about the details of each. She knew Anita's figure well enough to tell her which ones might need a little alteration.

Anita took the suits and went into a dressing room. Isabella left and came back with a blue two-piece bathing suit, which she held up in front of Ruth.

"Separates," she explained. "You probably need a D on top, right?"

"I'm really not interested," Ruth said. But even as she did, she thought that if ever there was a bikini that would fit her, this was it.

"A different color, maybe?"

"It's not that. I'm just . . . I'm feeling a little bloated today."

Just as she said that the big woman came into the room. "Honey, if you're bloated we're *all* in trouble."

"Listen," Isabella said, "why don't you just try it on? You don't have to come out of the dressing room if you don't want."

Ruth sighed. "Okay," she relented. "I'll try it on."

Because she had her period, Ruth left on her panties,

which were small enough to be concealed by the bottom
of the swimsuit. She got the top fastened, and stood back
to look at herself in the mirror.

Ruth blinked. Was this one of those trick mirrors, or
did her body really look that good? Her love handles were
gone. She turned to the side. No stomach flab. She'd lost
more weight than she realized. And Isabella was right. The
swimsuit was perfect for her. The top lifted her breasts to a
height they hadn't seen in years, creating two perfect bubbles of cleavage. And the bottom arched over her thighs,
making her legs look longer and leaner. She slipped into
her high heels and looked at herself again. Wow.

"How are you doing in there?" Isabella asked from the
other side of the curtain. "Can I come in?"

"Sure." Ruth parted the fabric.

She looked at Ruth and held her hands upward toward
the ceiling. "See? What did I tell you?"

Ruth's mother appeared behind Isabella. "Oh, honey! If
you don't buy that suit I'll buy it *for* you."

Isabella insisted that Ruth step into the outer area of the
dressing room where she could see herself in the mirror
from a distance. Okay, Ruth thought, standing back and
taking in the whole look, maybe a stupid bathing suit isn't
enough to lift my spirits, but it can't hurt. Just then, the
heavyset woman appeared behind her.

"Bloated? Ha! You look like a centerfold!" She grabbed
Ruth's hand and pulled. "Come on, I want you to get a
man's opinion. Hal!"

The woman dragged Ruth to the area where her husband had sunk even lower into the upholstered chair.

"Hal!" she shouted again. "Look at her! What do you
think? Is this a centerfold or what? I mean, look at that
figure. What do you think, Hal? Doesn't this girl look

great in a bikini? Tell her, Hal. Tell her how great she looks."

Hal looked Ruth up and down and then cleared his throat.

"C'mon, Hal," his wife insisted. "What do you think? Tell her. Tell her how she looks. Give her a man's opinion. Tell her, Hal. Say something."

"Hubba hubba," said Hal.

Driving back to the house with her mother, Ruth wondered if it was excessive to have bought the suit in all five colors. She'd have lots of opportunities to work on a tan, but why? She'd be thin and bronze and have no one to show off for.

"Are you planning on going to the Keys?" her mother asked.

When she and the kids came to Florida to visit her parents, Ruth usually took the opportunity to spend a night or two in the Keys, either alone or with an old girlfriend who lived down in Miami.

"I don't know." She sighed. "I'm kind of sick of the Keys."

"Someplace else, then?"

Poor thing, Ruth thought. She's trying so hard to think of some way to lift me out of my funk. She doesn't know that the only thing that would help is sitting alone in Marco Island.

"Oh, jeez!" Ruth said out loud.

"What is it?"

"I just thought of something."

"What?"

"Where can I get a road map of Florida?"

"Why?" her mother asked. "Where do you want to go?"

"The west coast," she answered, suddenly hopeful that she didn't have to let her new figure and new bathing suits go to waste. "Marco Island!"

The lounge chairs by the Tiki Pool of the Marco Island Marriott are situated so that you can behold a beautiful view of the ocean and still enjoy the civilized convenience of roaming waiters happy to take exotic drink orders. Ruth wore her new blue bikini and a tan she had acquired from several days at her parents' pool. She rubbed a sweet-smelling lotion onto her skin and relaxed into the lounge chair, her body welcoming the tropical sun like nourishment. Her plan was to spend the day deepening her tan. Then she'd have a relaxing massage before her appointment at the beauty salon, where she would get her legs waxed and her hair blown out as smooth as silk. She'd put on her new slinky floral dress before getting into her rented Mustang and driving over to Paul Capobianco's house for a surprise visit.

She was drifting into a dreamy sort of floatiness when she realized that a voice she had assumed was background noise might actually be addressing her. She opened her eyes, shielding them against the sun with her hand, and saw a blond man silhouetted in such a way that it looked like a palm tree was growing out of his head.

"Excuse me?" she said.

"I was just wondering what you were drinking," he said. "It looks so interesting."

Ah, she thought, a come-on. She sat up so she could get a better look. He was young, probably not more than thirty, with one of those carefully sculpted bodies. Except for some blond down on his arms, he had no body hair, and Ruth assumed that he probably waxed it off to better show his hard-earned muscles. It was an affectation of young men that wasn't to her liking. Vanity is for women, she thought, not men. Ruth was glad she didn't belong to a generation where the boys were just as appearance-obsessed as girls. How could she be a goddess if she had to compete with the person who was supposed to be pursuing her? No, if she slept with this guy she'd hate herself in the morning. Besides, Paul was the one she wanted.

"It's a frozen margarita," she said.

"Sounds refreshing. Do you mind if I sit down?"

"You're not going to come on to me, are you?"

He laughed, baring perfect white teeth. "I can't make any promises."

"Knock yourself out." She pointed to the empty lounge chair next to her. "But you're wasting your time."

"That's okay," he said, taking a seat. "I don't mind just sitting here and looking at you."

Oh, God, Ruth thought, this guy just oozes. "How old are you anyway?" she asked.

"Does it matter?"

"I guess not." Since you don't have a chance in hell, she wanted to add.

"I'm Jared Thomas," he said, extending his hand.

Jared, she thought. Dear God, he's probably even younger than thirty. She shook his hand. "Ruth Moss."

"What's a beautiful lady like you doing here all alone?"

"I'm not as alone as I look. I'm meeting someone later on."

"Too bad. If that doesn't work out, you should give me a call. I'd love to take you for a ride in my Carrera, Ruth."

She laughed. "That was pretty slick. You managed to

work into the conversation that you have a Porsche in under twenty seconds. That may be a record."

He grinned without a touch of embarrassment, which Ruth thought belied a sense of entitlement. A cocky kid used to getting whatever he wants.

"You're not easily impressed," he observed.

"Honey, I'm probably old enough to be your mother. Why don't you flirt with one of the pretty young girls on the beach?"

"I've *had* young girls."

"So I would make an interesting conquest, is that it?"

"I just find you attractive, Ruth. Is that bad?"

Ruth looked at her watch. "I have to go, Jared. You take care."

Throughout her massage, Ruth fantasized about her encounter with Paul. He'd be taken aback by her sudden appearance, but thrilled and horny. She could barely wait to see his face when she slipped out of her dress and showed him her trim, tan body. He'd go wild.

The salon did a great job on her hair. Silky and straight, it was a whole different look for her. Youthful. She shook her head and watched it flow across her shoulders.

She felt jittery as she slammed the door to her rented Mustang and set off for Paul's place, following the directions she had figured out using the map of the island provided by the hotel.

She found his community pretty easily, but there was one thing she hadn't counted on: a gatehouse. *Shit*. The whole drama of her surprise visit would be ruined if her arrival was announced. It would give Paul the few moments he would need to strengthen his resolve and greet her with that sober, I-told-you-we-were-through face.

This can still work, Ruth thought. I'll charm the guard, plead my case. He'll let me through. She rolled down her window.

"Hi." She smiled up at him, tossing her hair past her bare shoulder. "I'm here to see Paul Capobianco, but before you call him—"

"The party?"

"Huh?"

"He said to just let everyone through." He pushed the button opening the gate arm in front of her car. "Go to the first corner and make a right. His house is on the left. Have fun."

"Yeah, the party. Thanks."

She drove on, confused. Paul was having a party? The guard must be wrong. Paul wasn't a party type. Besides, he had once told her that his Florida vacations were his time for quiet contemplation. He always went alone and never invited anyone over. But when she neared the stucco house bearing Paul's address, she saw a line of cars and heard music coming from the backyard. This won't do, she thought, this won't do at all. She wasn't going to crash a party. The whole idea was to find Paul alone. She parked the car and cut the engine, considering whether she should just leave and come back tomorrow, or chance sneaking around the back and having a look. She decided on the latter.

She walked around the side of the house, her thin heels digging through the prickly grass into the soft ground. There was a tall hedge behind one of lights, providing a good vantage point. She looked through the leaves at the crowd, seeing face after face she didn't recognize. Finally, she saw a tall form emerge from the back of the house. Was that Paul? He walked over to a woman who was standing with her back to Ruth and handed her a drink. It can't be, Ruth thought. It just can't be. He put his arm around her in a proprietary way and she turned to kiss him. Dear God, it *was*. It was Margie!

Back at the Marriott's Tiki Bar, Ruth tried to quiet the fury with multiple margaritas, while telling one guy after another to get lost. By her third drink she had already been hit on by a fat man who wore his pants too high, a geriatric type with capped teeth who made a point of telling her he didn't need Viagra, and the dark-skinned bartender who told her, in a heavy Hispanic accent, that once you have black you never go back. He was, she thought, the Cuban version of Dan Aykroyd's wild and crazy guy.

"You are popular tonight," the bartender said.

"Lucky me."

She had never suspected that what was going on between Paul and Margie was serious enough for him to take her to Florida. I am truly pathetic, she thought, staring into her drink. I offer this guy everything I've got, I chase him to Florida, and for what? So he can choose a mousy little twit over me? I must be the most worthless piece of protoplasm slinking around this planet.

She threw a tip on the bar and downed the rest of her drink. Just as she put the glass down she heard a voice behind her and felt a hand gently touching her shoulder.

"Hey, sexy. What's a beautiful woman like you doing in a place like this?"

She pushed her stool back, ready to tell whoever it was

to fuck off. She was in no mood. But when she turned, she saw a familiar face. She exhaled.

"Hey, Jared."

He picked up a lock of her hair by the tips. "You look nice."

You, too, she thought. He wore a light blue collarless cotton shirt that made his designer tan glisten. She thought about the shape of his smooth muscled chest beneath. Don't do this, she warned herself. If you have one ounce of self-respect, do not sleep with this guy. You'll hate your-self like poison in the morning.

"Thanks. I was just on my way out."

He leaned in and kissed her neck. "Come to my room," he whispered throatily in her ear.

"No," she said, grabbing her handbag and standing, "you come to mine."

Chapter Twenty-two

The following week, Ruth awoke trembling violently. If I could just warm up, she thought, the throbbing in my shoulder might not seem so bad. If I could just warm up. A nurse draped a heated blanket over her.

"It's the anesthesia," she explained. "Everyone shakes when they first come out of it. Your surgery went well. Dr. Andréas will be here in a minute to talk to you. Can I get you anything?"

According to her surgeon, Ruth's torn rotator cuff was now officially fixed. There would be some pain, and it would take months of physical therapy to regain full use, but he was confident she'd wind up with close to one hundred percent mobility. That's all well and good, Ruth thought, but what will a healthy shoulder do for me now that my soul is shattered?

He sent her home with strong painkillers, which she took as much for the ache in her shoulder as the wound in her heart. If she could just anesthetize herself enough, she thought, she could manage to get through another day.

Despite her in-laws' attempts to care for her, and her friends' efforts to reach out, Ruth felt isolated in her physical and emotional pain. So when Lisa came by with a wrapped gift, Ruth thanked her, smiled weakly, and explained that she really needed some rest.

"It's a book," Lisa explained, pointing to the present. "*The Songwriter's Guide to the Marketplace.* I thought it might come in handy once you pick up your guitar again."

"Super," Ruth said, thinking that music was the very last thing she was concerned about. In fact, before the surgery she had put her guitar in the attic so she wouldn't have to look at it while she was recovering and unable to play.

"Call me if you need anything, okay?"

"I promise."

Maddie and Beryl were harder to chase away. They came bearing flowers, chocolates, and three George Clooney movies on DVD. Beryl parked herself in the living room, where Ruth had set up camp because it was too hard to sleep in the same bed as Keith, who thrashed about in his sleep, sending jolts of pain through Ruth's shoulder.

"Which one do you want to watch first?" Beryl asked, spreading the square cases out on the coffee table.

"Really, guys," Ruth said, "I just need to sleep."

"So sleep," Beryl said. "Maddie and I will watch the movie and wake you for the good parts."

"We're worried about you," Maddie added. "You seem so down."

"I'll call you when I'm feeling better," Ruth said. "I promise. Then you can come back with the whole George Clooney library, okay?"

"You have one week." Beryl pointed a finger in Ruth's face. "Then I'm dragging your ass out of bed and down to the Fishbeins' backyard so we can see what kind of kinky tricks they're up to."

"Fine," Ruth said, spilling a pill into her hand and chasing it down with a sip of water. It was as much for effect as it was for the pain. "I'll call as soon as I'm feeling better. Honest."

"One week," Beryl warned.

They left, and Ruth felt relieved to be alone so that she could just retreat into the blankness of sleep. She knew she would probably be bothered again soon—one of the pitfalls of sleeping on the couch in the living room—but what could she do? Her in-laws were sleeping in the guest bedroom and there was no other place for her. Besides, it was probably better for the children this way. At least they got to see her during her brief phases of complete consciousness. Depressed as she was, she still understood that they needed their mother.

Then one day her in-laws announced that they needed to get back home, and could she manage on her own. Sure she could. So she moved out of the living room and into the guest bedroom and tried to get on with the business of caring for the children and managing the house.

Fortunately, with Carmen cleaning and Marta taking care of Keith, there wasn't much that had to be done after the kids left for school. So, after getting them onto the bus, she would take a couple of painkillers and climb back in bed. Physical therapy, she told herself, could be put off until she was feeling a little better. So could getting the car washed, balancing the checkbook, returning phone calls, getting her hair cut, going to the dry cleaners, and all the other errands she normally ran in a day. Her schedule was to sleep from nine to two, and then get up and shower before the kids got home so she could carpool them to their various activities and see that they got their homework done before bed. It seemed like it took all the strength she could muster, and sleeping through the day was the only way she could fortify herself.

The problem was that Keith dogged her constantly, disturbing her rest with piddling problems. Either the *Times* forgot to include the Metro Section with the day's paper or he couldn't get the DVD player to work or Marta cooked something for lunch that he didn't like. Again and again, she told him not to wake her unless there was an emergency, but he just couldn't get it. The only relief she got from her melancholy was when she got so mad at him she wanted to scream.

One morning, she marched into the den where Keith was reading his newspaper.

"Listen," she said, "tonight is Morgan's concert at school, and if I don't get some rest now I'll never make it through. So whatever you do, *don't* wake me. Get it?"

"Unless there's an emergency," he answered.

"No, not even if there's an emergency."

"What if the house burns down?"

"Then I'll die of smoke inhalation and finally get some rest."

She marched out and went into the guest bedroom, where she closed the door and settled into bed with a pillow under her shoulder. She had hardly slept during the night and desperately needed the rest. Yet she was so agitated about the prospect of being woken that it was hard to unwind. Finally, after an hour of concentrated relaxation she floated into a dream state just below the surface of consciousness. She met Paul there. He wanted to know why he hadn't seen her in so long. She couldn't decide whether to tell him it was because of her shoulder surgery or because he had told her they were through. Then she noticed he was alone. *Where's Margie?* she asked him. He responded, but she wasn't quite sure what he had said. Her heart filled with hope. Perhaps they had broken up! *What did you say, Paul? About Margie?*

"Denny's Children's Wear called. They're having their midnight madness sale."

Ruth opened her eyes and saw Keith leaning on his walker in the middle of the room.

"What?" she asked, confused.

"Denny's called. They're having a sale."

It all became clear. Once again, Keith had managed to ruin her chances with Paul. He even got in the way of her dreams. "I told you not to wake me!"

"Everything is forty to fifty percent off," he said, as if nothing could possibly be more important.

Ruth yanked out the pillow that was supporting her shoulder and threw it at Keith's head. It missed.

"Drop dead!" she screamed.

Keith shrugged and shuffled out of the room. Exasperated, Ruth grunted and got out of bed to retrieve the much-needed pillow. She gave it one punch with her good arm to fluff it up and tried to get comfortable enough to fall back asleep. But no matter how much she tried to focus on something, anything, that didn't bring her down, her attention wandered, settling on the stuff that made her anxious or depressed. She tried to think about how well the children were doing in school, but wound up worrying about the social studies project Morgan hadn't yet finished and needed her help with. She tried to revel in Ben's extraordinary sweetness, but became agitated thinking about the creep who had broken into his locker and stolen his book fair money.

George Clooney, she thought, that's who I'll fantasize about. Maybe once they start filming the movie I'll flirt with him right in front of Paul, and he'll flirt back. Maybe we'll have a scandalous affair that will get the whole town talking. Maybe Paul will finally realize that he never should have let me get away.

Ruth wondered if George Clooney would be a better lover than Jared, who left her feeling sad and ashamed. More concerned with showing off his athletic prowess than pleasing her, he had strutted energetically around the room and approached lovemaking as if a team of Olympic judges were watching from the sidelines. Worst of all, he had kept his eyes closed almost continuously, as if he were trying to be someplace other than there, with her. *Look at me!* she wanted to scream, but didn't. Instead, she closed her eyes, too, and let herself climb the crest of orgasm and release. It wasn't even the need for sexual satisfaction that brought her there, but the desire to be done with the whole damn thing. Usually, Ruth considered her ability to climax easily a magnificent blessing. This time, however, she hated herself for letting go with this narcissistic lout. He didn't deserve her orgasm. She felt filthy and hollow.

"How long are you in town for?" he asked as he dressed to leave in the middle of the night.

Give me a break, she thought, hating him for going through the motions of asking that stupid, meaningless question. As if either of them thought they would ever see each other again. And hating him, too, for the smell of expensive aftershave he left on her skin, and the semen spilled from his condom and onto the sheets when he carelessly pulled it off. She rolled over the wet spot and onto her side to watch him pull his soft blue shirt over his beautiful head. All at once, she saw his whole future: the shallow, spoiled girl he would marry, the huge home he would buy, the expensive vacations, the pretty children, the package-perfect life of a handsome, privileged boy. Misfortune wouldn't touch him. He was just one of those lucky people who'd never find himself sleeping beside someone whose body and brain were ravaged by a stroke.

"Forget it, Jared," she said. "Just go have a nice life and try not to be too much of a shit to people along the way."

"You're funny," he said.

"Hilarious."

Later, when it was time to dress for Morgan's concert, Ruth had to summon all her energy just to find the strength. She had never fallen back to sleep and was even more tired and cranky than usual.

She went into the master bedroom, where an oversized walk-in closet housed her oversized collection of clothes. Keith was napping on the bed, snoring, with his mouth wide open. She ignored him and put on an outfit that hung loosely on her thinning frame. On the way out she stopped and watched him sleep, noticing the way his eyelids danced and twitched. He's dreaming, she thought. I should wake him now, just to be obnoxious. She looked at the TV remote on the night table. That would do it, she mused. I could turn the television on, full volume, and then leave, taking the remote with me! She picked it up and aimed it at the screen, but stopped before pressing the button. A better idea occurred to her. She gently placed the remote back down and tiptoed out of the room. She would let him sleep. And sleep and sleep. Right through Morgan's concert, which he wanted to attend. Would serve him right.

Just as she quietly closed the door, the telephone rang, and Keith woke up with a snort.

"Is it time to get ready?" he asked cheerfully.

Ruth sighed and shook her head, deflated. "Yeah," she said through the door. "I'll send Marta in to help you."

The concert brought Ruth's spirits down even more. All the other parents looked so happy to be there, greeting one another with laughter and smiles. Ruth felt like a fraud, going through the motions of a normal parent, when all she wanted to do was go back home and pull the covers over her head.

Before the lights went down in the auditorium, Suzanne Podobinski approached Ruth and asked about the shoulder surgery. This caught Ruth completely off guard, as Suzanne was the last person she expected compassion from. Ruth let down her armor and told her old tennis rival that she was having a rough time of it.

"I never thought it would be this painful," Ruth admitted.

"Look at the positive side," Suzanne said. "Now you have a great excuse for walking away from a tennis game when you're up a point."

I should have seen it coming, Ruth thought. But instead of rising to the challenge and hitting one back, she let out a long sigh and looked sadly at Suzanne. She no longer saw a powerful opponent, but a miserable little woman with bitter lines etched in the thin skin of her aging face. She thought about Suzanne's life of planned deprivation: diet sodas and salads with no dressing. Hours on the treadmill. And for what? Suzanne was nothing but a malnourished soul in size four pants.

• • •

A party was the last thing Ruth needed, but a few days later, Lisa, Maddie, and Beryl dropped in to remind her that the big movie project celebration party was that night.

"I'm really not up to it," Ruth told her friends.

"But it's your committee," Lisa said.

"And you worked so hard to get to this point," Maddie added. "It's your chance to shine."

Ruth laid her head down on the cool surface of the kitchen table. "Shine? I've never felt more matte-finish in my life."

"Listen," said Beryl, who was at the counter making coffee with Ruth's French press. "Podobinski is going to be there. You *have* to come, rub her nose in our success."

Ruth took a deep breath and felt it snag on something in her chest, as if her heart were blocking the way. Why didn't she even give a damn about Suzanne anymore?

Lisa rubbed her back. "Paul will be there," she said softly.

A rush of warm air filled Ruth's lungs and didn't move. "With Margie?"

Lisa looked to Maddie for guidance.

"No, I'm sure he's not bringing Margie. He wouldn't, would he?"

Beryl put a steaming cup of coffee in front of Ruth. "No way. He's not that much of a dick."

Ruth looked to Lisa, beseechingly.

"I agree," Lisa said. "He'll come alone. For sure."

Her scoop-neck red dress was the third outfit Ruth tried on. She eyed herself in the full-length mirror in her closet and decided it was all wrong. She pulled it off over her head and took out the stretchy black lace blouse that looked so good with her herringbone skirt. She'd need to wear her black bra with that one, so she unclasped the white one she was wearing and dropped it to the floor. As she glanced at her topless form, she remembered the time she undressed for Paul in his bedroom. Unlike Jared, he lay on his bed watching her intently.

"I could look at you forever," he had said.

"And not touch me?" she teased.

He smiled. "Come here."

"You have to catch me," she said, laughing.

His blue eyes burned dark as he leaped out of bed and caught her by the arm before she could run. Thrilled by the prospect of a chase, she tried to pull away, but was surprised by the strength of his grip. He threw her down on the bed and pinned her arms above her head. Furiously, he kissed, licked, bit, and sucked her body. She wailed with pleasure, expecting him to penetrate her hard and fast. But he spread her legs and stopped before entering her completely, moving his hips away in a tease as she brought hers up. She knew what he wanted her to do.

"Please," she begged. "Please, I need it. *Please!*"

And he gave it to her. *God, oh God.*

Ruth reached into her panties to touch herself when the phone rang. She paused, waiting for someone else in the house to pick up, but it rang again. And again.

Frustrated, she walked out of the closet, still topless, and picked up the phone by her bed. It was Paul. Was he going to try crawling back to her? Was he realizing how much more she had to offer than his prissy little Margie?

"How are you, Ruth?"

"Swell," she said, making the sarcasm obvious. She'd be damned if she was going to make this easy for him.

"What's the matter?" he asked.

She sat down on the bed. "For starters, I had that operation on my shoulder."

"Oh, the surgery! I meant to call, I'm so sorry. Did it go all right?"

"Except for the excruciating pain and long recuperation."

"Will you be okay for the party tonight?"

"I don't know. Maybe. Are you going?" She pictured arriving late, and seeing Paul's eyes widen at the sight of her trimmed-down figure in that black lace blouse with the plunging neckline.

"Yes," he said, "but listen, there's something I need to tell you. I'll be taking Margie with me. I thought you should know."

"You're taking *Margie*?" Ruth couldn't believe she had heard correctly.

"Yes, that's what I wanted to tell you." He paused. "We're engaged."

A surge of adrenaline rushed through her like an angry flood. She hesitated before reacting, but only for a second. "Engaged! You asked her to *marry* you?"

"Most people just say congratulations."

The nerve! How dare he chastise her for an ungracious reaction to news that separated the one string of hope that kept her from falling into the abyss!

"Fuck you, Paul!"

"Ruth!" he admonished.

"And fuck your holier-than-thou Catholic school bullshit!"

"Get a hold of yourself, Ruth. You're out of control."

"Yeah, well, it's better than being so *in* control all the time. What are you going to do with all that pent-up sexual energy, huh? Take it all out on Margie? Ha!"

"I think I've had enough."

"You can never have enough, baby," she seethed. "That's part of your problem. Maybe that's why you're marrying Margie. To tame that dirty beast *I* brought out in you. You can handle someone like Margie. But with me, you had to face the real Paul. The animal under the choirboy robe."

"Don't kid yourself, Ruth. I didn't leave you because our sex was too wild. I left you because you're *married*!"

She jumped up. "You mean, if my husband were stupid enough to go up on the roof in a rainstorm and get himself killed you would have proposed to me? That's crap and you know it!"

"It's not crap, Ruth. It's the truth! If you were a widow, I would have *begged* you to spend the rest of your life with me!"

Quiet. A deathly quiet, broken only when Ruth's arm reached out and slammed down the phone, which sent an unbearable pain tearing through her shoulder. It was a pain that made her drop to her knees as two thoughts collided in her head like freight trains traveling at full speed. Keith and Paul. Paul and Keith. Again and again they met and crashed with a deafening screech that was too much to bear. Make it stop, she thought. Make it stop!

She rose, dizzy, and heard Keith's voice from the hallway. "Are we going to the party soon?" he asked, pushing the door open. He stopped when he saw her half-naked form and stared, his slack jaw going even slacker.

"Yum-yum," he said.

"Get out of my way," she said through clenched teeth as she walked toward the closet to get some clothes.

He grabbed at her naked breast and squeezed. Ruth knocked his arm away and sent him tumbling in the process.

"I *said* get out of my *way!*" she screamed to her husband, now supine on the carpet. She went into the oversized closet and slammed the door. As she grabbed the first thing she found and pulled it on, she heard Keith's voice through the door.

"Are we gonna fuck now?"

Chapter Twenty-three

LISA

"Can I help you with that?" Maddie asked as Lisa pulled a tray of hot hors d'oeuvres from the oven.

"I'm fine," Lisa said, wishing she could get her friends to move into the living room. What kind of party is it if everyone stays in the kitchen the whole time? "There's hardly anything to do."

Adam picked up a bottle of wine from the counter and poured a glass for Maddie. He waved the bottle toward Beryl and her husband as a question, but they shook their heads and showed him their nearly full glasses. Adam turned his attention back to Maddie.

"So where is Bruce tonight?"

Oh, no, Lisa thought, not that. She almost kicked herself for not having filled him in before the party. She changed the subject as quickly as she could. "Adam, didn't Paul Capobianco and his friend say they wanted to see the house? Would you mind?"

Adam beamed, as she knew he would. The house was his pride and joy—tangible proof of his success—and giving people the tour was one of his great pleasures. He tipped his glass to Lisa and left to escort his guests around the property.

The doorbell rang. Lisa wiped her hands on a towel and said she would get it. "I hope it's Ruth," she added. Her friend had called from her cell phone earlier, sounding hysterical. Lisa pleaded with her to come straight over, but Ruth insisted on taking some time to herself to "sort things out first."

Beryl turned to her husband. "If it's George Clooney," she said, "I might ask you to get scarce for a while."

"If it's George Clooney," the portly Jonathan answered, "I'll put on lipstick and dance naked on this table."

But it wasn't George Clooney. And it wasn't Ruth, either. It was Jerry Murphy, the private investigator. Lisa had learned from Maddie that he actually *asked* for an invite, saying private investigators never get invited anywhere.

Lisa led him back to the kitchen to see the others.

"Oh, hello, *George*," Beryl said to Jerry. "Jonathan, have you met Maddie's friend George Clooney?"

"It's Jerry," Jerry said amid the titters. "Jerry Murphy. Don't you remember?" He looked like he was about to cry.

"She's just kidding," Lisa said.

"At my expense?"

"At *his* expense." Beryl pointed to her husband. "He said he would take his clothes off if George Clooney came, and that's a visual feast I shouldn't keep to myself."

Everyone laughed, even Jerry. The group chatted amiably for a while before the conversation splintered into small groups. Lisa was putting another tray of hors d'oeuvres in the oven when she overheard Jerry pull Maddie aside.

"I have good news," he said to her.

"I could use good news," Maddie said.

"That woman you thought your husband was sleeping with?" He leaned in. "She's a *lesbian!*"

Lisa, who knew the entire sordid story, including the

scene Maddie walked in on at the wedding, dropped the tray. It hit the hard tiles with a clang, and Lisa watched as frozen pigs in blankets rolled and skittered across the floor, several of them landing against the shoes of her guests. Now what do I do? she thought. Ask everyone to leave so I can clean up?

Beryl saw her expression. "Guess it's time to move this party to the living room," she said, ushering everyone out of the kitchen. As the group filed out of the room, Beryl leaned in to her husband and said, in a stage whisper loud enough for everyone to hear, "Ten bucks says she wipes them on her shirt and puts them back on the tray."

After cleaning up the mess, Lisa tiptoed into the den where she had left the children, in their pajamas, watching a DVD. Only Sarah and Simon were there.

"Where are the twins?" Lisa asked.

"Upstairs, I think," Sarah said, without looking up from the television.

Lisa tsked. "I told them to stay down here. Go on up and tell them they can either go right to bed or stay here where I can keep an eye on them."

"In a minute, okay? I don't want to miss this."

Lisa agreed, making a mental note to check back again as soon as she could. She tousled Simon's hair and left.

The doorbell rang again and Lisa headed toward it. Beryl beat her there and swung it open.

"That motherfucker got engaged to the little ferret-face!" Ruth announced in a booming voice.

Lisa looked behind her to make sure Paul and Margie weren't there. She and Beryl ushered Ruth into the kitchen to try to calm her down.

"Have you been drinking?" Beryl asked.

Ruth sat down heavily. "Can you blame me?"

"And you drove here?" Lisa said. "You could have gotten yourself killed or—"

"Spare me," Ruth interrupted, "I'm not going to turn into your mother, I promise." The sound of tires on the gravel driveway caught her attention and she turned toward the window. "Aw, shit, is that Podobinski's car?"

"That's her," Beryl said.

Ruth stood. "I'm going to tell her to get the fuck out of here."

Beryl pushed Ruth back into the chair. "You're going to sit down and shut up. She was invited to this party, remember?"

"Doesn't mean we can't throw her out."

Lisa took Ruth's hands in hers and stared into her bloodshot eyes. "I'm not throwing anyone out of my house, Ruth. Understand?" She paused, realizing she should tell Ruth that Paul and Margie were already there so she would be prepared. But Suzanne was pressing on the front door buzzer and no one seemed to be answering it.

"Just wait here," Lisa said. "Don't move. I'll be right back."

She let Suzanne in and then returned to the kitchen, where Beryl was making coffee to help Ruth sober up. Lisa thought that was a great idea, as she knew she couldn't keep Ruth from Paul and Margie all night. And in Ruth's current state, a huge confrontation was almost inevitable. The thought made Lisa's stomach coil in a knot.

"Listen, Ruth," she said gently to her friend. "I want you to promise me that you're not going to make a scene with Paul."

"Is he here already? Is the twatless wonder with him?"

Beryl laughed and Lisa was about to tell her to stop encouraging such outbursts when she looked out the window and saw a taxicab pull up. That could only mean one thing.

"Oh, no!" Lisa cried.

Beryl turned toward the window. "Is that Nancy? I thought you said your house was off limits to her."

"It is," Lisa said, rushing out of the kitchen. "She's not getting in here."

"Hey!" Ruth shouted after her. "I thought you'd never throw anyone out of your house!"

Lisa stood with her arms folded, blocking the doorway to her house. "What are you doing here?" she whispered through clenched teeth when Nancy approached, hoping she wouldn't have to make a scene in front of the room full of guests behind her.

"C'mon, Lisa," Nancy said, "don't be such a stick in the mud. It's a party. Let me in."

Lisa set her jaw and said nothing. You're not welcome here, she thought. It's what you deserve for every miserable thing you've done to me. For having been a selfish, useless mother. For loving alcohol more than you ever loved me. For coming back into my life and nearly screwing it up all over again. So go away. And never come back.

"Lisa? C'mon, baby. Let me in."

Lisa gently shut the door.

"You think it's easy staying sober!" she heard Nancy shout from the other side. "I could use your help, you know. Oh, sure, turn your back when I need you!"

And where were you when I needed someone? Lisa wanted to ask. She turned back to the room full of guests—including Paul and Margie—and saw Ruth come out of the kitchen and stop in the middle of the room, her eyes, hair, and dress alive in wild shades of red as if she had just burst into flames. She planted her feet apart for balance and glowered at Paul.

"You!" she seethed, an arc of saliva landing at his feet.

Paul grabbed Margie's hand with both of his, as if to protect her from an onslaught. Ruth's eyes seemed to lock onto the gesture, narrowing into a feral glare.

"He's so sweet and gentle in public, isn't he?" She addressed Margie but didn't take her eyes off Paul.

"He's always sweet and gentle," Margie offered.

Ruth threw her head back and laughed. "I guess he hasn't gotten you in bed yet! Think you can handle it, Margie? Did you know he likes it rough?"

"That's enough, Ruth," Paul said.

"I wonder if he'll tie you to the bedpost like he did with me."

Lisa glanced over to Suzanne Podobinksi, who stood against the wall with her arms folded, smirking in bemusement.

"C'mon, Ruth," Lisa said. "Let's get you back in the kitchen for a cup of coffee."

"He'll slap your ass till it's bright red," Ruth continued. "He'll bite your nipples till they're raw."

Beryl stepped forward and put her arm around Ruth. "He's not worth it, honey. Let's go."

Ruth pulled away. "I'm just getting started."

"Beryl's right," Maddie said. "I don't think you want to say anything else."

Suzanne Podobinski cleared her throat. "She doesn't need to say anything else. You people are done. Paul Capobianco is done. Having an affair with a member of the PTA is quite enough to get him fired." She took a step toward Ruth. "And I'm not just bringing him down. Your whole movie project follows right behind!"

Lisa felt the blood drain from her face. "You wouldn't!"
Suzanne beamed. "Watch me."

She picked up her purse as if she were going to waltz out the door, but just then, it burst open and Jill came rushing in, breathless.

"Fire!" she shouted to the astonished guests.

"What?" Lisa asked.

"Fire!" Jill said. "The white ranch house—it's on fire!"

Oh, no, Lisa thought. Not my precious ranch house! It's just not possible. Then she remembered all the flammable paint-removing solvents she had left in the hideous yellow kitchen and felt a shudder. But they couldn't just ignite on their own, could they? Then another thought occurred to her and an icy chill grabbed her by the throat.

"The twins!" she gasped. "Where are the twins?"

"What?" Adam asked.

Lisa remembered how often she had to chastise them for playing with the gas burners, and pictured their little hands reaching for the knobs in the white ranch house.

"The twins!" She shouted this time. "Where are the twins!"

"I'll go check upstairs," he said.

"And call 911!" she yelled as she bolted out the door.

She ran as fast as she could, unaware of the movement of her legs or the biting cold of the night air. Unaware that the party had followed her outside and someone faster than she had caught up and thrown a coat and scarf over her shoulders. A force that felt stronger than fire, stronger than anything, propelled her toward the burning house. She saw dancing flames push through the windows and taunt her. Black smoke filled the doorway and shimmied upward, disappearing into the night sky.

Yet that doorway was her target. Smoke, flames, she

didn't care. She was going in to get her babies. But as she neared, as she got close enough to feel the toxic fumes fill her lungs, someone grabbed her arm and held her back.

"The fire department is on the way," a voice said.

Lisa broke free and ran straight into the thick of it, her eyes stinging, her throat burning. Then she heard someone shout, "Is there a back door?" and Lisa stopped.

The back door! Since it was glass, she could break it with a rock and get in that way. She turned back and ran around the house, hoping the cruel black smoke hadn't yet reached it.

Dear God, she thought as she ran, her babies. Her precious babies. Had she failed them? Was this her fault? She should have checked on them sooner. She should have known they might wander outside. But how could they have gotten into the house? She had locked the front door, hadn't she? Lord, she hadn't!

Lisa wanted to scream. And scream and scream and scream. They'd be in there. They'd probably be dead. And it was her fault.

But she pressed forward. She would go in there no matter what. She would run in, grab their little bodies, and run out.

But as she neared the door, Lisa beheld an image that stopped her in her tracks. She blinked, trying to comprehend what she was seeing. Someone was emerging from the smoke that billowed out the back door. It was an adult. A skinny, familiar form. A woman.

Her mother.

As she drew nearer, Lisa saw that Austin was slumped over her shoulder and Henry was walking beside her.

Henry was okay! Thank you, God, thank you! But Austin. Sweet Austin.

Nancy stopped and laid him on the ground. "Does anyone know CPR!" she shouted.

Lisa glanced behind her and saw all her guests from the party.

Margie stepped forward. "I'm a nurse," she said, and kneeled beside the boy.

Lisa dropped to her knees and grabbed Henry and hugged him hard. "Are you okay?" she asked, looking up and down his body for any sign of burns, and then into his sooty face. He gave one hard pouty nod and dissolved into tears.

Lisa hugged him again and looked at Nancy, beseechingly.

"I think he's alive," Nancy said.

They both looked at Margie, who had her fingers pressed to his throat. "He has a pulse," she pronounced, and started breathing into his mouth.

There was a stillness then, and everyone else seemed to stop breathing as they watched the woman work, the reassuring music of distant sirens getting louder and louder in the background.

By the time the paramedics arrived, Austin had started groaning in low, hoarse whispers. Lisa insisted on riding in the ambulance with him to the hospital. And though he seemed fine, Henry needed attention, too, and was being led into a separate ambulance.

"Go with him, Adam!" Lisa shouted to her husband, who was standing back from the fire with Simon in his arms.

"I want Grandma!" Henry shouted.

And so it was decided. Nancy rode in the ambulance with Henry, and Adam would meet them all at the hospital later.

In the ambulance with Austin, one paramedic administered oxygen while another, a woman, checked his body for burns. Second degree, Lisa heard her say, left hand. That's it? Lisa thought. Relieved, she sighed and wept. It could be worse, so much worse.

"The smoke inhalation," Lisa said, "how bad is it?"

"His airway is open," the woman paramedic said. "We're giving him oxygen now. They'll be able to tell you more at the hospital."

When they arrived, the paramedic told Lisa that Austin would be going straight to Trauma. "You'll have to go to the waiting room," she added.

"I want to stay with him!" Lisa cried.

But it wasn't allowed. As her tiny son was wheeled away on a gurney, a kind nurse with a clipboard put her hand on Lisa's back and asked her to please come and fill out some paperwork.

Lisa heard a soft moan from the stretcher and leaned in. She thought he was trying to say something.

"Mommy," he whispered through the mask. "Mommy."

"Mommy's here, baby," Lisa said. "You're going to be fine."

And at once, Lisa knew it was true. He was going to be fine. And she collapsed in tears onto the shoulder of the kind nurse.

In the waiting room with Nancy, while both boys were being treated, Lisa asked her mother what had happened. Nancy explained that as her taxi passed the white ranch house she heard a loud bang and made him stop. She got out of the cab and saw flames. She assumed the house was vacant, and was just going to tell the driver to call 911 and be on her way, when she heard what sounded like a scream from inside. The smoke by the front door was already too thick to pass, so she went around back and tried the door, but it was locked. So she picked up a large rock and, with her coat wrapped around her hand so she wouldn't cut herself, smashed the glass and let herself in. She couldn't see a thing, but followed the sound of Henry's cries, and found him hovering over his brother near the back door. They were probably trying to leave, she figured, but couldn't get the door open. She grabbed them both and ran out.

By the time Nancy finished her account, Lisa was wracked with sobs. "You saved my children!" she cried, and embraced her mother. The two women held on tightly to each other, weeping.

"He's going to be okay," Nancy said.

Lisa released her mother then and looked at her. She noticed something on her arm—blood, seeping through the sleeve of her dress. "Mother!" Lisa said, pointing.

Nancy looked down. "Oh, jeez!" she said, and pulled up her sleeve to reveal a shard of glass sticking out of her forearm.

"Don't touch it," Lisa said. "Let's get you inside."

But as they walked toward the front of the room to see the triage nurse, Nancy pulled out the piece of glass and let loose a trickle of blood that quickly changed to a flow, spilling to the floor at an alarming rate.

Lisa stared, horrified. In a second, though, she got her wits and pulled off her scarf, wrapping it tightly around Nancy's wound as she led her quickly to the nurse.

"We need help here!" she shouted, and then, to Nancy, "You never listen."

Nancy was rushed into treatment, and Lisa was allowed to accompany her as a tall resident named Dr. Stewart cleaned and sutured her wound.

"He's cute!" Nancy whispered to Lisa, who saw the doctor smile.

"He *hears* you, Mom."

"Well, so what?"

"You just can't go flirting with every—" Lisa stopped herself. No, she thought. I'm not going to do this anymore. Maybe she never came through for me before, and maybe she never will again, but this once was enough. She saved my babies.

"Flirt all you want," Lisa said. "I don't care."

"It doesn't embarrass you?"

Lisa shook her head.

Nancy smiled. "Liar."

They both laughed.

"You forgive me now?" Nancy asked.

Lisa looked at her mother. What did she mean, exactly? Was she apologizing for stealing the rock? Or did she understand that that was merely the straw that broke the camel's back? Maybe she was sorry for everything. Lisa knew she should forgive her. Austin and Henry could have died. At this very moment, Lisa could have been weeping over two lifeless little bodies instead of watching her mother make a fool of herself with a young doctor. And yet, there was a part of herself that couldn't let Nancy completely off the hook.

"I guess," Lisa finally said.

"You don't. I can tell."

Lisa sighed. "I want to, Mom. Maybe it's just one of those things that's going to take a little time. But I'm going to try."

"You know what your problem is? You think you're so embarrassed by me. But it's you. You're embarrassed by *you.*"

Lisa had no desire to hear her mother's inane attempts at psychological insights, and grew bored enough by the conversation to become agitated. She looked at the ugly striped curtains that had been pulled shut around them. Someone, she figured, must have thought the discordant colors looked cheerful. "I wonder how Austin's doing," she said. "Maybe they'll let me in to see him now."

"Sure, change the subject. But there's something I've been wanting to say to you for a long time, and I want you to listen. You owe me that, at least."

Nancy looked hard at Lisa, who felt herself flush. Her mother was right, she owed her at least that much. So while she didn't want to hear what her mother had to say—not here, not now—she took a deep breath and told her to go on and say whatever was on her mind.

"Lisa, baby, when you were a kid, I did something really shitty to you and I want to apologize. And I don't mean the drinking and all that crap, though God knows I'm sorry for that, too. I mean about your singing. Lisa, honey, your voice. It's . . . it's . . ."

For heaven's sake, Lisa thought, does she really believe all will be forgiven if she admits I can sing? Does she think that's the source of all the strife between us?

"I know," Lisa said. "I know, it's nice. I have a lovely voice. It's sweet that you want to tell me, but you don't have to. Really."

"That's not what I was going to say," Nancy insisted, wincing in pain as the doctor continued to stitch her arm. "It's not just a nice voice, honey, it's magnificent. Beats the pants off mine. I know I never admitted that before. I was too jealous. So instead, I made you feel ashamed of it. Sometimes I think you've spent your whole life trying to be a dull little person so you wouldn't outshine me. I just want you to know that it's okay to be better than me. You understand what I'm telling you?"

Lisa blinked. What had her mother just said? The last thing she remembered was "Beats the pants off mine." The sentence seemed to ricochet around in her brain, bumping into every truth that held her world together. She heard the words that came after it, but couldn't comprehend their meaning. She realized she'd been staring straight ahead at the striped curtains, letting her eyes unfocus as the colors blurred together.

"I don't understand," she said.

"You're better than me, Lisa, and it's okay. I still love you."

Lisa let herself fall into the hard side chair next to Nancy's cot. She tried to steady her trembling hands on her knees.

Lisa tried to speak. I didn't know you thought I was better than you, she wanted to say, but couldn't quite get the words out. "I didn't know you thought that about my voice," she said instead.

"Of course you did. Somewhere inside you always knew that."

Did I? Lisa asked herself. A familiar fear gripped her stomach, providing the answer. Yes, of course! It was a truth that had been there all along, but was too terrifying for Lisa to face. She took a long, jagged breath.

"And you're okay with it?" she asked.

Nancy shrugged. "Hell, I'm no diva. Never was. Don't get me wrong, I can belt out a song. And maybe I even had five minutes where I was truly great, but I was too drunk to make it work for me."

Lisa felt a lightness, then, like the earth had released her of its gravitational pull. She held on to the arms of her chair as if she might float away. The sensation made her giddy, and she let out a giggle.

"What's so funny?" Nancy asked.

"I don't know," Lisa said, and her laughter turned to tears. She couldn't make sense of her emotions, but it was okay. She hugged her mother and cried. Nancy cried, too.

The nurse with the clipboard entered the room. "There you are," she said to Lisa. "Austin is awake and improving. We still have him on oxygen, but his levels are good. We brought Henry in to keep him company. You can come in now if you like."

"You're done," Dr. Stewart said to Nancy as he taped a bandage over her wound. "Just stop back here for aftercare instructions before you leave."

With that, the women followed the nurse to Austin's room. On their way there, Adam caught up with them. He held Simon in his arms and Sarah was beside him. He looked from Lisa to Nancy, their faces red and puffy from crying.

"Everything okay?" he asked.

"Everything's great," Lisa said, barely getting it out before she dissolved into sobs again.

Adam put his free arm around her and sniffled. Lisa let herself weep into his shoulder as Sarah grabbed her around the waist and started to cry. She heard Nancy whimpering, too.

Then, another voice spoke. It was tiny and soft, but distinct.

"Why evybody cwying?" it said.

They all fell silent and stared at Simon. Then, one by one, they each looked at one another to acknowledge what they'd heard before bursting into laughter. It was no hallucination. Simon had spoken!

Chapter Twenty-four

Austin's first night home from the hospital, Lisa slept on an air mattress on the floor between the boys' beds. The doctor had said he was fine, but Lisa felt the need for proximity.

She lay still, listening to the quiet of the dark house, trying to discern the shallow breathing of the twins' slumber. But all she could hear was the soft steady pulse of the electronic clock.

She sat up and looked over at Austin, watching his chest rise and fall, rise and fall. Then over at Henry. They were fine. Everyone was fine. Lisa lay down again and closed her eyes, waiting for the calm that would let her drift off.

That the movie deal was off didn't bother her. Not as much as it bothered the others, anyway. She had a lot to be thankful for and she knew it. But she worried about Ruth, who seemed to be slipping into a void, unaware that her friends were reaching out, ready to catch her at any time.

Lisa shifted, trying to get comfortable. She fought the

urge to sit up and look at the boys again. They're fine, she told herself. They're fine. Relax.

It occurred to her to try a trick she'd learned in the past to help herself sleep. She closed her eyes and imagined the people she loved right there in the room with her, just like the twins were. First, she put Adam on the bed next to her. She took her time and tried to sense his presence as if he were really there. It worked. In her mind, his warm body was right there next to her. Then she put Simon in bed with Austin, and Sarah with Henry. She saw them all sleeping blissfully. She was feeling happier and calmer, and drifted just below the surface of wakefulness. In that hazy state, she sensed another presence in the room. Her subconscious had placed someone in the rocker at the foot of her mattress. It was her mother.

They were all there, together. Lisa felt whole, and fell into a long, deep sleep.

The next morning, Adam took Simon to his preschool, and Lisa got Sarah and Henry off to school. Austin would be staying home another day or two, and Lisa looked forward to spending some time alone with him. She so rarely got to do that with one of the twins.

"My ride is here," Nancy announced.

Lisa was happy to have her mother back at the house. Glad to have found a way to be at peace with this crazy, annoying woman. She gave her a hug.

"Have a good day, Mom."

And then Nancy was off, taking a ride with a friend she had made at the treatment center.

Lisa and Austin spent the morning looking at his favorite books, and Lisa was happy to see how far his reading had come this year. After lunch, she could tell he was tired, and told him to close his eyes and get some rest. He quickly fell asleep and Lisa asked Bonnie to keep an eye on him while she went out for a little while. His teacher had called to say the children had made get-well cards for him, and Lisa wanted to stop by the school to pick them up. She knew he would be delighted by the cheerful wishes from his friends.

Her plan was to go directly to the school, but Lisa found herself slowing to a stop in front of the empty, no-longer-quite-white ranch house. She got out of the van and looked at the façade, bisected with a thick black scar where the exterior had charred. Yesterday, Adam had admitted the insurance adjuster, who said that the kitchen sustained most of the damage. The house was still structurally sound, and could indeed be restored. But Adam wanted to tear it down, and Lisa was inclined to agree with him. She didn't need it anymore.

Lisa got back in her car but stopped before she turned the ignition. She looked up at the house. Maybe one final good-bye, she thought.

She let herself in, and immediately smelled the awful, lingering odor of burnt chemicals. She cupped her hand over her mouth and surveyed the living room. The electricity had been turned off, so the house was now lit only by sunlight streaming through the windows. Its charm was hard to ignore.

She walked across the living room floor, carefully avoiding the puddles the fire hoses had left behind. When she got to the door of the kitchen, Lisa looked up. It was like a black, skeletal ghost of the room she had painted with such senseless abandon.

"At least the yellow is gone," she said out loud, making herself laugh. For the first time in so very long, Lisa felt genuinely happy.

She turned and made her way back to the front door, taking great, giddy leaps over the puddles of water. She shut the door behind her, taking one last look. There was something so homey about the place. It almost seemed a shame to tear it down. As she got into her van and closed the door, something occurred to her. At last, she realized the exact detail the kitchen had needed all along: a delicate stenciled border of cherries, just like the one she and Adam had had in their first home.

"Ah, well," she said, starting the engine. She adjusted her rearview mirror and took one final look at the ranch house. Then Lisa looked straight ahead and drove off.

The cards for Austin were in a cardboard box, decorated with colorful stickers and glued-on buttons. As she carried it out of the school and into the parking lot, careful not to damage the precious creation, a familiar car pulled in behind hers. It was Suzanne Podobinski, likely stopping there for some PTA business.

Lisa's first inclination was to hurry into her car and drive off, avoiding any kind of confrontation. But something inside her stirred. She didn't know whether it was the awakening jolt of almost losing a child or finally accepting her right to let her own light shine as brightly as anyone else's, but Lisa felt different. It was as if her spirit were no longer pinned down by a terrible weight.

Not that the fear was gone—the idea of confronting Suzanne made her heart race—but it finally felt like a tangible thing she could choose to ignore. How liberating!

The only problem was that there was nothing left to say. So Lisa just stood there and glared, feeling the pulse of anger in every beat of her heart, and doing nothing to suppress it.

Suzanne spotted Lisa and flipped her hair in the universal symbol of pretty-girl superiority. She hurried past Lisa on clicky high heels, adjusting the strap on the handbag swinging from her shoulder so that it hit the decorated box, sending buttons flying. Suzanne smirked and kept walking.

Lisa's fury boiled over. She put the box on the ground and hurried around Suzanne to block her entrance to the school.

Fear? Ha! Suzanne was a bug, a germ, a microbe. Lisa thought of the head lice invasion the school dealt with every winter, as hats and scarves and coats were shoved into cubbies, allowing the opportunistic parasites to jump from host to host. People like Suzanne were the same way. They'd always be there, reappearing year after year. But that didn't mean you sat by and let them take over. You fought.

Suzanne stopped and rolled her eyes. "*Excuse* me," she said dismissively.

Lisa didn't budge.

"Get out of my way."

Lisa nodded toward the strewn buttons. "That was supposed to be for my son."

Suzanne inspected her manicure. "Go call the National Guard."

Lisa took a deep breath, giving extra oxygen to the righteous indignation fueling her fury. Who knew anger could be so intoxicating? She narrowed her eyes and uttered the one word she'd been wanting to say to Suzanne Podobinski since that first day she tried to talk to her at the tennis club, only to be snubbed.

"Bitch."

Suzanne looked genuinely shocked. But she recovered quickly enough and laughed derisively. "Are you through?"

"Not by a long shot."

"What are you going to do? Beat me up?"

A good question. What *was* she going to do? Physical violence didn't seem all that far-fetched. But even as angry as she was, Lisa knew that wasn't the answer.

"I don't think so," she said.

"Then get out of my way, you stupid little twit." Suzanne pushed past Lisa into the building.

Lisa stood dumbly as Suzanne's heels click-clacked down the hallway.

"Wait!" she shouted.

"I'm in a hurry," Suzanne said without turning around.

"I saw!" Lisa blurted. "I saw. And I'm going to tell."

That got Suzanne's attention. She stopped and turned around slowly, clearly understanding the reference.

Lisa swallowed hard. "Give us back the movie project," she said, "or I'm going to tell everyone what I saw."

Suzanne sighed and shook her head, as if she barely had the patience to explain. "Go ahead and tell. You'll have to explain what you and your band of outlaws were doing traipsing around Donna's property. And once they find out you're a bunch of thieves, who's going to believe you? Face it, dear, the movie project is *over*. And so is Paul's career. I'll be dropping the bomb at next week's school board meeting, if you want to come. It should be a quite a show."

Suzanne pivoted and walked away, leaving Lisa with the impression that this confrontation business might not be so glorious after all.

Chapter Twenty-five

MADDIE

Days later, Maddie sat in the passenger seat of Ruth's Navigator, the heated upholstery powerless against the chill in her bones. Lisa and Beryl sat in the back, speaking softly.

"You don't have to do this, Maddie," Beryl said.

Maddie swallowed against the lump in her throat. "I do. I need to talk to him."

They drove across the flat terrain of eastern Long Island toward the New Montefiore Cemetery, where Jack was buried. Once they entered and passed the gatehouse, Ruth made lefts and rights down the narrow roadways of the vast grounds until she reached the designated intersection and stopped the car.

"Do you want us to come with you?" Lisa asked.

Maddie shook her head and got out of the car alone. She was greeted by a cruel wind that followed her as she walked past strangers' graves, looking for Jack's. Then she found it, a small metal plaque bearing his name. It marked the spot where, according to Jewish law, a tombstone would be ceremoniously unveiled in one year's time.

"Hello, Jack," she said out loud to the marker. Self-conscious, she looked around. The only people she saw were her friends in the car, who seemed to be passing around a cell phone, and an elderly couple, hundreds of yards away.

"I don't know why I'm here. I mean, we said our good-byes, didn't we?" Maddie looked down at the ground and remembered how deep the grave looked at the funeral. She thought about Jack, so far underground, and felt like a colossus looking down on him. She pulled her coat beneath her for insulation against the cold earth, and sat down, Indian style.

"This feels stupid," she said, thinking she wasn't really talking to Jack at all. He was gone. The dead cells in the box underground had nothing to do with her smart, funny, infuriating friend. She sat silently for a time.

"I called your mother," she finally said. "She's doing fine." Maddie picked up a pebble and rolled it between her fingertips. She flicked it away. "That's a lie. She's not doing fine, Jack. She's a wreck. She misses you. She told me parents aren't supposed to bury their children."

Maddie got quiet again. "Your father is your father," she continued. "You know, dealing with it in that weird way he has. When they were sitting shivah, he kept asking everybody if they wanted a plum. I said no, thanks, but I wish I hadn't. I wish I'd said yes. It would have made him feel better." Maddie sighed. "God, Jack. What's wrong with me? How hard would it have been to take the stupid plum?" She turned her collar up against the cold. "I'm so sorry about that, Jack. I'm sorry I didn't take a plum from your father."

She put her head down and sniffled, trying to fight the sadness that bore down on her.

"I fucked everything up, Jack. Bruce and I were just starting to work things out when Ruth called and explained what happened. Bruce, bless his heart, insisted we rush home to say good-bye to you. But then. Oh, God. Do you remember that conversation we had?"

Maddie thought back to the day she and Bruce rushed out of the hotel in Massachusetts so that she could visit Jack on his deathbed. He was home, receiving hospice care after the marrow transplant failed. A nurse greeted them at the door of Jack's home and explained that they had caught him at a lucid moment.

They entered Jack's bedroom together. An oxygen tank sat next to the bed, a thin tube leading to his nose. A breath caught in Maddie's throat as she saw Jack's still form, eyes wide open but blank with death. She froze, thinking he had already passed. Bruce ushered her into the room, his hand on her back.

"Jack?" he said. "It's Bruce and Maddie."

Jack's hollow face turned toward them and Maddie understood that he had already welcomed death. It was only the final mechanics of weakly pumping blood that separated him from the other side.

"Sit down," Jack said, his voice low and hoarse.

Maddie and Bruce approached his bed.

"I'm not going to stay," Bruce said. "You and Maddie probably need some time alone. I just wanted to say good-bye. You fought a good fight, Jack." He touched his sick friend's shoulder.

"Thank you," Jack said.

Bruce kissed the top of Maddie's head and told her he would wait in the car.

Still unable to speak, Maddie sat down by Jack's bed and pulled a tissue from the box on his night table.

"Alone at last," Jack said.

Maddie laughed and it was like a dam bursting. She wept into her hands.

"Mel," he said, his hand reaching toward her.

She grabbed it. "I'm sorry," she said. "I'm sorry things didn't work out between us."

He spoke slowly and deliberately. "I have no regrets. You belong with Bruce."

Maddie nodded. "You're right. I do."

"It's best we never slept together. But that day on your couch. I'm glad for that." His voice got stronger. "Sometimes, when I'm drifting off, that's where I am. Feeling your soft naked body under mine."

"I think about that, too," she said. "Your flesh against my flesh. I just didn't think that would be my last memory of you."

"I'm so tired."

"Do you want me to leave?"

"I'm sorry. I just have no strength to stay awake. Say good-bye to me, Maddie."

Maddie took a deep, deep breath. "I love you, Jack."

Jack smiled and closed his eyes.

She leaned forward and kissed him on the cheek, his skin so cool and dry to her lips. "Good-bye," she choked out.

Maddie pulled herself up from the chair and walked to the door. When she opened it, Bruce was right in front of her. Her heart froze.

"Bruce! I thought you were waiting in the car."

His face looked white. "I dropped my car keys in the hallway and had to come back for them."

Maddie stared at her husband and wondered if Jack's voice had been strong enough to carry into the hallway. Then she got her answer. Bruce turned and walked away from her.

Maddie followed after. No, not this, she thought. Not now.

"Bruce? Talk to me. What did you hear?"

He sped up and headed out the door to the car.

"Bruce? Don't ignore me. I need to explain this to you!"

He opened the car door and turned to Maddie. "I wish *I* was the one dying!" He got in the car, slammed it shut, and locked the doors.

Maddie pulled on the door handle. "Let me in! Let me explain!"

Bruce put his head down on the steering wheel and wept. She pounded on the window but he ignored her. Finally, he started the car and drove away. By the time Maddie arrived home by taxicab, he had already packed a suitcase and was heading out the door. There was nothing she could say to stop him.

Maddie felt the cold ground of the cemetery seeping through her coat, and realized there was nothing here at this grave that could help her. She rose to leave, but when she glanced toward the car, she saw that her friends had gotten out and were headed toward her.

"You okay?" Ruth said when she approached.

"No," Maddie said. "Jack is dead. Bruce is gone. I have nothing."

Beryl put her arm around her friend. "What am I? Chopped liver?"

Maddie laughed. "You're right. I have my friends. And I don't know what I'd do without you!"

They all hugged.

"Should we do something for Jack?" Lisa asked. "I mean, since we're here. It seems like we should do something."

"I wish I still had my guitar," Ruth said, her eyes filling with tears. "I'd play a song for him."

Lisa put her arm around Ruth, whose guitar had been

destroyed. She had left it in her attic while convalescing from her shoulder surgery, and carpenter ants had damaged it beyond repair. When her friends had suggested she replace it, she said she needed some time to mourn its loss.

The friends fell quiet and stood side by side by side, gazing down at the grave as if they understood that they each needed a moment of silence. It was broken, finally, by the sound of a crystal-clear voice wringing pain from a simple tune. It was Lisa, singing Ruth's song:

> *You sit alone in a room*
> *All alone with your pain*
> *All alone with your wounds*
> *And you cry out all day*
> *But they think it's a song*
> *Don't they know that it's wrong*
> *To leave you alone?*
> *You're bleeding . . .*
> *Ooh-ooh-ooh*
> *You need me!*

Ruth joined in for the chorus:

> *I'll stop the hurting*
> *I'll take your pain*
> *Give the song to Daddy, baby*
> *Give the song to Daddy!*

But there was no one to take Maddie's pain, and she wept, lavishly and indulgently, her friends gathered around, supporting her in her grief. She heard the sound of a car driving down the path, but she kept her face buried in Ruth's coat.

A door slammed. Footsteps approached. Still, Maddie didn't look up.

"Maddie," Ruth said gently. "Someone's here to see you."

"What? Who?"

"We called him," Beryl said, "from the car. We explained everything."

"He listened. He understands," said Lisa.

Ruth turned Maddie around to face the man walking down the path. "He loves you, Maddie. He wants you back."

Maddie put her arms out. "Bruce!"

Chapter Twenty-six

RUTH

At two a.m., Ruth tiptoed across her house, checking to make sure Morgan, Ben, and Keith were all asleep. Then she got dressed in layers for warmth, and quietly slipped out the front door.

What she was doing would shock everyone. She hadn't told her friends because she knew they would try to talk her out of it.

Ruth got in her car and headed for the school, hoping this act would obliterate the self-pity that had been crushing her spirit. She hated feeling sorry for herself, but everything in her life was going wrong at the very moment her friends were enjoying their happy endings. Maddie had reunited with Bruce and was getting her marriage back on track. Lisa's twins had survived the fire intact, and she had taken her mother back into her heart and her life. Even Beryl seemed to be getting on with it, using recent events as fodder for wisecracks and having as much fun as ever. But what was Ruth left with? She no longer had Paul, and she still had a damaged husband who could give her no intimacy, no companionship, nothing. She didn't even have the movie project anymore. There would be no chance to meet George Clooney. No chance to become the town hero. Hell, she didn't even have her guitar anymore. Just as well, she figured. Writing songs was a waste of time and energy. All that false hope that she'd get somewhere with her music was draining her spirit.

Of course, this act of defiance wouldn't make any of that any better, but she had to have some sort of victory over Suzanne Podobinski or she just wouldn't be able to go on. She was going to go through with this. Ruth was going to steal Applewood Rock—for good.

She turned into the school and drove around to the back, hoping to see Jerry Murphy's car, but he wasn't there yet. He was the one she called to help her do this, as she knew a private investigator could be trusted to keep his mouth shut. At first he balked at the idea of doing something illegal, but she talked him into it, promising a tidy sum and insisting she'd do it with him or without him.

"Besides," she had said, "I know I can trust you not to tell a soul."

It was probably the flattery that got him.

Though it was chilly enough to see her breath, Ruth got out of her car and walked over to the rock. She touched its cold surface, running her thumb along the roughness. All these years, this boulder sat here, impermeable, enduring rain, snow, wind, and generations of small children. A stoic, Ruth thought. It was exactly what she would need to be to survive.

She sat down on the rock and hugged her coat around herself, waiting for Jerry Murphy to show up. She tried to picture Suzanne's expression on learning that the rock had disappeared again. She'd grit her teeth and pace furiously, taking the news as a personal assault. Suzanne would suspect Ruth, of course, but lack of proof would leave her impotent to exact revenge.

Ruth searched for some tangible joy she could feel at the idea of trumping Suzanne one last time, but came up empty. Even now, she was simply going through the motions. Her passion had been drained, leaving her as cold and hard as the stone beneath her. She was counting on the aftermath of this caper to reignite her flame.

At last, Ruth heard a car driving around toward the back of the school and stood to meet Jerry Murphy. The vehicle came to a stop and the driver's door opened. Then the passenger and back doors opened, too. What was going on? Was Jerry Murphy bringing a crew to help?

Then three forms emerged from the open doors. Three female forms. Oh, dear, not this.

"What are you doing here?" Ruth asked as Lisa, Maddie, and Beryl approached.

"A little birdie tipped us off," Lisa said.

"A big birdie," Beryl corrected.

"Jerry Murphy," Ruth said. "That rat bastard."

"He was concerned about you," Maddie said.

Ruth hugged herself against the chilly night air. "Look, this has nothing to do with you. Go away."

She turned her back on the group and sat down on the rock. They approached and surrounded her. She knew they wanted to help her, but what could they do? Her life was in ruins.

Lisa crouched down before her and took Ruth's gloved hands in hers. "You were always the strongest woman I know."

"Not anymore. I don't even have the strength to cry."

Lisa glanced at the others and then stood, pulling Ruth by the hands. "Come here. We have something to show you."

Ruth stood slowly and let them lead her to the SUV

they came in. They brought her around to the back and opened the hatch. The interior lights shone down on a big, black object taking up the entire width of the space.

"A guitar case," Ruth said, touching it lightly with her fingertips.

"Open it," Beryl said.

"Whose is it?" Ruth asked.

Maddie laughed. "Yours."

Ruth pulled off her gloves, flipped open the fasteners, and slowly lifted the lid. What she saw inside made her gasp.

"A Martin! A vintage series Martin! I've been pining for this for years." She looked at her friends. "How did you know?"

"Your kids told us," Lisa said.

"But Keith footed the bill," Maddie added. "He insisted. We just did the legwork."

Ruth stroked the beautiful wood. They did all this . . . for her. She wanted to say something, but couldn't get out any words.

"Pick it up already," Beryl said. "Take it for a test spin."

Gingerly, Ruth pulled the magnificent instrument from its case. She strummed it, adjusted one of the strings, and strummed it again. Oh! That sound! She started plucking a tune that had been rattling around her brain, but as she found the notes and listened to the melody, the song surprised her. It wasn't the sorrowful, mournful tune she had expected, but a song filled with hope. She played and played, and only when she stopped to consider a musical bridge did she realize that she had walked over to the rock to sit down and work out the melody. Her three friends sat on the cold ground before her, in the middle of the school yard in the middle of the night. That's when she realized why her song of pain was ringed with joy. People loved her. Her husband, as sick as he was, wanted her to be happy. Her children were proving to be even more glorious than she had dreamed. And her friends. Was there anything they wouldn't do for her? Ruth played a few more notes. She didn't have everything she wanted in this life, and perhaps she never would. But maybe this was enough.

Chapter Twenty-seven

LISA

Lisa slipped an Aretha Franklin CD into her car stereo and wailed along with the music as she drove. She was on her way to Ruth's for one final meeting of the public relations committee. Not that they needed a formal excuse to get together anymore, but apparently Ruth had some last-minute business she wanted to discuss.

When she arrived, Lisa was glad to see that Maddie had brought Beryl along. It was fitting that they should all be together this day.

Ruth gathered them in the living room, and Lisa couldn't help noticing that her friend had regained her spark. In fact, she was positively glowing.

"Something's up with you," Lisa said, smiling.

"What do you mean?"

"Don't try to hide it. I can see it in your face."

Ruth blushed a bit. "That Rod Martin's been hounding me for a date."

"That producer?" Maddie asked.

"The one you said was such a prick?" Beryl added.

Ruth settled herself into a chair and picked imaginary lint from her pants. "He's growing on me."

Beryl laughed. "It's that alpha male personality. You're a sucker for that."

Ruth smiled and shrugged. "Yeah, but I'm just not sure I should be doing that sort of thing anymore. So I keep brushing him off, and he keeps coming back. If nothing else, it's great for my ego."

If Lisa had to bet, she'd wager that Ruth would eventually wind up sleeping with this guy. She knew that her friend had finally come to a kind of peace, accepting the love of her family and friends as the center of her life. But sex. Ruth wasn't the type who could walk away from that forever.

"You're wrestling with guilt," Maddie said. "Looks like Paul Capobianco had an effect on you, after all."

Ruth shrugged. "Maybe. At the very least, I'm feeling guilty that Paul's going to lose his job because I got drunk and shot my mouth off."

"It's not your fault," Lisa said. "Suzanne is a bitch."

"No, it *is* my fault. But I have an idea for a way to make it right. That's what I wanted to discuss. I don't think getting Paul fired is really what Suzanne is after. It's really about aborting the movie project so she can feel like she's won some sort of battle against me. So I was thinking that if we approached her and said we would *voluntarily* pull the project if she would keep her mouth shut about Paul and me, she might go for it."

Lisa nodded. "That sounds right."

"Are you all okay with that?" Ruth asked.

Lisa heard a sound coming from the hallway and she looked up. It was Keith, approaching the living room with his walker. He stopped at the doorway, and Lisa expected Ruth to shoo him away. Instead, she looked up and smiled.

"Hey, sweetie. We're talking about committee business. Do you want to come in and join us?"

Half of Keith's mouth went up in a grin. "Better view from here," he said.

Ruth winked at him and went on. "So what do you gals think? Should we approach Suzanne with that proposition?"

Keith made a gurgling sound and Beryl jumped on it.

"I think Keith would like to approach Suzanne with a proposition," she said.

He smiled and nodded, and they all laughed. Keith pushed his way into the room then and took a seat next to Ruth on the sofa.

Maddie turned the conversation back to business. "I'm okay with it," she said, "if it comes down to that. But do you really think there's no way we can get this project back on track?"

Beryl leaned in toward Ruth. "Can't we threaten Suzanne that if she gets Paul fired we'll tell everyone what we saw at Donna's pool?"

Lisa sighed. "I tried that. She said no one would believe us."

"Maybe they would," Beryl said, "if we all banded together."

Maddie shook her head. "Lisa is right. It's just our word against hers. Without proof, we have nothing."

"Proof?" Keith asked.

"We're talking about that scene we witnessed at the Fishbeins' pool," Ruth explained. "We have no proof of anything, so we don't think anyone will believe us if we tell them what we saw."

Keith pulled himself up on his walker and reached into his pants pocket. He pulled out his cell phone. "How about this?" he asked.

Ruth shrugged. "What do you mean?"

Keith pressed some buttons on his phone and turned it to face Ruth. "I took pictures. Look."

Ruth grabbed the phone from Keith, looked at the image, and let out a holler. "Oh, my God! It's them, by the pool!"

The others leaped from their chairs and gathered around the phone, laughing and screaming.

"Keith," Ruth said, "do you understand what this means? It means we have the proof we need to force Suzanne's hand. It means we're going to get the movie project back. Honey, you did it! You saved the day!"

Keith eased himself down onto the sofa and smiled. "I'm a hero!"

"You are," Ruth said, and kissed him gently on the lips.

He grabbed her ass with his good hand and gave a squeeze.

Epilogue

One crisp spring morning the following year, carpenters, technicians, prop people, and other crew members ran back and forth throughout a field behind the North Applewood Elementary School, rushing to finish the set before the star arrived. After several production delays, the George Clooney movie was finally being filmed.

Rod Martin, executive producer, watched from the sidelines, barking orders and shouting about the ineptitude of this idiot or that. When his cell phone rang, he answered it angrily, and finished even angrier.

"Goddamn it!" he yelled. "Jessica!"

"Problem?" asked the young woman he hadn't seen standing right behind him.

"Car service broke down on the way to the airport. I need someone to go pick up Clooney. Who's free?"

Jessica looked around and scratched her temple. "Everyone's pretty busy, Rod."

Rod Martin huffed and puffed like he was about to blow

something down, when the president of the PTA stepped to the rescue.

"I'll go," she said.

"Fine," the producer said brusquely. He slapped his Palm Pilot into Jessica's hand. "Handle this," he said to her, and wasn't more than a step away before he started screaming at someone else.

"You're a lifesaver," Jessica said to the woman. "If you give me a minute, I'll get you the flight information." She started tapping at Rod's PDA. "Let's see, it's a chartered flight coming into LaGuardia and . . . I'm sorry, what was your name again?"

The president of the PTA smiled. "Beryl," she said. "My name is Beryl."

Sobered by the possibility of what they could have lost, Maddie and Bruce opened the lines of communication and rediscovered the depth of their love. On the advice of friends, they went to see a marriage counselor, but realized after only two sessions that they already knew more about making their relationship work than any professional, and made a go of it on their own.

It worked. Bruce spent less time at work and more time telling Maddie how much he loved her. Maddie learned to trust his commitment to her.

With new clarity, Maddie regained her focus and decided that being a legal consultant would give her the kind of flexibility she needed. Essentially, she worked for the Applewood School District, but instead of being on its payroll, she billed by the hour and could come and go as she pleased.

She spent enough time in the main office to become pretty friendly with Paul Capobianco, who had indeed kept his job. Ultimately, it was Maddie that Paul went to for friendly sympathy when Margie announced she was leaving him for another widower from their church group. Someone, she said, a little less glum.

Maddie remained active in the PTA, and early one morning got a call from Beryl that sounded especially noisy.

"Where are you?" Maddie asked. "I hear cars."

"Stuck in traffic on the Grand Central."

Maddie looked at her watch. "Don't you have a PTA meeting today?"

"That's why I'm calling," Beryl said. "I'm going to be late and need you to get the meeting started for me. But I want you to give them a message. Hang on a sec."

Maddie heard whispering and the rustle of Beryl's cell phone being passed to another person.

"Hello, Maddie," said a masculine voice. "I want you to tell the PTA that I'm on my way and will be there soon. That is, if I can get this crazy woman to get her hand off my thigh."

Beryl's voice again. "He's lying. My hand's not on his thigh. It's on his crotch."

Maddie didn't need to ask who the man was. She recognized his voice. It was George Clooney.

After saving the movie project, Keith's renewed confidence enabled him to take a closer look at himself, and he gradually came to an understanding about his own impotence. In order to be at peace with it, however, he needed to know that Ruth's sexual needs were being fulfilled outside the marriage. The conversation was a relief to Ruth, who had been wrestling pangs of guilt over her decision on what to do about Rod Martin, with whom she had been developing a deep friendship.

Through the course of her conversations with Rod, Ruth finally figured out where she knew him from. His real name was Rodney Martin Rosenthal, and he had graduated from Ruth's high school just a year before her. He was genuinely bicoastal, dividing his time between his Beverly Hills home and his Manhattan condo. Once she got the green light from Keith and started sleeping with Rod, he bought a home in Applewood Estates just up the road from her. It was a perfect situation for both of them. He didn't have to give up his east-west lifestyle, yet had a steady relationship with a brash, sexy, challenging woman he had more in common with than all his L.A. bimbos put together.

Ruth found Rodney loud, arrogant, difficult, conceited, and self-centered. In short, a lot like Keith before his stroke. She also found him smart as a whip and funny as a pistol, and loved spending time with him. Besides, the sex was delicious.

Spending weeks or even months apart hardly bothered Ruth at all. She was awfully busy anyway, managing her new career as a songwriter.

Soon after recovering Applewood Rock, Nancy discovered that Chris was still involved with recreational drugs. She broke up with him over it, and learned that being sober and alone was okay. Her singing voice, unfortunately, had lost too much of its youthful vigor for her to continue making a career of it. She became a part-time caretaker for Keith, and satisfied her need to perform by volunteering to entertain elderly residents at a nursing home once a week. She combined her two jobs by bringing Keith with her to the home, where he made himself useful reading pornography to an elderly kindred spirit with failing eyesight.

At one of her AA meetings, Nancy ran into her old boyfriend, Naldo Reagan. They found they had more in common than ever, including a strong dedication to recovery from alcoholism. They started dating again, and eventually decided that they wanted to move in together. After house-hunting all over the tristate area, they realized that nothing appealed to them as much as a needy, burned-out ranch house in Applewood Estates, Long Island. So they went to Lisa and Adam with a proposal to pay a lower-than-market price to take the house as is. The Slotnicks agreed, with one condition. Lisa wanted to help with the renovation. A bottle of sparkling apple cider was uncorked and the deal was sealed.

Soon afterward, Lisa was contacted with another proposal. This one was from the director of the George Clooney movie. It turned out that after Lisa had passed Jill the tape her mother had recorded, Ruth had given Rod Martin a tape of "Give the Song to Daddy" that Lisa had recorded. The director of the movie agreed with him that it was just what the film needed. A pop diva was contracted to belt out the song for a music video that was played repeatedly on MTV and topped the charts for weeks. But they wanted a different kind of voice for the movie itself.

Before it opened nationwide, the new George Clooney movie previewed to a packed auditorium in Applewood, Long Island. There, in the darkness of the theater, as the opening credits rolled, it was the crystal-clear voice of Lisa Slotnick that filled the air.

A+

AUTHOR
INSIGHTS,
EXTRAS, &
MORE...

FROM
**ELLEN
MEISTER**

AND

AVON A

Interview With the Author

Shortly after I signed the contract for this book—my first—I was contacted by a writer named Steve Hansen, who I knew through the online writers' workshop we both belonged to. Steve wanted to interview me for Beverly Jackson's *Ink Pot*, a small but prestigious literary magazine (now, sadly, defunct). Since the readers of this journal were mostly writers, he thought they would be interested in hearing about my journey to publication. I agreed to the interview, and we arranged for a late-night, online chat. Here is the result:

Steve Hansen: After graduating college, you got a job in advertising. Were you writing ad copy? Or what were you doing? What do you remember most about those days?

Ellen Meister: My first job was actually not in advertising, but in the marketing end of publishing. I worked for a small medical book publisher and I think my title was "Promotion Associate." The business operated on such a small budget that I didn't even have my own garbage can. Honest. I had to improvise by taping an oversized envelope to the side of my desk and throwing my trash in there. My boss was so impressed with my ingenuity that she went out and bought me my very own trash can. It wasn't quite enough to entice me to stay, however, and I soon left to be an assistant to a literary agent. That was a terrible job for me as my secretarial skills weren't nearly good enough for the workload, and I left after a few months.

SH: Was the fact that you gravitated toward jobs in and around the publishing field a compromise (as it is for so many writers) between an unsure future of writing and getting a "real job?"

EM: Sadly, I wasn't writing any fiction at all in those days. So it wasn't a matter of getting a day job to make ends meet while I spent my evenings in literary pursuits. I was attracted to publishing and advertising simply because I liked words and books. And when I finally started getting copywriting jobs I was thrilled. I enjoyed that work. I was good at it, first of all, and loved that I did something for a living that ended with a tangible thing I had actually created and could put into a portfolio.

SH: So you weren't one of those people who knew practically out of the cradle they would be "A Writer." What turned you into one? Writing fiction is a long process if one is to master it. What kept you plugging away through what I affectionately call "the early years of drivel?"

EM: Ha! I actually *was* one of those people who always knew she wanted to be a writer. I'm just a terrible procrastinator. Writing was always something I was going to do later, when I had the time. For years I called myself a writer and didn't write a single sentence of fiction (unless you count advertising copy). Then one day I looked at my life and thought, if not now, when? What am I waiting for? Perhaps it was my own version of a mid-life crisis. But at any rate, I had three small kids at the time of this great epiphany, and virtually no time to pursue this dream. But I had the bug then, and knew there was a way to make it work. I simply had to. So I started getting up at five A.M. and writing.

Sometimes I regret that I waited so long to follow my dreams. But on the other hand, I think I would have been a terrible writer if I had started younger. I'm a late bloomer and I needed the maturity.

SH: But you were successful in other fields, copywriting, advertising, marketing, etc. Why did you "have to" write?

EM: I often think of writers as having a lot in common with exhibitionists. People who take their clothes off in public want to be *looked* at. They crave that attention. *Notice me and make me feel alive!* Don't we feel the same way about being read? We're baring as much of ourselves to the world as we can. And we want approval for it.

So I guess I "have to" write because I'm too shy to take my clothes off in public.

SH: Anyhow. You've recently garnered that ever elusive "approval" in the form of a big, fat book contract for your novel. What was the genesis of this book?

EM: The idea came shortly after I made the decision that I was going to get back to writing, no matter what. I had walked into a PTA meeting, smiling and nodding at all the other moms, feeling like I had this big secret. No one there knew I wanted to write. No one even knew I had an inner life. All they saw was this PTA face. Then I got to wondering if all the women in the room were thinking more or less the same thing. That's when I knew I needed to write about these women, and to explore the depth of their lives.

SH: You say you decided on writing the novel shortly after dedicating yourself to writing. Where did all those short stories you have published on the Web and in print come from? In between chapters of the novel you'd just pop one off or what?

EM: Remember how I said I was a terrible procrastinator? A lot of the short stories were an excuse to put the novel aside for a bit. But I'm not complaining. Writing short stories lets me flex different muscles, and ultimately makes me a better novel writer. Kind of like a baseball player taking time out to play basketball or hockey. (Good heavens. Did I just use a sports analogy?) Also, the road to book publishing is so very long that I needed the gratification of getting short stories published along the way. *(Editor's note: One example of Ellen's short stories follows this interview.)*

SH: Like Michael Jordan playing baseball? Hey. That was a disaster! Bad sports analogies aside, the ordeal you went through to get the novel published reads like Homer's *Odyssey*, and you are Odysseus. How'd you get through it? And, in discussing the rewrites that the novel underwent during that process, you talk about applying "Band-Aids" where "surgery" was needed. Can you be a bit more specific on what this means?

EM: How did I get through it? Well, I'm not sure I did, as I had at least one bona fide panic attack somewhere in the middle of the ordeal. It's not something I recommend. As far as the rewrite, I was lucky enough to land some brilliant agents. (Yes, that's agents, plural. I'm jointly repped by two people at the same agency.) They're as smart as they are ambitious, and they recognized, among other things, that the novel's "through line" needed to be stronger. That is, the central plot got lost in places where the subplots took on a life of their own. I agreed with them, but thought I could make the changes without doing major surgery on my chapters, which was an intimidating proposition since it's a big complicated novel, with three protagonists and lots of subplots. So I stuck Band-Aids all over the damned thing, and my agents kept coming back to me and saying I hadn't pushed it far enough. Finally I said there was nothing else I could do and so they submitted it.

Alas, the first editor who saw it rejected it for the very problem my agents had been complaining about. At that point I got off my ass and did the surgery required. And guess what? Once I got into it, it wasn't nearly as hard as I thought it was going to be. And of course, I'm happy with the finished product. The lesson learned is that it's a bloody process and I should have just done the surgery to begin with.

SH: Damn it, since you broached the subject a couple questions ago, I can't help but ask the question: Are all PTA women naughty "desperate housewives"? What's wrong with men these days that they can't satisfy their women? And are all these questions and more answered in your book?

EM: Yes, PTA women are terribly, terribly naughty. Something about those plant sale fund-raisers makes us lose all control.

I can't speak for all men and whether or not they're satisfying their women, but one of my more sexually charged characters is married to a man who was left half-paralyzed and completely impotent from a stroke. To make matters worse, the brain damage he sustained left him sexually uninhibited and unaware of his inability to perform. Hence, he has a tendency to ask strange women to fuck him. His wife copes by having an affair with the school superintendent.

Did I mention that there's sex in the book?

SH: Sex? What a novel selling point! Of course you'd put the poor *guy* through the torture of wanting it all the time, but not being able to "perform" as it were. Hey. Is that some kind of metaphor for all of us Neanderthals? You are naughty.

On a serious note, how has having three children and a knuckle-dragging husband to take care of affected your writing? Has it been a help or hindrance or combination of both?

EM: I don't think I could have written about sex and kids if I didn't *have* sex and kids. So as far as this novel is concerned, it's definitely been a help.

Honestly, I'm not the type who needs to be miserable and suffer for her art. I'm at my best when I'm happy. So having a loving, non-knuckle-dragging husband and three kids who make me laugh until I'm begging for oxygen is a good thing.

My schedule is tough, of course, but I'll have plenty of time to rest when I'm dead.

Steve Hansen is the editor-in-chief of *TQR (tqrstories.com).* He lives in Albuquerque, New Mexico.

Permission was granted to reprint this interview, which first appeared in *Ink Pot Literary Journal.*

Finding Cooper

A short story by Ellen Meister

Cooper was three when I lost him. And I don't mean lost him in the euphemistic, I-just-don't-want-to-say-dead sense. I mean lost him, as in, *God oh God, where's my kid? Has anybody seen my kid?*

The day started out typically enough. I went to pick up Cooper at the special preschool he attended for autistic kids, and saw him sitting at a table with the aptly named Merry, a new classroom aide who wore an idiotic smile almost continuously.

"Look who's here!" Merry said to him when she saw me standing at the door of the room. She pointed with her finger, but Cooper just looked at her hand. He didn't get the whole concept of pointing. Somehow, normal kids understand automatically that it's a directional cue, but to Cooper it was meaningless.

"Look who's here," she repeated, turning his face with her hands.

I stood and waited for recognition, knowing that if she just said the word "Mommy" he would think to look toward the door for me. Merry still had a few things to learn.

His teacher, Miss Nicki, looked up from the colored paper heart she was cutting. "Mommy's here, Cooper," she said.

That did it. My sweet-faced boy glanced quickly out the corner of his eye and came running to me. I kneeled to greet him.

"How was your day, Cooper?" I asked after hugging him. "Did you have fun in school?"

"Bub-bub," he said.

"Bubbles? You played with bubbles?" I looked at the aide who nodded in confirmation. "Yes, Mommy," I modeled, "I played with bubbles today." I stood and addressed Merry. "How was he?"

"Wonderful!" she gushed. "He wrote the whole alphabet."

I nearly rolled my eyes at this. Cooper had been writing the alphabet since he was eighteen months old.

"He said 'Zach' today," Miss Nicki added, walking toward us.

This was big news. Cooper's vocabulary consisted almost entirely of the names of inanimate objects. The fact that he'd said another child's name nearly constituted a breakthrough.

I bent over to face Cooper. "Did you say 'Zach' today? I'm so proud of you! Should I arrange a play date with Zach? Look at me, Coop. Do you want to play with Zach?"

He didn't respond, but I didn't expect him to. I rose and said good-bye to his teachers.

Merry laid a hand on my shoulder. "You're doing God's work," she whispered.

Tell God to do his own damn work, I wanted to say. *I'm just trying to have a life here.* Then I understood the beatific smile. She thought this was all part of God's design. I squeezed Cooper's hand and fought back my fury. How *dare* she. How dare she think the misconnected synapses that ruined this child's life are part of God's grand design!

I gritted my teeth. "C'mon Cooper," I said, as I pulled him down the hallway. I took a deep breath and tried to center myself. "We're going to the library."

It was Friday, the day we always went to the public library after school. Our routine was to go to the Children's Room first, where I would read to Cooper. If I let him pick out the book, he would choose *Trollo Takes a Train*. Every time. The story was starting to get on my nerves, and I even considered asking Mrs. Stiles, the persnickety children's librarian, if she would hide it on Friday afternoons. But I was pretty sure she'd have about ten strokes and drop dead at my feet if I asked her to do anything that wasn't etched in some ancient book of rules they kept hidden behind a ceiling tile somewhere.

When we got there, Cooper headed straight for the shelf where Trollo lived, while I tried to find something else he would like. I spotted an oversized alphabet book with big, lush illustrations, and thought it might do the trick.

"How about this one, Cooper? Want to read this one instead of Trollo today? Look. Look at the pictures."

Cooper shoved the Trollo book at me insistently.

"Okay," I relented. "We'll read Trollo first, and then we'll read the alphabet book. Does that sound like a plan?"

Cooper hit the front of his book with his palm, a signal to get started. He was getting anxious, so I opened it and read, silently editing as I went along.

"Trollo took a train. A train, a train, a train."

Mommy took some poison. Poison, poison, poison.

After we finished, I read him the alphabet book, not even realizing there was a picture of a train on the "T" page. Cooper went nuts.

"EEE-eee-ee!" he squealed, flapping his arms, which is what Cooper does when he's excited.

I grabbed his hand and gently stroked it. "Okay, Coop," I said. "Quiet down now."

I was, of course, a beat too late. The ever-vigilant Mrs. Stiles rushed over.

"Is there a problem?"

Yes, I wanted to say. My son is autistic. Apparently, according to some people, God thought it was a great idea to short circuit his brain so that this beautiful, creamy-skinned boy would find it excruciatingly difficult to learn simple things, like what it means when someone points a finger. And nearly impossible to make the natural human connections that you and I do a hundred times a day and take completely for granted. Things like looking another person in the eye or understanding that your mother isn't just an object that offers comfort and food and brings you to school, but a living, breathing feeling person who loves you so fiercely she would do anything for you. Anything. So yes, Mrs. Stiles, I guess you could say there is a problem.

"He's excited," I simply said. "He loves trains."

Mrs. Stiles brought her lips together, as if to say she's seen this type of indulgent parenting before and simply won't tolerate it. She turned her attention to Cooper.

"I bet you'd like to take this book home, wouldn't you?"

Her way of saying, don't let the door slam you in the ass on the way out.

"He likes to read them here," I explained.

"That's fine," she said, laying her hand on Cooper's arm, which he pulled away. "But you have to be quiet in a library."

Cooper patted the book again, indicating that he's done with her. He wants me to read. Mrs. Stiles straightened up and walked off.

After the Children's Room, we headed upstairs to where they kept the videotapes. My husband, Miles, and I liked to watch a movie on Friday nights after Cooper went to bed. It was our version of a date, since Cooper didn't do too well with babysitters, making it hard for us to get out.

This is where it happened. I held Cooper's hand as I scanned the cardboard videotape boxes for an interesting title. But he tugged in the opposite direction. Something had caught his eye and he wanted a closer look.

"Just a minute, Coop," I said. "Let me find a tape."

He was insistent, pulling and whining, and I feared he'd throw a fit.

"Okay, okay," I said. "Show me, Cooper. Show me what you saw."

I let him drag me toward the front of the aisle where he grabbed a box off the shelf and patted the title, indicating that he wanted me to read it out loud.

"Strangers on a Train," I said. "That's very good. You read the word 'train,' didn't you?"

He pulled from the shelf the plastic case that was behind the box, the one they keep the actual tape inside. The title was printed on it, and I think Cooper recognized that it said the same thing as the cardboard box. He held the two side-by-side, looking from one to the other. He sat down on the floor and laid them in front of him, transfixed.

"I'm just going to the end of the aisle, Cooper. Can you sit here quietly for a minute?"

He didn't respond, of course. So I just left him there while I walked about twenty feet away. I went back to scanning the titles, glancing back over at Cooper every few seconds. A certain tape caught my eye, and I picked it up to read the copy on the box. I guess I got engrossed for a moment longer than I should have, because when I looked up, Cooper was gone.

"Coop?" I ran to the end of the aisle and looked in both directions. "Cooper?" My heart started pounding, but I was sure I'd find him any second just around a corner. "Cooper!" I was getting louder, and people were starting to look at me. All at once I didn't give a shit. "COOPER!" I yelled. Nothing.

"My kid's missing!" I shouted to the air. "Did anybody see a little boy?"

"What does he look like?" someone asked.

Like a lost kid!, I wanted to scream. Somebody find him!

People started rising from chairs and looking around. I ran down the center of the room looking frantically into each aisle.

"Cooper!" I shouted. "Where are you?"

"Cooper!" I heard from people who had joined in the search. I did a quick lap around the perimeter of the room before dashing down the stairs. "Keep looking!" I shouted over my shoulder.

I almost ran smack into Mrs. Stiles. "Cooper's missing," I said.

"What?"

"My son, he's missing." I swallowed hard. "He's autistic."

Mrs. Stiles's face went white. "Lock the back door!" she shouted to a small woman behind the desk. "I'll get the front."

Now it felt real. I imagined headlines. Posters. Did I have a current picture of Cooper. *Oh God, what am I thinking?*

I ran to the Children's Room, where *Trollo Takes a Train* was still on the table where we left it. But the alphabet book was gone. Did that mean anything?

I imagined, for a second, my life without Cooper. But the picture was blank, like a sheet of photographic paper with no image developing. I'd wake up, have coffee, do stuff. Then I'd go to sleep and do the same thing all over again. What was the point? Without Cooper, my life had no shape, no color. Without Cooper, my life was a meaningless blank. I knew, then, that I needed him as much as he needed me.

I sat down on the floor and started to cry. The dam burst, and I covered my face as heaving sobs took over. And then.

Then I felt a tiny hand on my knee. I opened my eyes and saw Cooper sitting under the table with the alphabet book on his lap. *Thank you*, I thought. *Thank you, thank you, thank you.*

"Mommy sad," Cooper said.

Maybe it wasn't the hand of God that dropped a gift into my lap at that moment. But it was a gift just the same. I laughed and crawled under the table to hug him. It was his first sentence. But it was so much more. Cooper had recognized emotion. He had acknowledged me as a person. And, perhaps most important of all, he had felt the very human need to say it out loud. To me. To make a connection.

"Yes, Cooper," I said. "But I'm happy now."

Just then, Mrs. Stiles rushed into the room and saw us. "We found him!" she shouted to the crowd by the door. She kneeled down.

"What are you two doing under there?" she asked.

"God's work," I said. "We're doing God's work."

This story first appeared in *Nassau Review*.

ELLEN MEISTER grew up in the PTA-enriched heartland of suburban Long Island and spent her early career in publishing and advertising. She lives in New York with her husband and three children. This is her first novel.

www.ellenmeister.com

Ellen Meister